Capturing
THE
DEVIL

JIMMY PATTERSON BOOKS FOR YOUNG ADULT READERS

James Patterson Presents

Stalking Jack the Ripper by Kerri Maniscalco
Hunting Prince Dracula by Kerri Maniscalco
Escaping from Houdini by Kerri Maniscalco
Becoming the Dark Prince by Kerri Maniscalco
Gunslinger Girl by Lyndsay Ely
Twelve Steps to Normal by Farrah Penn
Campfire by Shawn Sarles
When We Were Lost by Kevin Wignall
Swipe Right for Murder by Derek Milman
Once & Future by Amy Rose Capetta and Cori McCarthy
Sword in the Stars by Amy Rose Capetta and Cori McCarthy
Girls of Paper and Fire by Natasha Ngan
Girls of Storm and Shadow by Natasha Ngan

The Maximum Ride Series by James Patterson

The Angel Experiment
School's Out—Forever
Saving the World and Other Extreme Sports
The Final Warning
MAX
FANG
ANGEL
Nevermore
Maximum Ride Forever

The Confessions Series by James Patterson

Confessions of a Murder Suspect
Confessions: The Private School Murders
Confessions: The Paris Mysteries
Confessions: The Murder of an Angel

The Witch & Wizard Series by James Patterson

Witch & Wizard
The Gift
The Fire
The Kiss
The Lost

Nonfiction by James Patterson

Med Head

Stand-Alone Novels by James Patterson

The Injustice (previously published as *Expelled*)
Crazy House
The Fall of Crazy House
Cradle and All
First Love
Homeroom Diaries

For exclusives, trailers, and other information, visit jimmypatterson.org.

Capturing
THE
DEVIL

KERRI MANISCALCO

JIMMY PATTERSON BOOKS
LITTLE, BROWN AND COMPANY
NEW YORK · BOSTON · LONDON

Copyright © 2019 by Kerri Maniscalco

Hachette Book Group supports the right to free expression and the value of copyright. The purpose of copyright is to encourage writers and artists to produce the creative works that enrich our culture.

The scanning, uploading, and distribution of this book without permission is a theft of the author's intellectual property. If you would like permission to use material from the book (other than for review purposes), please contact permissions@hbgusa.com. Thank you for your support of the author's rights.

JIMMY Patterson Books / Little, Brown and Company
Hachette Book Group
1290 Avenue of the Americas, New York, NY 10104
JimmyPatterson.org

First Edition: September 2019

JIMMY Patterson Books is an imprint of Little, Brown and Company, a division of Hachette Book Group, Inc. The Little, Brown name and logo are trademarks of Hachette Book Group, Inc. The JIMMY Patterson Books® name and logo are trademarks of JBP Business, LLC.

The publisher is not responsible for websites (or their content) that are not owned by the publisher.

The Hachette Speakers Bureau provides a wide range of authors for speaking events. To find out more, go to hachettespeakersbureau.com or call (866) 376-6591.

Photographs courtesy of Wellcome Collection: Bellevue Hospital, circa 1885/1898; post-mortem set, London, England, 1860-1870; Saint Michael the Archangel: the fall of the dragon and the rebel angels defeated by St Michael; Roses, Robert "Variae"; birds of the crow family: four figures, including a crow, a raven and a rook; Typical Victorian Pharmacy, Plough Court Pharmacy 1897.

Photographs courtesy of Shutterstock: Part One and Part Two images; New York City, circa 1889; gowns with beading and lace details; skull and rose tattoo image; map of Chicago, circa 1900; Vintage Post Mortem Tools; goat skull with smoky background; wedding invitation background.

Photographs courtesy of public domain: newspaper article circa 1893; H. H. Holmes circa 1880s/early 1890s; Court of Honor, World's Fair, Chicago; murder castle.

Photographs courtesy of Alamy: St. Paul's Chapel.

ISBN 978-0-316-48554-8

Cataloging-in-publication data is available at the Library of Congress.

10 9 8 7 6 5 4 3 2 1

LSC-C

Printed in the United States of America

Dear reader,
Beyond life, beyond death;
my love for thee is eternal.

For ever and for ever farewell, Brutus!
If we do meet again, we'll smile indeed;
If not, 'tis true this parting was well made.
—*JULIUS CAESAR,* ACT 5, SCENE 1

WILLIAM SHAKESPEARE

Good night, good night!
Parting is such sweet sorrow,
That I shall say good night till it
be morrow.
—*ROMEO AND JULIET*, ACT 2, SCENE 2
WILLIAM SHAKESPEARE

Our revels now are ended. These our actors,
As I foretold you, were all spirits and
Are melted into air, into thin air:
And, like the baseless fabric of this vision,
The cloud-capp'd towers, the gorgeous palaces,
The solemn temples, the great globe itself,
Yea, all which it inherit, shall dissolve
And, like this insubstantial pageant faded,
Leave not a rack behind. We are such stuff
As dreams are made on, and our little life
Is rounded with a sleep.
—*THE TEMPEST,* ACT 4, SCENE 1

WILLIAM SHAKESPEARE

PART ONE

NEW YORK CITY

1889

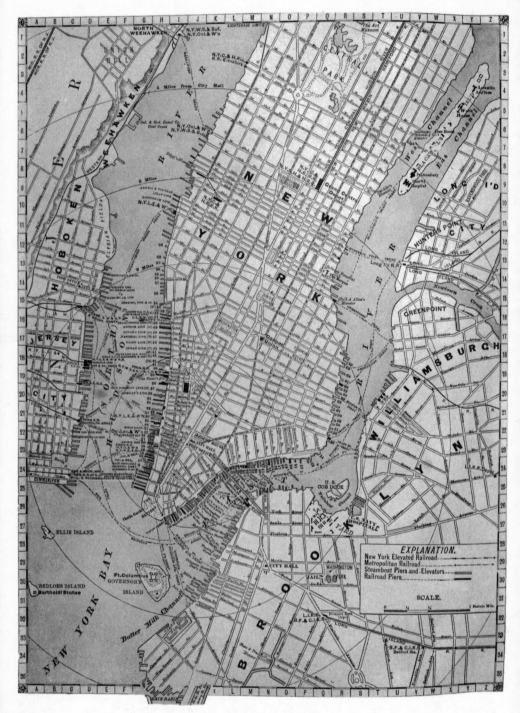

New York City, circa 1889

ONE
DEATH COMES SWIFTLY

WEST WASHINGTON MARKET
MEATPACKING DISTRICT, NEW YORK CITY
21 JANUARY 1889

A blast of frigid air greeted me as I unlatched the carriage door and stumbled onto the street, my attention stuck on the raised axe. Watery sunlight dribbled off its edge like fresh blood, tricking me into recalling recent events. Some might call them nightmares. A feeling akin to hunger awakened deep within, but I quickly swallowed it down.

"Miss Wadsworth?" The footman reached for my arm, his focus darting around the throng of dirt-speckled people elbowing their way down West Street. I blinked, nearly having forgotten where I was and who I was with. Almost three weeks in New York and it still didn't seem real. The footman wet his cracked lips, his voice strained. "Your uncle requested you both be taken directly to the—"

"It will be our secret, Rhodes."

Without offering another word, I gripped my cane and moved forward, staring into dull black eyes as the blade finally came down, severing the spinal cord at the neck with a wood-splintering thwack. The executioner—a sandy-haired man of around twenty years—worked the axe free and wiped its edge on the front of his bloodstained apron.

For a brief moment, with his shirtsleeves rolled back and sweat dotting his brow, he reminded me of Uncle Jonathan after he'd carved open a corpse. The man set his weapon aside and yanked the goat's body backward, neatly separating the head from its shoulders.

I drew closer, curious that the animal's head didn't tumble off the butcher's block as I'd imagined—it simply rolled to the side of the oversize board, gaze fixed permanently toward the winter sky. If I believed in an ever after, I might hope it was in a better place. One far from here.

My attention drifted to the goat's carcass. It had been killed and skinned elsewhere, its exposed flesh a map of white and red, crisscrossing where fat and connective tissue met with tender meat. I fought the growing urge to quietly recite the names of each muscle and tendon.

I hadn't inspected a cadaver in a month.

"How appetizing." My cousin Liza finally caught up and looped her arm through mine, tugging me out of the way as a man tossed a stuffed burlap sack across the sidewalk to a younger apprentice. Now that I was paying closer attention, I noticed a fine layer of sawdust around the butcher's feet. It was a good method to easily soak up blood for sweeping, one I was well acquainted with thanks to time spent in Uncle's laboratory and at the forensic academy I'd briefly attended in Romania. Uncle wasn't the only Wadsworth who enjoyed cutting open the dead.

The butcher stopped hacking the goat apart long enough to leer at us. He crassly slid his gaze over our bodies and offered a low, appreciative whistle. "I can snap corsets open faster than bones." He held his knife up, his attention fixed on my chest. "Interested in a demonstration, fancy lady? Say the word and I'll show you what else I can do to such a fine figure."

Liza stiffened beside me. People often called women of supposedly questionable morals "fancy ladies." If he thought I'd blush and run off, he was sorely mistaken.

"Unfortunately, sir, I find I'm not terribly impressed." I casually slipped a scalpel from my wristlet clutch, enjoying the familiar feel of it. "You see, I also eviscerate bodies. But I don't bother with animals. I butcher humans. Would *you* care for a demonstration?"

He must have seen something in my face that worried him. He stepped back, his calloused hands raised. "I don't want no trouble, now. I was just havin' some fun."

"As was I." I gave him a sweet smile that made him blanch as I turned the blade this way and that. "Shame you don't feel like playing any longer. Though I'm not surprised. Men such as yourself boast in a grandiose fashion to make up for their...*short*comings."

Liza's jaw practically hit the ground as she angled us away. She sighed as our carriage finally rumbled off without us. "Explain to me, dearest cousin, why we left that warm, lavish hansom in favor of wandering through"—she motioned at the rows of butchers' blocks with her parasol, each stall featuring different animal parts being wrapped in brown paper packages—"all this. The smell is positively horrendous. And the company is even more foul. Never, in all my life, have I been spoken to in such a wicked manner."

I kept my skepticism on that latter point locked away. We'd spent more than a week aboard an ocean liner cavorting with a carnival known for debauchery. Being acquainted with the ringmaster for five minutes proved he was a devil of a young man. In more ways than one.

"I wanted to see the meatpacking district for myself," I lied. "Perhaps it'll give me an idea for the perfect main course. What do you think of roasted goat?"

"After witnessing its beheading or before?" she asked, looking like she was moments away from vomiting. "You do know that's what cookbooks are for, correct? Inspiration without the labor. Or carnage. I swear you miss being surrounded by death."

"Don't be ridiculous. Why would you even think such a thing?"

"Look around, Audrey Rose. Of all the neighborhoods in this city, this is the one you chose to stroll through."

I tore my attention away from a plucked chicken that was seconds away from joining the dismembered goat, my expression reserved as I took in our surroundings. Blood steadily dripped down many of the wooden blocks lining the storefronts, splattering onto the ground.

Judging from the multihued stains, the streets weren't washed even after a busy day of hacking animals apart. Veins of crimson and black wound through cracks in the cobblestones—tributaries of old death meeting the new. The scent of copper mixed with feces pricked my eyes and thrilled my heart.

This street was death made tangible, a murderer's dream.

Liza sidestepped a bucket of frost-coated offal, her warm exhale mimicking steam rising off a boiling teakettle as it mingled with the cold air. I wasn't sure if the amount of entrails or their near-frozen states offended her more. I wondered at the darkness swirling within me—the secret part that couldn't muster up an ounce of disgust. Perhaps I needed to take up a new hobby.

I feared I was becoming addicted to blood.

"Honestly, let me hail another hansom. You shouldn't be out in this weather anyway—you know what Uncle's said about the cold. And look"—Liza nodded toward our feet—"our shoes are sopping up snow like bits of bread in soup. We're going to catch our death out here."

I didn't glance down at my own feet. I hadn't worn my favorite pretty shoes since the day I'd taken a knife in my leg. My current footwear was stiff, boring leather without a delicate heel. Liza was correct; icy dampness had found its way in through the seams, soaking my stockings and causing the near-constant dull ache in my bones to intensify.

"Stop! Thief!" A constable blew a whistle somewhere close by and several people broke off from the crowd, scattering like plague rats rushing down alleyways. Liza and I moved aside, lest we become the unwitting victims of fleeing pickpockets and petty thieves.

"A whole roasted pig will be more than enough food," she added. "Stop worrying."

"That's precisely the issue."

I pressed closer to the building as a young boy ran by, one hand on his newsboy cap, the other clutching what appeared to be a stolen pocket watch. A policeman followed, blowing his whistle and dodging through vendors.

"I can't stop worrying. Thomas's birthday is in two days," I reminded her, as if I hadn't already done so one hundred times over the last week. The constable's whistle and shouts grew further away and our slow procession down butchers' row resumed. "It's my first dinner party and I want everything to be perfect."

Mr. Thomas Cresswell—my insufferable yet most decidedly charming partner in crime solving—and I had danced around the subject of both courtship and marriage. I'd agreed to accept him, should he ask my father first, and hadn't expected everything to unfold quite as quickly as it had. We'd known each other for just a few short months—five now—but it felt right.

Most young women of my station married at about twenty-one years, but my soul felt older, especially after the events on the RMS *Etruria*. With my approval, Thomas sent a letter to my father, requesting an audience to make his intentions clear. Now that my father, along with my aunt Amelia, was en route from London to New York, the time was fast approaching when we'd begin an official courtship followed by a betrothal.

Not long ago, I would have felt invisible bars closing in at the thought of joining myself to another; now I irrationally worried something might bar me from marrying Thomas. He'd almost been taken from me once, and I'd kill before I allowed that to happen again.

"Plus"—I pulled the letter from the premier chef of Paris from my purse and waved it playfully at Liza—"Monsieur Escoffier was *quite* specific about obtaining the best cut of meat. And Uncle isn't the one who'll deal with a stiff leg," I added, leaning a bit more heavily on my cane. "Let me worry over that."

Liza looked ready to argue but held a perfumed handkerchief to her nose instead, her gaze snagging on the mechanical canopy above us. A conveyor belt with hooks swept by, a constant loop of gears clicking and metal clinking, the noise adding to the clamor of the streets as butchers staked hocks of fresh meat to it. She watched the dismembered limbs jostle their way into the buildings where they'd undoubtedly be broken down further, seemingly lost in thought.

Likely she was searching for another reason I ought to stay inside and rest, but I'd done plenty of resting in the weeks we'd been in New York. I needn't hear from others what I could and could no longer easily do. I was more than aware of that.

While it was true I wanted Thomas's eighteenth birthday to be special, it wasn't the whole truth behind my obsessing. Uncle hadn't permitted me to leave my grandmother's home much for fear of fracturing my leg further, and I was going mad with inactivity and boredom. Throwing Thomas a party was as much for me as it was for him.

Though I was grateful for my cousin—she and Thomas had taken turns entertaining me by reading my favorite books aloud and playing the piano. They had even put on a few plays, much to both my amusement and my dismay. While my cousin had the voice of a nightingale, Thomas's singing was atrocious. A cat in heat held a note in a more pleasant manner than he did. At least it proved he wasn't limitlessly skilled, which pleased me to no end. Without them or my novels, things would have been much worse. When I was adventuring between the pages of a book, I wasn't sad over things I was missing outside.

"Your grandmother's kitchen staff is capable of doing the shopping to Mr. Ritz's instructions. Wasn't he the person who recommended Mr. Escoffier? These are not the sort of scenes one should be subjected to prior to a dress fitting." Liza nodded at the eyes being pried from the goat's skull and set in a bowl, while its belly was sliced open to remove organ meat. "No matter how accustomed you may be to macabre things."

"Death is a part of life. Case in point"—I jerked my chin toward the fresh meat—"without the death of that goat, we'd starve."

Liza scrunched her nose. "Or we could all learn to simply eat plants from now on."

"While that sounds valiant, the plants would still need to die for your survival." I ignored the tweak of pain in my leg as a particularly icy blast of wind barreled over the Hudson River and slammed into us. The sky's gray belly bulged with the promise of more snow. It seemed like it had been snowing for a month straight. I was loath to admit that Uncle was right: I'd suffer the consequences of today's activities later this evening. "Anyway, my fitting is in twenty minutes, which gives us plenty of time to—"

A man in a dark brown cutaway coat and matching bowler hat jumped aside as a bucket of waste splashed onto the street from the tenement window above, narrowly escaping a most unpleasant bath. He crashed directly into me, knocking my cane to the ground along with what appeared to be a medical satchel filled with familiar tools. Forgetting about his bag, he held fast to my arm, preventing me from tumbling onto our items and potentially getting impaled on anything sharp.

While I steadied myself, I eyed a rather large bone saw peeking out from where it had come undone in his bag. There was also what appeared to be an architectural drawing. Perhaps he was a doctor building his own medical offices. After he made sure I wasn't in danger of falling, he let me go and quickly snatched up his satchel, stuffing the medical tools back in and rolling the drawing back up.

"Apologies, miss! M-my name is Henry. I didn't mean to—I really should learn to watch where I'm going. I've got my mind full of a million things today."

"Yes. You should." Liza swiped my cane from the ground and gave the man a scowl Aunt Amelia would be proud of. "If you'll excuse us, we must be on our way." The man turned his attention to my cousin and snapped his mouth shut, though I couldn't be sure if that was due to her beauty or her temper. She openly scrutinized him while he seemed to collect his thoughts. "If you'll pardon us, Mr. Henry," she said, latching onto my arm once more and tossing her caramel-haired head back in a most haughty manner, "we're late for a very important appointment."

"I didn't intend—"

Liza didn't wait to hear about his intentions; she led us through the maze of butchers and vendors, her pale sage skirts and parasol in one hand, and me in the other. We were moving at a pace much too difficult for me to manage when I finally wriggled free of her grasp and steered her off West Street.

"What in the name of the queen was that about?" I asked, indicating the man we'd practically run from. "He didn't intend to bump into me, you know. *And* I believe he was quite taken with you. If you weren't so abysmally rude, we could've invited him to the party. Weren't you saying just yesterday that you wished to find someone to flirt with?"

"Yes. I did."

"And yet... he was polite, a bit clumsy, but harmless and seemed to have a sweet temperament. Not to mention, he wasn't unpleasant to look at. Don't you enjoy a man with dark features?"

Liza rolled her eyes. "Fine. If you must know, *Henry* is too close to *Harry* and I'm quite through with men whose names begin with the letter *H* for a while."

10

"That's absurd."

"So is walking through a butchers' alley in January in a pale dress, yet do you see me complaining, dear cousin?" I raised my brows. "Well, I can't help it!" she cried. "You know how nervous I am to see Mother again, especially after I very *briefly* ran off and joined the carnival."

At the mention of the Moonlight Carnival we both grew quiet for a moment, silently recalling all the magic, mischief, and mayhem it had brought into our lives in just nine days aboard the RMS *Etruria.* In that respect, the carnival certainly lived up to its show-bill claim. Despite the trouble it caused, I'd forever remain grateful for Mephistopheles and the lesson he'd taught me, intentional or not. By the end of that cursed voyage, any doubts I'd had about marrying Thomas disappeared like a magician casting an elaborate illusion.

Certainty was empowering.

Liza wrapped her cloak about herself and inclined her head down the next street. "We ought to hurry over to Dogwood Lane Boutique," she said. "Any dressmaker who studied under the House of Worth won't appreciate it if she's kept waiting. You don't want her to take her annoyance out on your poor gown, do you?"

I craned my head around, hoping for another glimpse down the butchers' alley, but we'd already left that blood-splattered street behind. I took a steady breath in and slowly exhaled. I wondered if boredom and Thomas's party were truly the only reasons behind my fascination with one of the goriest districts in New York City. It had been almost a month since we'd worked on a murder case. Three blessed weeks without death and destruction and witnessing the worst the world had to offer.

Which ought to have been cause for celebration. Still, I worried over the strange sensation lingering in the pit of my stomach.

If I didn't know any better, I'd think it felt like a twinge of disappointment.

Gowns with beading and lace details.

TWO

FIT FOR A PRINCESS

DOGWOOD LANE BOUTIQUE
FASHION DISTRICT, NEW YORK CITY
21 JANUARY 1889

Liza took my cane and set it against the fleur-de-lis wallpaper of the dressmaker's parlor, her eyes alight with a million romantic daydreams. I, on the other hand, imagined I looked half ready to faint. The smaller dressing lounge located off the main room was stiflingly warm. A large fire burned perilously close to racks of dresses made of chiffon, silk, and gauze. Though perhaps I was roasting because of the heavy layers of the extravagant gown I was trying on. It would be stunning for Thomas's birthday, as long as I didn't ruin it by sweating so much.

Bric-a-brac littered the marble mantel, inviting and homey, like much of the décor. A young woman brought in a piping-hot tea service and set it on an end table with scones, jam, and clotted cream. Two champagne flutes promptly joined the treats on a silver tray for us. Raspberries floated to the top, turning the beverage a delightful pink. I managed to shift most of my weight to my uninjured leg, though the effort was slightly exhausting as I focused on not wobbling.

"Stop fidgeting," Liza ordered, slightly out of breath while she fluffed what layers she could on my dress. The gown was a beautiful blush color, the skirts a voluminous tulle with a beaded overlay that began from the bodice and cascaded to either side like a glittering waterfall made of crystal. Liza tugged the ribbons on my bodice a bit tighter, then covered them with the pink ruffle, which reminded me of the petals of a peony. "There. Now all you need are your gloves."

She handed them over and I slowly tugged them up past my elbows. They were a cream so rich I wanted to dip a spoon in and taste them. I had my back to the giant looking glass and fought the urge to turn around and see the final result. As if plucking that very thought from my mind, Liza shook her head.

"Not yet. You need to put the shoes on first." She hurried into the next room. "Mademoiselle Philippe? Are the slippers ready?"

"*Oui, mademoiselle.*" The dressmaker handed my cousin a pretty teal box with a satin bow, then rushed back out to the main room, ordering her employees to add more beads or tulle to other gowns.

"Here they are." Liza approached me with a devilish grin. "Let me see your feet."

"I'd rather not—"

I would have argued—my shoes of late had been more utilitarian and clunky than to my liking—but when Liza opened the lid and held up my new slippers, tears stung my eyes. If it were possible, the shoes were even more enchanting than the gown. They were flat silk shoes embroidered with roses and embellished with gemstones. A pale pink so exquisite I could hardly wait to wear them. When I touched them, I realized they weren't silk—they were made of a buttery leather, so soft I could practically sleep on them. Liza helped steady me while I slipped them on, her own eyes misting as I wobbled and held tighter to her shoulder.

I couldn't help but laugh. "Are you all right? I didn't think the shoes were *that* awful."

"You know that's not..." Liza sniffled and swatted at my backside. "I'm just so happy to see you light up again. I know how much you missed wearing your favorite shoes."

Hearing it spoken aloud, it seemed such a silly thing: to mourn the loss of frilly, insensible shoes. But I loved them and had taken for granted the choice to wear whatever I pleased. I lifted my skirts so I could admire my gleaming foot attire.

"You did a marvelous job designing them. I cannot think of one detail I'd change."

"Actually"—Liza stood and dabbed at her eyes with a handkerchief—"this was Thomas's idea."

I glanced up sharply. "Pardon?"

"He said if you could no longer wear shoes with heels, there was no reason he couldn't have some made that were equally beautiful. If not more so." I stared, unblinking, like a fool. She grinned. "He designed them himself. He even had extra padding added to the soles to help soften any discomfort. He noticed you often wince when you first stand. These, while they're gorgeous, also function in a way that might ease some of your pain."

I blinked several times, finding myself unable to formulate any sort of decent response that didn't include crying into my pretty new skirts. It might not appear to be of much consequence to anyone without an injury, but to me it meant the world.

"They're highly impractical," I said, looking down at them. "They'll get dirty and ruined—"

"Ahh, about that." Thomas emerged from around the corner with more boxes stacked in his arms. He paused long enough to run his gaze over me, his attention slow and meandering. Heat rose in my cheeks and I subtly patted the front of my bodice down, physically checking to see if wisps of smoke were coming from my person. He finally met my eyes and grinned in satisfaction. "I had a few extra pairs made."

"O-oh...what a delightful surprise, Mr. Cresswell! However did you know we'd be here?"

At this, I rolled my eyes skyward. Liza was almost as abysmal at acting as Thomas was at singing. She kissed my cheeks and smiled warmly at Thomas. The two co-conspirators had planned this moment out. I could have hugged them both. "I'll be back in a few minutes. I saw this darling little robe I need to inquire about."

Thomas nodded as she moved past him and promptly started up a loud conversation with the dressmaker in the next room. "You look stunning, Audrey Rose. Here." He set his armful of boxes down on the settee and then took my hand in his, guiding me around to peer into the looking glass. "You're a vision. How do you feel?"

I didn't wish to sound vain, but when I first saw myself standing there, dressed in a gown fit for a princess, with shoes designed by a handsome yet wickedly charming prince, I felt as if I'd stepped out of the pages of a fairy tale. It wasn't the sort of story that placed me in the role of the helpless maiden, however. This tale was one of triumph and sacrifice. Of redemption and love.

"I didn't know you were such a talented cobbler, Cresswell."

He tucked a stray piece of hair behind my ear, expression thoughtful. "I find myself striving to learn new talents, especially when the result is you looking—"

"Radiant?" I guessed.

"I was going to suggest 'like you wish to destroy my virtue at once,' but I suppose yours isn't a terrible deduction, either."

Thomas pressed his lips to mine in a gesture that was meant to be sweet and chaste. I was almost certain he hadn't intended for me to pull him near, deepening our kiss. And I sincerely doubted he'd planned on lifting me into his arms, skirts puffed around us, as he walked us over to the settee and maneuvered me onto his lap, careful to mind my leg. There was truth in his assessment after all.

I ran my fingers through his soft locks, allowing myself a few moments of unfettered bliss. Times like this, when I was curled into his arms, safely tucked away from murder and corpses, I found stillness and peace. Staring into my eyes as if I offered him the same respite, he brought his lips to mine again. Recalling where we were and the danger of having someone walk in and find us in such an indecent position, I slowly forced myself to sit back. I laid my head against his chest, enjoying the solid beat that matched my own.

"It's your birthday and yet you're the one surprising me with gifts. Somehow, I don't think that's how it's supposed to work."

"Oh? I thought the one with the birthday had the right to choose whatever he wanted. Maybe you'll want to ravish me for being so irresistible."

And humble. "Thank you for the shoes, Thomas." I looked at the stack of boxes, teetering precariously close to the edge of the settee now. He caught my stare and nudged them back to safety. "All of them. It was very sweet. And highly unnecessary."

"Your happiness is always necessary to me." He tilted my chin up and kissed the tip of my nose. "We'll find new ways of navigating the world together, Wadsworth. If you can no longer wear heels, we'll design flats you adore. If you ever find those no longer work, I'll have a wheeled chair made and bejeweled to your liking. Anything at all in the universe you need, we will make it so. And if you'd prefer to do it on your own, I will always step aside. I also promise to keep my opinion mostly to myself."

"Mostly?"

He considered that. "Unless it's vastly inappropriate. Then I'll share it with gusto."

My heart gave an involuntary flutter and I was sure if I didn't keep making light of the situation, I'd tackle him to the ground immediately and never be asked back to this boutique again. "Eighteen." I sighed dramatically. "You're practically ancient. In fact"—I breathed him in, trying to hide my smile—"I believe I smell grave dirt on you. Terrible."

"Wicked thing." He nuzzled my neck, prompting gooseflesh to rise in the best of ways. "I'm actually here to invite you to the slums, per your uncle's request."

Our warm moment came to a sudden halt. I took in his serious expression and the scientific and cool persona that he often donned before we examined a corpse. For the first time I noticed his dark clothing, the black coat and matching leather gloves peeking out from his pocket—perfect for attending a murder scene. My treacherous heart picked up its speed once more.

"Has there been a murder?" A muscle in his jaw tightened as he nodded. "Have you already been to the scene?" I asked, wiping my own expression clean.

He watched me carefully before answering. "Yes. Your uncle called for me shortly after you and Liza went out this morning. I was already planning on surprising you here, but you'd just left and Liza asked that I give you both at least an hour. I decided to go to your uncle first."

"I see."

"Actually," Thomas said, "I don't think I've expressed myself clearly. Your uncle quite nearly bit my head off when he noticed I hadn't brought you with me, and sent me out again straightaway." He stood and held his hand out. "Shall we see about solving another gruesome murder, my love?"

I didn't want to be so excited by those words, yet I couldn't deny the subtle thrill running through me, as if tiny lines of electricity had replaced my veins. I craved solving another murder almost as much as I craved Thomas's kisses. And I craved those frequently.

I took my cane from him and went to grab my cloak when Liza marched back into the room, a stern look upon her face.

"Oh, no. If you believe I'm allowing you to rush out that door in *that* dress to investigate some blood-soaked murder scene…"

She closed her eyes as if the very thought was too much to bear. My cousin turned on Thomas, pointing to the door, an army general addressing her unwieldy troops.

"She'll meet you in five minutes in the main sitting room. Unless you'd prefer for her to show up at your party in old rags or her petticoats." Thomas opened his mouth, likely to quip about my undergarments, then shut it at the warning look Liza flashed. "This is non-negotiable. Now, go."

THREE

ROOM 31

EAST RIVER HOTEL
LOWER EAST SIDE, NEW YORK CITY
21 JANUARY 1889

While Liza and I had taken shelter in the dressmaker's shop, winter had decided to run amok in the streets. The skies, which had appeared pregnant with precipitation earlier, finally gave birth to a shrieking storm. Wet snowflakes plopped against the roof of our carriage, cocooning us in a layer of frigid cold. Wind howled as it rushed through the alleyways, forcing people to pull their collars up and run as quickly as they dared over ice-slicked streets.

Even though I'd purchased new stockings and was wearing one of the warmer pairs of shoes Thomas had had made for me, my teeth began to chatter. I clamped my jaws together, hoping to will the chills away through sheer stubbornness alone.

It was impossible. My teeth clacked in the most embarrassing way. Thomas eyed me from across the hansom, then checked the warming brick at my feet, face grim.

"It needs to be reheated over a fire," he said, half unbuttoning his overcoat.

I watched as his own body trembled before I reached over and stilled his movements. "What happened to body heat being the most effective way of preventing frostbite? If you take that coat off, you'll freeze before you can valiantly assist me."

He glanced up, the seriousness leaving his features at once. I swore stars danced in his golden-brown eyes. "What did you think I was doing?"

"Removing your overcoat to place about my feet?"

He shook his head, his expression laced with mischief. "I was planning on stripping bare and having you do the same. *That* is the best way to share body heat. I paid the driver to go around the block a few times if necessary. Figured we might sneak back to your grandmother's house instead of frolicking around another murder scene. Since she's traveling and the house is empty, I imagine I could get you warm soon enough."

He dragged his gaze over me in a way that felt more searing than a simple touch. His look promised what months of flirtations had hinted at. And there was little humor in how serious he was about pleasing me. Despite the plummeting temperature in our carriage, I felt the sudden need to fan myself. He pulled his attention back up to mine, lips quirked upward.

"Perhaps you'll be the one getting me warm. I'm not opposed to either scenario, really. Ladies' choice."

My cheeks pinked. "Scoundrel."

"I love when you whisper sweet nothings to me." Thomas maneuvered himself across the carriage and sat beside me. He opened one side of his coat, then wrapped an arm about my shoulders, drawing me near. I noticed his attention had moved to the frost-coated window, all signs of flirtations melting faster than the snow outside would. Whatever he'd seen earlier had to have been gruesome for him to not elaborate on any details and to flirt so brashly. He was doing his best to keep me distracted, which was never a good sign for the victim. We rumbled past Catherine Slip and turned down Water Street. "It won't be much longer now."

I nestled into my collar, breathing in the warmth of my own body. The buildings had gone from gleaming, pale-colored limestone to brick covered in grit and all kinds of sludge. Cobblestone streets gave way to muddy ones, frozen in parts and treacherous-looking for more than one reason. I spied groups of children huddled together between buildings, their faces and limbs gaunt. It was a brutal morning to be outside.

Thomas, never missing a detail, held me tighter. "They're mostly children from Italy. Either they've run from their families or have been turned out to earn money for them."

A lump rose in my throat. "They're so young. How on earth can they make a wage?"

Thomas grew very quiet. Too quiet for a young man who enjoyed sharing facts on every subject imaginable. I noticed his fingers weren't tapping their usual incessant beat, either. I looked out the window again and suddenly knew what he couldn't bring himself to say. Those boys—those children—would have no choice but to turn to a life riddled with crime. They'd fight, steal, or subject themselves to worse horrors in order to survive. And some would not.

It was a fate I could not imagine for my worst enemy, let alone a child. Even though Thomas had once mentioned the world was neither kind nor cruel, I couldn't help but feel it was unjust to so many. I stared, unseeing, as we rode by, feeling helpless.

Neither of us spoke again until we reached our destination. As our carriage rumbled to a halt, chills erupted down my spine for an entirely new reason. If the meatpacking district had been a murderer's dream, then this building was the seat of Satan's kingdom. The exterior appeared rougher than the men and women slumped against it, and twice as mean. It was a far cry from the dressmaker's shop, which was filled with lighthearted warmth and decadence.

Reporters in black overcoats circled in front of the door, reminding me of vultures hovering over their next meal. I shot a glance at Thomas, noting the same dark look in his eyes. It seemed murder was the newest form of entertainment. Jack the Ripper had awakened a need in spectators that was almost as frightening as the crimes we investigated.

"Welcome to the East River Hotel," Thomas said quietly. "We're heading to room 31."

Inside, the hotel appeared uninhabitable to anything other than vermin. Even the roaches and mice would probably seek better-smelling accommodations soon. Anyone who charged one cent for room and board ought to be sent directly to the workhouse. Rats scuttled under the stairs and crawled into the walls, unhurried and undisturbed by our presence.

Droppings were scattered everywhere. I took a careful step into the entry, trying not to think of disease clinging to my hemline as my skirts swished over the muck. Father's fears of contracting illnesses were a hard habit to break. It was dark enough that I was either blessed or unfortunate to not know the full extent of the squalor. The only light in the entryway was from shafts of wan sunlight creeping between slats of rotten wood in the upper level.

Bits of graying plaster on the walls either crumbled on their own or were the unfortunate victims of angry patrons. It was hard to tell if they'd punched the wall or if they'd been shoved into it. Perhaps both scenarios were true. Wallpaper lay half ripped from the hallway, and the rest was stubbornly hanging on. It was dark like the rest of the interior. As dark as the deeds that we were about to investigate.

I made the awful mistake of looking down again and spotted drops of dried blood. Unless the victim had been attacked here, our murderer must have exited this way. My stomach gave an involuntary flip. Perhaps I wasn't as anxious to study another loss of life as I'd imagined earlier. Maybe nearly a month free from the worry of destruction wasn't enough of a respite at all.

Thick layers of dust and cobwebs gathered in the corners, adding to the crawling sensation along my back. Buckets of refuse attracted flies and other vermin I didn't wish to inspect too closely. It was a horrendous place to live and an even more abysmal place to die.

"Which direction?" I asked, half turning to my companion.

Thomas motioned toward the back end of the building, down a narrow corridor. There were more rooms off to each side than I'd have thought could fit on this floor. I raised my brows, surprised there was no desk clerk station in the main entry. Peculiar for a hotel.

As we moved forward a few steps, I also noted that the door numbers began at twenty and furrowed my brow. "Is this not the ground-floor entrance?"

"There's a stairwell through that door that leads down to the first floor," Thomas said. "The body is in the last room on the right. Watch your step."

It was an odd configuration. One that lent itself nicely to hiding a murderer or aiding them with escaping detection from witnesses. Before I stepped into the corridor, I dared a glance up, noticing people staring down, their expressions as bleak as their surroundings.

A mother rocked a baby on her hip while several young boys and girls watched with empty stares. I wondered how many times they'd witnessed police coming into their borrowed home, removing another body like yesterday's rubbish.

I recalled my earlier worry over Thomas's birthday party and shame crept in. While I was fretting over dessert courses and French delicacies and mourning the loss of frilly shoes, people were struggling a few blocks away to simply survive. I swallowed my revulsion, thinking of the person who'd been slain here. The world needed to be better. And if it wasn't possible for *it* to be better, *we,* its inhabitants, needed to *do* better.

I gathered my resolve and moved slowly down the corridor, using my cane to test the creaking floorboards to ensure I wouldn't fall through. A policeman stood outside the room and, much to my surprise, nodded as Thomas and I drew closer. There was no scorn or mockery in his gaze. He didn't view me and my skirts as unwelcome, which bolstered my first impressions of the New York City Police Department. At least for the moment.

"The doctor's been waitin' for you both." He pushed the door open and stepped back. "Careful, now. The room's a wee bit crowded."

"Thank you, sir." I managed to step into the quarters, but there wasn't much space to spare. Thomas moved behind me, and I paused long enough to run a cursory glance around the room. It was sparsely decorated—one bed, one nightstand, one tattered, blood-soaked quilt. In fact, as I edged farther inside, I saw the bedding wasn't the only thing splattered in blood.

Uncle stood over the tiny bed frame, pointing to the victim. My pulse slowed. For the briefest moment, I felt as if I'd been transported back to the scene of Miss Mary Jane Kelly's murder. It was the last Ripper crime and the most brutal. I didn't have to move closer to see this woman had been practically eviscerated. She was unclothed from the neck down and had been stabbed repeatedly about her person.

I felt, more than witnessed, Thomas moving around behind me and shifted to glance at him. The rogue was almost dancing in place, his eyes alight in the most abhorrent manner.

"There is a body," I whispered harshly. It was incredible that he could carry on as if it were a regular afternoon stroll by the river.

Thomas drew back, his hand clutching his chest. He looked from me to the body, his eyes going wide. "Is that what that is? Here I was convinced it was a Winter Ball. Shame I wore my best suit."

"How clever."

"You do say you like a man with a rather large—"

"Stop." I held my hand up. "I beg of you. My uncle is *right* there."

"Brain." He finished anyway, grinning at my reddening face. "You truly astound me with the direction your filthy mind travels in, Wadsworth. We're at a crime scene; have a care."

I gritted my teeth. "Why are you so flippant?"

"If you must know now, it's—"

"There you two are." Uncle had the look of a man on the verge of a rampage. I could never quite tell if death was a balm or an irritant to him. "Clear the room!" Policemen inside paused, staring at Uncle as if he'd possibly lost his good senses. He turned to a man in a suit and raised his brows. "Inspector Byrnes? I need a few moments alone with my apprentices to examine the scene. Please have your men wait in the hall. We've already had half of Manhattan trouncing through here. If anything else is disturbed, we won't be of much use to you."

The inspector looked up from the victim, taking in my uncle and then me and Thomas. If he, an American inspector, was annoyed that an Englishman was tossing him out of his own crime scene, it didn't show. "All right, boys. Let's give Dr. Wadsworth some time. Go ask the neighbors if they've seen or heard anything. The housekeeper said she saw a man—get me a description." He glanced at my uncle. "How long's she been here?"

Uncle twisted the ends of his mustache, his green eyes scanning the body in that clinical way he'd taught both me and Thomas. "No more than half a day. Maybe less."

Inspector Byrnes nodded as if he'd suspected the same.

"Witnesses say she rented a room between the hours of ten thirty and eleven last night."

Uncle observed the victim again and seemed to stare through her into that calm place necessary to locate clues. People in London thought him heartless. They didn't understand he needed to harden his heart in order to save them the pain of never knowing what happened to their loved ones.

"We'll know more once we perform a postmortem," he said, motioning for his medical satchel, "but an initial glance—based on the current state of rigor mortis—indicates she might've perished between the hours of five and six. Though that may well change once we've gathered more scientific fact."

Inspector Byrnes paused in the doorway, his expression unreadable. "You inspected the Ripper murders." It was a statement of fact, not a question. Uncle hesitated for only a moment before nodding. "If this is the work of that sick bastard . . ." The inspector shook his head. "We can't let this news get out. I won't have any panic or riots in this city. I said it before; I'll say it again—this ain't London. We're not going to muck this up like Scotland Yard. We *will* have a suspect—or Jack the damn Ripper himself—in the jug in thirty-six hours or less. This is New York City. We don't mess around with depraved killers here."

"Of course, Inspector Byrnes."

Uncle shifted his gaze to mine. He'd never asked me directly about the events of last November, but he knew as well as I did that Jack the Ripper could not be responsible for this murder. We were privy to something neither Inspector Byrnes nor anyone else knew.

Jack the Ripper, scourge of both London and the world, was dead.

FOUR

OLD SHAKESPEARE

EAST RIVER HOTEL
LOWER EAST SIDE, NEW YORK CITY
21 JANUARY 1889

"Describe the scene, Audrey Rose." Uncle shoved a journal into Thomas's hands. "Record everything and include a sketch. Inspectors have photographed the body, but I want every detail, every speck, on paper." He jabbed the paper, punctuating each point a bit more emphatically than the last. "We will not have another mass hysteria on our hands. Is that understood?"

"Yes, Professor." Thomas moved to do as he was bid.

I rolled my shoulders back, slipping into that familiar cool calm as I stared at the body and divorced myself from imagining her alive and well. What was left of this woman was a puzzle to solve. Later, once her murderer had been caught, I might remember her humanity.

"Victim is a woman roughly fifty-five to sixty years of age." I glanced around the crime scene, no longer sickened by the blood that coated nearly everything like a layer of macabre rain. A small wooden pail lay upturned on the ground near my feet. Judging from the strong scent of hops and barley, it had been filled with beer. Another swift appraisal of the room suggested she may have been well into her cups—alcohol thinned the blood and made it hard to clot. Which explained why there was an excess of it splattered everywhere.

"She was possibly too inebriated to fight off her attacker." I pointed to the upturned pail. Uncle—despite the ghastly scene surrounding us—seemed pleased by this observation and motioned for me to continue. I bent over the body, ignoring the pitter-patter of my pulse. She'd sustained so much trauma that a foul odor was already present. Even with coldness seeping in from cracks near the window, the putrid scent hit the back of my throat.

I swallowed rising bile quickly. There was no preparing for that tangy-sweet smell and no forgetting it. The stench of human rot haunted me almost as much as the victims we inspected.

"Bruising around the neck indicates strangulation." I reached for the clothing covering her face and paused, turning to Thomas. "Are you through with this part of your sketch?"

"Almost." He went back to his journal, holding it up and angling it, comparing the scene before us to his drawing. After adjusting the drape of the clothing, he looked up. "All right."

Without hesitation, I removed what turned out to be a dress from her face and pulled her eyelids back, searching for conclusive proof strangulation was the cause of death.

"Petechial hemorrhaging is present. Our victim was strangled before other…" I paused while Uncle rolled her carefully onto her side. My gaze halted on two Xs carved into her buttocks, momentarily distracting me from my observation. I took a quick breath. "Before other nefarious acts were performed on her person."

"Excellent." Uncle leaned over, inspecting the corpse for the same clues, then carefully placed her back as she'd been found. "What do you make of the dress draped over her face?"

I stared down at her body, naked except for where the murderer had laid her bloodstained clothing over her head. Whenever we conducted a postmortem on a corpse in the laboratory, Uncle used bits of cloth to cover victims. They were ice-cold and lying on our sterile slab, but they deserved respect. Her indecent state was another way the murderer tried—quite literally—to strip her of her humanity.

"Perhaps he felt ashamed," I said, looking upon the body as if I were the killer. Sometimes it was too easy to do. "There could've been something about her that reminded him of someone else. Someone he possibly cared for." I lifted a shoulder. "She might even *be* the person he or she was fond of."

Uncle twisted his mustache. He looked like he wanted to pace around the room, but it was too small with the three of us inside. "For what end? Why would a person—who so brutally carved open a body—be concerned with covering her eyes? What might that say about him?"

I glanced at Thomas, but he was lost to his own investigation again, sketching everything as Uncle had requested and more. He knelt down, capturing each stab wound, each angle the blade had entered from perfectly. It reminded me of the time he was practically nose-deep in one of the Ripper victims. A chill tickled my spine. I did not enjoy the similarities of the cases.

I drew my own focus back to the scene before us, contemplating this murderer. Perhaps he also wished to shame her. "I imagine he— or she—didn't want to look upon the face of his victim," I said. "It's possible he didn't want to think of her as a person."

"Very good," Uncle said. "What else?"

Ignoring the blood smeared on the body, I focused on the stab wounds. Whoever had committed this act had been enraged. There were so many punctures, it appeared as if they'd struck her again and again and again. Each encounter with the blade more brutal than the last. They were furious, but whether or not that fury was directed at the victim or simply projected onto this woman was a mystery.

The murderer could have slit her throat in one clean swipe. He didn't choose that merciful route. He craved pain—it delighted him.

"Most of the knife wounds were made postmortem. Along with *X*s that have been carved into her...buttocks." I squeezed my eyes shut for a moment. Miss Mary Jane Kelly, the last Ripper victim, flitted through my mind once again. "Our victim was also disemboweled, though we'll know which organs—if any—were removed upon our internal examination. Given the sunken appearance of her lower abdomen, however, I believe something has been taken."

"All right. Let's get this next part over with, then." Uncle took his spectacles off and rubbed the bridge of his nose. "What makes this murder different from the murders in London?"

I snapped my attention to Uncle's. "You're not honestly considering this is one of Jack the Ripper's victims, are you?"

As if being dragged away from a particularly engrossing book, Uncle shifted his attention away from the corpse and met my stare. I wasn't sure why neither one of us ever broached the subject, but somehow, despite the grotesque and horrendous things we subjected ourselves to on a near-daily basis, Jack the Ripper was a topic we dared not touch.

"What is a lesson I try and impress upon you with each case, Audrey Rose?"

"To look at facts," I answered automatically. I focused on releasing the tension in my muscles, finding that my mind cleared with the task. "To remove emotions and read clues left behind before coming up with a hypothesis based on assumption."

Uncle nodded. "Part of that includes ruling out options. We're in the unique position of having examined the Ripper victims. We have intimate knowledge of how those bodies were left, what injuries they'd sustained. That gives us something to compare and contrast, doesn't it?"

"Ah. I see." Thomas sat back on his heels, tapping his pen against his journal. "If this were a scientific experiment, then we'd have the control and variables."

"Measuring the differences will assist with eliminating Jack the Ripper as the murderer," I said, understanding Uncle's methodology better.

"Good. Both of you. Now, then"—Uncle pointed to the neck again—"what would the Ripper have done? What *did* he do with each of his victims?"

For a brief moment my heart lurched into that dark space I'd fought so hard to overcome. I despised thinking of the Ripper case, but I could no longer hide my grief or ignore the evil that had been done last autumn. It had been five months now since his first murder; it was time once and for all to face the truth and move on.

Thomas half turned in my direction, running his attention over me in a swift, analytical way. I knew he'd not interrupt or offer his opinion unless I gave the signal to do so. While it was tempting to have him confront that monster for me, it was my duty. He might be heir to a dynasty saturated in blood, but so was I.

I clutched my unoccupied hand at my side, holding tightly to my cane with the other. "Jack the Ripper strangled his victims before slitting their throats. Every one of them. Even Miss Elizabeth Stride."

"Indeed. He'd been interrupted during that murder, but he still slit her throat before attacking Miss Catherine Eddowes later that same evening. This murderer"—Uncle motioned to the victim lying before us—"had more than enough time to commit his darkest fantasies. He was presumably here with her for hours, more than enough time to carve her up. Miss Mary Jane Kelly's corpse was nearly unrecognizable as human. There were similar circumstances with that crime when compared to this one. It was committed inside. Miss Kelly was a prostitute. She'd been drinking. Yet this murderer did not follow that same familiar technique of slitting her throat and viciously cutting her up. Yes, this victim may have an organ missing, but it's not in the same careful manner as our previous cases in London. Now, tell me, what else doesn't fit with Jack the Ripper?"

I mulled over details of the Ripper case. Each murder scene had been burned into my memory—I didn't have to dig too deeply to recall their facts. I doubted I'd ever forget those crimes. I stared down at this victim. The bruising on her neck was different. Instead of the Ripper's long fingerprint blossoms of crushed flesh, this pattern was more akin to striations. I noticed a pair of torn stockings on the floor.

"This victim, given the marks on her neck, was likely strangled with her own stockings. The Ripper committed his crimes by use of his hands." Uncle's expression shifted once again to pride. His acknowledgment was welcome, yet felt a bit strange given the circumstances. I wasn't sure I wanted my premier talent to be deciphering corpses, but there were worse titles to hold. "The knife"—I nodded toward it—"is also another difference. Jack the Ripper never left a weapon behind."

"Excellent." Uncle inhaled deeply. "What is a more obvious difference?"

Thomas pushed himself into a standing position and tucked his journal into an inner pocket on his jacket. "This victim is older than each of the Ripper victims by at least a decade."

I stopped listening to Uncle and Thomas as they traded theories like weather statistics. A hint of a memory tried surfacing from the depths of my mind. It was hazy, however, similar to squinting at an object through thick fog. I could almost make out the shape of it . . .

"The unsolved murder from the *Etruria*," I said as the memory finally broke free. "That crime was similar in nature to this one."

In fact, if I recalled correctly, Thomas and I had worried we'd unleashed a Ripper-inspired murderer in America. The conversation between my uncle and Thomas halted immediately. Both men slowly blinked at the connection. For a few cursed moments, the only sound was our breath juxtaposed with the utter silence coming from the victim splayed out on the bed.

"What we need to do is get a look at the passenger log of the *Etruria*," I continued when it became clear my uncle and Thomas were flummoxed by my deduction. "It might be the best way of hunting down this murderer."

"Assuming the murderer used his actual name." Thomas looked skeptical. "Proof is not required when booking passage across the sea."

"You're right. I doubt he used his true name," I said, leaning on my cane. "But, at the very least, it could potentially give us an alias that might be his undoing."

Uncle stared at the room and I wondered what he was actually seeing. After a minute he motioned toward the corpse. "Let's finish with our inspection. I'll ask Inspector Byrnes to send someone over and fetch any information they can get from the *Etruria* passenger manifest."

With that settled, I faced the body and tried calming the excited thrum of my pulse. I licked my lips, hoping the hunger didn't show in my face. It was hardly the time to appear flushed and bright-eyed. Though if Thomas could dance around earlier as if we'd been invited to a grand ball, then I ought to be forgiven for this transgression in decorum.

I felt the pressure of Thomas's look almost as acutely as if he'd reached over and touched me. Uncle might be preoccupied, but Thomas never missed any shift in my mood.

I glanced at him, unashamed. His eyes were dark with worry. He had cause to be afraid; I hardly recognized myself. I shouldn't delight in such violence, yet there was no denying how extraordinarily alive I felt while studying death.

Perhaps it was the devil in me, begging to be set free. Without further ado, I obliged.

FIVE
A HAUNTED PAST

Before we left the hotel, Inspector Byrnes promised to call on us with more details of who the victim was, and without permission to perform or observe the postmortem, Thomas, Uncle, and I retired to our home to await the news. After supper, I excused myself to change and noticed an envelope postmarked from London waiting on my vanity.

Curious, I slit it open with a swift flick and read the neat, unfamiliar script.

> *Word has reached me about your upcoming nuptials.*
> *I am en route to New York and shall arrive in two*
> *weeks' time. Do tell Thomas I wish to speak with*
> *him before the wedding ceremony.*
> *It's of the utmost importance. I have something*
> *he needs.*

Odd. Neither Thomas nor I had spoken to anyone other than Liza and my father about our hope to marry. And my father certainly wouldn't have told anyone we wished to be engaged without granting Thomas an audience with him first. There were certain customs that needed to be met in the correct sequence. Once my father agreed, Thomas would need to write to his family. Until all of the necessary paperwork had been drawn up, no one outside of our immediate families would be privy to an engagement. And yet... someone else knew it was possible. In fact, they seemed already convinced a wedding was in our near future.

Rubbish.

I crumpled the letter and fed it through the ornate grate covering the fireplace, watching as its edges shifted from black to orange before fully catching fire. I waited until it had disintegrated to ash before turning away. An uneasiness settled into my stomach, making itself quite cozy. There wasn't anything menacing about the note, but the lack of signature was troubling.

If it were Thomas's sister, Daciana, she would've surely signed her name, and the note would've been as warm and friendly as she was. I imagine she'd send a letter directly to her brother if she had a message specifically for him. It made no sense that she'd write to me instead, asking me to pass her wishes along. If not Daciana or her beloved Ileana, then who would ask to speak with Thomas before our wedding?

Part of me worried it was something devised by the impish ringmaster with whom I'd played a dangerous game of illusion. Would Mephistopheles have spies in New York? I inhaled deeply. There was no way the ringmaster would trouble himself with our lives anymore. He knew my heart belonged only to Thomas. He wasn't *that* much of a devil.

A soft knock came at the door, dragging my mind away from its endless circling. My imagination often crafted elaborate tales. This was likely another one of them. "Come in."

Liza waltzed in with a fragrant cup of tea, then stopped short, crinkling her nose as she waved her free hand about her face. "It smells like burnt parchment in here. You're not setting our plays on fire, are you?"

I set my cane against the settee and plopped down. I traced the brocade pattern on my aquamarine skirts, hesitating. It all seemed so silly now. "I received a letter."

Liza crossed the room and handed me the tea. "Yes, I imagine with a possible wedding coming up you'll receive quite a few of those. Did you burn this particular letter?"

I nodded, taking a quick sip. There was an earthy yet spicy taste to it that wasn't at all unpleasant. I managed to drink a bit more before answering. "I—It seems I'm the recipient of a possible veiled threat. Though the more I think on it, the more I *may* be overreacting. Perhaps I'm suffering from jitters before Father gives his blessing. That's normal, isn't it?"

At this confession, Liza's eyes nearly popped from her head. She hurried over and—after setting my tea down—clutched my hands in hers, face alight with excitement. "A scandal! Intrigue! You do get to have all the fun. Do you believe it's a scorned lover, seeking revenge?"

"What? Why would you believe that?" I stared into my cousin's expectant face and finally relented. "Well, to be truthful, Mephistopheles *did* cross my mind. He enjoys meddling, but we were hardly lovers. And while I might have had a momentary lapse in judgment, there was never any true danger of me falling in love with him."

Liza looked at me sadly. "Sweet cousin, I know you didn't harbor feelings for Mephistopheles. I was actually talking about Thomas."

I opened my mouth and shut it as I turned the notion over. "Thomas has not..." I shook my head. "He's not courted anyone before."

There was an uncomfortably long beat of silence that stretched between us.

Liza plucked at the frills of her skirts. "Are you certain? Has he actually said those words to you, or are you guessing?"

"I—" I went to argue, but—as was the case where matters of the heart were concerned—my cousin was blastedly correct once again. "I imagine he would've mentioned by now if he'd courted anyone in the past. He's always been so serious about his work with Uncle." Liza seemed ready to say something else but pressed her lips together instead. I sighed. "This is ridiculous. Thomas doesn't have a former lover who's seeking to ruin our wedding. Say that were even possible, how might she know of our betrothal plans?"

"Rumors. Gossip. You know there's nothing quite as scandalous or delicious as a good romance. Especially since you and Thomas have become well-known in London. A butler or servant might've seen correspondence and started a chain of ill-kept secrets."

"If we'd sent out invitations or even letters to our families, that might be." I picked my tea up and let the fragrant steam soothe me. "Maybe it's Jian or Houdini or someone else from the Moonlight Carnival who's playing a rather cruel joke. I wouldn't be surprised if they sent an anonymous letter to someone. You know their sense of humor is a bit warped."

The more I rambled, the more unlikely my guesses became and the more uneasy I felt. My cousin's expression hardly helped mend my worries. Liza plastered on a smile. "You're probably right. I'm sure after ten days of annoying you, kissing you once for all of *two* seconds, then running off to the next city to find another conquest, the ringmaster has set spies on you and wishes to ruin your hypothetical wedding by sending notes to newspapers across the pond."

Bloody hell. I regretted telling her about the unfortunate kiss. Thomas, however, took it all much better than I deserved. He only wished I'd kneed Mephistopheles in a sensitive body part for taking advantage of me.

"Brat." I finished off my tea, grabbed my cane, and headed for the door with as much confidence as I could muster. "I'll simply ask Thomas about any romantic entanglements right now."

"Excellent idea." Liza eyed the bookshelves near my fireplace. "Would you like me to stay until you return?"

I knew she'd like nothing more than to curl up with a good romance novel, and I didn't want my worries to stop her from enjoying her evening. I shook my head. "I'll be fine, thank you."

It was much harder to creep around a house I was unfamiliar with at night, and my cane clicking against the thin carpet didn't aid my stealthy pursuit. I cringed each time it made contact with the floor, praying Uncle was preoccupied with sleep. Though after our morning of investigating, he was likely awake studying his journal entries, hoping Inspector Byrnes would still send word at this hour.

Mrs. Harvey was staying on the same floor as Liza and me and wouldn't mind if she did catch me sneaking around. In fact, she might push me off toward Thomas's chambers all while humming pleasantly to herself. During our time on the RMS *Etruria,* she'd gone as far as practically encouraging me to sneak off to visit Thomas after she'd given me a note from him requesting a midnight meeting.

I was extra grateful that my father and aunt hadn't arrived yet. There would be no predicting where either of them would be at this hour. Ever since Mother's death several years ago, Father rarely slept and wandered the halls of our home late into the night like a restless ghost.

When I came upon Thomas's door, I found it partially open. I peered in through the crack, curious as to what he might be doing. It wouldn't have surprised me if he'd deduced my unannounced arrival.

The lamp on his bedside table was on and the fire was softly crackling in the corner. The room itself was a deep blue, like the darkest part of the ocean.

With its carved mahogany furniture and strong color scheme, it fit Thomas perfectly. I tried to keep my attention from lingering on his bed, but its rumpled state was hard to ignore. Papers lay scattered about it and journals were stacked in chaotic towers. I half expected to find him propped up against the headboard, dozing like a tired prince resting on a throne of books.

My stomach turned a few times when I recalled he was reading Jack the Ripper's entries. He'd mentioned it once in Romania and had tried again while we were crossing the Atlantic. I still wasn't ready to know what my brother had to say about his crimes. I felt relief knowing the journals were with us, though, safe from anyone who might harm them or share their secrets.

Feeling like an intruder, I knocked. "Thomas?" I called softly. The aromas of cinnamon and sugar wafted nearby. I pushed his door open wider, mindful of any creaking hinges. "Cresswell?" I craned my head into the room. "Where in the—"

"Please tell me all of my salacious dreams are finally coming true."

I jumped backward and cursed as my cane clattered to the floor. I spun around as gracefully as I could and glared. "What are you doing sneaking about corridors at this hour?"

A sly grin slid across Thomas's features as he motioned me into his chambers. "You realize the irony of you asking that whilst you are, in fact, sneaking about the corridor at this hour as well, don't you?" At my annoyed sigh, he held up a plate stacked with treats and eased the door shut with his foot. "The cook made cinnamon buns slathered in melted butter and sugar. Apparently they're for the morning, but I couldn't help myself." At my incredulous look, he added rather indignantly, "You try turning down the scent of cinnamon and sugar and my ultimate love: butter."

I snatched a piece of the dessert bun off his plate and groaned in sheer bliss as it melted on my tongue. The well-balanced flavors and sweetness were enough to make me forget why I'd initially marched down here at this hour. Thomas set the plate on a dresser and eyed me with the same sort of hunger and devotion he'd gazed at the pastries with.

Without taking his attention from me, he reached over and wiped a bit of icing from the corner of my lip; then his mouth was on mine. It was warm and sweet. And wholly unexpected. The pastries had been good, but this was *much* better. He slowly backed us into the dresser so I could sit against it, taking my weight from my leg. While we kissed, he gently cradled my face between his hands as if I was the most precious thing in his world.

Somehow, both his consideration and our new position awakened something untamable in me. I longed for more. I pushed off from the furniture and leaned him against the bed, enjoying the flash of surprise as I deepened our kiss. Thomas recovered quickly, opening his mouth to taste me, his hands running along my spine. After a moment or two, neither one of us seemed satisfied with the distance remaining between us. His hands drifted down to my hips, gripping them in a way that was both sweet and possessive. I slipped mine under his jacket and went for the cravat at his throat, before he leashed himself.

"Wait," he said, breathless.

I drew back, startled. "I—Is this too much?"

Thomas hooked an arm around me and tugged me near, dropping kisses from my lips to my heart and back again. Like his demeanor in the laboratory, his attention to detail was slow and deliberate. He listened to each thrum of my heart, each inhalation of breath, and used his powers of deduction for my pleasure. When he finally managed to pull away again, his breathing was as heavy as his lids. "No, Wadsworth. It's not too much at all. It's just—"

"It's your virtue, isn't it?" I teased. "You want to wait until we're properly married."

"God, no." He snorted. "I've wanted to ravish you for an indecently long while. If I was a more selfish creature, I'd take you right this moment if you'd have me." My attention moved from his mouth to his bed, considering. "However"—he sat down on the mattress and patted the spot next to him—"you might not wish to take things any further tonight. I—"

My earlier worries came rushing back and I interrupted him before I lost my nerve. "Have you courted someone else?"

"I—" He studied me in that swift deductive way of his. I expected to see mirth; instead he leaned over and kissed me chastely. "I have never officially courted or asked permission to court anyone. Only you."

I breathed out, though relief was short-lived. One little distinction caught my attention. He and I weren't *officially* courting, either. At least not until my father agreed to it. Thomas ran a hand over his face and I finally noticed the worry he'd been hiding.

"There's something you ought to read," he said. "I found this earlier and have been debating the best time to show you."

Something akin to hysteria writhed in my gut. He must have received an anonymous letter, too. My palms were suddenly damp and my mouth bone-dry. Someone was targeting us for reasons I dared not consider. "What is it?"

"It's—I think it's best to see for yourself." He flipped through a journal and removed an envelope, eyes downcast as he handed it to me. For a moment, it seemed as if the entire universe had drawn a breath, waiting for my response. My panic only increased when I removed the letter and was struck immobile at the handwriting.

It couldn't be.

I blinked, certain I must be hallucinating. It was not written in the same hand as the letter I'd received. This one was much more familiar. I'd know it anywhere.

"What is this?" I asked, my voice betraying my fear. Thomas shook his head and remained silent. I steeled myself. His demeanor indicated it would be worse after I read it.

Blood rushed in my ears as I began reading. I now understood precisely why Thomas had held back from our clandestine moment. My limbs felt weak and I couldn't decide if I wished to scream or cry or do some mad combination of the two. I fought the upheaval of emotion swirling in me, hoping I wouldn't be sick this very second. Like a golden sun rising on the horizon, a new nightmare was dawning bright.

My beloved brother had one more secret he'd been keeping.

And it changed everything I thought I knew.

Dearest Sister,

if you are reading this letter, it means i've either been arrested or have already met with justice. What a pity. i suspect the queen and Parliament have been waiting to rip me apart for the trouble i caused. i imagine it's been a hard time for you, but i ask that you remain strong of will and mind. Despite whatever circumstances have led us to this point, i hope this note finds you well, though perhaps you'll feel a bit sick after you've finished it. it is one more regret to add to the list, i'm afraid.

i know there's a strong chance you'll not be pleased by my deeds, but i have one final confession to make. i liked to fancy myself as Jekyll, really. My colleague, well, let's call him Mr. Hyde, is returning to America soon and he's promised to continue our work there.

i love you, no matter what anyone may say—know that as truth. i'm sorry for what i've done, but i swear you will soon see the value of my work, even if you disagree with the methods. One day you'll understand the truth of who Jack the Ripper is. Do not forget about my journals, dear sister. i wrote them for you and our family's legacy.

Love forever and always,
Nathaniel Jonathan Wadsworth

SIX

A VICIOUS DISCOVERY

THOMAS'S ROOMS
FIFTH AVENUE, NEW YORK CITY
21 JANUARY 1889

There were two of them.

I trembled violently, almost crushing the letter in my fist as I leapt from the edge of the bed. Pain lashed up my leg like a fiery whip, reminding me to be gentle with my body, though there was no protecting my heart. I tried to ignore the angry throbbing by reading the note again. And again, my pulse raced with each treacherous sentence.

There were two of them.

It couldn't be true. It couldn't. And yet...I couldn't breathe. I could barely *think* through the cacophony in my head. I wanted to claw my corset off and set it on fire. I wanted to run from this room and my life, and never look back.

"Audrey Rose?"

I held up a hand, stalling Thomas from whatever he was about to say. An enormous pressure kept building under my ribs and the air suddenly felt too thin or too heavy. This had to be a nightmare. Soon I'd wake from it and all would be well. Soon I'd remember my beloved brother was Jack the Ripper and he was dead and my family was shattered, but we were slowly piecing our lives back together. We were broken but not defeated. We were—I pinched my arm and cried out. I was awake and this was happening. I swallowed hard.

I could not accept this letter. I couldn't. The implications were too much to bear. Without preamble, I dropped onto the mattress, head spinning. Though perhaps it wasn't my mind that was under attack—my heart was close to breaking. Again. How many times would this case haunt me? How many secrets did my brother keep? Just when I thought I'd solved one mystery, another took its place, more brutal and vicious than the last.

I focused on drawing in a slow breath and exhaling. A feat more difficult than it should've been. Jack the Ripper hadn't committed his crimes alone. His reign of terror was not yet complete. That thought ripped the rest of my heart from my chest. Jack the Ripper was alive.

All this time...all of these *months* I'd convinced myself that his horrors were over. That his death might offer a bit of solace to the spirits of those he'd slain, though keeping his secret didn't offer me the same peace in return. Every ghost of the past I'd worked to fight against, every demon in my imagination—*everything* was rallying against this news, clawing its way up my throat, taunting me with an *I told you so*. His death was one more lie to choke down. Tears burned my eyes.

Jack the Ripper was two depraved, twisted men acting as one. And I knew—I *knew* with every molecule of my body that he'd been with us on the *Etruria*. That crime was too much like him for me to have overlooked it. I committed the same mistake I had during our first case—I ignored the facts because I didn't *want* to see them for what they were. I drew in one ragged breath after another.

Jack the Ripper lived. I couldn't stop repeating it in my mind.

"Wadsworth...please, say something."

I clamped my mouth shut. If I opened it now, I might start screaming and never stop. I didn't know who my brother or the real Ripper was. I barely recognized myself in this moment. Who else in my life wasn't what he or she appeared to be? I closed my eyes, forcing myself to become a solid block of ice on the inside. Now wasn't the time to fall apart.

"On the ship," I said through gritted teeth. "He'd sat in the shadows, night after night, watching, lurking, probably enjoying the chaos of another career murderer putting on a show." I shook my head, anger filling the space where hurt had resided moments before. I wondered if my rage was hot enough to set others on fire. "Does he know me? Was he stalking me across the sea, or was it simply a twist of fate that our paths crossed once more?"

I set the letter down and gripped the rose knob of my cane until my fingers went numb. I wanted to bash it into the Ripper's skull. I wanted—

Thomas slowly placed his hand over mine. He held it there until the violence left me. "There's more, I'm afraid. In his journals."

I fought a bitter laugh. Of course there was more. It seemed this nightmare was only just beginning. Each time I thought I closed a chapter, there was a new twist waiting to reveal itself. I didn't bother asking for details. If there was more, it involved another person, and another tragic loss of life. Another brutal murder to add to the Ripper's blood-soaked résumé.

"Who?"

"A Miss Martha Tabram. She was a prostitute who earned a living in the East End." Thomas watched me carefully before rummaging through the stack of journals, finding the one he'd been reading. "Nathaniel saved several newspaper clippings discussing her death. Apparently she'd been stabbed thirty-nine times with two different knives. One was thought to be a pocketknife, and the other was described as a dagger. Judging from what we know of the other Ripper killings, it was probably a long, thin surgical knife."

I turned the information over in my mind. The urge to scream was still present, but the need decreased as I shifted into mystery solving. "Did Uncle attend the murder site?"

"No." Thomas shook his head. "A Dr. Killeen was called to inspect her body at the scene, and another coroner is quoted in a second article. I'm not sure why Dr. Wadsworth wasn't consulted."

"Probably because Scotland Yard had no need of his expertise yet." I stared at the headline. My uncle was a brilliant professor of forensic medicine and often assisted on a case when invited, but he was not an official member of Scotland Yard. "As you're well aware, prior to Jack the Ripper, a repeat murderer was practically unheard of. I imagine they used whichever coroner was available and didn't give it a second thought."

Neither one of us mentioned a more glaring reason why they hadn't called in an expert: our society was unkind to women. Especially those who were forced to survive any way they could. Sure, the papers would claim they'd exhausted all possible inquiries, but it was another filthy lie told to enhance their tale. To sell their papers. To make them sleep better at night.

I inhaled deeply, channeling my returning rage into something usable. Anger wouldn't resolve problems, but action would. I inspected the first article with a cool head.

THE HORRIBLE AND MYSTERIOUS MURDER AT GEORGE'S YARD, WHITECHAPEL ROAD.

" 'The August Bank Holiday murder took place in George Yard Buildings.' " I read the first few lines of the article aloud. "Her body was discovered in the morning of the seventh of August." My blood chilled. "That's nearly three weeks prior to Miss Mary Nichols."

The first—supposed—victim of Jack the Ripper.

"What's interesting," Thomas said, grabbing another journal

from the pile, "is Miss Emma Elizabeth Smith was also murdered during a bank holiday."

I closed my eyes, recalling all too clearly that she'd died on the fourth of April. My mother's birthday. Another fact from her case rose to the surface of my mind. "She lived on George Street. This murder took place in George Yard. It might mean something to the killer."

Thomas seemed intrigued by this new thread. He got off the bed and sat at a small writing desk, jotting notes down. While he lost himself with that task, I turned my attention back to the newspaper clippings regarding Miss Martha Tabram's death. My brother didn't claim her murder in his journal—at least he hadn't done so in this volume—but his interest was no coincidence.

The *East London Advertiser* proclaimed:

The circumstances of this awful tragedy are not only surrounded with the deepest mystery, but there is also a feeling of insecurity to think that in a great city like London, the streets of which are continually patrolled by police, a woman could be foully and horribly killed almost next to the citizens peacefully sleeping in their beds, without a trace or clue being left of the villain who did the deed. There appears to be not the slightest trace of the murderer, and no clue has at present been found.

I rubbed my temples. I hadn't heard of this murder, though if I recalled correctly, the first part of August had been unusual in my home. My brother was preoccupied with his law studies, and my father was in one of his especially gruff moods. I'd attributed Nathaniel's absences to Father's growing agitation and had thought my father was upset by the approach of my seventeenth birthday.

Every morning, he'd taken the newspapers and had them burned before I could read them.

Now I knew why. It wasn't madness, but fear. I turned the next page of the journal and silently read a quote clipped from an article.

"The man must have been a perfect savage to inflict such a number of wounds on a defenseless woman in such a way." This from a George Collier, deputy coroner for the district.

Hastily scratched below, in Nathaniel's frantic hand, was a passage from our favorite gothic novel, *Frankenstein*.

> . . . if our impulses were confined to hunger, thirst, and desire, we might be nearly free; but now we are moved by every wind that blows and a chance word or scene that that word may convey to us. We rest; a dream has power to poison sleep. We rise; one wand'ring thought pollutes the day. We feel, conceive, or reason; laugh or weep, Embrace fond woe, or cast our cares away; It is the same: for, be it joy or sorrow, The path of its departure still is free. Man's yesterday may ne'er be like his morrow; Nought may endure but mutability!

I'd read the book so many times during chilly October evenings that it took only a few moments to place the scene. Dr. Victor Frankenstein had traveled to a land of snow and ice to confront his monster. Before his meeting with the creature he so despised, he'd hinted that nature could heal a man's soul. Did my brother fancy himself as Dr. Victor Frankenstein?

I'd always thought he'd considered himself the monster based on previous passages he'd underlined months ago. How well could I claim to know him, though? How well did any of us truly know one another? Secrets were more precious than any diamond or currency. And my brother had been rich with them.

I found a nib of ink and began scribbling my own furious notes on a blank page, adding dates and theories that seemed as unhinged and untamed as Frankenstein's monster. Perhaps I was becoming my own mad, feral creature.

Movement caught my attention a second before Thomas knelt in front of me, his expression uncharacteristically kind. For a fleeting moment, I wondered how I looked through his eyes. Did I seem as wild as I felt? My heart thumped as quickly as a rabbit's, but my instincts weren't to flee; I wished to draw blood. Thomas touched my brow, then traced his finger across my hairline, soothing a knot I hadn't realized was forming. I relaxed at his touch. Marginally.

"You've got a certain aura of murder that's—quite honestly—a strange mixture of alluring and troubling. Even for me. What is it?" he asked. I turned the journal around, pointing out the *Frankenstein* passage. He read it, then searched my face. "I remember your brother was intrigued with Galvani's experiments with electricity and dead frogs, and Shelley. But that isn't what's bothering you."

"In one article the wounds described on Martha's body were focused around her throat and lower abdomen."

Thomas's gaze moved back over the *Frankenstein* passage, his own brow creasing at my seemingly abrupt change in subject. "Emma's wounds were thought to be too different from the five murders that took place in Whitechapel," I said, growing more confident as I spoke. "Her attacker neither went for her throat nor stabbed her."

Thomas swallowed hard, no doubt remembering with vivid detail the atrocities that had been done to her. "No, she'd been brutalized in other horrific ways."

"Indeed." Someone had ruptured her peritoneum by inserting a foreign object into her body. We'd never been sure if it was machinery or something else that had done the damage. Gears were found at the scene, something we later realized were part of my brother's plan to pass electricity into dead tissues. "Nathaniel speaks of Jekyll and Hyde in his letter," I continued, "but this passage points back to his preoccupation with Dr. Frankenstein and his monster."

"I'm afraid I'm not quite following, Wadsworth. Do you believe your brother was using gothic novels as his source material for his killings?"

"Not entirely. I believe Nathaniel might be responsible for Miss Emma Elizabeth Smith's death. He was obsessed with fusing machine and human together. Her attack fits with that. It also fits seamlessly with Galvani's experimentations. Dr. Galvani demonstrated that a dint of electricity could make a frog's muscles twitch postmortem. Nathaniel tried to improve upon his theory and take it even further by bringing humans back to life using a larger electrical charge."

"I thought we established Miss Smith as a likely Ripper victim," Thomas said carefully.

"We did. But it doesn't fit. Even if his method of killing shifted as his deadly talents grew, her murder was not the ultimate goal. Not like the others. She'd been brutalized, but I don't believe he wished to slay her. He wanted her to live. That was his entire point. Nathaniel wasn't interested in killing things. He longed for a way to bring them back."

Thomas was quiet and perfectly still.

"Nathaniel killed Emma, but he was never Jack the Ripper, Thomas. He was the man who *made* Jack the Ripper. Or perhaps befriended him."

Thomas glanced at the dates I'd hastily scrawled. A battle of emotion crossed his features. "If Nathaniel attacked Emma in April, perhaps her death disturbed him. It would seem that there may have been a part of him that couldn't cross that line again. At least not himself." He looked me over carefully. "Did he exhibit any early behaviors that would hint to savior ideologies?"

At first I went to shake my head, but a memory surfaced. "When we were children, he used to become physically ill if he couldn't save a stray cat or dog. The thought of something dying was unbearable to him. He'd lie in bed for days, crying or staring at the ceiling. It was terrible and there wasn't anything I could do to bring him out of that dark place." I inhaled deeply, trying not to get lost in thoughts of the past. "If Miss Martha Tabram is the first true Ripper victim, that means Nathaniel had nearly four months to create his own monster. He says in his own words"—I jabbed the letter—"that he worked with another. I imagine my brother urged these killings on and profited scientifically from the organs acquired, but another person actually committed the rest of the murders."

"That does not make your brother innocent," Thomas said gently.

I lowered my head. If my theory was correct, Nathaniel had forged a person into a blade, making him far from innocent. And yet confronting his guilt—yet again—caused a visceral ache I didn't anticipate. We humans could not help loving our monsters. "I know."

Thomas rolled his head from side to side. "There's still a possibility Nathaniel only followed the murder of Miss Smith from the papers. Perhaps the true murderer sought him out, or vice versa. At present, we're speculating. You know what your uncle says about that."

Speculation was pointless. Facts were what we needed. I looked at the stacks of journals on Thomas's bed. My brother had written volumes of notes. I feared it would take years to unravel each new thread he'd knotted away. Thomas stood behind me and placed his hands on my shoulders, slowly working the tension from them.

"It's only a puzzle in need of solving, Wadsworth. We'll figure it out together."

I fought a fresh wave of tears and reached up to hold Thomas's hand in mine. "I—"

"If you're both so inclined to join us," Uncle said, entering the chamber, eyes flashing at Thomas's other hand still touching my shoulder, "Inspector Byrnes is in the parlor."

Bellevue Hospital, circa 1885/1898

SEVEN

MISERY LANE

GRANDMAMA'S PARLOR
FIFTH AVENUE, NEW YORK CITY
21 JANUARY 1889

Inspector Byrnes stood with his large hands clutched behind his back, staring at a portrait of my grandfather that hung like a warning over the fireplace. Judging from the straightness of his posture and the way his muscles looked ready to spring forward at the smallest hint of trouble, his news wasn't good. Not that I expected it to be.

"Thank you for calling on us so late, Inspector," Uncle said by way of greeting. "Would you care for a drink?"

The inspector turned and removed a folded newspaper from his coat. He leaned over and slapped it onto a rather delicate end table, his cheeks deepening to near purple as he read the headline through clenched teeth.

JACK THE RIPPER HAS COME TO AMERICA.

"This abomination of a headline will be shouted by every news-boy in the city come dawn. I don't know what happened in London, but it won't stand here!" He straightened and took a moment to compose himself. "I won't let Jack the Ripper strike fear into the heart of my city, Dr. Wadsworth."

A muscle in Uncle's jaw twitched, the only indication he was getting annoyed. "I am a man of science, not a portending device. If you'd like to give me more details, perhaps I can help craft a better understanding or profile of who this killer is. Differences in wounds left on the victim could help alleviate hysteria. Unless you share your findings, I'm afraid I have nothing else to offer."

"Fine. You want more facts? We confirmed the victim's identity as a Miss Carrie Brown, a local wh…prostitute," Byrnes said, clearly shifting his words because of my presence. What a pleasant gentleman. I all but rolled my eyes. "Friends called her Old Shakespeare, since she used to quote him when she was deep in her cups."

Thomas and I glanced at each other. Now that there was a significant potential that the Ripper was alive and well, ignoring the parts that fit with his previous killings was difficult. He was known for victimizing prostitutes who'd been heavy drinkers. Just like this murderer.

"A friend of hers came forward, an Alice Sullivan," Byrnes continued. "Alice said she saw Carrie twice that day. Carrie hadn't had a proper meal in days, so that afternoon Alice got them sandwiches at a saloon. She claims they met up again for an evening meal at the local Christian mission before going their separate ways to do their business."

"When was the last time she was seen?" Uncle asked.

"Alice said around half past eight that night. Saw her with a man named Frenchy."

"Was Alice the last person to witness her alive with him?" I asked.

Inspector Byrnes shook his head. "Mary Minter, the housekeeper at the hotel, saw her take a man into her room later that evening. She said he wore a black derby hat and had a thick mustache. Real dodgy. Didn't look anyone in the eye, kept his face down. Like he was trying to not be noticed. We can't confirm if it was Frenchy or someone else."

"Has someone tracked down Frenchy?" Uncle asked.

"Apparently, she was seen with two different men named Frenchy last night." At Uncle's confused look, he clarified, "Frenchy is a popular nickname around that neighborhood. One man is called Isaac Perringer. We're still lookin' for the other. For now we're callin' them Frenchy Number One and Frenchy Number Two. I've got my best men out searching for them. We'll round them all up and show them to the witnesses."

"Most hotels, even more questionable ones, require a ledger to be signed," Thomas said. "Did anyone on your staff inquire about it?"

"Course. What kind of fools do you think we are over here?" Byrnes gave Thomas a scathing look. "He registered them as a C. Nicolo and wife."

"Do you have a photograph of the ledger?" I asked.

Byrnes frowned. I was unsure if it was our inquisition about his police work, or if the question caught him off guard. "Can't say that I do. Why?"

"An analysis of the writing might prove this murder cannot be connected to the London Ripper," Uncle said, giving me a swift nod of approval. "If you're so keen to quiet the papers, it'd be an excellent way to show the person in question's hand is different from known Ripper letters. Between that and securing a witness to place either 'Frenchy' at the murder scene, it ought to be easy enough to tamp down Ripper hysteria."

"You're expecting a drunken lot, most of whom lack proper intelligence during the best of times, to be reliable witnesses." Byrnes buttoned his overcoat and donned a bowler hat. I fought the urge to remind him that *he* was the one who'd suggested "rounding them up," not Uncle. And it was their circumstances, not their intelligence, that made them turn to the bottle. "You're either incredibly naïve, or hopeful, or both, Dr. Wadsworth." He tipped his hat and headed for the door. "Good night."

"Inspector?" Uncle asked, stepping into his way. "Will we have access to the body?"

Byrnes paused, considering. "She'll be in the morgue at Bellevue until they take her to Blackwell's Island along with the other unclaimed bodies. If I were you, I'd go tonight. Sometimes corpses don't make it 'til morning. Especially not on Misery Lane."

The morgue on 26th Street—appropriately referred to as Misery Lane—ought to have been called a crypt. One from the likes of Poe's macabre imagination or the beginnings of a sinister vampire tale. It was dark and dank and smelled of rot and human waste. If I allowed my mind to wander, I might convince myself I could hear the faint beating of a buried heart.

Located one story below the foreboding hospital above, bodies lay stacked in heaps on wooden tables. I'd never seen such disregard for the dead before and swallowed my horror down. Corpses were shoved so closely together, I wondered how they'd moved new bodies onto adjacent tables without knocking the others over in the process.

Uncle paused at the threshold, his gaze landing on each body in various states of decay. He removed a handkerchief from his inner pocket, eyes watering. One corpse nearby had already begun to bloat, and the fingers and toes were the blackish blue of death.

A man in a butcher's apron glanced at us, then went about his business of inspecting the bodies. Candles burned ominously close to the corpses. Two young men dressed in black stood in the shadows, watching the coroner with bored interest. He snapped at them, motioning to a cadaver that seemed quite fresh. "This ought to do. Take it and be off with yourselves now."

Their boredom transformed into a gleam of hunger I knew well as they stepped forward and claimed the proffered dead. They hoisted the elderly male corpse onto a wheeled stretcher, hastily tossing a sheet over it as they pushed it out of the room. The sound of wheels turning rumbled down a corridor. At my furrowed brow, Thomas leaned in to whisper, "Medical students."

"Interns." The old man turned back to us, eyeing my uncle with thinly veiled annoyance as he pulled a pocket watch out. It was nearly midnight. "You the professor from London?"

"Dr. Jonathan Wadsworth." Uncle glanced around the room again, the flickering light reflecting in his spectacles like flames. I fought a shiver. He looked like a vengeful demon. "I'm told the body of Miss Carrie Brown is here. Would you mind showing it to us?"

"The whore?" The coroner's sour expression said he most certainly minded the interruption, especially for someone as lowly as a prostitute. I clenched my hands. "If you must." He jerked a thumb down one long, narrow aisle of cadavers. "This way."

Thomas, ever the gentleman, swung his arm toward the two men retreating down the row of the dead. "After you, my love."

I gave him a tight smile and followed Uncle, my cane clicking in alternating soft and hard thumps as I walked over mounds of sawdust on the tile floors. I wasn't frightened of the corpses—those I found strangely comforting. The atmosphere and disregard for their scientific study made my skin crawl. Well, that and the maggots wiggling around the bits of bloodied sawdust, which hadn't been swept away in quite some time.

At the end of a row of bodies, close to where a lone bulb buzzed above us, we stood over the remains of Miss Carrie Brown. Much to my dismay, she'd been washed. Swathes of pale flesh marbled with deep blue veins were marred only by the stab wounds. Uncle closed his eyes for a moment, likely trying to collect his anger. "She's been cleaned."

"Course she has. Won't do us any favors to keep her dirty and stinking while she's here."

A blatant lie. None of the other bodies had been cleaned. He'd probably tried tidying her up to sell to the doctor in the operating amphitheater above. A potential Jack the Ripper victim would be quite a draw. Thomas reached for my arm as I took an unconscious step forward. I wouldn't resort to violence, but part of me wished to strangle this man. Miss Carrie Brown had already been forced to sell herself in life; these men had no right to auction her flesh in death.

"Did you photograph the body before wiping away evidence?" I asked.

"You a nurse?" The coroner squinted at me. "Doctor's sending all sorts down to collect his specimens now."

My nostrils flared. Thomas carefully stepped beside me. He was worried for the old man's safety, not mine. "Miss Wadsworth is exceptional with postmortem studies. Her inquiry is a valid point, sir. Blood evidence is often overlooked, but we've found instances where studying it proves most beneficial to tracing a murderer's killing blows."

"Did that fancy London schooling help Scotland Yard find Jack the Ripper?" He shook his head. "You've got thirty minutes before the meat cart comes for her. Unless you'll be following her to the island of unclaimed bodies, I suggest focusing on what you came to do."

Uncle held a hand up, both a command and a request for my silence. Fuming at the ignorance of that rude man, I silently counted to ten. Fantasizing about all the ways I *could* flay him open until I found peace once more. Uncle pulled an apron from his medical satchel and handed it to me, his focus straying to my leg. "If this is too much—"

"I'm fine, sir." I set my cane against the cadaver table and tied the apron about my person. "Shall I make the first incision or assist while you do it?"

Uncle took in the determined set of my jaw, the defiance flashing in my eyes, and gave me a small nod of approval. He'd taught me well.

"Don't forget to hold the skin taut."

EIGHT

BARON OF SOMERSET

GRANDMAMA'S PARLOR
FIFTH AVENUE, NEW YORK CITY
22 JANUARY 1889

"Care to sit on my lap?" I whirled around and the corner of Thomas's mouth lifted in a half smirk. "Your pacing's having a curious effect on my pulse. If we're going to remain distracted from our research, there are more exciting ways to pass the time that will keep our heart rates up."

"This is hardly the time for such . . . pursuits, Cresswell."

"This might be the perfect time for *those* pursuits. Your uncle's escorting Liza around the city. Mrs. Harvey, bless her predictability, is napping. Which means you and I have the house to ourselves. If we were to compare it to some killer's motivation, this is an opportunity too perfect to pass up. Shall I kiss you or would you prefer to kiss me first?"

"Oh, yes. Now that you've compared our romantic tryst with a murderer, I feel precisely like kissing." I shot him my most incredulous look. "In the last twenty-four hours, we've discovered Jack the Ripper might not be who we thought he was and is still alive. A woman was brutally murdered. My father will be here in mere hours, deciding our fate, and you're lounging in that chaise, sipping coffee, nibbling on petit fours, and making untoward innuendoes as if nothing is wrong."

"They're only untoward if you're uninterested. Judging by the flush creeping into your face, and the way you keep glancing at my mouth with that ravish-me-now look in your eyes, I'd say you were quite keen on ruining me this moment."

"Have you no morals?"

"Don't be ridiculous; of course I've got morals. One or two, perhaps."

"Honestly, Cresswell?" I couldn't believe he was making light of our situation when I was certain the universe was caving in around us.

"You're right. Three at most."

Thomas popped another petit four into his mouth and stretched his legs out in front of him. His chest rose and fell in even intervals. It was maddening that he could be so calm and collected while I felt as if a storm was lashing about my insides.

He grinned.

"Your father, Lord Wadsworth, the great Baron of Somerset, adores me and wishes to see *you* happy. There's nothing to worry over there. We're one step closer to uncovering the truth behind the Ripper murders. Which is cause for celebration. This"—he held his cup up— "is actually a strange—yet not entirely unpleasant—herbal tea concoction Liza offered me before she left." He took a sip of it and continued to drink me in as he did so, his gaze sweltering enough to nearly burn a hole in my resolve. "And it was a genuine request, not an innuendo."

"Gentlemen don't offer such crude suggestions to their loved ones."

Trouble sparkled in his eyes. "Scoundrels do and they have entirely more fun."

Part of me longed to fall into his arms and kiss him until all our worries melted away, but that was impractical. I snuck a quick look at him, admiring the deep blue of his suit. Thomas might be more scoundrel than gentleman, but he always dressed the part of a prince.

This morning was no exception. My focus moved from the swirls on his waistcoat to the careful knot of his cravat and traveled up to his full lips. The ones that were quirked in wicked delight. My face heated as I realized I'd been caught admiring him.

"I promise not to bite or nip at you in any untoward manner. Please." He patted the seat next to him, expression devilish yet innocent. "I have something for you."

"Thomas—"

"Swear it." He crossed his heart. "Here."

He leaned over and pulled a package out from where he'd hidden it behind the chaise, a look of triumph flashing in his face. The charcoal-colored box was long and thin, with a beautiful black ribbon. Intrigued, I crossed the room and settled next to him, exchanging my cane for the box. Unable to help myself, I shook the present a bit. Whatever it was, it had been secured within an inch of its life. There wasn't so much as a rattle.

Thomas laughed. "Go on and open it."

Needing no further encouragement, I pulled the ribbon free and removed the lid. Inside, on a bed of crimson velvet, a gleaming new cane caught the light. For a moment, my heart stilled. I'd thought my ebony rose knob had been spectacular, but Thomas had found yet another way to impress me. I removed it, marveling at the fine craftsmanship.

The wooden shaft was dark, nearly black, with hints of crimson. A wrought silver dragon with rubies for eyes coiled around the handle of the cane, mouth open, as if it were about to set its enemies on fire. I felt an immediate kinship with it.

"It's rosewood. My mother had a chess set made of it. We'd play sometimes when I had trouble falling asleep." Thomas reached over and pressed a ruby eye, releasing a hidden stiletto blade that flicked open at its end. "I thought you'd like it. It reminded me a bit of Henri, the dragon I told you about from our home in Bucharest." His voice was shy, uncertain. I studied the way he bit his lip and fiddled with the blade. "It may be presumptuous, but I-I'd hoped you might enjoy carrying a symbol of my family. If you don't wish to, I've got another on order, so please don't feel obligated. I—"

"I adore it, Thomas." I ran a finger over the dragon's scaled head, words stuck in my throat. "I am honored you wished to share your family's legacy with me."

"I didn't want you to think it was claiming territory."

I laughed outright. "Oh, Thomas. I truly love you."

Whatever shyness or uncertainty he'd felt earlier was gone. His attention was sure and steady, and he boldly inspected me. He moved his gaze from my eyes to my lips, where it lingered a moment. I swore the boy possessed the ability to set a person ablaze using one smoldering look. "I want you to always have choices."

Choices. Those would be grand. I glanced at the mound of journals waiting for us on the table. There was much work to be done. So many mysteries left to unravel. My head knew we needed to focus on solving these crimes, but my heart wished to curl up in front of the fire, pull Thomas into my arms, and kiss him until we were both blissfully happy. I permitted myself one more moment of this fantasy life—pretended we were the sort of couple who needn't trouble ourselves with anything other than reading the paper and tending to the house.

A mental image of a woman lying split open snapped me back to reality.

Ever in tune with me, Thomas helped me to my feet and sighed. "You start in on the journals; I'll fetch us more tea."

I snagged his arm and kissed him deeply. I ran my hands through his hair, then stepped back, pleased by his tousled, surprised look. "Bring some scones and clotted cream, too. And maybe a few more petit fours. I adore those little candied flowers on top."

Around four o'clock, I gave up on the journals. Nathaniel had scientific notes mixed with quotes from Dante, Milton, and Shelley. His train of thought was hard to follow and it appeared as if madness had overtaken him, though I had a nagging feeling that I was missing a crucial clue hidden within his ramblings. No matter how hard I tried, I kept reading the same sentence, my gaze returning to the second hand of the clock as it anxiously ticked along.

Uncle had left nearly an hour ago to meet my father and aunt at the docks.

Each time a carriage rattled by, my heart pounded through my body in a wild, thrashing beat. I moved my new cane from one hand to the other, focusing on the smooth rosewood and fierce dragon to soothe my nerves. Liza and I had changed into finer dresses, and my lavender skirts were quite the contrast to my menacing, red-eyed dragon cane.

"Remember, your father worships me, Wadsworth." Thomas dragged me from my spiraling worry, expertly reading each shift in my mood. "Leave charming him to me."

My lips twitched upward. "Yes, well, if that's true it's a clear indication Father's abusing his tonic again."

"Or he's got horrible judgment," Liza added, grinning at Thomas's scowl. "Don't be cross, Mr. Cresswell. I'm only stating facts. You know, those bits of logic and hard truth you adore subjecting the rest of us to *incessantly*?"

"Wonderful," he said, "you're both hilarious now."

"You started it," I said, now focused entirely on him and not my nerves.

Thomas offered an amused grin from behind the journal he'd been engrossed in all day. I very maturely stuck my tongue out, and his eyes darkened in a way that had my pulse speeding for other reasons. Despite my best efforts, my cheeks flushed warm and the rogue winked, turning his attention back to his reading material. I all but rolled my eyes.

Liza stood several times, drawing back the heavy velvet drapery, staring down into the street. She sat beside me, picked up her needle-work, then tossed it down and practically ran to the window the next time wheels clattered by. Her skirts seemed to increase in volume depending on her mood, and today they were ruffled and fluffed to within an inch of their lives. She was as nervous as I was. Perhaps a little bit more. Aunt Amelia was a force to be reckoned with on a good day. I feared today would not be one of her more gracious days.

"This is ridiculous," Liza muttered. "It's not as if our parents are going to murder us." She glanced sharply at me over her shoulder. "They wouldn't get away with murdering their own children, would they?"

"Depends on how well they dispose of your bodies." Thomas just managed to dodge a pillow that flew by his head. I smiled as Liza huffed a few unladylike curses under her breath.

In a continued effort to give me freedom, my father had granted me permission to sail to New York with Uncle Jonathan and Thomas to assist with a forensic case, but Aunt Amelia had been worried into a fit when Liza vanished without so much as a note. Learning that her well-bred daughter had in fact run away to join a floating carnival likely turned all that fear into a raging fury. I suspected my aunt might become hysterical upon seeing Liza. She might very well lock her away in a tower.

I pasted on my brightest smile. "Your mother is going to be very relieved to see you."

Likely *after* she let loose a litany of admonishments and chained Liza to her rooms for the remainder of her natural life. My cousin gave me the sort of look that called me on my lie, but she turned her attention back to the street, her face turning deathly pale.

"They're here."

"Very funny."

"Truly." Liza held a hand to her center. "Your father is stepping out from the hansom now."

I wondered at the sudden void of nerves. It seemed as if my heart either skipped a beat or had ceased to move entirely. I snuck a peek at Thomas, hoping for him to appear as uneasy as my cousin and me, but he sprang to his feet with a jaunty hop.

I stared, openmouthed, as he bounced from foot to foot.

He caught my eye. "What? Can't a young man enjoy a good hop every now and again without judgment?"

I shook my head. "Aren't you the least bit worried?"

"About what?" he asked, a crease forming between his brows. "Seeing your aunt and father again?"

For a near genius, he could be quite obtuse. "Oh, I'm not sure. How about that small task of asking my father for my hand in marriage?"

"Why should I worry over that?" Thomas helped me to my feet, his smile returning in full force. "I've been waiting for this day like a child counting down the moments until Father Christmas arrives. If it were humanly possible, I would've swam to England and flew your father here on da Vinci's ornithopter the second you told me your wishes."

"You're—"

"Impossibly handsome and utterly charming and yes, yes, you'd love to ravish me right this moment. Let's hurry, now, shall we?"

My cousin snorted from her position by the window. "Now I understand why Audrey Rose calls you insufferably charming, with much emphasis on *insufferable*."

Thomas tossed an arm around Liza and steered us both through the doorway and into the corridor. "If you find me intolerable now, just wait until we're cousins, too. I have a special talent for annoying family members most. Just ask my father."

At this my cousin seemed to shed her nerves. Thomas didn't

speak often of his family and it was cause for great intrigue. "When will we be meeting your father?"

Liza didn't seem to notice the moment of hesitation, or the quick tightening of his jaw, but I'd been carefully watching. It was there and gone within the same breath. I didn't know much of his father's side of the family, but I'd gathered enough from Thomas's stories to know theirs was a relationship with much strain.

"Whenever he feels the need to show up and woo us with his charm," Thomas said. "If you think I'm extraordinary, wait until you have the luxury of meeting Lord Richard Abbott Cresswell. He puts me to shame. Which he will remind you of. Often."

Liza abruptly halted, her mouth dropping open. Worries of her mother's scorn were now the furthest thing from her mind. "The Duke of Portland is your father?" She flashed an accusatory glare at me. "You knew his father is a duke?"

I slowly shook my head. Thomas's mother had a distant claim to the Romanian throne, and I imagined his father—who he'd said married for business, not love—would have chosen his bride carefully. Lord Cresswell was not the type of man who'd marry below his station. Though I'd never asked outright, I'd assumed he was either an earl or possibly a duke.

There were a few Cresswells in the aristocracy; I just didn't know Thomas's father was the highest ranking of them. A twinge of worry crept under my skin. Society would whisper about me even more once they found out. I'd be called all sorts of unpleasant names.

As if she were privy to my thoughts, Liza exclaimed, "If you and Thomas marry, you'll be deemed an upstart!"

At that very moment, the front door opened. The smile that had been on my father's face faltered. "Who will dare to call my daughter that?"

NINE

A DESPERATE REQUEST

GRANDMAMA'S GRAND FOYER
FIFTH AVENUE, NEW YORK CITY
22 JANUARY 1889

Aunt Amelia stood behind my father's formidable form, likely crossing herself against the thought of societal condemnation. It hadn't taken but thirty seconds for me to draw her singular focus. I glanced at the ceiling rose, wishing it would magic me out of this situation. Liza shot me an apologetic look but bit her tongue. Her mother's attention would now be solely devoted to polishing any imperfections out of me. Aunt could never resist a charitable project.

"After I soak in a warm bath and remove the stain of transatlantic travel, we ought to spend time practicing your stitching," Aunt said by way of greeting. "Volunteering for the less fortunate will also help mend any rumors. Perhaps you may put your medical interests to use. You might aspire to be the next Clara Barton."

Uncle, who'd been patiently silent while everyone crowded into the foyer, rolled his eyes. "Yes, dear sister, that's a wise suggestion indeed. If Audrey Rose were at all versed in the field of nursing, it might be an even wiser idea. Since she tends to the dead, we'll have to search for other charitable means for her. Corpses aren't in need of medical supplies or darned stockings."

Aunt sniffed indignantly, turning her nose up. "Your grandmother's home is lovely. Will Lady Everleigh be joining us this evening?"

"No, Aunt. She was in India according to her last letter, but insisted we stay here while I…" I glanced at my cane. I hadn't mentioned my injury to my father in any letters, and he'd been too quiet since entering the home. Seeing his attention directed at my leg with a furrow in his brow, I knew why he'd been silent. I had much to explain. "I—"

"It's so good to see you both," Liza said, snapping into action. She rushed forward to kiss her mother's cheek, fussing like a hen when she stood back. "It feels like ages have passed! How was your voyage? The weather has been a fright! All the snow and sleet has been miserable. The hems of my dresses have seen better days."

For a moment that stretched uncomfortably into the next, my aunt didn't deign to respond. She scrutinized her daughter as if she were a stranger offering her a bouquet of dog poo. Liza had never openly disobeyed her mother before; she rebelled in her own subtle ways. I was the one Aunt Amelia had to save, what with my corpse fascination and poor judgment in young suitors. When Liza abandoned London to sail across the Atlantic with Harry Houdini without so much as a word, I can't imagine my aunt ever saw that betrayal coming.

Before she could comment, Liza called for the butler. "Have someone draw a bath for Mama immediately. I've also got dried lavender and rose oil in the washing room." She turned a radiant smile on her mother. "Lavender is so soothing, wouldn't you agree? I've been reading up on herbal blends. Who knew there were so many uses for petals?"

As slick as anything, my cousin looped her arm through Aunt's, steering her up the stairs and away from me. Thomas stepped forward and dipped his head politely at my father. "It's wonderful to see you again, Lord Wadsworth. I trust you journeyed well?"

Uncle sidestepped our little trio and shook his head as he disappeared down the corridor. He muttered something that sounded an awful lot like "good luck to you both" followed immediately by "pompous ass." I glared after him. I'd thought he and Father had put their feud aside when they'd worked together to get me into forensic school in Romania. Apparently there was still much work to be done on their relationship as well.

Thomas feigned ignorance over my father's belated response. I, however, was ready to toss myself out of the nearest window; my nerves were near bursting. Father inspected Thomas for another heart-stoppingly long moment before nodding. It wasn't quite the warm welcome I'd hoped for, but it certainly wasn't the worst given the circumstances. He'd entrusted Thomas with watching over me—no matter that my broken leg was a result of *my* choice and there wasn't a thing Thomas could've done about it. On the contrary, sometimes I'd catch him watching me limp and wondered if he wished he'd taken the knife and possibly died instead.

"We journeyed well indeed. Though I cannot say the same for my daughter." He pointedly glanced at my cane. "I imagine there's quite a story behind this." He met my gaze, his expression softening. "If you don't mind, I'd like a few moments to speak with Audrey Rose. Alone."

"Of course." Thomas offered another polite bow, then straightened. He winked at me and hummed his way along the corridor Uncle had disappeared down, leaving me alone to deal with the many questions and worries I saw flashing in my father's eyes.

I drew in a deep breath. It was time to plead my case about a possible betrothal. "Shall we move to the sitting room?"

It was hard to fathom that nearly two months had passed since I'd last seen my father. He was more robust than I remembered—his face had more color and his eyes were bright. Gone was the ashy pallor that clung to him like a second skin. I exhaled slowly. I hadn't realized how worried I'd been that he'd fall back into his addictions in my absence. Sadness still crept in around the edges, but he seemed in command of it now instead of the reverse.

He sat at an oversize writing desk, fingers steepled as he took in this new version of his daughter. I stood as still as I could manage. "You didn't mention the cane in any of your letters."

I swallowed hard, focus fixed on the dragon's-head knob. A thought struck as I pulled strength from this symbol of Thomas's house—he'd found a way to be with me, to ease my nerves while I spoke with my father. He truly thought of everything.

"I apologize, sir. I didn't want you to be upset unnecessarily. I—"

"Sweet girl." My father shook his head. "It was not an admonishment. I'm worried. When you left, you were whole, and now…"

"Make no mistake, Father. I am still whole. Neither a limp nor a cane will slow me down."

"I did not mean to offend." He smiled gently. "I can see you're adapting well. Give me time to do the same. You know I can be a bit—"

"Overbearing?" I asked, not unkindly. "All I require is love and acceptance."

"Then you shall have both in abundance." His eyes misted. "Well, now. Since that's settled, on to other matters. Jonathan tells me you've been taking to your forensic studies quite well. He believes your skill will surpass his in the near future."

I blinked at the sudden pricking sensation. "He hadn't mentioned that to me."

"I daresay he won't, either. Not until he's sure it won't go to your head. The fool." Father's eyes twinkled. "He also tells me that Thomas is a fine suitor. I must admit, when I agreed to send you to Romania, I didn't anticipate receiving a request for an audience with him. At least not so soon. I don't know if it's wise to entertain thoughts of courtship or betrothal now. You are young yet."

Here it was. I gripped the dragon a bit more tightly. "To be honest, sir, I hadn't planned on feeling so strongly for another. I-I tried fighting it, but I truly believe I've found my equal. I cannot imagine a more perfect partner to walk hand in hand with through life."

"Please. Sit." Father indicated the tufted chair across from him. Once I perched on its edge, he continued his inspection. "You're almost of age, but I fear there's much you'd be giving up. Why not come back and ask me this in a year's time? If your love is true, it won't be hindered by another few months. If anything, it will blossom further."

It felt as if someone had struck a blow to my chest. Each time I imagined this scenario, I didn't see my father pushing off our betrothal. A few months ago, he'd been secretly trying to match me with a detective inspector who hailed from an impressive family. Now he wanted me to wait. Neither of those spoke of what *I* desired.

"With all due respect, Father, Thomas and I have withstood events most couples will never face. We've been tested, and each bump, twist, and crack hasn't broken us. It's only made our bond stronger. I could wait another year or two or ten, but it wouldn't matter. The truth remains that I am in love with Thomas Cresswell and I choose to share my life with him."

"What of your studies? Will you give up what you've fought so hard for simply to become a mistress of a house?" Father took a sip of wine from a goblet I hadn't noticed. "Granted, Thomas hails from quite a lineage, so your home will be grand. Is that what you want from life? If you choose not to marry, you'll be heir to our property." He looked at me closely. Here was yet one more choice. One more bar being removed from my cage. "Once you marry, all of that will revert to your husband. And he will be fit to do with it as he pleases without your counsel. Are you certain that's what you wish? Do you know Thomas enough to trust him with such matters?"

I waited for it, the tremor of fear. The familiar thrum of hysteria building in my body, urging me to flee. It didn't come. If anything, my resolve turned molten hot before hardening into something unbreakable.

"I trust him entirely. He hasn't simply told me things to win my affections and trust with words; he's shown who he is through his actions. Never more so than when we traveled here last month. Thomas and I will write our own rules. I won't stop my studies and he won't stop his. Ours is a love built on mutual respect and admiration. I love Thomas for who he is. He doesn't wish to change me, or cage me, or turn me into a perfect doll to tout about." I took another deep breath. "In the event our marriage dissolved, he would never take my home or property from me. But," I quickly added, seeing my father about to seize on that thread, "I do not believe ours will be an unhappy union. On the contrary, I believe this is the beginning of our story. We have countless adventures ahead of us."

Father sat back, the leather of his chair creaking, and took another sip of wine. We stayed in comfortable silence, regarding each other for a few moments. It wasn't unpleasant. A fire crackled in the corner; the scent of leather and sandalwood wafted about. It was cozy and it felt good to simply be around my father again. Finally, he took a deep breath, seeming to come to his decision. His expression was utterly unreadable.

"Please have Thomas come in."

"Sir?" I asked, hating the edge of worry in my voice. "You will agree, won't you?"

"I may."

Relief sluiced through me. I practically stumbled out of my seat and threw my arms around my father's neck. "Thank you! Thank you so much, Father!"

He held me close, chuckling. "Now, now, child. Save your thanks for a little while more. Let's first hear what your Mr. Cresswell has to say."

Post-mortem set, London, England, 1860-1870.

TEN

CORPSE DELIVERY

I snuck into the parlor and cracked the door open, watching Thomas stand outside the sitting room, squaring his shoulders as if readying for war. I supposed it was a battle of sorts—he'd be fighting for my hand against a father who didn't wish to relinquish it just yet. It took all of my self-control to not go to him. He appeared determined, yet the way he stared at the closed door hinted at his own nerves. Not much ever subdued Thomas's swagger, though it appeared that my father's presence was doing a wonderful job of it. I'd made one more request to my father, and now it was up to Thomas to win this scrimmage for us both.

Uncle came around the corner, apron in hand. "They're bringing a body 'round the back. I've set up the carriage house for the autopsy. Gather your tools and meet me there at once."

My cheeks flushed as Thomas canted his head in our direction. So much for stealth.

"Are you—can it not wait?" I motioned to the room Thomas finally disappeared into. Uncle knew precisely what was happening and how important it was. "Thomas is—"

"Wasting time with matters of the heart when we've got a more important duty to uphold." His eyes flashed in warning. "Do not remind me of his wayward priorities. Unless you'd like to both be taken from this case or any future cases, I suggest you realign your focus. The two of you are acting like lovestruck young adults instead of serious students of forensic medicine. Settle your personal affairs on your own time."

With that he stormed past me and slammed the front door. I bit my lip, stealing one more look at the parlor. I longed to rush to Thomas and find out exactly what my father decided, but Uncle was right. This case was the most important of my life. If Jack the Ripper lived, I needed to set that straight before any more talk of weddings or love took place.

I called for my medical bag to be brought outside and made my way to the carriage house and the new body waiting to tell us its secrets.

⤙⟶⤚

"Focus! The left kidney weighs how much?" Uncle asked, practically snarling.

Another young woman lay on our makeshift examination table, silent, unlike the muffled street noise working its way into the carriage house. Wooden wheels clattering over cobblestones and another ravaged body weren't the only causes of my distraction, however. My leg ached terribly. I'd removed my overcoat and gloves in favor of working efficiently, and it was unforgivably cold. My breath puffed in little white clouds as I weighed the organ, teeth chattering.

"O-one hundred a-and sixteen g-grams, sir."

Uncle's attention snapped from the opened corpse to me, swiftly noting the shivers I was no longer able to hide. My heavy velvet charcoal gown with scarlet trim was warm enough for sitting indoors with a hot cup of tea and a good book, but it was January in New York and the weather was as wicked as the person leaving bodies like fallen bits of snow around the slums.

"Grieves!" Uncle shouted for the poor stable boy he'd snagged for this most gruesome task. The young man appeared in the doorway, stealing glances at the slain woman, his complexion almost tinged green. "Tend to the fire. But mind it doesn't get too warm. We don't want to accelerate the decomposition of the body, do we?" The boy shook his head, no longer appearing just green; he now looked quite ready to vomit at the thought of a rotten corpse in his mistress's carriage house. Whether it was from fear of my grandmother or the corpse, it was hard to discern. He'd already paled to an unhealthy hue when Uncle had demanded he remove all three of Grandmama's carriages and replace them with an examination table. Perhaps he worried he'd end up like the cadaver we were carving once Grandmama found out. "Off you go, then!"

Horses quietly nickered and neighed from the next building, stamping their feet in either appreciation or annoyance as the boy added coal to the elaborate iron stove in the corner. Grandmama's property was quite luxurious for city dwellings—having both a carriage house and stables. The fireplace warmed the space marginally where we worked, though the ground still seemed to delight in sending blasts of icy air up my skirts. I worked the numbness from my fingers, knowing I'd be of no use if they remained as stiff as rigor mortis.

"Ready?" Uncle asked, pursing his mouth.

"Yes, sir." My leg throbbed, though I gritted my teeth and kept quiet about it, lest Uncle remove me from my task. "The right kidney is a bit larger—it's one hundred and twenty grams."

He held out a specimen tray and I deposited the slippery organ, heart racing as it nearly tumbled off the surface of the slick metal. "Easy, now."

Uncle set it next to a specimen jar. I eyed the formalin waiting to be used and wiped my blade down with carbolic acid before choosing another tool from the bounty laid out on a small tray table. It was time to remove the stomach and sift through its contents to see what secrets it held.

A few slices in the correct areas had the stomach out and on the table, ready to be explored further. I hesitated, meeting my uncle's hungry gaze across the body. For the first time I recognized his expression for what it truly was—curiosity. It was an inherited trait, after all. He nodded toward the organ, doing a poor job of keeping that insatiable thirst for knowledge in check. I cut carefully down the center of the stomach, doing my best to avoid having the blade sink too deep and destroy any evidence that might be present.

Uncle handed toothed forceps over, pointing to the two flaps I'd made. "Good. Now pull them back—excellent. Well done." He pushed his spectacles up his nose. "Note any scent lingering."

Though it was hardly the most appealing part of our job, I leaned close, drawing in a large breath. "Honestly, it smells a bit of ale. Is that...possible?"

Uncle jerked his head once in affirmation. "Indeed. In instances where a victim's ingested too much to drink prior to death, it's not unheard of to smell the alcohol in their blood."

Without meaning to, my lip curled. Some scientific facts, no matter how intriguing, were horridly gruesome. "Why didn't we notice that in Miss Brown's room, then?"

"It might have been too faint with the ale that had spilled. Or we might have thought it was simply the upturned pail." Uncle adjusted his apron, retying its strings. "It's imperative to always take into account the scene. Little details which might seem unrelated often are pieces we've yet to fit into the puzzle."

Thomas marched into the carriage room, his face an unreadable mask. I stood there, apron splattered with innards, trying to dissect any hint as to how his meeting with my father had gone. It was like the months of learning his quirks vanished at once. Apparently, he'd granted me those insights and had now withdrawn that luxury.

I tried catching his attention, but he stubbornly pretended not to notice. I couldn't help but feel a slight sting. Thomas Cresswell could still be that same cold person in the laboratory and society; I just hadn't expected him to be that way with me anymore. Especially not on the day he asked my father for my hand. His attention finally flicked to me, before landing on the cadaver. Clearly it was business as usual.

"Who's this?" he asked, tone neutral, curious. "Is it another..."

He needn't inquire aloud what we all feared. I wiped my own expression as clean as my blade, then lifted a shoulder. "At first glance? No. However"—I moved from the stomach to her head, pointing out the marks on her person—"she's been strangled. Petechial hemorrhaging is present. As are slight abrasions around her neck. See?"

Thomas drew closer, attention fixed on the injuries. "Where was she found?"

"Not far from where Miss Brown's body was discovered," Uncle said. "Though she was dumped in an alleyway near Mulberry Street."

"The Italian slums?" he asked. "Do we know her identity?"

Uncle shook his head. "Police haven't been able to locate anyone who knew her. Might be a new arrival."

"I see." Thomas's face betrayed the slightest hint of emotion. "They won't do much searching, will they?"

I turned my attention back on her, brow crinkled. "Why wouldn't they? She's got every right to the same sort of investigation as anyone else."

Uncle offered me a sad look. "They aren't always keen on wasting time on immigrants."

"'Wasting'?" Something red-hot and boiling bubbled inside me. I was shaking so hard my hand slipped and I almost cut myself with the scalpel. "She's a person who deserves to have her story told. What does it matter where she was born? She's a human, same as the rest of us. Doesn't that grant her a proper investigation?"

"Would that the world lived by that notion, we might all find peace." Uncle motioned to a journal. "Now, then. Be sure to write down every detail, Thomas. Let's give the police more than enough reason to keep searching for her family or loved ones." Uncle turned his gaze back on me, narrowing his eyes as I slowly returned my focus to the stomach. "You ought to stand by the fire awhile, else your leg will be in a miserable state later."

I was already in a right miserable state; I didn't see any reason why my leg shouldn't join the celebration as well. I lifted my chin. "I'll live."

"Not as long as you'd like to, should you keep that attitude up," Uncle replied coolly. "Now, then. If we're all feeling less ornery, let's continue with the internal examination."

Annoyed with my uncle, Thomas, and the ways of the world, I picked up my blade and sought justice the best way I knew how.

Skull and Rose Tattoo

ELEVEN

SKULL AND ROSE

I was too stubborn to admit it, but Uncle was correct again—tonight my bones ached worse than they usually did. Standing for extended periods was difficult enough without wintry weather sinking its claws in, wreaking more havoc on me.

After we'd sewn up the last cadaver, I made my excuses to my family and had the kitchen send a dinner tray to my room, hoping my warm quarters and thick blankets might help. Once I finished eating, I sat in front of the fireplace, scalding tea in hand, and accomplished only burnt fingers. The aching chills refused to leave. Knowing I'd hurt worse in the morning, I limped to the bathing chamber and turned the copper faucet, filling the bath for a good, hot soak.

I stepped out of my robe and gingerly maneuvered into the water, wincing a bit until I acclimated to the heat. I leaned my head against the lip of the porcelain tub, my hair piled in a messy knot, and inhaled the pleasing herbal scent. Liza had taken to concocting more than tea blends—she'd made the loveliest aromatic salts for me, claiming medicinal properties would help different ailments. This particular blend would assist with drawing out toxins and calming my nerves, amongst other things, she told me.

Whether that was true or not, it smelled divine. Steam rose in fragrant tendrils of lavender, lemon balm, and eucalyptus, relaxing both my muscles and my soul. I was constantly moving as of late, always rushing from one problem to the next without pausing to restore myself. I wasn't used to taking careful note of each of my movements, and found the learning of it to be tedious at best. Though my body was a stern professor—it let me know when it had had enough and would continue teaching the same lesson until I became an apt pupil. I must learn to pace myself or suffer the consequences.

Death. Murder. Even while relaxing I couldn't escape such horrors. I closed my eyes, trying to erase images of the most recent mutilated corpse from my mind. I loathed that a woman might be brutalized by her killer and then again by the men investigating the crime. It was an unfair world—one that showed no mercy for those who needed it the most.

Hoping the bath salts might draw those thoughts away, I sank lower, the water now tingling against my earlobes. A door to my outer rooms opened and closed, the soft click reminding me of a bullet sliding into the chamber of a pistol.

I sighed. So much for stealing a few restorative moments alone. Was it the chambermaid coming to stoke the fire? I silently prayed my aunt hadn't come to read any passages of scripture. I dipped further into the water and pretended I hadn't heard her enter, focusing instead on unkinking each muscle. Soon enough, footsteps approached and I wished a thousand unpleasantries upon the intruder.

"Wadsworth?" Thomas called quietly, then pushed the door open, halting as I nearly splashed him in my haste to cover up. Of all the—

I crossed my arms in a feeble attempt at modesty. "Have you lost your senses?"

"If I hadn't before, I certainly have now." He blinked slowly, trying and failing not to stare at me in the tub. He didn't have the courtesy to even blush—he looked positively dumbstruck. As if he'd never encountered a body without clothing before. Perhaps just not one with a still-beating heart. I'd be flattered by his obvious response if I wasn't so flustered.

"Get out!" I whispered harshly. "If my aunt or father sees you in here—"

"It's all right. We're engaged." He shook himself from his stupor and knelt beside me, a small devilish smile playing on his lips. "That is, if you'll still have me?"

"Father agreed?" Forsaking propriety, I almost leapt from the water into his arms, stopping myself at the last moment. "I can't believe you kept that from me all afternoon!" I sat back and his focus shifted to where my bare shoulders met the water. His gaze darkened in a dangerously seductive manner, awakening a growing need in me. "At least be a gentleman and turn around."

His expression hinted that he was far from a gentleman at the moment, and a quick inspection of my face confirmed I liked it. Excitement thrummed through me. I couldn't deny enjoying the power of his deductions when he directed them at me, and I wondered what that extreme attention to detail focused entirely on my body would feel like.

"As a properly engaged couple, we're permitted a few more liberties. For instance, we might spend time alone, behind closed doors." He purposely scanned the bathing chamber, nodding toward the door. "Seems a shame to let those liberties go to waste."

The scoundrel had the unmitigated *gall* to indicate joining me in the bath. As I turned that thought over, my entire body heated up, having nothing to do with the steaming water. I found the idea of bathing together to be—I splashed water onto my face. When I looked at him again, I noticed a slight furrow in his brow. "Was there something else?"

"Other than informing you that we're finally, truly engaged, dear fiancée?" I nodded, the word sending a little thrill through me. As if recalling he had a purpose more important than flirting, he pulled a small royal-blue pouch from his jacket pocket, his attention now fixed on it. "My sister arrived bearing gifts."

I almost jumped from the bath again, but settled for craning my head around Thomas to see if his sister was making an appearance in my chambers, too. "Daciana's here?"

"She and Ileana arrived shortly after supper. I meant to surprise you." He ran his thumb over the velvet pouch, seemingly lost in another place and time.

"Cresswell?" I gently prodded, my concern growing. "What is it?"

"A letter."

He sounded so sad, my heart nearly broke. I motioned to the little pouch, wanting to drag him from his despair. "That's the strangest letter I've ever seen."

He glanced up through thick lashes, humor flickering in his eyes before he looked away. "Instead of being terrified of her imminent death and thinking only of darkness, my mother wrote us letters. She wouldn't survive to see either of us married, but..." He shook his head, swallowed hard. His emotions were on full display, unlike earlier, during the autopsy, when he'd seemed so cold and remote. "She wrote one for me to read upon my engagement."

Forgetting about any cursed rules of the world, I reached over, water dripping onto the hexagon tiles, and laced my fingers through his. "Oh, Thomas. Are you all right?"

A single tear slipped down his cheek as he nodded. "I'd forgotten, almost, what it was like. Listening to my mother's advice. Her voice. The soft accent that was never quite British or Romanian, but somewhere in between. I miss her. There isn't a day that passes where I don't wish for another moment with her. I'd hoard it away forever, knowing how precious it was."

I gently squeezed his hand. In this most unfortunate circumstance, we understood each other too well. I missed my own mother terribly. While I was thrilled Father had finally agreed to our engagement, the wedding planning and celebration would be difficult to go through without her. Her absence—along with Thomas's mother's—played a large role in our second request to my father. I hoped he'd consented to that as well.

"It is a gift, having her letters to look forward to," I said. "They're invaluable little mementos—proof that some things are truly immortal. Like love."

Thomas swiped at his nose, smiling, though his expression was still too despondent for my liking. "Beyond life, beyond death. My love for thee is eternal."

"That's beautiful. Was it in the letter?"

"No. It's how I feel about you." I swore my heart stuttered a moment. The young man who London society claimed was nothing more than a cold automaton had created poetry. Thomas quickly opened the velvet pouch, tipping its contents onto his palm. A gold ring set with a large crimson jewel lay there like the deepest drop of spilled merlot or crystallized blood. I gasped as he held it up to the light. The unblemished stone was quite literally breathtaking.

"Red diamonds are the rarest in the world." He turned it one way, then the next, showing off its magnificence. I couldn't stop staring at it. "My mother told me to follow my heart, no matter what others might counsel, and give this to whoever I choose to wed. She said this stone represents an eternal foundation, one she hopes is built on trust and love." He inhaled deeply. "I'd already jotted down those lines for you, *'Beyond life, beyond death; my love for thee is eternal.'*"

At this admission, he blushed. "When Daciana brought me this letter today—the very day your father gave us his blessing—and I read that line, it felt as if my mother was here, offering her own blessing not just for me but for you, too. She would have welcomed you as her daughter."

He took my left hand in his, his gaze now locked onto mine. I knew him well enough to realize how serious he'd become, how important these next words would be. His coldness this afternoon in the makeshift laboratory was self-preservation; he was preparing to open himself more fully than the corpse we'd flayed apart.

I remained still, as if one unexpected movement might frighten him away.

"This ring is a gift from my mother, passed along from her mother and so on. It was once owned by Vlad Dracula." Without breaking my stare, he nodded toward the jewel. "It's yours now." Gooseflesh rose along my arms, catching his attention. "I'll understand if you'd rather have another diamond. My family legacy is rather—"

"Majestic and incredible." I cupped his face, noticing a slight tremor go through him. I knew it hadn't anything to do with the bathwater. Thomas Cresswell still didn't believe he was worthy of love. That his lineage was some sort of dark curse. I thought he'd banished his doubts by the end of our voyage here. Some monsters were harder to slay, it seemed.

"Thomas, I had chills because I'm honored you'd share your deepest fears with me." With this bloodred diamond, he was giving me another piece of his heart. It was a gift rarer and more precious than the stone he wished to place upon my finger. "I will wear it proudly and cherish it forever."

I worked my mother's pear-shaped diamond off and put it on my other hand, pulse racing as Thomas slipped his family heirloom onto my ring finger. It fit like it was always meant to be mine. He kissed each knuckle, then drew my arm around his neck, uncaring that he was getting his shirt wet.

"I love you, Audrey Rose."

Without prompting, I placed my other arm around him. My shoulders were now completely out of the bath and I was perilously close to being exposed further, but I didn't care. Thomas's body was both shield and comfort as he pressed it firmly against me.

"I love *you*, Thomas." When we kissed, I swore the earth shook and the stars burned brighter. Thomas moved out of my grasp long enough to hop into the tub, fully clothed, and pulled me onto his lap. Heat shot through me at the unexpected but welcome contact. "Are you quite mad? I'm not wearing any clothes!" I whispered, laughing as he dunked under the water, then shook his head like a dog. Droplets pelted me. "My aunt will die from the scandal!"

He brushed a piece of hair from my face, then slowly moved his lips from my jaw to my ear and back, kissing my bare skin until I was convinced we soaked, unhurt, in a pool of fire, and each of my fears and worries of being caught burned away. "Then we ought to be very quiet."

He lifted me higher and I stared into his eyes, losing myself in the sensation of running my fingers through his damp hair. He looked at me like I was a goddess—like I was fire and magic and spell work combined in human form. I traced a finger down to his collar, teasing the first button open. I suddenly wanted to see more of him; I *needed* to. I tugged his jacket off, leaving his shirt on, though it might as well have been off. Soaked through, it left little to the imagination. A faint image on his upper chest bled through the fabric. I leaned in. "What is that?"

He glanced down as if he hadn't a clue, then shrugged. He unbuttoned the first few buttons and pulled his shirt open, revealing a tattoo. They'd become quite popular with the upper class, but I hadn't thought he'd be interested in such fads. Not that I minded. It was...tantalizing. I touched it with my fingertips, careful to avoid the red splotches around its edges indicating it was fairly new. He watched me, his attention intent and focused, while I inspected it.

"A skull and rose?" I finally asked. "It's beautiful. What does it mean?"

"Oh, lots of things." He drew back, exhaling, a self-satisfied smile in place. "Mostly it's a study in contrasts; light and dark, death and life, decay and beauty." His expression turned thoughtful. "To me it also symbolizes good and evil. Placing it on my heart proves love conquers everything. Naturally I needed a rose on my body forever, too." He kissed me, slow and sensuous, as if to make sure I didn't misinterpret his innuendo. "When you saw Prince Nicolae's tattoos you seemed intrigued, so I deduced you'd enjoy it. I hope that's true."

I gave him a bemused look. "You're free to ornament your body however you'd like. No permission needed."

"Truthfully, I thought it'd be a good reason for you to take my shirt off."

I grinned. Thomas enjoyed saying shocking things to gauge my response. There was no reason I couldn't match him in that area. "Your deductions might not be as sharp as you think if you believe I lack motivation, Cresswell."

His jaw practically hit the floor. Immensely satisfied, I bent my head, kissing the inked area above his heart. With or without the rose tattoo as a permanent marking, Thomas Cresswell was mine. When a small gasp escaped him, I covered his mouth with my own, claiming him fully.

TWELVE
BIRTHDAY SURPRISE

"It's so good to see you again!" I wrapped first Daciana, then Ileana in a warm embrace. "I've missed you both terribly. Please sit." I motioned to the settee in the parlor.

Thomas's birthday party was a few hours away and I wanted time for just the girls, so I'd arranged for a tea service. I couldn't help but recall the many times my aunt had wished for me to host high tea and how uncomfortable I'd been. True friends made all the difference.

"How's the academy faring after all that happened?" I asked. Ileana had pretended to be a maid to help uncover who might be murdering people in and around Bran Castle. It was where we'd first met, and it felt like ages rather than weeks had passed since I'd last seen them.

Ileana perched on the edge of the settee and Daciana sat beside her. "They're recovering well enough. Moldoveanu is as attentive to his students as ever."

I smiled. It was a polite thing to say, considering the headmaster was as pleasant as a head full of lice. I poured them both cups of tea. "And the Order of the Dragon?"

Daciana's eyes lit up as she took the offered cup of Earl Grey. "It's always interesting. Though it would be doubly so if you and Thomas joined our ranks. I know he didn't seem all that interested before, but we'd love to have you both. There are so many cases, we're overtaxed."

Tempting though their offer was, I did not wish to belong to any organization, even a secret one that sought justice as much as I did. We'd be required to travel wherever the Order deemed necessary and infiltrate places like Ileana had. I'd learned aboard the *Etruria* how hard it was to go undercover and knew acting was a talent I didn't possess.

"I'll keep that in mind for the future, though you shouldn't rely on it," I said carefully, not wanting to offend. "I'm quite content with picking my own forensic cases. But I'm always here to listen and offer advice if you need it."

Daciana set her teacup down and gathered me into another hug. I squeezed her back, fighting a sudden prickle of tears. "Join or not, but please come back to Bucharest. The house is lonely without you."

A moment later, Liza waltzed into the room, a small gold-foiled box tucked under each arm. She brandished the boxes like they were spoils of war. "Who would like some chocolate?"

We spent the better part of the morning talking about our work and our lives, and Liza had them howling with stories from her misadventures in the country. For the first time in a long while, I was surrounded by a boisterous, happy family. Death and sadness did not invade this sacred space—it was a time for laughter and living well. I wanted to capture this moment and hold it close to my heart forever. I had an uneasy feeling it wouldn't last.

I glanced at the clock in the parlor, pulse mimicking the rhythm of the second hand as moments ticked by. I'd checked the dining room twice already—everything was perfectly set. The roasted whole pig lay proudly on a bed of herbs. But the true gem was the dessert station.

It was piled high with tortes and petit fours and French macarons in petal pinks, icy blues, and pale yellows and greens. The chef had even managed a stunning lilac shade I'd never seen before. There were lemon cakes with lavender-infused frosting, puddings, cinnamon buns smothered with icing, and candied plums. I'd also seen to it that a Catherine Basket would be brought out later, the frozen cream fruit confection laid atop a silver service tray covered in fern fronds. It wasn't the only iced-cream treat I'd commissioned—I'd designed a near-life-size replica of a swan to add a bit of whimsy to the table. The perfect dessert offering for a man with an insatiable sweet tooth.

"Miss Wadsworth?"

I turned at the sound of the butler's voice. "Yes?"

"The mail just arrived." He handed me a letter. It was a heavy cream envelope with no return address. I raised a brow.

"This is postmarked last week," I said, turning it over.

"Weather has been difficult on the postal service, Miss Wadsworth." He pointed a gloved hand toward a stately piece of furniture. "An envelope opener is in the top drawer of the secretary."

"Thank you." I waited until he'd closed the door again before making my way over to the ornate piece of furniture. Like everything else in Grandmama's home, the edges were covered in a fine lace filigree made of gold. I found the letter opener and tore into the mysterious envelope.

It's been too long, but worry not, I'll see you soon enough. Be ready.

I flipped the card over, searching for any clue regarding the sender, but that was it. Two lonely lines. It was written in a hand I didn't recognize, but it had a feminine feel to it, if such things could be applied to ink on parchment. I cursed myself for sending the previous letter up in flames. Now there was no way to be sure if it had been sent by the same person.

Daciana and Ileana were shopping for their presents for Thomas, so I'd inquire about it when they returned. Since the post was delayed, they'd probably arrived first. I exhaled. That was likely it. My nerves over Thomas's party—and our engagement announcement—were granting my imagination permission to act out.

To ease my worry, I returned to the dining room, checking it over once more. Aunt Amelia walked in, her sharp gaze landing like a blow on each detail of the room. I went to fumble with my gloves, then stopped. The birthday party would be a success because we were celebrating Thomas. Little did my aunt know, we'd also be celebrating our shared news. I didn't want to ruin my evening by developing an acidic stomach because the linens weren't pressed within an inch of their lives.

Tonight, the only thing that would stand out in our memories was being surrounded by our loved ones. In ten years, I'd think back to the butterflies fluttering in my center, the quiet anticipation of unveiling the dessert table along with my ring.

Bolstered by what truly mattered, my own gaze swept across the room as surely as it assessed the dead. I was confident in the laboratory. I would be here, too. There was no reason I couldn't marry the two parts of my life together as well.

"It's lovely, isn't it?" I asked cheerfully. My aunt pursed her lips but nodded. "Thomas will be pleased with the whole roasted boar. Though I suspect he'll be mesmerized by the sweets." I lifted my cane, pointing out the table filled with desserts from all over the world. "I imagine he might skip the main course entirely."

Aunt Amelia drew in a long breath. The idea of eating only

sweets obviously broke all sorts of polite society rules, though she was too well-bred to argue if Thomas wished to dine on pastry. He outranked everyone in the house, though he never acted as if he did.

She cleared her throat delicately. "The iced-cream swan is exceptional. I can't imagine the artistry involved with crafting the mold. The details of the seeds for eyes is..." Aunt wet her lips, seeming to think long and hard about her next words. It was a miracle. "It's a feat even Her Majesty would be inspired by, I'm sure."

"Thank you." I flushed, pleased by her hard-earned praise. I walked over to the life-size sculpture. It *was* grand. Liza had chided me for fussing, but the end result was magnificent. "Those are actually licorice drops. I hired a confectioner as well."

At this my aunt appeared rather impressed. She lifted her chin in approval. "Lovely touch. Have you seen to the wine list? You'll need to pair it well with each course. Although"—she strummed gloved fingers across the linen—"you may wish to not serve red tonight."

I'd given my cousin as much freedom as she wished in choosing the pairings. I had focused on ordering champagne and rose petals for our toast. I didn't know why my aunt was opposed to a red blend. Before I could inquire, she continued, crinkling her nose.

"No one needs to be reminded of blood. Especially after that horrid article."

My focus snapped to my aunt. "What article?"

Seemingly irritated for having brought it up, she marched over to the sideboard and pushed a newspaper into my hands. They trembled ever so slightly as I read the headline.

ATROCIOUS MURDER.
Another Crime of the "Jack the Ripper" Type in New York City.

Without giving me a chance to finish the dreadful piece, she plucked the paper from my fingers. "I'll mention the wine situation to the butler. You're certain everything else is ready?"

"Yes, Aunt." My response sounded wooden even to my own ears, but I feared the mask of calmness I'd donned was slipping. This was a nightmare. No matter how far I traveled or how hard I pushed it from my mind, Jack the Ripper stalked me, invading every aspect of my life. Before she could whip my nerves into a bigger tizzy, I dipped my head. "Excuse me. I need some air before the festivities begin."

A small courtyard sat behind Grandmama's home, bordered on all sides by the buildings that comprised her property. Snow-dusted ivy crawled along the walls, and I imagined in the summertime it was alive with wildflowers, swaying in the breeze off the Hudson River.

Too soon, my thoughts twisted into something sinister. I pictured those same vines wrapping about the neck of an unsuspecting victim, strangling the life from her before thorns dug greedily into her skin, spilling blood. My vision became so real, I almost smelled the unforgettable scent of copper.

"Jack the Ripper is truly here," I whispered to myself, breath puffing in the cold. I shuddered to think what my mind might conjure up now that the Ripper was up to his dark trickery again. Last time, werewolves and vampires had haunted me.

A pale marble statue of an angel grabbed my attention, startling me with its size. I caught my breath, chiding myself for being jumpy. It blended in with the snow and stone walls, though now that I was looking closely, I couldn't fathom how I'd glanced over something that majestic.

Feathers were carved with a careful hand, the raised wings reminding me of a dove in flight. Snow slipped down the angel's face, resembling tears. There was a sadness in its face that made me wonder if it was truly an angel. Perhaps it was one of the fallen.

The clomping of boots alerted me to his presence before I turned. I quickly pulled myself together, hoping the remaining tremors would be mistaken for a reaction to the cold. I shifted around to face Thomas, my expression neutral. I knew I wouldn't fool him with a smile, but my nerves could easily be the result of his party. He knew I was more comfortable with a scalpel in hand than I was reciting a toast, and he adored me all the more for it. I was surprised he wasn't alone.

A cat as black as night trotted along behind him. I squinted at it, noticing there was a patch of white under its neck. "Cresswell, there's a cat following you." I searched the courtyard for a broom or some other object to shoo the beast away with. I tapped my cane on the ground as a last resort, eliciting an annoyed flick of the cat's ears. It looked at Thomas, and either my delusions had begun in earnest, or the stray was about to strike. "It's going to pounce on you."

"Actually, he's waiting to be invited. Observe." Thomas patted his shoulder once. Without hesitation the cat leapt from the ground, perching on his shoulder, and stared smugly at me. "Wadsworth, meet Sir Isaac Mewton. Sir Isaac Mewton, this is that special human I told you about. You'll be nice to her or there won't be any more belly rubs in your future."

I opened my mouth and shut it. Words abandoned me. At least I was no longer on the brink of falling into the Jack the Ripper abyss... Thomas had once again managed to yank me from my doom. Except this time, he wasn't aware of his assistance.

"Sir Isaac *Mewton*?" I closed my eyes. "Do you honestly expect me to address that creature that way? Where did you even find it?"

"Don't be absurd. You don't call me His Royal Eminence Lord Thomas James Dorin Cresswell, do you? Sir Isaac will be quite adequate. He found me a few streets over. His command over gravity rivals his namesake's."

I might start calling Thomas His Royal Pain in My Arse. "We cannot keep it."

"Sir Isaac," he corrected.

I sighed. "We cannot keep Sir Isaac. How can we care for him on our many travels?"

Thomas frowned. I thought he'd see the logic in my statement; apparently, I was wrong. "Do you expect me to turn my back on this face? Look at the cunning in his eyes." He petted the cat, which still perched on his shoulder, its golden eyes watching me warily. "Are you denying me my one true birthday wish?"

"I thought the gift of my presence was your one true wish," I said blandly.

He made a face. "Imagine, coming home from a long day's work, tossing your blood-splattered apron off, grabbing a warm mug of tea. Then Sir Isaac hops into your lap, circles, once, twice, possibly thrice, before curling into a ball of warmth and fluff." He scratched the cat's head, drawing a purr so loud it might alarm the neighbors. "Tell me having a cat's affection and a good book doesn't sound like an ideal evening."

"Is that really all you'd like me to picture? If that's an ideal evening, then how, exactly, do *you* fit in?"

"You'd be scantily clad in *my* lap; Sir Isaac would be in yours." Thomas held fast to the cat as he ducked the snowball I tossed at him. "What? It's my fantasy of our future!"

I wiped the snow from my gloves, giving in. "Fine. Sir Isaac stays. I suppose he's a Cresswell-Wadsworth now."

Levity vanished from Thomas's expression. "Are you thinking of taking my name—in part? I didn't think—is that what you want?"

I picked at imaginary fuzz on my gloves, stalling. "No, I don't believe I will." I flicked my attention to his, noting the slight flash of disappointment before he wiped it away. I smiled. "At least not in *part.*"

He looked up quickly; hope slipped in between the cracks of his emotional armor. His reaction made me all the more certain of my decision. "Does that mean...?"

I bit my lower lip, nodding. "I've thought about it a great deal. If the choice was never offered, I might feel differently. But, I—I'm not sure how to describe it. I want to share a name with you. Thomas doesn't quite suit me, although you'd make a lovely Audrey Rose."

His laugh was full and rich. The cat twitched its tail and hopped to the ground, annoyed it was no longer the center of Thomas's world. Once my love collected himself, he stepped near, holding my hands in his. "I would take your name, if you wanted to keep it."

He meant it, too. I pulled him to me and kissed him lightly. "Which is precisely the reason I'm happy to become a Cresswell. Now, let's go. We've got a birthday party to attend and a rather fun announcement to make." I looked at the cat. "You, too, Sir Isaac. Let's be on our way. I have to put my gown on and I'm sure I can rustle up a rather dapper ribbon for you."

Lord help me, but the cat seemed to perk up at the thought. It was a Cresswell through and through.

THIRTEEN
CHAOS UNLEASHED

GRANDMAMA'S DINING ROOM
FIFTH AVENUE, NEW YORK CITY
23 JANUARY 1889

I threaded my arm through Thomas's, leading him into the dining room, where our families waited, milling about. My betrothed abruptly halted, nearly making me lose my balance as he took in each of the dessert tables. Sir Isaac Mewton hissed from his shoulder, displeased with either his frosty-blue silk bow or Thomas's sudden halt. He hopped to the ground and skirted around us, heading straight for the bowl of cream I'd asked the footman to leave for him.

"You beautiful, brilliant, wonderful woman," Thomas whispered, eyes going wide as he stuck his finger in the closest cake and tasted the frosting. I shook my head. He had the manners of an alley cat and the disposition of a child. "My God. Is that espresso frosting? I've never—" He inspected me in that Cresswell way of his. "Your creation?"

"It was just an idea—I know how much you favor coffee, and it goes so well with chocolate..."

Thomas kissed me, hard and deep, only stopping when someone cleared their throat across the room. We broke apart, both of us flushed, and waved shyly at our family members. Aunt Amelia, the likely culprit for the admonishment, *tsk*ed.

"Thank you for joining us for Thomas's birthday celebration," I said, once we'd all taken our seats around the large mahogany table. "Please raise your glasses in a toast. Mr. Cresswell is now eighteen. If only he were a bit wiser to match his old age."

"You may be waiting on that day for all eternity, Audrey Rose." Daciana elbowed her brother, smiling tenderly. Chuckles went around the table.

We feasted on the roasted boar and herbed potatoes, forgetting about proper dining protocol on who needed to speak to whom, and simply enjoyed being together. After the desserts began arriving in earnest, Thomas caught my attention and raised his brow. It was time.

Suddenly, glancing into the faces of our loved ones, my nerves came back with a vengeance. I wasn't sure why my mouth was now bone-dry, or why my heart beat three times too fast. These people loved us; they wouldn't pass judgment. And yet I couldn't stop the flutter of my pulse. The last of the sweets were making their way to us, and I had no choice but to stand up and announce our betrothal. It was all so real, I—

Thomas grabbed my hand under the table, weaving our fingers together in the same way our lives would soon become entwined.

He squeezed reassuringly, then let go and stood, raising his glass of wine. "To Audrey Rose, for her time and careful planning of this evening. I'm quite possibly the luckiest person who ever lived. And not simply because she had every dessert known to humanity baked for my pleasure." Everyone raised their own glasses, clinking them merrily. Thomas cleared his throat, his nerves finally showing. "It brings me the greatest honor to announce our engagement. Through some means of magic and mystery, she has accepted my proposal."

The silence I feared never happened. At once, our families clapped and congratulated us.

"Oh, joyous day!" Mrs. Harvey practically fell backward in her excitement. She rushed around the table, tottering a bit, and hugged me close. "Congratulations, my dear! I knew you and my Thomas were a smart pair! The way he looks at you—like he's seeing under all those layers and—"

"Thank you, Mrs. Harvey!" I clutched Thomas's chaperone back fiercely, meeting my father's glistening eyes across the table. He smiled, warm and proud. He clearly missed where Mrs. Harvey's train of thought was heading. Thank goodness for small favors. Once Thomas managed to wrangle Mrs. Harvey back into her seat, I stood at his side. I motioned for the champagne to be brought out, waiting as everyone took their rose petal–infused flutes.

"We have one more tiny announcement," I said, drawing in a deep breath. Thomas clasped his free hand in mine again, giving another encouraging squeeze. There was no time like the present to unleash some chaos. "We wish to marry within the next fortnight."

There was a new scientific theory that claimed sound ceases right before an explosion occurs. I hadn't put much thought into it before, but I imagined it was similar to how silent the dining room became after I'd made that last statement. Weddings normally took a length of time to prepare for—mostly due to all the legal matters that needed sorting. Two weeks was unheard of. Once the shock of our upcoming nuptials passed, everyone began clamoring at the same time.

"A fortnight?" Aunt Amelia cried. "Impossible!"

"The flowers!" Liza added, appalled. "The menu…"

"The dress," Daciana said, sipping from her champagne flute with gusto. "It's madness, hosting a wedding that quickly. Unless…" Her sharp gaze landed on my belly.

I scowled, earning a sheepish look of apology. I was not with child. Thomas and I hadn't—my heart raced when I recalled our scandalous bath last night. Though he'd explored *much* more of my body than he'd ever done before, we had not crossed that line.

Thomas stood beside me, shaking his head. "Given the nature of our work, we may need to travel alone. Quite soon. It would be easiest for us to do so if we were married."

"Of course!" Aunt Amelia tossed her hands in the air. "Your careers. How unreasonable of us to have forgotten that Audrey Rose has chosen dark pursuits in place of tending to a proper home." She rubbed her brow. "This party was planned so well. I thought you'd grown out of that morbid, unbecoming fascination."

Thomas bristled, but I put a hand on his arm. I recognized my aunt's scolding for what it was—nerves and worry. "I know it's asking a lot of everyone, Aunt," I said calmly. "However, if anyone can accomplish an impossible task, it's the people present in this room." I looked from my aunt to Liza, Mrs. Harvey, Daciana, and Ileana. Warmth filled the void of sadness I'd felt, missing my mother. "My mother would be extremely grateful for the love and support you've all shown to me." I turned to Thomas, smiling shyly. "To us."

"Since it's such a short timeframe to accomplish a wedding," Thomas added, "we'd like for it to remain very simple. Our only wish is to be surrounded by those we love. And cake. Most specifically, that chocolate coffee concoction that has stolen my heart and my senses entirely." I nudged him. "*Almost* entirely. A bit of macerated cherries or raspberries would also be welcome. Do feel free to bring us samples. Often."

Liza appeared as if we'd requested to dance across a crescent moon during Samhain splattered in sheep's blood. "*Simple?*" she sputtered, glancing around for assistance. "What, shall we sew the table linens together for your dress?" Her pitch was rising to a worrisome level. Father and Uncle both lifted their heads, staring up at the ceiling in a manner I was all too familiar with. "I cannot work under such conditions and limitations! It is unreasonable to ask that of us."

I opened my mouth, stunned. "Liza…we don't want to be any trouble. It's—"

"—our God-given duty as your family to make this as spectacular as possible. How dare you believe, for one instant, we would ever feel *troubled* over making your day beautiful!"

With that, she turned to her sisters in arms, plotting our wedding. Thomas leaned in, a smile in his voice. "Remind me to never cross your cousin. She's more fearsome than my father."

Everyone spoke in rushed spurts, nodding one moment, shaking their heads the next. It was fascinating to watch. They truly were like an army, assembling a plan of attack as swiftly as if they'd practiced this formation for years, unbeknownst to me or Thomas.

"She can alter the dress she's wearing," Ileana offered, nodding at the blush ensemble I wore. "It's close to a wedding gown already. The beadwork is exceptional."

I glanced down at the princess gown I'd had made at the highly acclaimed Dogwood Lane Boutique. It *would* be quite lovely. Liza and Daciana both drew back, holding their hands against their hearts. "No! Absolutely not!" they said in unison. Then Daciana elaborated, "Her gown ought to be new—made specially for this most treasured day. It'll be white, like the queen's was, with layers of flowing gauze and crystals sewn into the bodice."

Arguments went back and forth so quickly, I felt dizzy. I found an empty seat next to my father and uncle. "Thank you, Father. I know you're not entirely comfortable—"

"I've found I am most content when my daughter is happy." He hugged me. "Plus, your Thomas is quite the brave young man. Look how he's challenging your cousin on the colors of the flowers." My father shook his head, smiling. "He's unique. Unique enough to keep you looking this happy for the rest of your lives, I'm sure."

Uncle grunted. "I knew pairing the two of you together would be trouble."

"Well, I'm pleased you played such an important role." I kissed him on the cheek, surprising us both. Uncle flushed bright red. "Meeting that annoying student in your laboratory last autumn turned out to be one of the best chance encounters of my life."

Uncle muttered something and quickly exited the room.

After he'd gone, my father laughed, shaking his head. "My dear girl. If you believe it was a chance encounter, you have much to learn. Especially about your uncle."

Sounds of friendly chatter and clinking forks against porcelain plates faded into the background while I mentally turned his words over. "You must be mistaken. The night I met Thomas, he'd come uninvited."

Father's eyes danced with mirth. "Sweet daughter of mine. Jonathan's more apt at reading people than Thomas is. He knew long before that boy ever walked into that laboratory that the two of you had the potential to change the world together. Know this—he took Thomas on as an apprentice because he is and always has been the Wadsworth who believed love could bridge the barrier between life and death. If you think me a romantic old fool, my brother is twice as much on both counts."

Twelve days came and went; time slipped through our grasp like a wily career murderer. The women in our families—along with my father, who, surprisingly enough, rather enjoyed all the preparations and shopping—worked from sunrise until sunset, planning and ordering and amending their lists. Thomas and I tried assisting but were shooed away. Murders didn't slow in the city, though no more seemed to be committed by the Ripper's hand. It ought to have proven joyful, but the churning unease in my center knew otherwise.

If Jack the Ripper was no longer in New York, he was stalking another city. I did not delude myself into believing he'd simply given up killing. If anything, he'd been experimenting with new variations on his methods. Unusual, and troubling for a killer. He'd already been an efficient murdering machine; with more practice and altered methods, we might never stop him.

Uncle tossed his scalpel into a bucket of carbolic acid, careless of what else got splashed with the liquid. "Nothing! It's as if he's disappeared."

I set my cane down and picked up the bucket, fishing the medical tool out. Uncle's anger had been simmering for days and was coming to a full, maddening boil. I'd never seen him take his frustration out on his blades before.

"I—" I paused to gather my courage. "I may know of a place we might learn more."

Uncle's attention shifted to me. "How?"

I glanced at Thomas, suddenly unsure I wanted to share this fact with Uncle. My betrothed nodded, giving me his support, but wouldn't offer an opinion on the matter. This was my secret to reveal and mine alone. It was strange, feeling as if I was about to betray my brother. I couldn't reconcile my innate urge to protect the person who hadn't protected others.

"Well?" Uncle asked, losing his already fraying patience.

I steeled myself against any more fits of his rage. "Nathaniel's journals. They—they contain quite a lot of information. Regarding the murders."

I didn't need to elaborate on which murders.

Uncle's eyes grew distant, his posture straightening. "Your brother knew nothing worthwhile regarding those murders."

"I'm quite certain he—"

"He was yet another unfortunate victim, though I know many would find that hard to believe."

I pressed my lips together, refusing to argue when he was clearly in denial. I knew the feeling all too well and wouldn't steal his stubborn peace from him, misplaced though it might be.

Whether Uncle wanted to confront his own truth or not, the fact remained: Nathaniel knew more about Jack the Ripper than any of us.

FOURTEEN
COURTING A CRESSWELL

"Have you decided how you're wearing your hair tomorrow?" Daciana asked, poking her own updo in the looking glass. "If you style it like this, you can show off that striking neckline of yours."

"Or you might keep it loose and not give a care about what others think," Ileana added, her Romanian accent as lovely as ever. She gave Daciana a pointed look as she combed through her own locks. "Your veil will cover it up anyway."

"Yes, but *after* the ceremony she'll be strutting around without all that fabric nonsense." Daciana added a flower to her hair. "Perhaps our friend here might prefer to have her hair up and out of the way for post-wedding activities."

She waggled her brows suggestively and, without even glancing over my shoulder, I was quite certain Aunt Amelia was about to fall over, crossing herself furiously on the way down.

"Miss Cresswell!" My aunt snatched a fan off the dresser, frantically waving it before her reddening face. A vein in her forehead throbbed in the most troublesome manner. "Language, please."

"Apologies, Lady Clarence. Miss Cresswell is fond of the truth." Ileana heaved a sigh, almost coaxing a smile to my lips despite my best efforts. She alone knew what it was like to court a Cresswell and live to tell the indecent tale of it.

"They'll be married soon enough," Daciana said. "I imagine they'll do more than hold hands in bed. The way they stare at each other when they *think* no one is looking could impregnate her on the spot. Now, *that's* downright indecent, especially over the soup course."

The entire room seemed to suck in a breath at once. Daciana lifted a shoulder and went back to inspecting her own hair as if she'd not hinted at such private matters and nearly caused an embolism in my aunt. Mentioning anything close to pregnancy or the science behind how such a thing happens was simply not done in polite company.

Ileana rolled her eyes skyward, as if silently communicating that teaching subtlety to a Cresswell was a lost cause.

"Here. This will be perfect." Liza had opened a fashion magazine, pointing out an illustration of a complicated hairstyle to distract everyone. "See how loose waves fall naturally over her shoulder, yet the top half is braided into a coronet? It's so decorative and fun. I'm certain we can weave orange blossoms in your braids and then set jewels into it, too. You'll look like you're wearing a crown made of flowers and precious stones."

I inspected the hairstyle, biting my lip. It might be deemed high fashion, but it reminded me of a rather messy sparrow's nest. All that was missing were some twigs and dried leaves. I said a silent prayer of thanks the wedding hadn't been scheduled for the fall, else I might've ended up with those very embellishments stuck into my hair. Thomas would fall off the altar from laughing so hard. Which might almost be worth it.

Realizing Liza was waiting on a response, I stumbled over the best compliment I could offer. "It's very...interesting."

Daciana and Ileana snorted, but a swift glare from my cousin had each of them holding their hands against their mouths, doing a terrible job stifling their giggles. I flashed them my most pleading look; all of the plucking and primping was beginning to set my teeth on edge.

"If you'll excuse us." Daciana gracefully hopped to her feet. "I'm going to check on my brother, then retire for the evening." She took both of my hands in hers and kissed my cheeks. "Good night, Audrey Rose. Sleep well. Tomorrow we shall officially become sisters! I cannot express how happy I am to have you as part of my family. I'm not sure if Thomas or I am more thrilled!"

Ileana sighed at Daciana's "Cresswell" theatrics and hugged me good night. "We'll see you in the morning. Try to sleep soundly. Your wedding will be unforgettable, I promise."

I took a steadying breath. "You think so?"

She nodded. "You're simply walking to Thomas in a beautiful gown, sharing vows, eating some cake, then beginning a new chapter of your lives. Together. Everything will be wonderful, you'll see."

"Thank you." I clutched her close.

Once they'd left, Liza tapped the image in the magazine again. "Well?"

I swallowed hard, hoping my expression didn't betray my growing horror. "Perhaps keeping the hair simple might be best. The dress is already so decorative—with all that beading and embroidery—and the diamond tiara is another bold statement..." I trailed off, noticing how both my aunt and cousin seemed to be mentally crossing themselves at my lack of vision. "You're right. Let's set the hair and we'll see how the waves look in the morning before we decide."

With that crisis settled, my cousin ushered me onto the velvet bench in front of the vanity and got to work twisting and pinning small sections of my hair into place. I tried not to wince as she inadvertently yanked some strands out with her overzealous twists.

"You mustn't squint so much," Aunt Amelia scolded, leaning over and pinching color into my cheeks until I was certain each of my blood vessels had popped and I might, in fact, internally bleed to death before sunrise. "You'll cause wrinkles and will look like an overcooked goose before you're twenty. Do you wish to have a husband who no longer desires you so soon?"

I inhaled and allowed myself the mental count of three before responding.

"Because he'll desire a Christmas goose instead?" I raised my brows. "They do say the best way to a man's heart is through his stomach."

Liza coughed a laugh away, abruptly returning to my trunk to rummage through my things. I took another deep breath and counted until I felt the next retort dissolve on my tongue. I highly doubted anyone was having such a discussion with Thomas the evening before our wedding. Men prided themselves on aging. They might lose their hair and expand their bellies and still be deemed a wondrous catch, marrying twenty years their junior. Yet heaven forbid a young lady grow into old age and be proud of the lines on her face; the very lines that told a story of a life well lived. The nerve of us to live happily and without apology. I scowled at my reflection.

"Sit up straight." Aunt Amelia gently swatted my backside with the fan. "Your posture is all wrong. If you slump tomorrow, your tiara will tumble right off that smart head of yours. You want to appear pleasing to your bridegroom, don't you? I cannot—"

"What Mother is *attempting* to say is she loves you and is only fussing because she's worried something will go wrong and you won't have a marvelous day. Isn't that right, Mother?" Without waiting for a response, Liza handed me a box with a big red ribbon. I held it up, curious. Judging by its weight, it felt like some sort of garment. "It's a little something I saw in the fashion district. It's for your wedding night, but you might want to try it on to make sure it suits you before then." I went to untie the ribbon but she placed her hand on mine, stopping me. "Open it later."

Pretending as if she didn't hear that last instruction, Aunt Amelia went about tying my hair up in small sections and securing it with pins with swift efficiency, though I could have sworn I saw the slightest bit of wetness on her lashes before she blinked it away. I reached up as she placed the last pin and clutched her hand in mine.

"Thank you, Aunt," I said, meaning it. "Tomorrow will be perfect."

FIFTEEN
YOURS TO GIVE

Once Aunt Amelia and Liza retired to their chambers, I sat in front of the vanity, adjusting the hundreds of pins they'd stuck in my hair for the sake of fashion, wondering if the end result of soft, "natural" waves would be worth the discomfort of sleeping on them tonight. Without a doubt, it was not. Much of the wedding felt as if it were now a spectacle, like Mephistopheles and his crew had taken over its design and created another revel for the Moonlight Carnival.

While I couldn't deny the extravagant hothouse flowers and the princess dress were quite lovely, I wished to walk down the aisle as myself. I simply wanted to be with Thomas, and that didn't require pomp and circumstance. I'd be content saying my vows without an audience present, though I knew my family and loved ones had worked hard to make the day special for us, and I wanted to share in their celebration and good cheer. With limits.

I began taking the hairpins out, watching sections of my dark hair uncoil like ebony rope, falling against my collarbone. It was much better to enjoy my sleep and feel well rested for tomorrow rather than suffer and pretend to be cheerful in the morning.

"Appear pleasing to my bridegroom, indeed." I shook my head. Aunt Amelia didn't understand Mr. Thomas Cresswell at all. I snorted at the very thought of him requiring me to behave or look a certain way in order to be pleased.

Thomas wouldn't mind if I showed up to the church in my laboratory apron, sawdust clinging to my hems, scalpel in hand. In fact, the rogue might prefer it. He truly loved me for me.

There was none of that "he loved me in spite of" nonsense. Thomas saw who I was—flaws and all—and I was more than enough for him, as he was for me. We needn't *complete* each other; we *complemented* each other. He and I were whole on our own, which made us so much stronger when combined than two symbolic halves coming together to create one. Our bond had double the strength. Nothing could tear it apart. And after tomorrow, nothing would.

I allowed my focus to fall upon my new dressing gown, or lack thereof. The moment my family had left, I'd unwrapped the present, immediately understanding why Liza had warned me to wait. She'd gifted me with a sheer cream-colored robe embroidered with strategically placed wildflowers to hide certain parts of my anatomy. It came with a matching nightgown made entirely of sheer lace. Worn together, the garments hinted at nakedness, but worn separately they unabashedly flaunted my form.

Instead of feeling as if I were a walking scandal, I felt confident when I tried them on. My silhouette was visible as firelight flickered behind me. I tied the ribbons at my low neckline, then ran my hands down the sides of my soft curves, staring at my reflection. In less than a day, I'd wear it to my marital bed. The clock chimed off twelve bells, promptly derailing thoughts of tomorrow's sleeping arrangements. I went back to my task. It was getting late and I needed to attempt to sleep before dawn.

Halfway through undoing my hair, I leaned forward, inspecting this pre-wedding version of myself in the looking glass, searching for any trace of panic or urge to flee. The only emotion I saw staring back was excitement. Pure and radiant. My cheeks were flushed, and there was an undeniable sparkle in my green eyes. I'd finally become the rose with soft petals and sharp thorns Mother always said I could be. The constant pang of nerves that plagued me at the thought of marriage was replaced with a serene calmness. An absolute void of worry or doubt.

I was ready to become Lady Audrey Rose Cresswell.

The name gave me power—perhaps because I'd chosen it for myself, it was no longer something I'd been born into, or something expected of me by my husband. Thomas had made it infinitely clear that I was free to be whoever I wanted to be, and the world could simply swallow an egg if it didn't like it. My father didn't seem particularly keen about the idea but deferred to my future husband, who refused to force his will upon anyone but himself. There was power in choice. And I'd choose Thomas in each and every lifetime, if such things were possible.

I smiled to myself. "You've truly bewitched me, Cresswell."

"Always nice to hear, though not entirely surprising, Wadsworth." I startled back and dropped my last hairpin, meeting Thomas's mischievous expression in the looking glass as he slipped into my room and quickly shut the door behind him. "Have you seen how handsome I look in this suit?"

I held a hand to my pounding heart as I recovered from the shock of him answering a sentiment he wasn't meant to hear.

"Audrey Rose." He bowed deeply, then stood, his gaze snagging on my robe. Whatever quip he'd been about to say abandoned him as I swiveled on the bench, allowing the firelight to illuminate the outline of my body. I tried not to laugh at the slight flush creeping past his collar, or the way his throat bobbed as he quickly swallowed. "I—" He exhaled slowly, as if collecting his thoughts. "You—".

"Yes?" I prompted when nothing else seemed forthcoming. I never thought I'd see the day when Thomas Cresswell was without words, and I relished this clumsy version of him.

"I realized I won't be able to call you Wadsworth anymore."

"Oh? And you decided sneaking into my sleeping chamber at midnight to tell me was the best course of action?" I patted the space next to me on the vanity's bench. After the slightest hesitation, he crossed the room and joined me. I watched the fire crackle in the hearth across from us. "Are you the one whose feet are getting a bit chilly now?"

A smug look replaced whatever nerves he'd shown.

"Apologies for any disappointment, my love, but my toes are exceptionally warm this evening." Thomas lifted his legs up, wiggling his shiny shoes around. He pulled back his trousers, exposing a thick pair of knitted socks. "It's simply going to be an adjustment, calling you Cresswell. I'm going to believe I'm talking to myself, not that I'm a bad conversationalist. I rather enjoy having heated debates with myself most days."

He paused, fidgeting. I realized he was avoiding looking in my direction for too long. Of all the times he'd brashly flirted with me, I couldn't believe how shy he was when confronted with a nightgown. He wasn't nearly as flustered during our bath. Maybe it was the bed, looming silently beside us, that made him nervous.

"I tried calling Sir Isaac 'Wadsworth' earlier." He flashed a quick smile. "He wasn't very agreeable to it, I'm afraid."

I huffed a laugh. "Why does that not surprise me?"

Thomas took my hand and gently turned it over, tracing the

lines of my palm, his expression suddenly serious. His jaw tightened. "There's still time, you know—if you've changed your mind. About…all this. I know this has all gone much faster than you'd have liked. Most engagements are at least six months; then there's the matter of age. If you'd prefer to wait…"

I shifted so I could take his face in my hands, ensuring his gaze was locked onto mine. I ran my thumb against his jaw, marveling at how good it felt to simply touch him.

"I've never been more sure or ready for anything in my whole life, Thomas Cresswell." He seemed ready to argue, so I lightly kissed him. "In fact, the morning can't come soon enough. We've never done anything by anyone's rules but our own. Why start worrying now?"

He looked skeptical. "Are you certain?"

"Of us? Most definitely so."

"How do you know you're ready?"

"Well, there are lots of reasons," I said carefully.

"Tell me the most scandalous one." His request was meant to be lighthearted, but the edge of worry was there. Thomas hadn't relinquished his fears of inadequacy.

I leaned into him, breathing in the scent of coffee and a hint of rich spirits. I wondered if my father had offered him whiskey, or if he'd been anxious enough to pour some himself.

"I want to fall asleep against your chest and wake up in your arms. I long to be free to hug or kiss you whenever I choose, for as long as I choose. I want to know the sound of your breath as you slip into sleep. I want to—" I sat back, any further flowery declarations wilting on my tongue. The fool was practically bouncing in his seat. "Why are you smiling like that? I'm trying to have a serious moment and you appear as though you either need to use the loo or have inexplicably sat on an anthill in the middle of my room."

"Apologies." He fell to his knees before me, the goofy grin stuck in place as he took both of my hands in his. "I'm not making fun; it's just—you didn't drop your gaze or increase the pressure in your grip at all."

I glanced skyward, wondering if I even wanted to ask for clarification. "What in the name of the queen does my grip have to do with my declaration of love, Cresswell?"

"Everything."

"I—"

He captured my mouth with his. Unlike other stolen kisses, which began slow and sweet, there was a passionate heat in this one. Each time our lips or tongues came together, another spark ignited, until soon my entire body felt as if it were ablaze. Judging from the growing intensity of his kiss, and the daring places our hands touched, neither one of us wanted to control it any longer. We were on dangerous ground, which only made the fall more thrilling.

Thomas still knelt before me, so I pulled him closer, his arms circling my waist as he instinctually pressed his body against mine. Soon he abandoned my lips in favor of kissing my neck, his hands trailing up my sides, leaving no place unattended. I nearly lost my remaining senses as he gently angled my head back, exposing my throat for better access, his fist knotted in my hair. Either he or I made the next move, I wasn't certain, but suddenly his jacket was on the floor and my robe joined it.

A chill danced across my skin and I couldn't help but gasp. The robe had been the only item of clothing keeping me semi-decent. My nightgown left nothing to the imagination. Even in dim lighting, my form was plainly visible. As if he'd just realized this himself, Thomas rocked back on his heels, his breathing quick and uneven, much like my own.

For a fraction of a heartbeat, he seemed uncertain.

"Is this all it takes to silence that wicked mouth of yours?" I raised a brow, hoping the quip covered my growing nerves. We were alone in my bedroom, scantily clad, the night before our wedding. I was struggling madly to find a reason to send him away. "If I'd known, I would have worn this ages ago."

Thomas's attention snapped to my face. His expression was filled with such raw longing, I lost my futile battle with Victorian morals. He looked like a man who'd discovered his heart's deepest desire in the flesh and wished to claim it immediately. I realized that his respect for me and my choice was the only tether holding him in place. One little nod would unleash him.

My pulse raced as I silently gave him permission, wanting him to touch me again so badly it almost ached. Thomas Cresswell never disappointed. He leaned into me, his body snug between my thighs.

"Your nightgown is lovely, but your mind is what attracts and captivates me." His eyes traveled from mine, meandering down the road of delicate lace, igniting a new wave of desire as he gripped the sheer fabric at my hip. His touch was intoxicating. I couldn't stop myself from arching into it, craving more. "Your body..."

His focus lingered on the ribbons. I enjoyed the elegance of the garment and how I felt both bold and soft while wearing it. Thomas seemed to appreciate it for other reasons, and he was no longer masking how much he wanted me. I drew in a deep breath and fought the urge to completely disrobe him. If he kept looking at me that way, I'd lose control.

"Your spirit."

Thomas dragged his scorching gaze down every inch of me, leaving no part neglected, his breath hitching the lower it sank. If looks could consume, he'd just devoured me. And I wanted more. A warm sensation started in my toes and moved like honey up my body. It seemed as if Thomas had deduced exactly where the warmth was spreading and wouldn't mind following the line of sweetness with his mouth. That image almost stopped my heart. I gripped the sides of the bench in a fruitless attempt to rein myself in.

Misjudging my response, he froze. "I ought to go—"

I stared at his mouth, trying to corral my emotions. He *should* go to his chambers. And I should let him. Our virtues could go to hell in just a few hours, *after* we were wed.

But instead of agreeing, I reached for the waistband of his trousers, pulling him against me. I didn't want to wait any longer. I needed him. Suddenly shy at what I was asking, I averted my gaze.

"Stay here with me tonight. Please."

He tilted my chin up, staring deeply into my eyes, and I knew with utter certainty that he'd give me everything I wanted and more. "Forever, Audrey Rose."

This time when our kissing began, it was careful and deliberate— yet unrestrained. There were no tethers tying us back. Nothing keeping us from our base instincts. Seeing me naked and vulnerable unleashed a part of Thomas I wasn't sure he'd known existed. I thought of nothing except the feeling of his fingers and lips. Each place they touched, explored, caressed. Society vanished. Rules vanished. There was no one and nothing except the two of us, completely lost in our own little universe, our bodies uncharted galaxies to explore.

When Thomas drew back and met my gaze, I knew he saw the answer to his unspoken question reflected in my eyes. Without speaking, he lifted me off the velvet bench and laid me on the bed, his body settling comfortably above mine.

Neither of us had done this before—had loved so fiercely or freely—and instead of worrying over details, I gave myself over to my feelings completely.

"I love you, Audrey Rose."

His hand trailed from my ankle to my calf, leaving goose

bumps—and the most glorious tingle in its wake—as he pulled my stocking off. The smoothness of his action felt like it was the most natural act in the world. He repeated the motion with my sore leg, taking extra care to be as gentle as possible, which only made me long for him more. He brought his lips to my scar, showing every piece of me tender affection.

With slightly trembling fingers, I undid the buttons of his shirt, marveling at how beautiful he was both inside and out. His tattoo was completely healed now and was truly a work of art. As if he needed any other ornamentation to refine his already exquisite body.

"How is it you're so…defined?" I asked, running my hands over his surprisingly hard chest. "Do you take secret sword lessons I ought to know about? This"—I motioned to him—"makes no sense."

"Truthfully?" Thomas laughed, seeming to release a bit of his own nerves. "I pick up cadavers every day in the laboratory. All that body-hauling business keeps me quite fit and healthy. Plus"—he kissed from my neck down to my collarbone, spending extra care and attention on the area nearest my heart—"I do take fencing lessons, as per my father's wishes." At my shocked look, he grinned. "I've warned you—expect a lifetime full of surprises, my love."

A rush went through me at those words. We truly would have an entire lifetime to unravel each mystery the other possessed. I pushed myself up onto my elbows and pressed my lips to his skin, exploring his expanse of chest. His breath caught and I found myself echoing the sound as he pulled the ribbons of my nightgown apart, his attention never leaving my face, constantly searching for any hint of hesitation, any silent plea to stop.

He wouldn't find it, not even while using his most impressive Cresswell deductions. In a few hours we'd be married, and I was ready to claim him entirely.

In what seemed to be only seconds, we'd both stripped bare. A new sensation of heat began, almost indescribable in its intensity, as Thomas deepened our kiss and slowly, carefully lowered himself. Our bodies came together—and I was wholly cast under the spell of our love.

Heart pounding, skin aflame; each touch and caress was a hundred different feelings vying for my attention at once. Without effort, our bodies knew precisely what to do, how to react, and any hint of discomfort disappeared as we moved together, getting lost in our kisses. I'd imagined being clumsy or stilted as we fumbled through the science of it, petrified my mind would turn to thoughts of anatomy diagrams, taking me from the moment by fretting over mechanics. But I needn't have worried. I was much too consumed by the sensation of our skin pressed together without restrictions between us. Of the feeling of him. Of us. I gripped the sheets beside me, doing everything in my power to not call out his name.

"Audrey Rose," he whispered, pausing briefly.

My answer was a kiss, a plea. The careful attention Thomas paid to his deductions was focused entirely on me now—each inhalation, each exhalation. He listened in earnest, reacting and shifting to elicit the same waves of rapture until I was certain I must've left my body and become a star shooting across the vast universe.

SIXTEEN
A TANGLE OF LIMBS

AUDREY ROSE'S ROOMS
FIFTH AVENUE, NEW YORK CITY
5 FEBRUARY 1889

After, we lay in a tangle of limbs and bedsheets, our chests rising and falling in unison. Thomas drew idle circles across my stomach. I closed my eyes, allowing pure contentment to settle over me like a blanket. I couldn't imagine a more perfect experience. It saddened me to think young noblewomen were sometimes instructed to lie back and "think of England" when consummating their marriages. Love ought to be a mutual delight.

Thomas shifted his focus from my stomach to my hair, now running his fingers through my unbound locks, the motion soothing enough for my lids to suddenly feel too heavy to keep open. I closed my eyes, enjoying each careful stroke. I should love to spend eternity falling asleep *and* waking to this.

"I don't think I've ever been more content."

Thomas leaned over and kissed the top of my head. "Well, I can think of at least one other time *I've* felt perfectly content. And it may have been when you ravished me in the bathtub. Or that one time in the library." I swatted at him, drawing a deep chuckle. "Right, that only happened in my dreams. This is by far one of my happiest memories."

I wrapped my arms around him. "I'm sorry I've been so afraid, Thomas."

"You know, I'm extraordinary when it comes to puzzling things out, but this is a bit of a mystery even for me. Also, it's not at all what I'd imagined you saying directly after our first physical expression of love." He played with my hair for a few quiet moments, twirling locks around his fingers as if they were the greatest marvel of the nineteenth century. "What, exactly, have you been scared of? Me? Or my intimidating manhood?"

"Of course not you." I shook my head, glancing up, not bothering to acknowledge his other, wicked comment. "Falling. I'm—I fear it."

A smile curved his devilish lips. "I've never taken you for the clumsy type, Wadsworth."

"Don't be daft." I nestled closer to him. "You know what I mean."

"It would be nice to hear, though. For the sake of proving myself correct, of course."

I sighed, but relented. "It's...I find it's much easier to be brave when it comes to trusting my mind. I know what I'm capable of. What I can improve upon. Learning and making mistakes doesn't terrify me—it...I'm not sure. It fuels me, I suppose. But love? Letting go and falling completely petrifies me. When I'm vulnerable I feel as though my stomach has plummeted through my knees and the world is spinning out of control. Unlike science and mathematics, there are no formulas I can use to create an absolute outcome. Falling is chaos."

"It scares you even knowing I'm right there beside you?"

"I believe that scares me more. It terrifies me to think of you loving me as much as I love you. What happens when either one of us dies? We work in death nearly every day. I've lost so many people I've loved—losing you, sometimes if I think about it I'm unable to breathe. If I open myself up to loving you, to falling completely and without hesitation, I fear what may happen. Not from something you or I do, but life. It feels much safer to be insulated from that."

"Nothing in life comes with a guarantee, Wadsworth." Thomas took a deep breath. "Outside forces will always be out of your control. One thing you can control is how you choose to live. If you wake up fearful of every bad thing that *might* happen, you miss out on the good. Death will come for us all one day. Worrying about tomorrow only accomplishes ruining today."

He rolled onto his side and held my hand against his heart.

"Love is immortal. Death can neither touch nor steal it. Especially when it's true. Let's add another promise to our tally," he said. "Promise me to wake each day and find joy wherever you can, no matter how small it may be. There will always be hard times and trying times and times for sorrow, but we won't let those days destroy the here and now. Because right now? I'm here." He kissed the top of my head. "And you're here." He pressed his lips to my knuckles. "And the present is more glorious than the future and all of its unknowns."

"How have you not figured out a formula for love yet?" I teased.

"Have you no faith in my mighty brain? Of course I've worked out an equation only for us." Thomas smiled. "My love for you will be a constant in a sea of unknown variables. We may fight or be cross with each other, but our love will never fade or wilt. Trust in that. Trust in us. Forget the future. Forget worry. The only thing that terrifies me is the possibility of living with regret. I don't ever want to wake and wonder what life could have been like with you in it. I don't ever want to regret holding myself back from loving you as fully and openly as possible."

He searched my eyes and part of me wished to fall into the depth of adoration I saw within his expression and swim in the feeling forever.

"Unless you've changed your mind..." He quickly looked down. "I—"

"Thomas, never—" I tilted his chin up until our eyes met and held. "I love you. Now and always."

Before he could doubt or argue it, I kissed him. A few moments later we were exploring our newest form of silent communication, and the rest of the world and worry faded away. We celebrated our love until the sun rose and we could no longer risk being wrapped in each other's arms. In a few short hours we'd officially become husband and wife.

Then we could stay in bed for eternity.

Thomas reluctantly got up and pulled his trousers on, his hair mussed in a way that had me checking the clock to be sure we couldn't linger for a little while longer. He caught the look in my eye and beamed. "You are an absolute fiend, Miss Wadsworth. It's a good thing you're making an honest man out of me soon. My reputation is in tatters. If you keep gazing at me that way, we're never going to make it down the aisle."

"You adore it," I said, slipping my arms into my robe and sliding out of bed. "And I love you." I pulled him to me and kissed him properly. "Now, go. I'll see you in church soon."

He stared at my robe, his gaze declaring all sorts of trouble as he leisurely took me in.

"I'm sure we can make time...all right! All right, I'm going." Thomas paused, his fingers tapping the door as he openly admired me one last time. "Do you remember when I teased you about getting you to church?" I nodded, thinking back to our first case together. He smiled, that boyish, vulnerable smile. "After I said it, I'd never hoped for something more."

My heart felt ready to burst at the seams. Perhaps we could steal a few more moments...

An hour later, Thomas finally crept from my room, whistling quietly as he left me to get some sleep. We'd both need to be up soon to prepare for our day. The next time I saw him would be at the end of an aisle, when we began a new chapter.

One where we wrote our own rules from now until forever.

I slid back between the covers, convinced I'd never be able to sleep, and fell into an immediate and deep slumber. A lovely dream began—a preview of our upcoming nuptials. I was dressed in my wedding gown, my veil trailing like a cloud behind me.

The young man waiting at the altar was dressed in black. From his midnight suit to his shadowy form. Even up to the tips of his twisted horns, gleaming like twin obsidian blades.

My blood prickled. That wasn't...

I thrashed about, trying to wake myself. The man waiting for me had no face, no discernible features other than the horns on his head. In my dream I began trembling, the bouquet of roses I held pricking my hands. Blood dripped on my dress and onto the ground, mixing with the petals already strewn there. He didn't speak or move; he simply waited. Silent. Foreboding. Radiating menace. I dug my heels into the smooth marble of the chapel. But it was no use. I was pulled to him as if he were a magnet tugging me closer against my will.

He was only a silhouette, but I recognized who he was. Our destinies seemed fated for this moment. As if we'd been set upon this course our whole lives and all of my choices leading up to this had been mere fiction for his amusement. I wanted to scream, but couldn't.

It was the first night I dreamed of the devil, and I feared it wouldn't be the last.

NOT CAUGHT YET.

Many Arrests, but the New York Ripper Is Still at Large.

Detectives in Private Clothes

Newspaper article, circa. 1893

SEVENTEEN
STILL AT LARGE

AUDREY ROSE'S ROOMS
FIFTH AVENUE, NEW YORK CITY
6 FEBRUARY 1889

I sat perfectly still, my tea untouched, as Liza and Daciana worked my hair into perfection. My wedding gown was covered with a large blanket to keep anything from spilling on it, though a few layers of the pale blush and white skirts managed to sneak out.

Made of silk and tulle, the long-sleeved dress was exquisite—something straight out of a fairy tale, with glittering gemstones sewn both into the bodice and at different intervals in my skirts. When I walked, it looked like stars were winking in and out of the sunlight, too excited to wait until nightfall to remain hidden. Tiny blush petals were also clustered around the edge of my modest neckline, with more tendrils reaching for the floor, marrying the two colors of tulle expertly. It was extravagant, but elegant. A shining beacon of wonder.

Unlike my darkening mood.

No matter how much I wished otherwise, the glow I'd felt when Thomas left this morning had been replaced by a shadow. Its talons scraped against my good mood. Between the nightmare and the news I'd just learned, I could not settle my racing thoughts.

Even on the morning of my wedding, Jack the Ripper haunted me. I'd requested the newspaper along with my breakfast tray to be served in my room. I don't know why I hadn't considered the latest sensation making front-page news. I regretted not tossing it in the fireplace immediately. I wanted *one* day free from death. I longed to think only of life as we celebrated our union. Now I could hardly think of anything else with the article glaring at me.

NOT CAUGHT YET.
Many Arrests, but the New York Ripper Is Still at Large.

"See?" Daciana fluffed my hair over one shoulder. "Partially down is a bit softer. It matches the feeling of the gown. So ethereal." She tugged one of my braids, drawing my attention up. She raised her brows. "You appear as if you've seen a ghost."

I tried offering a smile but worried it was closer to a grimace instead. Judging from the slight narrowing of Daciana's eyes, she didn't believe my poor acting. "Liza?" she asked, her tone especially sweet. "I forgot the strand of pearls in my room. Would you mind getting them? They'll look exquisite tucked into her hair, don't you think?"

"Oh!" Liza clapped her hands. Her dress was a flowing blush that matched the petals sewn into my many layers. "What a wonderful idea!"

She dashed out the door, intent on embellishing every inch of me until I sparkled more than all the diamonds and jewels woven into my ensemble. I sighed. And here I thought Daciana was on my— I leaned forward, noticing the pearls on the vanity, and flicked my gaze up. "You lied."

"As did you." She gave me a conspiratorial smile. "Now, tell me, what's got you looking so dreadfully pale?"

"It's nothing. It's…" I scrambled for one of my worries. I didn't want to open up a discussion about the Ripper murders; that would lead to too many other inquiries. And I didn't want to share the details of my silly nightmare. Which left one inquiry I'd had for her anyway. "I received an odd letter or two that hadn't been signed. I was just remembering it now."

"A letter?" she asked, adding a few pearls to my braids. "Do you mean the note I sent along to you?" She laughed. "Apologies, dear sister. Ileana and I were in such a rush, I barely had time to scratch a note out to let you know we were coming."

"But it mentioned having something Thomas needed."

She picked my hand up, turning it about so the crimson diamond caught the light. "I wanted him to propose with Mother's ring. He's so sentimental, though he never lets it show. I knew how much it would mean to him, having her letters and blessing. I adore you and I love my brother immensely. I didn't mean to cause any strife."

I let my breath out in a whoosh. At least that was one less thing to worry over. My gaze slid to the newspaper before I tore it away again. Now if I could only stop allowing Jack the Ripper to step from my nightmares into reality, I'd be fine.

Liza huffed back into the room, her face flushed. "Are you certain the pearls were in there? I couldn't find them."

Daciana held the strand up, a sheepish look on her face. I studied the way she bit her lip and crinkled her eyes. She was quite convincing. "I must have brought them in and forgot I'd set them on the vanity already."

Ileana slipped into my chamber, eyes glistening when she saw me fully dressed. "You look so beautiful!" She hugged me close. "I wanted to give you something. Well, it's actually from Thomas," she amended, grinning at my confusion. "Here. He had these made."

I opened the box she held, pulling a stunning pair of robin's-egg-blue shoes from tissue paper. Diamonds were sewn across them, shimmering like stars in a cloudless sky. I clasped my hand over my mouth, trying to not cry off the kohl Liza had so carefully put on.

"They're incredible."

"Something blue and new," Daciana murmured. "Your ring is something old."

"Oh!" Liza rushed about the room, nearly tripping over her skirts. "I almost forgot!" She held up a diamond necklace with a solitary stone that was the size of an eyeball plucked from someone's head—a charming image for a wedding day. "This is from Mother. She said you may borrow it for the ceremony."

Daciana lifted my hair and fastened it. "You're all set."

Liza, Daciana, and Ileana stepped back, clasping their hands together as they inspected me. Their eyes shone with unshed tears. My family. If they kept this up, we'd all be sobbing messes together. A knock came at the door and suddenly the newspaper article was the furthest worry from my mind. My heart raced as I pushed myself to my feet.

Daciana let my father in and he halted when he saw me. It was hard to tell the exact emotions playing across his features, but the hitch in his voice was unmistakable. "Are you ready, Audrey Rose?"

I drew in a deep breath and slowly exhaled. "I am."

It was finally time to meet my husband at the altar. Neither the devil, nor a nightmare, nor any other nefarious thing would ruin our day.

St. Paul's Chapel, New York City

EIGHTEEN

MY VOW TO YOU

Father clutched my arm, his eyes misting as he placed the veil over my face. "You're a vision, my sweet child. Your mother would be overcome with pride. You look very much like her today." He adjusted his diamond-pinned cravat and leaned in, whispering, "There's a carriage waiting in the alley in case you've changed your mind. I'll take care of the details."

I laughed, then quickly blinked tears away. Once I was certain I wouldn't ruin my kohl, I looked at my father and smiled. He'd take me from this chapel at once, no questions or judgment, should I choose a different fate. And I loved him for it. I tried not to focus on the sudden overwhelming sadness of closing one chapter and stepping into a new one. No matter how much I'd longed for freedom, it was a strange sort of thing to no longer be under my father's roof. Another bout of emotion welled up, threatening to spill down my cheeks. I uselessly fanned my face, picturing how angry Aunt Amelia would be if I cried my makeup off.

As if he'd crafted some magical tool to see into my mind, my father hugged me near, patting my head. "There, there, Audrey Rose. You'll always be my darling baby girl. If you're happy, then I am, too. I just wanted you to know that you have choices. Options. Whatever you'd like, I will make happen. As I ought to have done for you a long while ago."

I accepted a handkerchief and dabbed at my eyes. "I scarcely know why I'm crying," I said, unable to stop the flow of tears that had begun. Aunt Amelia would definitely murder me if she wasn't preoccupied with last-minute arrangements. "I want this. More than anything. It's...everything is going to be different now, is all."

"Ah." Father gently took the handkerchief from me and tucked it back into his pocket. "Part of growing older means letting go. You can't move forward if you never take those first few steps onto new ground. Now's the time to be brave, Daughter. Walking into the future means trusting in yourself even when you can't see around the bend. As long as you're certain this is what you want, all will be well."

First Thomas and now my father. If this had been one of Liza's novels, I'd probably have to face this question another dozen or so times before my journey was complete. I listened to the steady beat of my heart, waiting for a whisper of doubt or a niggle of uncertainty.

Standing in my wedding gown, hair flowing most scandalously down my back in loose waves, with a braid of flowers and pearls twisted into a coronet about my crown, I glanced at the scarlet diamond glittering from my finger.

"When I imagine my life without Thomas, that's the only time I worry." I hugged my father. "I'm quite sure about us, though I'm sad to leave you."

"Me, too. We shall both visit often." Father sniffled and gave me a short, curt nod as he straightened. "Let's see you two off, then, hm?"

"I love you, Father."

He looked at me once more, his eyes filled with emotion, and I wondered if the same memories were playing through his mind. Me climbing onto his lap while he'd crafted mechanical toys in his office. The two of us dashing through the gardens and hedge maze at our country home, Thornbriar. Our whole family—Mother, Nathaniel, Father, and me—sitting out on the lawns of Hyde Park, enjoying a picnic along with the fairies Father had claimed were all around us. He swore folklore held kernels of truth—that evidence waited for curious little children to unravel the mystery of the Fair Folk and other, darker mythological creatures.

All of it seemed as if it had occurred yesterday. And yet it also felt as if a hundred years had passed. I glanced down at my bouquet, at my mother's heart-shaped locket, which Liza had thoughtfully woven around the stems. I hoped there was an ever after, and that my mother and brother were both smiling down upon me now. I certainly missed them and all the memories we never had the chance to make.

"Ready?" Father asked, squeezing my hand gently.

I took a deep breath and nodded. It was time to create new memories together. We'd do it for ourselves and our loved ones. As we stepped up to the aisle, a pipe organ began playing Mendelssohn's "Wedding March." My hand tightened on Father's arm ever so subtly as everyone in attendance turned to watch us enter the room. I paused for a moment, breath stolen, as I finally got my first glimpse of the chapel.

From the flowers to the lush greenery and colors chosen, it was gorgeous yet somehow a bit dangerous. Light with a hint of dark. Like dappled sunlight slipping into a moss-covered forest deep in the woods of Ireland or some other more magical land.

"It's like the enchanted forest you used to tell us about," I whispered to Father. I blinked tears away. Liza must have recalled how much I'd adored those stories as a child. Back before I'd been altered by death.

Garlands made of fern fronds, eucalyptus greens, lamb's ears, and white cabbage roses were strung along the pews. Strings of peonies hung in varying intervals from the rafters like a canopy of petals. On the altar, a large decanter with red roses sat majestically—a centerpiece that demanded attention. Instead of setting the flowers right side up, Liza had opted to put the blossoms in the water, leaving the stems and thorns pointing heavenward. It was strangely beautiful and wholly unique.

Orchids and more peonies in purples and petal pink were also woven into the floral design. My favorite flowers mixed with Thomas's, each coming together to create something magnificent. There was so much to see, yet the only thing my gaze was desperate to find was—

Thomas.

The priest stepped aside, revealing my love in all his splendor. I suddenly forgot how to breathe. I felt everyone's gaze as it landed on me, heard their intake of breath, but could only concentrate on not grabbing my skirts and rushing to the young man standing at the end of the enchanted aisle. My dark prince.

Somehow, my father and I finally reached the end of the petal-strewn pathway. I took the final step, kissed my father good-bye, and barely breathed as he placed my hand in Thomas's waiting grasp. It did not escape my notice that he appeared to be the heir to a dynasty.

Thomas Cresswell looked more regal than Prince Albert. His black suit was tailored perfectly to his frame, hugging the angles and lines that were so sharp they made one consider sinking to one's knees in supplication. Surely he had to be an angel sent directly from Heaven.

His hair was styled with pomade and his eyes were filled with a steadiness I didn't know I'd been craving until I drank it in. I spied an orchid dusted with glitter—my favorite flower—pinned to his lapel, and any remaining tension left my limbs at once. That dear detail was all Thomas, and I had to remind myself to not kiss him senselessly. It looked like a painting he'd created of an orchid with stars within its petals. After deducing how much I favored the flower, he'd married our two loves together. Much like we were about to do.

I clasped his hands and he took a deep, shuddering breath. My gaze immediately dropped to his lips and lingered. I wondered if flashes of last night were playing across his mind, or if I was truly the only devious one.

"You are exquisite, Audrey Rose," he whispered.

I allowed one more, indecently long assessment of his form, much to the priest's dismay. His suit stretched across broad shoulders, and silver thread trimmed the collar, matching the silver whorls in his dark gray waistcoat. He was utterly magnificent. I recalled another time I'd had similar thoughts back in Romania. I hadn't been truthful then. I'd not keep my heart from him now. "You're devastatingly handsome, Thomas."

His grin was so radiant, he practically beamed. The priest cleared his throat, holding his prayer book up, likely reminding us we were in a house of God and were not yet married. If he was that put out by our appreciative glances, he'd likely go up in fire and brimstone if he knew we'd already consummated our marriage. Three times last night.

And once this morning.

"Will you, Thomas James Dorin cel Rău Cresswell, take Audrey Rose Aadhira Wadsworth to be your wedded wife, to have and to hold, from this day forward, for better, for worse, for richer, for poorer, in sickness and in health, to love and to cherish, till death do you part?"

Thomas gently ran his thumb over my knuckles. "I will."

The priest nodded. "Very good. Audrey—"

"I will love and honor you every second, every minute, every hour of the day," Thomas continued, stepping closer. "I vow to seek your counsel on all matters, both big and small, and to cherish you with each breath in my lungs. I promise to never make the same mistake twice, to make it my daily duty to see you smile, and to hold your hand through each challenge, each victory, and each new adventure this life brings our way." He slipped a wedding band next to my engagement ring, never taking his gaze from mine. "From this day until my last, I vow to love and hold you, as my equal in all ways, Audrey Rose."

Someone gasped from the pews at his shocking declaration. Distantly I heard a door open and close, but I couldn't tear my attention away from Thomas. A woman was supposed to honor and obey her husband in all things. What Thomas had promised was freedom and respect for the remainder of our lives. He'd said as much plenty of times in private, but to do so in front of an entire chapel full of witnesses...

I swallowed hard, tears welling, as he offered me an encouraging nod. I could practically see the words he'd said to me a thousand times before dancing across his expression. *Expect a lifetime full of surprises.*

"Yes, well." The priest turned to me, face stern. "Audrey Rose Aadhira Wadsworth, will you take Thomas James Dorin cel Rău Cresswell as your wedded husband? To have and to hold, from this day forward, for better, for worse, for richer, for poorer, in sickness and in health, to love, cherish, and to *obey* him till death do you part?"

My heart felt as if it were ready to burst through my chest as I stared into Thomas's eyes. I took his other hand in mine and stepped near enough to require tilting my head back as I slowly placed a ring on the tip of his finger, waiting until our vows were complete before I secured it on him. We'd chosen matching bands—two serpents entwined in an infinity symbol.

And if someone knew to look carefully enough, they'd recognize they were actually dragons, symbolic of his mother's lineage. Thomas smiled down at me, his expression unabashedly open. I lightly squeezed his hands as I drew in a deep breath.

"I will." I pulled him nearer still, ignoring the disapproving grunt from the priest. "I promise to love and challenge you, to remind you to don warmth as much as you wear that cool, scientific exterior I adore so much. I vow to always remain the woman you fell in love with. I will honor you by never being afraid to express my opinion, to love you without limits, and to tell you each day of our lives how incredible you are. How kind and gentle and intelligent. I promise to love you with every part of me now until our next lifetime. I love you, Thomas James Dorin cel Rău Cresswell, now and forever more."

Footsteps sounded behind us, but I didn't quite care who we'd offended with our proclamations. Let them leave. This moment was ours. Despite the enchanted forest setting, standing here, in front of Thomas, it was the simple wedding we'd wished for all along—a day where we could speak to each other from our hearts as if it were just the two of us.

The priest drew in a long, measured breath. "If no one sees fit to object to this... *ceremony*... yet, then I now pronounce you husband and—"

"Pardon my interruption," a new voice said. "I'm afraid this wedding cannot continue."

Thomas and I—along with the rest of the church—turned, the combined sound of rustling silks like bird wings flapping in the chapel. An attractive young woman in a claret traveling dress was halfway down the aisle, advancing on the altar with an envelope clutched in her gloved hands.

"Who is that?" I swiveled my attention back on Thomas, expecting a shrug. Instead, he'd gone exceptionally pale. His reaction set off shrill warning bells in my head. "Thomas?"

His throat bobbed as he swallowed down some emotion—fear? "Merciful God above."

"What?" I asked, looking between him and the young woman. My heart had now taken full flight. It was pounding so hard I felt faint. "Who is she? What's happening?"

He stared, unblinking, for what felt like a full minute before mustering up a response. Perhaps he thought this was some dream. Or a nightmare, given the way he'd stopped breathing.

"That's Miss W-Whitehall."

"Not for long, silly." Miss Whitehall, who'd continued her slow march toward us, turned a dazzling smile on the priest. "You see, Thomas and *I* are betrothed."

"What?" My voice echoed around the chapel. Thomas's ring fell from my hands, the tinny sound much too loud for such a grand space. No one moved to pick it up. I swore the earth tilted on its axis or perhaps Liza had pulled my corset too tight. It sounded as if she'd said she was betrothed to Thomas. *My* Thomas. The man I gave myself to last night. The man who—moments ago—swore to love me forever. The man I'd just exchanged rings with. Well, almost. I could still faintly pick out the sound of the gold band as it rolled to a stop. It was odd, hearing something so insignificant while my heart cracked wide open.

I glanced at him, but his attention was fixed on what Miss Whitehall was carrying, the muscle in his jaw strained. I closed my eyes briefly, hoping this *was* a nightmare. That my subconscious was torturing me with fears before our day. Surely this could not truly be happening. Not when I'd finally overcome my reservations.

Not after we'd spent the night together...

Unimpressed by the deadly stares from our friends and family, Miss Whitehall walked up the last few steps to the dais and handed the priest the envelope she'd been waving about like a declaration of war. I could only watch, horror-struck, as the priest opened the cursed letter.

"I've got official correspondence as proof. See?" She leaned her blond head over the document, pointing out a line for the priest. "It says so right...there."

He fumbled for control, or perhaps an answer from God on how to proceed. I watched him scan it twice, as if he'd hoped what was written there had changed. "Er...it does say you two are—" The priest glanced at us, brows tugged close. "When did you and Miss Wadsworth become betrothed?"

My heart thumped wildly. Thomas held fast to my hand, addressing the priest. "I made my intentions for courtship known in December. Miss Wadsworth agreed to our betrothal in January."

I gripped Thomas's hand until I was sure it must have been painful, but he didn't seem to mind or notice. He held me with equal force, as if by clinging to each other our bond could not be broken. We waited, fused together, as the priest's gaze dropped back to the letter, his mouth tightening.

"And the announcement?" the priest prodded, his expression growing grimmer by the second. "When did you formally declare your engagement?"

Thomas stared at the broken seal on the envelope, his tone clipped. "A fortnight ago."

"I-I'm sorry." The priest shook his head, glancing from the letter to us. "This is postmarked the first week of December. I do not have the legal authority to marry you today." He swallowed hard, and I saw true regret enter his eyes. "Nor ever, if this remains a binding agreement."

Miss Whitehall shifted her attention to my fiancé, smiling demurely.

"Surprise, Mr. Cresswell. I do hope you're pleased to see me again. I've certainly missed you."

NINETEEN
DASHED TO BITS

AUDREY ROSE'S ROOMS
FIFTH AVENUE, NEW YORK CITY
6 FEBRUARY 1889

I perched on the edge of my bed, voluminous skirts of tulle cushioning me in case I pitched forward, giving in to the shock still settling in. Honestly, I was surprised I felt anything other than the emptiness where my heart once beat. I could not fathom how the events of the last hour had unfolded. A day full of hopes and dreams, dashed to bits in an instant.

Liza had filled me in on pieces of the story I missed after I'd fled to my rooms. Even now the tale was disjointed and filled with conjecture. Apparently Thomas's father made the cursed arrangement, but a letter was allegedly signed by my fiancé requesting permission to marry Miss Whitehall. At present, there was a great debate on its authenticity.

Thomas and I were so certain of each other, so confident that we'd battled against our own doubts and were now victorious. We didn't consider enemies sneaking in, destroying the life we'd envisioned building together. The future that was so close I nearly clutched it in my grasp. My jaw clenched as the scene played back in my mind, each dreadful detail cutting like a knife.

Thomas was betrothed. To another.

It couldn't be true. And yet...each time I closed my eyes, I saw Miss Whitehall waving that portent of doom about, an expression of glee upon her face. Until this morning, I'd never heard her name uttered. Not once. I'd looked to Thomas for answers, but he'd donned that icy exterior, permitting no one a glimpse into his heartbreak. The absolute elation I'd seen in his eyes had disappeared, gone so quickly it was as if it never existed. The young man standing at that altar no longer resembled the affectionate, loving man I'd shared my heart—and body—with. This Thomas was remote and cold. Something I recognized as his emotional shield, though it didn't stop the sting of him leaving me to deal with my devastation alone.

Once the priest had declared Miss Whitehall and Thomas's betrothal standing and ours invalid, my aunt and cousin sprang into immediate action, whisking me from the church, buffeting me against the dawning horror that our wedding day had been ruined.

I, too, was now ruined. At least in society's tiny little mind. My hands were clammy and cold as I curled them into fists, my nails creating crescent moons in my palms. I'd discarded my gloves somewhere on the way back to my chambers. They were likely stained beyond repair now, too. Just like—I could barely draw in breath.

This *couldn't* be happening. Thomas and I had exchanged our virtues the eve of our wedding, never dreaming everything would go to hell in a few short hours. *He'd* be all right. Not that I'd wish otherwise; my anger lay elsewhere. Society never condemned men for their part in untoward romantic encounters. Women were harlots and upstarts while men were experienced and savvy. Oh, how I loathed the world.

When I pictured our secret tryst accidentally being exposed...

my thoughts immediately shifted to Liza; this could affect her own future. People would whisper of her lowly, wanton harlot of a cousin. She'd be made a jester in her social circles.

Not that she'd be invited anywhere, because of the scandal. I covered my face, as if that might block the growing sickness of just how much had gone wrong. It seemed a cruel twist of fate, that something born of love could evoke such hatred.

Father and Uncle stayed behind, arguing facts and sorting out the situation, according to my aunt's endless chatter when she'd come in to check on me at some point. There was another debate brewing on whether or not Miss Whitehall had shared the news with her extended family. If there was no public proof of her supposed betrothal to Thomas, then it could go away without involving the courts. If she'd sent letters, then there was nothing we could do until it was solved through proper legal measures. *If* it could be solved through legal channels. Thomas might be unable to break the agreement.

I couldn't retain anything anyone said after that declaration. Betrothals were so rarely created out of love; they were business maneuvers, and as such there were many rules and regulations once one had entered into them. To imagine Thomas legally bound to another—I leaned over my skirts, praying I didn't vomit on my gown.

First the shock of my brother and a second Jack the Ripper... and now this. I rubbed my temples.

Aunt Amelia and Liza had left me in my room with promises of tea and spiced wine and other things that would not mend my shattered heart. Nothing they could bring would calm the growing storm raging inside me. If only we'd waited a few more hours, this would be wretched, but at least I'd have one less thing to feel ill over. One less life I'd ruined.

Shoving aside worries over my forsaken virtue and how it could affect my family if anyone found out, I had no idea what to make of the situation. I hadn't thought Thomas courted anyone else. Yet he knew who Miss Whitehall was immediately upon seeing her. They had to have had *some* interaction or encounter. She certainly seemed both familiar with and fond of him. And the way she'd smirked at me as if I was an opponent...

I rubbed my temples a bit harder, trying to recall exactly what he'd said when I'd inquired about his romantic history. I was fairly certain he'd claimed to have loved only me. But what did that mean in truth? If I dissected it, there was no mention of *interest* in another. He very well could have indulged in a romance with her. Perhaps it was meaningless to him, but clearly feelings were involved for her. Or, at the very least, finances.

I swiped at my tears. I wanted to take the vase of orchids some- one had placed on my nightstand and smash it against the wall. It was startling, how quickly my emptiness filled with anger. My hurt needed an outlet, and fury at least made me *feel* something other than hollow. I didn't care if there *had* been anyone else—the lies or falsehood was another matter. Especially after I'd directly asked Thomas about it a few weeks prior. He might not have agreed with my spending time with Mephistopheles, but I'd warned him first. Thomas knew my plan to infiltrate the carnival and get close to the ringmaster; he simply didn't like that decision.

Which had been the entire source of my sliver of doubt. It was the first time I worried he might not be the person he claimed to be. That his insistence I proceed in another manner was a preview of what life would become, the more comfortable he was around me. I feared it was only going to get worse, that he'd start exerting his command in small ways until I eventually looked to him to see how I ought to feel. Men in our society were bred to falsely believe they knew best. Of course a sliver of doubt had crept in. He'd unintentionally gouged a hole in my deepest fear. But this? This was unthinkable.

I may have stumbled a bit, had fears of trusting in us, but I never pretended away my indecision. Even when admitting my hint of doubt, I'd told Thomas the truth. It had nearly broken us both, but I'd told him each fear in my heart, sparing no detail. I'd given him the choice, whether or not he could still love me, despite my confusion. My choice had never centered on another person. Though Mephistopheles certainly tried his hand at manipulating my feelings. My struggle was always on the direction of my life and how well I knew myself.

Miss Whitehall was not a direction. She was a living, breathing reminder that Thomas and I had known each other for only a few months. There was much about him that I still didn't know. I almost cringed at the thought of what other secrets he'd yet to reveal.

"What have you gotten us into now, Cresswell?" I whispered.

It was medically impossible, but I swore my heart rattled instead of beat, the jagged pieces cutting me with each cursed movement. Inside I was a torn, bloody mess. Outside I feared I wasn't faring much better. I couldn't settle on which emotion was winning out: anger or pure emptiness. How silly of me to believe in happy endings when I lived and breathed in darkness.

I ought to have known better. Fairy tales don't end well for the imposter princess. No amount of artistry or cunningly placed pieces of moss and flowers could make my enchanted forest a reality. I was a damned thing. I might as well be the devil's heir. At least then I wouldn't have to hide who or what I was.

"How are you?" Liza entered my bedchamber without knocking, her expression the most solemn I'd ever seen it. In a way her mood was a relief—it certainly felt as if a part of me had died and we were mourning it together. I laughed, the sound hysterical to my own ears. Of course. I'd be the one who'd planned a wedding but ended up with a funeral. I was the queen of death. A princess of corpses. Everything I touched decayed.

My laughter immediately cut off, replaced by uncontrollable sobs. I was thankful my tears didn't spill over. I only hiccupped and choked them back down. Liza's gaze paused on my face, her own mirroring the devastation I felt. I wondered how red my eyes were. How beaten I must look. There was no pretending, no mask to hide behind. My heart was wholly broken.

Liza took my hand in hers, squeezing until I tore my attention from the petals that had been sewn into my skirts. It was such a lovely gown. I longed to take my scalpels to it.

"Will you help me out of this dress?" My voice was scratchy and rough, sounding as if I'd swallowed mouthfuls of seawater. I had no idea how long I'd been sitting there, lost in the prison of my misery. It felt like centuries. "It chafes."

My cousin hesitated, her hand dropping to her side.

"This is a momentary hurdle, nothing more." She sounded firm, though I detected a slight tremor of worry that belied her resolve. There was no guarantee this would be reconciled. At least not in a favorable manner. Liza knew that as well as I did. "Clearly a mistake has been made, and Thomas will rectify it at once. You should have seen him. I was unaware he could be quite so . . . intimidating." I flicked my attention up at that. "Not to us. His anger was directed entirely at the situation. He's writing a telegram to his father now."

I drew in a ragged breath, not quite ready to know the answer to my next question, but unable to keep myself in the dark any longer. "Was there . . . is there truly a written agreement? Between Thomas and . . . and her?"

Liza pursed her lips; clearly this wasn't news she wanted to share. Not while I probably looked like a talking corpse. "Yes. Thomas told your father he's never seen it before. That a mistake has been made, but confirmed it was his signature." She watched me closely and I dropped my attention back to my dress. "If you saw the way Thomas was, you'd know there was nothing to worry over. Signature or not, he will fix this."

I nodded, my head wobbling along of its own volition. I wanted to have the same faith my cousin was in possession of, but at my core sat mathematical unease. The numbers didn't quite add together. Clearly Thomas's father had entered into a written agreement with Miss Whitehall, meaning there would be legal repercussions involved with sorting it all out.

If he even *could* sort it out.

My head spun as the same conclusion whipped around my mind again and again. Miss Whitehall would take Thomas and we'd no longer belong to each other and he'd end up marrying her and—my skin seemed to catch fire. I tugged at the neckline of my wedding gown.

"Please," I ground out, pulling the material away from my body. I swore it came alive and delighted in choking me. Blotches of angry red welts appeared like petals on my skin. My own personal bouquet of regret. "Get this dress off me before I rip it off!"

Startled by either my tone or the welts, Liza began unlacing my bodice as quickly as she could manage. My deep breaths weren't helping; my ribs expanded more and more until she reached around and pulled me into a fierce hug. I shook beneath her touch, unable to control my flood of tears. Thomas was promised to another. Our wedding was a mockery. I was losing him. I couldn't breathe. I choked on tears that refused to cease.

"Breathe. You must breathe, Audrey Rose." Liza held me fiercely. I closed my eyes, trying to command my lungs to breathe in time to my cousin's steady breaths. It took a few tries, but I managed to collect myself again. Liza spun me around, shaking me a little. "Be still. *Think*. What is this?"

Tears threatened to spill again; my lips wobbled. "The worst day of my existence."

"Yes, but *think*. Be still and think about it without emotion." I flashed her an incredulous look. As if I could turn my emotions off *now*. She set her jaw, determined. She would be my strength when I couldn't summon my own. It almost brought on another round of tears. I'd heard that brides cry at weddings, but this wasn't how I'd imagined it. "This is a mystery for you both to solve. Understand? And, in case you've forgotten, your Mr. Cresswell is one of the best at solving mysteries. Do you truly believe he'll let this stand? He seemed ready to unleash Hell upon the world. Satan himself would tremble. Have heart, Cousin. All will be well."

Despite her reassuring words, I caught a flicker of doubt crossing her features, sending me tumbling into my own worries once more.

TWENTY

INCONVENIENT ARRANGEMENT

AUDREY ROSE'S ROOMS
FIFTH AVENUE, NEW YORK CITY
6 FEBRUARY 1889

An hour or possibly five later, I huddled into my silk robe, sipping another herbal tea concoction Liza had brought before she slipped away to talk with our family. As I inhaled the fragrance and concentrated on the different herbal notes, I guessed at the deeper meaning behind them.

Though she didn't inquire into my personal affairs, I'd wager anything that Liza was concerned about pregnancy and the tea would prevent it. I'd been ingesting it for weeks, so chances were good that I could cross one worry off the growing list. My cousin was truly a master of reading people and working her magic for romantic entanglements. I didn't know whether to laugh or cry, but I was grateful beyond measure for her keen sense.

She'd suggested sitting in my room eating chocolate and drinking champagne, but I'd begged her to go downstairs and keep everyone away, unable to deal with their pity. Or their words of hope. I wasn't sure which stung more. Their belief that all would be well, or my grappling with the truth that it would not.

Thomas could work out impossible equations, but even he couldn't make two and two equal five. I sipped my tea, relishing its sharpness. It was almost as bitter as my mood. I'd grown used to the taste of fresh herbs and looked forward to breathing in the aromatic scent.

It was especially calming as I sat in the center of my own disaster. My wedding gown lay discarded beside me, a heap of tulle and petals and whimsy. Which was a contrast to my reading material. Nathaniel's journals lay strewn across what should have been my marital bed, his notes scattered and dismal like my current thoughts. I glanced at the pile and winced. I'd accidentally smudged ink on my wedding gown. It was one more loss to add to the day's tally.

I shook my head. Death invaded even the most sacred of spaces in my life.

If it was intent on joining me in my darkest hours, I might as well welcome it. I flipped through an entry, reading but not actually absorbing the information. I'd been so certain Thomas would visit me, but as the hours grew later, I couldn't stop wondering if his devotion was another fantasy I'd concocted.

When the knock finally came, I sat straighter in bed, my fingers twisting my bedsheets as the door creaked open. He halted by the doorframe, leaning against it as if he were held there by some magic spell, a wary expression on his face.

After his initial inspection of me, he wouldn't meet my gaze. How different it was from this morning, when he'd stared unabashedly into my eyes, our bodies melded into one. A thousand images fought their way into my mind—his hands in my hair, his lips on my throat, my fingers on his back, our hips pressed together. It had all been so wonderful, and now...

I clamped my jaw shut to keep from crying in front of him. The same fears were circling like vultures again, picking at the bones of my sadness. My reputation, my future. What did any of it matter? I didn't want to think of marriage to another. Let the whole world talk of my wicked ways; they already did anyway. My lips trembled, snipping whatever cords had held Thomas in place.

In a few strides he was across the room, wrapping me in his arms. "I'm so sorry, Audrey Rose. I...I understand if you hate me or—or wish to end our—"

"Hate you?" I pulled out of his embrace, searching for any hint regarding his true emotions. His expression was carefully controlled, even now. "How could I hate you? You were unaware of the betrothal, weren't you?"

Thomas released me to tug the letter Miss Whitehall had brandished from his jacket, holding it up by two fingers as if it were a stinking hunk of rotten meat he wished to toss away. I'd witnessed him nearly nose-deep inside more than one putrid corpse and his demeanor hadn't been so distressed. He ran his free hand through his hair, tousling it in a most un-Thomas-like manner.

"I swear I had no inkling my father had arranged that betrothal."

He tossed the paper to the floor, glaring as if his infernal stare might set it ablaze. An ounce of my worry dissipated. Only an ounce, however. Even though Thomas was disgusted by this news, depending on the terms of the betrothal, there might not be anything he could do about it—his signature was on the letter. In England, a letter requesting an engagement was as acceptable and binding as if Thomas had done so in person.

I wanted to fire a hundred questions at him, but I refrained. I watched as his icy exterior slowly melted, revealing the true depth of his own despair and worry.

"Though, given one of our last arguments in August," he continued, "I'm not as surprised as I ought to be. Father had been rather put out that I hadn't made more of an effort to court Miss Whitehall.

I hadn't—" He shook his head. "I hadn't considered his motivations for doing so. Clearly, a mistake on my part. She's the daughter of a marquess. My father believes marriage is nothing more than a wise business transaction. It was a lesson he was trying to teach me the night I met you, actually."

"How..." I felt my emotions bubbling up again. A marquess was several ranks higher than my father's lordship in the British peerage. For Thomas's father, himself a duke, allying with my family would be a much poorer match. I drew in another deep breath. "How did you meet Miss Whitehall? I thought you hadn't courted anyone."

I glanced up in time to see him flinch. "It was never—" He rubbed his face. He looked tired, almost haggard. "My father requires I attend certain gatherings throughout the year. Mostly just one or two horrendous parties hosted by his friends. I met Miss Whitehall at her coming-out ball."

He hesitated, which only made my nerves rattle more. When it seemed no further information was coming, I gathered my strength. I deserved to know. "And?"

Thomas stood up and prowled around my small room, almost as if he were subconsciously searching for an escape route. "I knew my father wanted me to show interest, but it was the furthest thing from what *I* desired." He snuck a glance at me, his lips almost quirking. "I wanted to be left alone. I considered science my one true love. Miss Whitehall was grating. She cornered me by the buffet, asking question after question." At this memory, a full smile flashed across his face before he seemed to recall the horror of our day. "She agreed with everything I said, annoyingly so. Her eyes kept sliding over my shoulder, toward another young man. I began to understand that she was interested in my father's title. That she'd tell me anything I wanted to hear. When I imagined how our life would unfold, I could think of no greater misery for either of us. I knew I needed to end her pursuit at once." He inhaled deeply. "I suggested we run naked through the streets and she fainted into her dessert. I left soon after, not expecting to ever hear her name or see her again."

I took a few moments to absorb his story. "So you never—there was never any...fondness...on your part?"

"Never. I hardly spent an hour with her. And our interaction was mostly me being obnoxious and her half listening." Thomas settled next to me on the bed. "Are you sure you aren't angry with me?"

I considered his story and how I felt.

Finally, I took a deep breath. "When you promised a lifetime full of surprises, this wasn't exactly what I had in mind."

Thomas snorted as if the weight he'd been carrying had suddenly lifted. "If it's any consolation, it isn't quite what I had in mind, either." He tentatively picked my hand up, tracing the outline of the red diamond I still wore on my ring finger. "Do you...regret what happened between us?"

My cheeks heated as memories of our bodies coming together in the most intimate way crossed my mind. His lips and hands paying homage to me in ways I'd never dreamed possible. How unbelievably good it felt, giving myself to him completely.

"No, not"—I swallowed hard, stalling—"not entirely."

He stiffened and I wished to cram the words back in, but I couldn't deny my racing emotions. Even though it might make him uncomfortable, we ought to share our innermost fears. If I'd learned anything from our time with the carnival, it was the power of sharing the parts of myself I worried might scare him away. I twined our fingers, putting emphasis on the strength of them woven together as one.

"I do not regret sharing a bed with you. Not now or ever. I-I'm uncomfortable not knowing what comes next. What if you *must* wed

Miss Whitehall? What happens then?" I took a steadying breath. "If you share her bed, I cannot be your mistress, Thomas. I will not do that to myself, no matter how much of my heart you possess."

He was quiet a moment. Almost as silent as the dead. I gathered my courage and looked at him, seeing just how tense he'd gotten. "Do you believe that's something I would do to you? That I'd allow my father to do to us?"

The dangerous calm of his tone sent gooseflesh racing along my spine. Liza was right. I'd never seen this side of Thomas. I didn't fear him; I feared the war he might wage for me. Thomas was a young man who'd found happiness, and he'd clutch at it until his body turned to dust.

"What are the terms of the betrothal?"

"None that cannot be broken," he said, his voice as cool as ice chips.

I didn't believe his bravado for a moment. I glanced up sharply, studying him. There. In the slight curve of his frown. "May I see the letter myself?" He hesitated, a moment too long, but bent to retrieve it. I read quickly and silently, cursing as I finished. It was much worse than I'd feared. "Thomas...he will disown you. You will have no title, no money, no home."

The enormity of the situation threatened to knock me over.

"You cannot—" I forced myself to sit straight, to turn my spine to steel. "You cannot give that up. Not for me."

Thomas stood, bending down to look in my eyes. "He might take my English title, but my mother's ancestral home does not belong to him. She saw to it that it would pass to Daciana before I came of age. Much as he might wish he could, he cannot take my Romanian lineage from me. If the choice is between you and a title I don't care for? My answer is simple."

"Is it something you can truly live with giving up?" I asked. "Or

will a seed of resentment be planted here"—I touched his heart—
"growing over time until you regret your decision?"

Silence crept in the spaces between our breaths, waiting to be
banished, but it seemed he welcomed it. I wanted Thomas to deny
my fears, call them ridiculous, but he stood there, fiddling with my
ring, bereft of words. It was easy to believe you could forsake your
name in favor of love—in theory. When faced with the consequences
that tumbled like stones falling down a cliff, it wasn't quite as simple. Blessedly—or yet another cursed act; it was hard to distinguish
between the two—someone knocked at my door.

No longer caring who witnessed us sitting alone together, I called
out, "Come in."

Daciana swept in like a storm descending on the shore, eroding
the remainder of my calm. Her eyes flashed. "You're not the only one
who our dear father wrote to." She clutched a letter in her fist, holding it up for us to see. "He's threatened me."

"Don't be absurd." Thomas's light tone did not match the fearful
look in his eyes. I imagined another stone falling from the avalanche
his father had started.

"You underestimate our father." A tear slid down Daciana's
cheek. "If you do not agree to his terms, I will be married to that old,
rotten friend of his immediately."

I glanced between them, noticing the remaining color drain
from Thomas's face.

"Who?" he asked, his voice already laced with dread.

"The one whose previous wives have gone missing." Daciana
seemed more inclined to gouge someone's eyes out rather than cry
now. "And our home in Bucharest will revert to my new husband as
the law decrees. You and I will have nothing left of Mother."

TWENTY-ONE
AN IMPOSSIBLE POSITION

AUDREY ROSE'S ROOMS
FIFTH AVENUE, NEW YORK CITY
6 FEBRUARY 1889

Thomas went preternaturally still, reminding me of the vampire rumors that ran in his family. Hair at the nape of my neck stood on end. A strange energy crackled in the space around us, a charge waiting for the tiniest spark to explode. He stood, hands unmoving at his sides, chest hardly rising. I imagined on the inside he was a tangle of chaotic energy. It was the only explanation for how frightfully calm he was. Thomas always tapped his fingers or paced. He was never still. Not like this.

Finally, he blinked. "I'm eighteen. Father's threat is meaningless. As of Mother's decree, the property is now mine. And since I'm in charge, I say you can refuse the marriage and live in our family's home forever. Ileana, too." He looked at me, a glimmer of hope entering his features. "Wadsworth and I will live there as well. If she chooses to. We needn't worry about London society or courts or pledges of unrequited betrothals. We can leave all of it behind. Father won't follow us to Romania. If anything, he'll be pleased his problems have been resolved."

Daciana's eyes watered. I let out a sigh. Thomas and I could still be together. We'd move to Romania. All would be well. If this had happened just weeks ago, we'd all be in a world of trouble. I was still unsure how I felt about God; however, if He resolved this so swiftly—

"You misunderstand." Daciana's voice quavered. "His threat isn't only to me." Her hand trembled slightly as she held the letter out. "He's threatened Ileana. If we do not bend to his will, he's going to tell her family about our relationship."

I'd always imagined Thomas's irises being warm like melted chocolate. Currently they reminded me of burning coals. They were nearly black with his sudden rage. "He cannot prove—"

"He's been reading my letters," she said. "He's made copies by tracing them. It's how he knew about your growing affection for Audrey Rose." Thomas released a litany of curses. "And Ileana...she's a Hohenzollern, Thomas," Daciana whispered. "The scandal will not only destroy her family but her place in the Order. She will be banished from their ranks. It would—the disgrace would destroy her."

"Did you say she's a Hohenzollern?" I nearly pitched forward. I'd known Ileana was a member of the Romanian nobility, but I hadn't a clue how far up the ranks her family was. She was a princess of Romania. Our situation had gone from bad to passable back to hopeless in a few breaths. What his father was doing was deplorable.

I glanced at Thomas, tensing at the pained expression on his face. If this were a game, his father had successfully outmaneuvered him. There were no other cards for us to pull, no tricks we could use to wriggle out of this mess. Thomas would marry Miss Whitehall, or everyone he loved—aside from me—would be ruined. I was only ruined in a different way.

It was an impossible position. If he picked me, he was damning his sister and her beloved and losing both of his ancestral homes.

He'd also lose his title. And he'd lose his future. If he did as his father commanded, he'd break my heart and his own. There were no winners in this game.

Except his father and Miss Whitehall. They'd get everything they desired.

I waited, pressing my hands hard against my center, wondering when it would feel like my heart had been punched out again. I ought to feel better, knowing Miss Whitehall was only after a marriage of convenience. That his father didn't dislike me, but longed for status more than his son's happiness. Neither of those realizations dulled the growing ache.

I peeked at Thomas and the hole in my chest expanded. He appeared to be grappling with this same understanding, weighing out each decision and its consequence. In his face I saw the absence of hope. Our future was doomed.

Daciana collapsed onto my settee, head in her hands. "There's no way around this. If only Ileana and I had been more discreet—"

Thomas was before his sister at once, expression fierce. He gently clutched her wrists, drawing them away from her tearstained face. "Do not ever blame yourself or Ileana. You have every right to love each other as freely as anyone else. He's playing this game as filthily as possible because he has no options left. If he did, he'd have saved these threats for some other terrible scheme. Father is twisted and brutal and this is *his* issue, not yours. Agreed?"

She sniffled, turning her pleading gaze to me. "Audrey Rose, I cannot apologize enough, if only—"

"Thomas is right." I interrupted before she lost herself to hysterics and I joined her. "This isn't your fault. This isn't anyone's fault." I ran my hand through my hair, tugging it a bit to ease the headache that was forming. "Please don't apologize or feel responsible."

Thomas sat on the floor, lost in thought. Liza had been

correct—he'd never stop trying to unravel this puzzle until he found a way to solve it. He'd run himself through before he gave up.

"What if…" Daciana rubbed her temples. "What if you married Miss Whitehall," she asked, holding her hand up when Thomas appeared ready to launch himself into a tirade, "then you'd neither consummate it, nor ever live with her. It would be a marriage in name only. Then you and Audrey Rose might live in Bucharest together. Or travel the Continent. You needn't stay in one place, lest your supposed 'wife' come searching. Who knows? If you don't consummate it, perhaps she'll beg for an annulment. It's rare, but it has happened."

Now it was my turn to go very still.

Thomas opened his mouth, then closed it. I watched a range of emotions play out across his features—he was too rattled to bother with masking them or adopting that cool exterior. Or maybe he didn't choose to do so in front of me and his sister. We were the only two people in the entire world he could be himself around. He nibbled on his thumb.

"It's not ideal by any means," he said at last. "And I'd much prefer to gouge an eye out with a rusty spoon, but it might be the only way for us all to live as we choose. I'd gift you with the Bucharest house; you'd never permit Miss Whitehall to enter."

"I'd be more than happy to uphold that bargain."

Both Cresswell siblings looked at me, brows raised. I stared at each of them, taking careful pains to mind my tone. Their matching expressions of hope were going to be hard to break. I glanced at my ruined wedding dress. The smeared ink looked like dried blood and seemed to portend a promising future that died a violent death. "You'd have me as your mistress, then?"

Thomas blanched. "Not—n-not in my heart. You'll forever remain—"

My look silenced him. Strange, considering I hadn't meant it to.

My tenuous grip on my emotions was slipping; I needed to try harder to replace my own mask.

"I'll forever remain a blight in society. Not that I particularly care what others think, but what about my family?" I asked quietly. "What of my father? Or Uncle? And especially Liza? Will my stain of bedding a married man leach out and dirty her prospects? Should I condemn her to a life of scorn as well?" I shook my head sadly. "I might not care what the world whispers behind *my* back, but how could I forsake everyone I love?" I pushed myself off the bed, moving unsteadily toward him, pausing as he got to his feet, eyes glistening. I could see he knew I was right, though he loathed it. "The reason you have to marry Miss White-hall is the very same reason I must decline your offer. No matter how much I wish not to. I cannot curse my family any more than you can curse yours. I am many things, but to be that selfish? It's inconceivable."

A tear slipped down his cheek. I reached up, brushing it away first with my hand, then with a kiss. He pulled me close, burying his face in my hair, my neck, his breath warm and ragged on my flesh. He whispered his deepest fear. "Do you not love me?"

I wrapped my arms tighter around him, trying to memorize how good his body felt so near mine. The coffee and sugar and cinnamon scent that was so Thomas. These were only a few of the things I'd miss terribly once they were gone. But they must be cut away, sliced like a tumor before it could grow. Though it killed me, I had to push him away. For both of our sakes. If not, we'd both travel down a path of hurting the ones we loved. I would not let him turn into a devil, no more than I'd allow my own darkness to take control.

"I will love you until the world stops spinning or my heart ceases to beat, Thomas Cresswell. Even then I'm not sure my love will ever be content to leave you. But I won't ever share a bed with someone who belongs to another. No matter how much I long to. Please do not ask that of me."

I heard the rustling of skirts—a reminder that Daciana was still present—and went to pull out of his embrace. Thomas held fast, unwilling to have this moment end.

"I'll leave you two." Daciana's footsteps moved across the room, pausing. "If you need me, Audrey Rose, please don't hesitate to find me. No matter what time."

The soft click of the door indicated we were alone again. Together in our shared misery. Thomas's tears dampened the collar of my robe, causing tiny goose bumps to rise with each of his unsteady exhalations.

His hand moved from my waist to my hair, knotting itself in a most pleasant manner. He kept it there, not quite pulling my head back, but his meaning was clear. He was asking for us to spend the night together, wrapped in a cocoon of covers and a tangle of limbs. He wished to pour our worries into kisses and caresses, pushing them away for tomorrow. Putting off the inevitable, when we'd have to say good-bye to our romance.

He was pretending no one had invaded our world and flipped it upside down. I wanted nothing more than to join him in his fantasy. To go to bed and wake up as if today had never happened. It would be so easy, returning to how we used to be. I curled my fingers around his collar, fighting what felt natural. It was hard to recall that only a few hours had passed since we'd laughed and kissed in this very bed. Back when our world was blissfully simple.

All I had to do was lift my chin and his lips would be on mine, claiming me as I'd claimed him. I wanted it. More than anything. I wanted to hold him and feel safe in our embrace—sheltered from the outside world and each invasion that threatened to wrest us apart. But it would only make our separation harder, and it was already unbearable. Because no matter how much I wished for it to be different, we *must* separate. The thought was enough to have me dig my fingers into his suit jacket. Imagining my world without his crooked smile and his sweet kisses…I buried my head against him.

We'd forever be bound—through our work and Uncle—and sharing any more of myself would tear my soul out. I wanted him, but I needed to take care of myself. I brought my palm to his chest, resting it against his heart for a few precious beats, imagining the tattoo there, then pushed myself away. I swallowed my own tears, relieved in a sense that I'd cried so hard earlier. It seemed I was finally empty now. Thomas made to reach for me again, his own tears only just beginning, but I stepped back, shaking my head.

It was the hardest, most treacherous act I'd ever been forced to commit. Though in truth I had not done this to him. That blame rested solely on his father.

"We must both be strong." I stared at my feet, at the slippers he'd so lovingly had made. These new ones were pale blue with tiny white orchids. "I cannot bear it otherwise. I cannot—" I swallowed hard. "Please, Thomas. Please do not make this harder than it is. I fear I might collapse."

Thomas stood for another moment, hands limp at his sides. I didn't believe he knew what to do or where to go next, either. We'd fought for each other, had been through so much and had grown together, only to have our future snatched away in an instant by an enemy we hadn't seen coming. He was eerily quiet. I dared a glance up, meeting his fierce expression. There was a look of battle in his gaze that startled me. I waited, breath held, for him to speak. To declare this was not how our love story ended.

He offered a jerk of his chin and walked stiffly to the door. I kept staring as he disappeared through it, his footsteps receding down the corridor, and discovered I'd been wrong once again. I was capable of many more tears. One drop, followed by another, hit the tops of my satin slippers, staining them a deeper hue. I kicked them off and plunged under my covers, listening as my heart snapped in half.

On this day, one we were supposed to cherish for eternity, I wept on top of Jack the Ripper's journals. I could not control my sorrow, and I cried until the sun rose, turning the sky a vicious, deep red. Once I'd exhausted myself, I fell unwillingly into a fitful sleep.

There, the devil waited, his lips pulled into a sneer. I'd once again fallen into my own personal Hell. This time I couldn't tell what was worse—my dreams or my reality.

Saint Michael the Archangel: the fall of the dragon and the rebel angels defeated by St Michael

TWENTY-TWO
A QUEEN ARRIVES

GRANDMAMA'S DINING ROOM
FIFTH AVENUE, NEW YORK CITY
7 FEBRUARY 1889

After much internal debate, I walked into the breakfast room, head held high, ready to face Thomas in the aftermath of our failed wedding—and almost tripped over my velvet skirts at the unexpected sight that met me there. I bit the inside of my cheek to be sure I wasn't hallucinating. A shock of pain indicated I was indeed awake. I almost preferred to be conjuring up images again.

There, looking like a queen on her throne, sat Grandmama. And she did not appear pleased. My gaze traveled to the newspaper set before her, quickly scanning the headline.

OUR JACK THE RIPPER.
HE DISEMBOWELS A WOMAN
IN NEW-YORK.

He Leaves His Mark In the Shape of a
Cross Cut on the Spine—Police Mystified, but
Working Hard.

"Grandmama." I offered my most humble curtsy. I wished to run to her, fold myself into her arms, sit in her lap, and have her smooth each of my worries away. But she wouldn't tolerate such acts. At least not in front of the others in the room. "What a wonderful surprise."

"You lie like a Wadsworth."

My smile remained frozen in place. I did not think her sour mood was entirely due to the unpleasant news of a mutilated corpse. I had no doubt she'd been informed of yesterday's events, and dread filled me. First Miss Whitehall, now Grandmama. If Thomas's family arrived next, I might turn to religion after all.

While she inspected me from crown to toe, I subtly did the same. Her silks were deep turquoise with silver stitching, the details of the design reminding me of fabrics from her native India. Diamonds sparkled at her wrists, ears, and neck in the light. She'd dressed impeccably, as always. I let out a silent prayer of thanks for choosing my own dress with care. While I'd felt like donning a burlap sack to match the new bags under my eyes, I'd ultimately gone with a daring French-inspired design from Dogwood Lane Boutique.

It was deep scarlet edged with delicate gold lace, the colors bringing out the green in my eyes and the blackness of my hair. I'd slipped on one of the extravagant—yet functional—pairs of shoes Thomas had had made: black with gold flowers and vines embroidered on them, the toes peeking out in their own dazzling way.

If I were destined to be jilted, I'd look my best in the process. It was petty, especially since this situation was not entirely her fault, but imagining Miss Whitehall seeing me dressed like a goddess of the underworld offered a twinge of satisfaction I desperately needed.

Grandmama continued scanning me, her expression impossible to decipher. I straightened under her scrutiny, hoping I appeared less nervous than I was. Her gaze was watchful and sharp like a hawk's. And I was done feeling like prey.

"How was your trip?" I asked sweetly. "It's been a while since you've returned to India."

She motioned with a gnarled hand to come closer, as if she hadn't already inspected me within an inch of my life. Arthritis had plagued her for years and now seemed to pain her greatly. After each movement, I noticed a flash of a wince.

"You look as if you've been sent to chop onions as a punishment. Your eyes are too red." She grabbed my collar, tugging me close enough to sniff dramatically. "You smell like lemon verbena. And sorrow."

"I drank a cup of tea in my rooms," I lied. "It scalded me."

We stared at each other a moment, her brown eyes rich as mocha. I caught a whiff of the peppermint candies she was fond of sucking on, the scent bringing me straight back to my childhood. Looking into her lined, light brown face, it seemed a lifetime ago.

"How did you sleep?" Liza asked cheerfully, trying to shift the subject. I dared a glance around the room. Aunt Amelia had the social graces to stare into her cup of tea, pretending nothing was amiss and a wedding hadn't been ruined and my grandmother wasn't interrogating me. In this moment, I felt like hugging her. "Would you like me to make some of that herbal tea you like?"

"No, thank you." I smiled wanly. "I'd like some gingerroot. My stomach is a bit queasy this morning."

Liza's gaze dropped to my stomach, as if she might locate the cause of my ailment through careful analysis. My suspicions regarding her herbal blend had been correct. I was heartbroken, not with child. Aunt Amelia clucked, swatting at her daughter's hand. "How's your mending coming along? I'd like to visit the orphanage this morning."

"Honestly, Mother?" Liza asked, exasperated. "Are we going to carry on as if nothing upsetting happened yesterday? Audrey Rose needs our support."

I poured myself some tea and added a scone from the sideboard to my plate, slathering it generously with clotted cream and raspberry preserves before joining them at the table. I wasn't sure what it was about them, but sweets always seemed to go down easily, no matter how much one's heart ached.

"Actually," I said, between bites, garnering a swift look of reproach from both my aunt and my grandmother, "I'd much prefer to pretend nothing happened." I glanced around the room, relieved it was only the four of us. "Where is everyone?"

I silently hoped Miss Whitehall had had a change of heart during the night and withdrawn her end of the betrothal. Perhaps Thomas, Daciana, and Ileana had been kind enough to send her and her trunks back to England. Alone.

"Your father had business to tend to; Jonathan is in the study—throwing books around if the noise is any indication." My aunt pressed her lips together; clearly she disapproved of such antics. Father's business was likely an excuse to be free from Grandmama's scowl. She didn't care for the Wadsworth side of the family, and not much had softened her over the years. Honestly, I never understood why she'd disliked my father. It certainly wasn't because he was English. She'd married an Englishman herself, after all. "Thomas and his sister, as well as Ileana, left in a coach this morning. They only said they'd return this afternoon."

I considered the odd combination of relief and disappointment I felt. It was maddening how I could experience both in equal measure. A treacherous thought elbowed its way into my mind. I wondered if they *had* gone to call upon Miss Whitehall. Then I wondered where she'd gone after the chaos she'd unleashed.

Truthfully, I hadn't paid attention to anything other than remembering to breathe. I imagined like in most cases of trauma, once the initial shock wore off, I'd need to face plenty of unpleasant questions. A few snuck through the barriers I'd erected, bringing with them a sudden renewal of fear. Was Thomas trying to dissuade her from their betrothal? Or had he decided to do as his father bid? It felt as if the walls were sliding closer together. My head swam with worry.

I concentrated on breathing, though it did little to slow the rapid pounding of my pulse. I knew my family was pretending not to notice, and that only made me feel worse. If I could not act decently in front of them, I shuddered to think how I'd be around Thomas.

I pushed a piece of scone around the clotted cream.

"Stop frowning," Grandmama scolded. "You won't accomplish anything but wrinkles."

My aunt harrumphed in agreement and I almost rolled my eyes. It was shaping up to be a tremendously long day and it wasn't much past nine. Perhaps escaping upstairs to mend socks would be fun after all. I sipped my tea, focusing on the spicy flavor of ginger.

At least Grandmama managed to distract me from my growing internal hysteria. I could feel her probing stare and pretended not to notice. We hadn't seen each other in a few years and—just as I know I haunted my father—I probably reminded her too much of my mother. The older I got, the more I bore a striking resemblance to her.

"Who is this boy who's betrothed to another?" she finally asked.

I set my cup down, the porcelain clinking in the sudden quiet. "His name is Thomas Cresswell," I said primly. It was best to answer with as little detail as possible.

Grandmama struck her fork against the teapot, the clanging loud enough that my aunt jolted in her seat. "I asked *who* he is, not what his name is. Do not toy with me, girl."

I followed her gaze as it landed on my cane. Without really thinking of the symbolism, I'd grabbed the dragon's-head knob today.

I flicked my attention up to hers. Grandmama truly missed nothing. Thomas had some competition in the deduction area. I couldn't decide if it would be interesting or downright terrifying when they finally interacted.

I looked at my aunt and cousin, both of whom were politely sipping from their cups, appearing to have intensely taken up the art of tea-leaf reading. Though I knew they were listening with keen interest. Thomas's lineage was his story to tell. He'd been careful with what people in London knew, and I didn't wish to be the one who divulged his secret. I still had much to learn about his family. My aunt meant no malice, but she enjoyed chatting with acquaintances over tea. I did not want her to inadvertently make Thomas the center of more gossip.

"Well?" Grandmama pressed. "Will you tell me who he is before I go to my grave?"

"He's the son of a duke."

Her eyes narrowed. Though she'd fallen in love with an Englishman with a title of his own, she did not care for the English or their peerage. She never let anyone forget that the English—most of them, anyway—were nothing but colonizers who wished to obliterate cultures instead of enrich their own by learning the ways of others. She spoke the truth freely, which made others uncomfortable. Confronting demons was never a pleasant task, especially when they were your own.

"Duke?" she echoed, lip curling.

"The Duke of Portland," I said, purposely misunderstanding her meaning. "He's quite a formidable man, from what I've heard."

"I imagine that's true, considering how loathsome he must be, ruining his heir's happiness. What sort of devious person arranges a betrothal of such a dubious nature?" She shook her head. "It's for the best you didn't marry into that household. They'd be the sort who'd steal the silver and peddle it off to the gambling halls. Think of all the pounds you'll save not having to replace the silver."

I sighed, staring longingly at my scone. The raspberry preserves now looked as if I'd dragged the bloody remains of my heart across my plate. I pushed my breakfast away. It was one more casualty of the last twenty-four hours. "How was India?"

"Would that Her Majesty, the imperial empress and giant donkey's ass, decided to stay out of our affairs, it might have been well."

Aunt Amelia subtly crossed herself. Speaking ill of the queen was treasonous, but I had to agree with my grandmother on this point. Invading another country, warring with its people, and then forcing them to adopt your ways was the epitome of barbarous. A term often thrown around regarding the innocent people who'd been conquered by the true barbarians. My grandmother loved my grandfather wholly, but that did not mean she ever forgot who she was or where she hailed from. I believe he'd loved her all the more for her conviction.

"I've heard—" I snapped my mouth shut as Uncle banged the door open, spectacles askew. I recognized his look immediately. Either a new body lay waiting for our scalpels to explore, or there was a new development in our Ripper-like case.

"I need to speak with you." He jabbed a finger in my direction. "At once!" he barked when I hadn't moved instantly. As if noticing the other women in the breakfast room, he nodded, his attention pausing on my grandmother. "Good morning, Lady Everleigh. I trust you're well?"

"Hmmmph," she grunted, not bothering to elaborate. "Mind your manners, Jonathan. They're abysmal."

"Yes, well." Uncle turned on his heel, letting the door shut behind him. As if my life hadn't already reached a crescendo in turmoil, things were boiling over everywhere I turned.

I bid my grandmother good-bye and hurried after Uncle, my cane clicking in time with my heart. The day had only just begun, and I already wished for the comfort of my bed.

⁓◦⁓

"That bloody fool arrested a man." Uncle slammed the newspaper down on the large writing desk in Grandmama's library. "Apparently, Frenchy Number One was the unfortunate pick."

EXTRA.
Frenchy No. 1

Is He the Man Who Murdered
Carrie Brown in the
East River Hotel?

Arrested Last Friday and at
Police Headquarters
Ever Since.

Blood-Stains on His Hands and
Clothes and in His
Room.

I scanned the *Evening World* newspaper article, shaking my head. "They mention blood being found on his doorknob, but that isn't true."

I thought back to the crime scene. The papers alleged that the man who'd been arrested, a Mr. Ameer Bin Ali, had rented the room across from Miss Brown, and they'd found bloodstains on the interior and exterior of his door. The only blood I recalled outside of the victim's room had been droplets found in the corridor, leading very much *away* from the crime scene and the supposed killer's own door.

"Did they inquire about his profession?" I asked, remembering the butchers' row located not far from the hotel. "For all they know, it might be animal blood. If there was in fact blood present."

Uncle twisted his mustache, attention focused inward. After another moment of inner debate, he slid an envelope over. "This arrived from London. It's late in finding me, as it traveled to Romania first before getting forwarded here in New York."

A plain, otherwise unremarkable envelope with a large red CON-FIDENTIAL stamped across it indicated its importance. I flicked my attention to Uncle and he motioned for me to open it. Inside was a postmortem report signed by a Dr. Matthew Brownfield. I read it quickly.

Blood was oozing from the nostrils, and there was a slight abrasion on the right side of the face....On the neck there was a mark which had evidently been caused by a cord drawn tightly round the neck, from the spine to the left ear. Such a mark would be made by a four thread cord. There were also impressions of the thumbs and middle and index fingers of some person plainly visible on each side of the neck. There were no injuries to the arms or legs. The brain was gorged with an almost black fluid blood. The stomach was full of meat and potatoes, which had only recently been eaten. Death was due to strangulation. Deceased could not have done it herself. The marks on her neck were probably caused by her trying to pull the cord off. He thought the murderer must have stood at the left rear of the woman, and, having the ends of the cord round his hands, thrown it round her throat, crossed his hands, and thus strangled her. If it had been done in this way, it would account for the mark not going completely round the neck.

I knit my brows together. "If this was prepared by Dr. Brownfield, why does he refer to 'he' in the text?"

Uncle tapped the section I'd inquired after. "Dr. Harris, his assistant, examined the scene. Dr. Brownfield wrote the report after." He shifted his finger, pointing out the date of the attack. "The twentieth of December."

Thomas and I had still been in Romania attending school, and Uncle had likely been getting ready to come fetch us. Which explained why he hadn't attended the scene or known about it.

"This is all unfortunate," I said slowly, glancing over the report once more, "but I'm afraid I don't understand. Why did Scotland Yard send this to you with such urgency?"

"Blackburn sent this." Uncle turned his attention on me, his expression dour. Blackburn was the young detective inspector who'd worked on the Ripper case with us. He'd tried to court me as part of a secret agreement with my father, which did not end well for Detective Inspector Blackburn when I'd discovered their plan. "The victim was a prostitute by the name of Rose Mylett. Known as Drunken Lizzie by some. She was murdered not far from Hanbury Street, her limbs positioned in a way as to remind the police sergeant who'd found her of the Ripper." My blood chilled. "He also felt her strangulation, though hard to detect with the naked eye, was quite reminiscent of Miss Chapman's injuries."

I circled the desk until I came upon the chair and slumped into it with all the grace of a sack of potatoes. "If Jack the Ripper was in London on the twentieth of December, that means he very well could have been on the *Etruria* on the first of January. With us."

It also meant my brother could not have committed that crime.

Uncle nodded slowly. "It does not escape my notice that this victim was named Rose. I hope it wasn't meant as a warning, but we will tread most carefully in the days and weeks to come."

I met Uncle's eyes. For a brief moment he appeared almost as frightened as my father once looked. It quickly passed. Ignoring chills that dragged spindly fingers down my flesh, I turned my attention back on the report. It was yet more proof that Jack the Ripper lived.

Perhaps some monsters were immortal after all.

Rosa syluestris flore &c pleno.

Roses, Robert "Variae"

TWENTY-THREE
WHAT'S IN A NAME?

GRANDMAMA'S SITTING ROOM
FIFTH AVENUE, NEW YORK CITY
7 FEBRUARY 1889

I felt silly loitering in the corridor outside my grandmother's private sitting room, but I couldn't quite bring myself to cross the threshold. I stared at the door, pulse racing as I lifted my hand to knock, pausing just before I made contact with the carved wood. Again. Which was so foolish I could have screamed. I wasn't *afraid* of my grandmother. I'd missed her terribly. However, I was unsure that I could withstand more questions about Thomas or the wedding.

Knowing Grandmama, I was certain she wasn't satisfied by my lack of exposition on the matter and would demand to know each painful detail. I released a breath. There was no escaping this conversation, so I ought to face it straight on. At least Thomas was still out; it would make it easier, knowing he wasn't lurking too close. I shook myself out of my hesitation and lightly rapped my knuckles against the door. Best to strike quickly before I lost my nerve.

"Come in, Audrey Rose Aadhira."

I pushed the door open and was immediately struck by the colorful palette Grandmama had chosen for this room. Turquoise and fuchsia, sparkling greens and rich yellows. All edged in gold, all utterly decadent yet still inviting. From the finely woven rug to the shimmering wallpaper and tapestries, it was like stepping into a vivid dream.

A silver tea set released a pleasantly spicy aroma into the air. It was also beautiful—intricate swirls resembling vines and coriander leaves decorated the entire set of the teapot, creamer, and sugar bowl. Something she'd brought from India, no doubt. She watched me in that appraising way that said she'd missed nothing. Warmth entered her features.

"It's yours, if you want it." She motioned to the tea set. "I didn't get a gift for your wedding. Though I also didn't receive an invitation."

She puckered her mouth as if she'd sucked on a lemon, and I couldn't help but laugh. I nearly dropped my cane in my haste to throw my arms around her, breathing in her comforting scent. This time, without an audience, she embraced me affectionately. It felt good to hold her; too many years had passed. I knew it was hard for her—between her dislike of my father and the loss of my mother, she never stayed in England for long. Grandfather had passed on a few years before my mother had, and I could only imagine how deep her own pain went. I nestled beside her on her settee, which was covered in a rather gorgeous peacock fabric.

"Your invitation was sent, Grandmama. I cannot help that you're harder than a ghost to track down." My brief levity popped like a deflated balloon when I pictured Miss Whitehall marching in with her letter. "Plus, the wedding…" I swallowed a lump that suddenly formed. "You know it was…"

My grandmother drew back, and her gaze softened. "You love him very much."

"Yes." I fiddled with my gloves, unable to meet her eyes for fear I'd start bawling again. "I love him in ways that sometimes frighten me."

She pulled me into the circle of her arms, stroking my hair as she used to do when I was a child. I didn't recall them starting, but tears now streamed silently down my face. Grandmama pretended not to notice as she cooed to me.

"There, there, child. Much as I dislike admitting it, you were named for two fierce women. Your grandmother Rose and me." She held me tighter as the sobs grew worse. "Your mother loved the name Audrey, you know." I could hear the smile in her voice, and while I'd heard this story many times before, I found myself straining to listen again, as if it were the first time. " 'Noble strength.' Malina wished for you to be strong of will and mind. I think she would be pleased, seeing you pursue your passions. She wanted you to be kind like your grandma Rose. As outspoken as your favorite grandmother, me. And unafraid to be yourself. Like her. Do you remember what she used to say, about roses?"

I swiped the last of my tears and nodded. "They have petals and thorns."

"Do not be afraid now, child." Grandmama's confident voice was a balm to my broken heart. "You hail from a long line of women with bones made of steel. Your mother would tell you to be brave when you feel anything but. She would want to see you happy."

"I miss her," I whispered, realizing I hadn't said it aloud in so long. "Every day. I worry if she'd be pleased with the life I've chosen. It's not conventional—"

"Bah! Convention." Grandmama batted the word away. "Do not trouble yourself with something as boring as convention. I know my daughter. She was proud of you and Nathaniel. You were the brightest stars in her universe. She loved your father without question, but you children were the twinkle in her soul."

We were quiet for a while, each of us probably lost in our own memories of her. My last ones haunted me. My mother had stayed by my side while I'd burned with fever, several years ago. She'd refused to give the task to someone else, insisting on tending to me personally.

Thanks to her tireless nursing, I'd recovered from scarlet fever. She hadn't. Her already weakened heart couldn't fight the infection. She'd battled long enough to see me well before she passed away in my arms. Even surrounded by my father and brother, I'd never felt so alone as I did that day. Her death was my main motivating factor for pursuing science and medicine.

Sometimes, in my most private moments, I'd wonder who I might be if she'd lived.

Grandmama finally exhaled, and I tensed for what I knew had been the true reason for this visit.

"I've made certain...arrangements...to my will," she said. My focus shot to hers. This was not at all what I thought she was about to say. She gave me a sly smile. "It was to be shared between you and your brother evenly, but now with him gone..." She inhaled. Her sharp gaze cut into me like a knife—we'd kept details of Nathaniel's death from her, and her expression let me know she was more than aware of it, but she'd allow me to keep my secrets. For now. "You will need to guard yourself against anyone who whispers pretty words in your ears."

"What on earth do you mean?" I couldn't even consider carrying on a flirtation with anyone. It was unthinkable. "Who will be wooing me so soon?"

Grandmama snorted. "Hopefully not soon. I don't have any plans on departing the world just yet. But when I do, many moons from now, you will become an heiress. All of this"—she motioned around the room, though I knew she was also speaking of the house—"will be yours. As will the properties in Paris, London, India, and Venice."

My heart rate slowed. "Grandmama...I cannot...that is very generous of you, but—"

"But what? Will you have me stuff my pockets on my deathbed and carry my money into the next life?" She sniffed as if injured. "The correct response is 'thank you.'"

I shook my shock away and clutched her hands in mine. "Thank you, Grandmama. Truly."

By remaining unmarried, I'd inherit my grandmother's property in full. I might not marry the love of my existence, but I would be happily wed to my profession and live comfortably, dependent upon no one. I got choked up again for an entirely new reason.

"There, there. Don't cry on the silk, dear." She handed me a handkerchief that was a yellow so bold it almost dared anyone who used it to remain sad. "Tell me about your Thomas."

I sagged against the settee, letting my head drop back. I stared at the ceiling—it had been painted to match the night sky. I picked out constellations before I recognized some from the orchid painting Thomas made for me while we were in Romania.

"As you know, he's betrothed to another," I said, not wishing to elaborate. She pinched my knee and I yelped in surprise. Glaring, I rubbed out the throbbing spot and gave in. "It isn't the most pleasant subject for me at the moment," I said. "What does it matter if you know more regarding him or not? We cannot proceed with our marriage. He belongs to her by law. Thinking about it is only making me feel worse than I already do. And I'm exceptionally miserable."

"Good." She jerked her chin in approval. "You need to let those rancid emotions out. They'll only fester the more you lock them up. You don't want infection spewing into other areas of your life, do you?"

My lip curled in disgust. What an attractive thought. Comparing heartache to an abscess in need of lancing. "What's done is done. I have no more control over the situation than Thomas does. He cannot go against his father; the duke has made it nearly impossible.

So then what, pray tell, do you suggest reliving those putrid emotions will do? It only makes it worse—dwelling on things I can never have."

Grandmama grabbed my cane from me and stamped it against the floor imperiously. "You fight. You fight for what you want. You do not wallow or surrender. The lesson is not in lying down and allowing yourself to be stabbed, child. It's in pushing yourself up and battling back." Her eyes flashed. "You fell down. So? Will you stay there, weeping over skinned knees? Or will you brush off your skirts, adjust your hair, and carry on? Do not relinquish your grasp on hope. It's one of the best weapons anyone possesses."

I shut my mouth. There was no need to argue. Grandmama clearly didn't understand how impossible our situation was. I sipped my tea and forced a smile. I wouldn't destroy her optimism the way mine had been destroyed. She shook her head, not fooled by my performance, but we didn't speak of impossible things again.

TWENTY-FOUR
A STUDY OF CONTRASTS

GRANDMAMA'S GRAND FOYER
FIFTH AVENUE, NEW YORK CITY
7 FEBRUARY 1889

The sun had long since relinquished its reign to the moon when Thomas returned to my grandmother's house. Silver shafts of light played across his face, giving him an otherworldly look as they cut jagged lines in his already angular features. Light and dark. A study of stark contrasts, much like our work.

If he hadn't walked in of his own accord, but required an invitation, I might soon believe vampires roamed the earth. He seemed to have aged a thousand years since the last time I saw him. I wondered if I appeared the same.

Tension swarmed in as if it had followed him in from the cold. His overcoat dripped melted snow onto the hexagon tiles in the foyer, nudging a slight frown onto the butler's face as he took the offending garment and derby hat.

I'd been caught halfway between the corridor leading from the parlor and the grand staircase when he'd barged in, his attention falling on me instantly. For a moment, we both stood frozen, unsure of what to say. He didn't look like he'd hoped to see me so quickly.

A piece of my heart withered. Thomas and I were never at a loss for words.

Silence stretched uncomfortably as I took in his wary expression and the slight tightening around his mouth. I swallowed down my sudden rush of emotion.

"My grandmother is home and wished to say good night to me." I held up a cup of tea by way of explanation, making the situation even more uncomfortable. "Rose and hibiscus with a spoonful of honey. It's quite nice for a winter's night."

Thomas didn't so much as blink. His face was devoid of all emotion, leaving me nothing to read. I should have left him alone, clearly that's what he wanted, but I couldn't help but draw out our time together for one more moment.

"Where are Daciana and Ileana?" I asked, trying to sound pleasant. He lifted a shoulder, toeing at the floor his eyes were now fixed upon. I gave up. It was difficult enough being in his presence without his cool behavior. "Well, then. I-I'm glad you're home. Well." I silently cringed. I needed to flee immediately. "Good night."

"Audrey Rose, wait." He held his hand out, nodding at my refreshment. "May I?" I longed to be alone in my misery but passed the cup over, watching as he winced a bit from the temperature. "Where would you like me to bring this?"

I waited half a beat before responding. Surely my Thomas would have some inappropriate quip, some untoward suggestion. He'd hint about my bedchambers or other more salacious nooks and crannies to steal kisses in. His expression remained perfectly blank.

Unshed tears stung my eyes. I couldn't stop imagining him calling on Miss Whitehall. Spending an afternoon getting to know her, giving her the smile he'd used on me.

"There's a study on the second floor," I said, slowly making my way up the stairs. It was particularly drafty tonight, and the cold seeped into my bones, causing my ever-present stiffness to worsen. "You can leave it there; I'll be in shortly."

Footsteps above pitter-pattered back and forth, followed by the sound of a door opening and closing. I tilted my head, hoping Aunt Amelia was looking for her bedtime spirits. I internally shook myself. Things were truly horrid between us if I was wishing for my aunt's interruption. We halted on the second-floor landing and I nodded to the right. "It's the second door down."

Fire crackled and snapped as Thomas opened the door. I stood on the threshold, admiring the room while a bit of heat kissed my face. The chamber was quaint in size and cozy, though the furnishings were straight out of a gilded palace—the fire blazed cheerfully, chasing any hint of coldness away. It was the next best thing to soaking in a tub. My muscles unwound in increments, though my leg still bothered me.

I settled onto a cushioned settee and accepted my tea. "Thank you."

Instead of rushing from my newly acquired sitting chambers, Thomas glanced around the space. He might have been carved from marble, given how cold and unreachable he seemed.

I examined everywhere his focus darted. From the bronze wallpaper to the intricate weave of the Turkish rug. Each chair had a rich emerald pattern that blended together enchantingly with the gold and silver thread. The most dramatic piece, however, was the settee I sat upon. Curtains of cobalt velvet hung from the ceiling, gathered in the center by a golden crown, then flowed to either side, appearing almost as if I were tucked into a waterfall.

His attention skipped over me, which only increased the pressure mounting in my chest. I wished he would speak or leave. This remote Thomas was almost as unbearable as the thoughts and questions that kept swirling about my head.

Where have you been? Why won't you look at me?

He stepped toward another wall that featured floor-to-ceiling shelves stuffed full of jewel-toned leather spines, their titles etched in gold. Books ranging in subject matter from science to philosophy to romance—Grandmama collected them all. Liza had already chosen several romances and locked herself in her room to read the blustery night away. I would have joined her, but I had much more macabre things to study and didn't wish to ruin her good time.

"Uncle shared a rather interesting new find about the Ripper today."

"Your grandmother must love books," Thomas replied, his voice stiff. Formal. Unfeeling. He ignored the Ripper matter altogether. I wondered if that meant he'd decided he wouldn't be assisting with the case anymore. A knife twisted in my gut.

"My grandfather used to gift her with a book from each place they traveled," I said. "He didn't realize she'd already gifted herself with ten or more by then, but he never complained when they'd have an extra trunk or two packed entirely with books." I lifted my cane, pointing out the shelves, though it didn't matter. He still wasn't looking at me. "These are the extra volumes, the ones that don't fit in the main library downstairs."

Sir Isaac slinked in and found the pillow I'd left for him on the floor. He inspected it thoroughly before plopping down to wash. I didn't wish to say so aloud, but I'd been comforted by his little catly presence all afternoon. He helped fill in that wretched hollowness as I fretted over Thomas and Miss Whitehall and all the terrible thoughts about them that assaulted me.

After scratching behind Sir Isaac's ears for a bit, Thomas walked over to the shelves, running his fingers across the spines. "Are you going to inquire about my day?" he asked, not looking at me. "You're not the least bit curious? I've been gone for hours."

His question caught me off guard with its directness. Was he foolish enough to believe I hadn't nearly gone mad with wondering? My mind conjured up all sorts of scenarios. From him confronting Miss Whitehall to them discussing their future to him grudgingly accepting their fate. I'd barely remembered we had other massive issues—such as the Ripper-like murders—to contend with. Or the news of Rose Mylett's brutal killing that Uncle had shared. Almost every one of my waking thoughts today had centered on where he was. I loathed how distracted I'd been.

"Of course I'm curious, Thomas! I . . . I fear if I discover one more unpleasant thing—" I inhaled deeply, collecting myself. "My heart already feels as though it's been forcibly removed. Is it not enough, having our wedding destroyed? Must I now suffer by hearing about Miss Whitehall?" I could feel tears building, hot and embarrassing as they spilled down my cheeks. "Unless you're about to tell me that she has abandoned her scheme to marry you, I don't wish to discuss her, or your father, or hear any more suggestions about having an affair behind your betrothed's back. I cannot take any more disappointment. It is *destroying* me."

"Do you think I was with *her* today? Carrying on a courtship? After what happened yesterday? Have you gone mad?"

I bristled at his tone. "How should I know when you haven't been around? What am I supposed to think?"

"You shouldn't think; you should *know* I love you." Thomas spun around, his eyes wild. "What if I don't follow through on the marriage and stay betrothed? Why won't you consider being with me, no matter what? Why is it that Mephisto's brand of debauchery and lifestyle was less appalling than my offer? Do you regret not leaving with the carnival? Do you regret leaving him? No matter that he used manipulation tactics, preyed upon your goodwill, and would have continued doing so. Why is my offer not enough?"

If he'd slapped me, it might have stung less than the utter

devastation I heard in his voice. My pulse raced. His untamed behavior was much worse than his coolness. I now realized he'd been using it to cover up the depth of his own hurt. Thomas had finally lost his grip on his emotions and it seemed they were pouring out.

"Thomas…" I stared at the ceiling, searching for cracks or fissures. Surely it was about to come crashing down like everything else around me. "We've been through this. I cannot change the fact that I made mistakes during that investigation. I thought I could playact a certain role, and I lost myself in the process. Clearly it was the wrong decision. I am not perfect, nor have I ever claimed to be. All I can do is try my best to learn from my mistakes and grow."

"That doesn't answer my question." His voice was too quiet.

I dropped my attention back to him. He was staring at me intently. "Do you honestly wish to speak of Mephistopheles? Now?"

He jerked his head in what was supposed to be a nod. "Why would you toss away society's rules for him and not me?"

I exhaled. He was hurt and I'd helped to inflict this wound. I wished there wasn't such a gaping chasm between us. I wanted nothing more than to take him in my arms and kiss his fears away. And I wanted him to hold me close, too, to make me forget the pain and misery of the last twenty-four hours. But those were not appropriate actions for us now. I needed to remember that.

Even if it went against every natural urge in my body.

"You know I never truly considered Mephistopheles as a suitor. It was never *him* that I'd been taken with. It was the idea of completely living outside of society. Tossing each rule and restriction in the rubbish bin and living life on my terms and my terms alone. Sure, he might have been the one who introduced me to that idea, but I'm afraid you and I are forever going to relive that week. Mephistopheles didn't almost win my heart. He wasn't so clever and beautiful and mysterious enough to entice me away from you. If you want the whole truth, I was afraid of the kernel of doubt in my heart. I was terrified that *I* might not ever be good enough for *you*. You're so sure of us and have had romantic experience—"

"I've had no experience where love is concerned, Wadsworth."

"Oh?" I raised a brow. "Miss Whitehall simply sprang forth from our imaginations, waving that betrothal agreement about?" I sighed as his shoulders slumped. We were not mending our broken hearts this way. "The truth is, yes, he was able to use my naïveté against me. Until recently, I've lived a terribly sheltered life—I had no friends aside from Liza. You were the only young man I'd ever spoken to apart from my brother. I'm still learning about myself. While I was playing that role, trying to garner information about the murderer, I... it was the first time I'd made other friends. People outside of my tiny little part of the world. They liked science and they danced without a care, and they were so extraordinarily free. A part of me wanted to be like them. Even if it was a lie and it made a mess of things. I wanted to forget about who everyone wanted or expected me to be. I'm dreadfully sorry you were hurt in the process."

He glanced up sharply. "You are free to choose; I've always said—"

"Yes, yes." I waved my hand about. "*You've* always said. My father's always said. Uncle has *always* said." Unable to meet his gaze directly, I stared down at my hand, realizing I hadn't yet returned his family ring. I stopped looking at it and focused on Thomas again. "It's one thing for others to *tell* you what's best, but without experience of your own?" I shook my head. "I am not perfect, nor will I ever aspire to be. Flaws are what build character. They make us more human. More—"

"Susceptible to heartbreak?"

"Well, yes, I suppose that's true." I met his gaze full on. "If I lived out the rest of my days worrying about perfection or achieving *The*

Angel in the House standard of what women ought to be—that is a cage I will not set myself in. I'm sorry I hurt you, Thomas. I cannot apologize enough for my doubt, momentary though it might have been. But my struggle was always between what *life* I wanted for myself, not which *man* I wanted to spend it with. You accuse Mephistopheles of manipulation, and you're not wrong. He never pretended his bargains weren't in his favor. He told me directly he is an opportunist. I knew that. He is flawed, but show me a person who isn't. My hope for him is to learn his own lesson in the future. He's scared of being vulnerable; I should think you know a thing or two about that."

"What of my offer of living outside society with me?"

"I decline your offer because there is another who is officially committed to be your wife, Thomas. Were you unattached, and if it wouldn't harm our families, I might consider living our life however we wanted to live it. No rules. No society terms. Just you and me. I would take you without a ring or a home or any document declaring you were mine. That is not the situation we find ourselves in at present. And that is the *only* reason your brand of debauchery doesn't suit me. No matter how hard he tried wooing me, *I* never pursued a courtship with Mephistopheles. It's always been you for me, even when I didn't know who I was anymore. It will *always* be you, Thomas. No matter who tries to come between us. You are my heart. No one can take it."

Thomas gazed at me for a moment, then dropped into a chair, his head in his hands. "I despise this."

"It's a horrid situation, I know. But we will get through it. We have to."

"No, no." Thomas glanced up. "I despise being the one having an emotional dilemma. It's much more enjoyable being the one consoling you. You haven't even offered to let me sit on your lap. You're terrible at this."

We tentatively smiled at each other. Our grins were both gone as quickly as they'd come, but it was a start. As sick as it made me to think of beginning anew with Thomas Cresswell.

"Well." I searched for something else to do or say in the awkward silence. The curious part of me that always seemed to win could no longer contain itself. "What did you do today?"

He assessed me from head to toe, paying careful attention to my face. I knew he was studying every miniature movement and plucking apart my emotions. His own impenetrable mask was back in place. I hoped I appeared strong enough to withstand whatever he said. The slight frown he let slip made me think otherwise. "I...I did pay a visit to Miss Whitehall—"

"All right." I abruptly held up a hand. He closed his mouth, his expression strained. "Please. I don't mean to be rude, but I feel a little ill. I-I can't hear about this now or I may vomit. It's too much."

Thomas's attention strayed to my stomach, a line of worry creasing his brow.

For the love of the queen, I was *not* with child. My ever-vigilant cousin had been making me drink those herbal blends for weeks. Well before Thomas and I had consummated our—I exhaled. We needed to find another pursuit.

"Would you...I'm going to study Nathaniel's journals. You're welcome to join." I looked up in time to notice him wince. "If you'd like."

He tapped an anxious rhythm on his thigh while he considered. Finally, he dragged his chair closer and pulled a journal in front of himself. He might jest about my curiosity, but his was equally piqued. A tiny sense of relief blossomed. Things were easier between us when we had a mystery to solve.

"*Le bon Dieu est dans le détail,*" he said, his tone reverent. At my knitted brow, he amended, "Flaubert."

"I meant the sentence, Cresswell." Unable to help myself, I rolled my eyes. Leave it to Thomas to quote the author of *Madame Bovary*—in French—at a time such as this. His theatrics truly knew no bounds. " 'The "God" is in the detail' ought to be shifted to the 'devil.' "

He laughed. "True. There's certainly nothing holy about the notes in these devil's journals."

TWENTY-FIVE
VIVISECTIONS AND OTHER HORRORS

GRANDMAMA'S UPSTAIRS STUDY
FIFTH AVENUE, NEW YORK CITY
7 FEBRUARY 1889

A few hours later, Thomas and I had fallen into a familiar, peaceful work rhythm. Sir Isaac tried assisting in our endeavor a few times by batting my nibs of ink off the tables. I glared while Thomas howled with laughter. After he'd stolen Thomas's favorite pen, the cat found himself back on his cushion, washing himself without a care in the world.

Though that was where our levity ended. Our reading material made my stomach twist into intricate knots. I could barely bring myself to read this secret and hideous part of my brother. On more than one occasion I had to close one of his journals, steeling myself once more before pressing onward. It was a monumental task—there were over one hundred notebooks, some filled entirely from cover to cover with small script, while others had bits and pieces of ideas sprinkled every few pages. The handwriting shifted with Nathaniel's moods. The more wild and outlandish the idea, the more illegible the script became.

His sketches, however, remained eerie in their precise lines and careful shading. My brother was always a perfectionist. From his carefully pomaded hair to his finely tailored suits. Despite what he'd done, I missed him.

My rose and hibiscus tea sat untouched, its steam having long since stopped breathing fragrant wisps into the air. Now it looked like a cup of chilled blood. A memory of another time and place played across my mind. Nathaniel had had a bottle of congealing blood in a bottle in his laboratory. I wondered now if it had been animal or human.

"I cannot believe he performed so many ghastly experiments." I tugged a chenille throw blanket tighter. "Vivisections." I nearly gagged at one of his sketched images of a live animal flayed open; my brother spared no detail of its torture. "I don't understand. My brother loved animals. He was the one who'd cry himself to sleep if he couldn't save a stray. How could he have done this? How could I have not seen the wickedness in him sooner?"

Without lifting his head from his book, Thomas sighed. "Because you loved him. It's normal to reason away oddities in his behavior. Love is wonderful, but as with most forces of nature, there's lightness and darkness within it. I believe in some instances the greater the love, the more we ignore facts that are obvious to others. You did not see the signs because you *could* not. It's not inadequacy on your part—it's simply self-preservation."

I snorted. "Or denial."

"Perhaps." Thomas shrugged. "If you accepted the truth of your brother, you'd be forced to confront your own darkness. You'd discover your morals aren't defined in terms such as black or white, good or bad. Most shy away from that level of introspection. It makes us realize we're villains. At least in part. We also all have the capacity to be heroes. Miss Whitehall might think me a villain for trying to break our engagement, while you believe me to be a hero for that very same act. At some point, we're all someone's hero and another's villain. It's all a matter of perspective. And that changes as frequently as the cycles of the moon."

It was quite a morbid thought. One I did not wish to expand upon.

"Here." I slid the envelope marked CONFIDENTIAL over to him. "Uncle received this earlier. It strongly suggests another Ripper murder occurred on the twentieth of December."

Thomas read the report while I went back to Nathaniel's journals. Or tried to.

"Tell me everything your uncle said." His tone was calm enough for me to realize an internal storm was raging. "I need to know every detail."

"All right..." I told him everything I could remember regarding Miss Rose Mylett's death. He listened carefully and quietly, his jaw set and his expression perfectly placid. He politely demanded to know what Uncle had said about Blackburn, then pored over the journals, reading through them with the singular focus of a starving dog gnawing on a bone.

He didn't say so aloud, but I saw the same fear etched into his features that had flashed in Uncle's face. Somehow Rose Mylett might've been a subtle warning directed at me. Whether or not that was true, I refused to yield to some madman who preyed upon women.

An hour ticked by, the clock on the mantel chiming ten bells. I lifted my hands above my head, stretching one way, then the next. I creaked these days more than some wooden chairs.

"I'm not sure if we'll find anything useful for Jack the Ripper's identity or possible location in these," I said. "Thus far it's simply disturbing."

"Not nearly as disturbing as another potential Ripper murder." Thomas ran his gaze over me as if to be certain I was still there, sitting beside him, scowling.

Another half hour flew by. I blinked, surprised to find a plate piled high with slices of cake and two forks before me. Chocolate with chocolate espresso icing and macerated raspberries in the center. A frothy glass of milk sat next to it.

Part of me longed for a bite, until I remembered it would've been served at our wedding. Aside from that, I was appalled by the thought of eating while reading such grotesque passages, but after a while, I gave in and ate two pieces myself.

Thomas smiled. "Terrified of clowns and spiders, but not devouring chocolate cake whilst elbows deep in morbid journals. You truly are my match, Wadsworth."

The corner of my mouth lifted, but the easy retort quickly died. I might be in his heart and he in mine, but I was no longer his match. At least not the way we both wished to be.

His own smile faded and he returned to his work, the carefree moment floating away like a leaf on the wind. I resumed my own research, focused entirely on locating any hint or clue that might assist in our locating the real Jack the Ripper. Thus far, Nathaniel had been careful not to name his murderous comrade.

An icy fingertip traced a shiver along my spine when I turned to another disturbing section with pages upon pages of diagrams featuring intricate mechanisms fused with living tissues and organs. A heart with gears, a pair of lungs made from the leathery hide of an animal. Other organs were harder to place, though one resembled a uterus. Then there were hands, eerily similar to the steam-powered one I'd found in our home. In some ways his sketches reminded me of Mephistopheles, who was exceptionally talented at engineering. In another life they might have been friends. I swallowed hard, suddenly overcome with emotion.

Thomas set his journal on the table, head canting to the side. "What is it?"

I pinched the bridge of my nose. "You're not going to enjoy my thoughts."

"On the contrary, I find them quite alluring. Especially when they're untoward."

This, at least, coaxed a smile to my lips. Reading about mad science and detailed murder seemed to be just the tonic Thomas required to continue flirting shamelessly. My smile disintegrated. "I was thinking about Ayden."

"Mephisto?" Thomas narrowed his eyes. "Well, then. I hope you were picturing him fully clothed in one of his ridiculous masks and gaudy jackets." He smiled, much too sincerely, and I braced myself for what had brought about such a contented look. "Covered in maggots might be fun, too. Remember when that happened to Prince Nicolae? It was one of the top moments of my life, really. I swear, sometimes I replay his expression as they shot out of that cadaver onto him and my mood is lifted all day. You ought to try it whenever you're feeling glum. There"—he grinned widely—"I'm doing it right now and it's marvelous."

"Honestly? I scarcely remembered that, and with good reason." I shook my head. "Also, by the by, we're in the midst of an investigation and you're still annoyed about Mephistopheles's choice in sequins?"

"No." Thomas bristled. "I'm annoyed I forgot mine and couldn't strut around in my carnival best, too. Aside from his mediocre jokes, he truly had nothing else going in his favor. Perhaps it was best I didn't upstage him in that regard as well."

At my eye roll, he held his hands up. The scoundrel had definitely lightened my heavy mood and he knew it. Perhaps we could make this post-wedding friendship work. It wouldn't be easy, but most things in life weren't.

"All right, all right," he relented. "What were you really thinking?"

"That he and Nathaniel would've been good friends." I flipped the journal open, resuming my scan of the dark material. "Perhaps if my brother had found someone else who enjoyed crafting mechanisms... maybe he would have put his skill to better use. Maybe he'd still be alive." I traced his writing. "Perhaps those poor women would never have been killed."

Thomas was up and out of his seat in the time it took me to blink. He sat next to me, wrapping an arm about my shoulders. "Do not travel down that path, Wadsworth. It will only lead to heartbreak. *Maybe, perhaps, what if, if only;* they all ought to be stricken from the world. At least in our world they ought to be outlawed." He pressed his lips to my temple, their warmth shocking and pleasant. "Nathaniel made his choices. Regardless of any infinite number of paths he *could* have taken, he might always end up in that laboratory, flipping that lever. Those women, as brutal as it may sound, would always be in danger based on the nature of what they'd been forced to do to survive. If your brother didn't kill them himself, if someone else was truly wielding that knife, then their fate might have always been decided. No amount of altering a few facts might change that."

"Do you truly believe that?"

"I do." Thomas nodded fiercely. "You spoke of choices and mistakes earlier. Nathaniel chose his path. Granted it was a mistake that turned out to be fatal, but he had every right to make it. No matter how wrong we know his actions to be."

"Yes, but—"

"If it's true for you and me and anyone else who makes mistakes," Thomas said, "then it applies to your brother as well. Just because his were on a grander, more wretched scale, doesn't negate that basic fact. If you can forgive yourself and learn, then see this for what it is. A terrible mistake—on many levels—that ended in tragedy for many people."

Something deep inside uncoiled slowly at first, then more swiftly.

Guilt. Only in its absence did I realize how tightly I'd been holding on to it. Guilt had stalked me since my mother died, and had followed more closely after my brother passed on. I'd blamed myself for both their deaths. I'd grown so used to it, I was almost terrified to let it go.

Forgetting about secret fiancées and all the reasons I ought to keep my distance, I sank against Thomas, using his steadiness as support.

"It's hard," I said, swallowing hard. "Letting go."

"You don't ever have to let go of *them*." Thomas rubbed my arm soothingly. "But you must learn to part ways with both guilt and blame. If you do not, they will latch on like thirsty leeches, bleeding you dry."

"I know. Sometimes I wish I could change the past. Just once."

"Ah. That might be a mathematical impossibility for now, but you can alter the future. By taking what you've learned yesterday and putting it to practice today, you can build better tomorrows." He leaned closer, smiling against my neck. "Speaking of a better future. I've been thinking of solutions for our problem. At least for—"

"Father will be here within the hour," Daciana said by way of greeting. Her face flushed a brilliant scarlet as she stepped into the room. "He's come to take you back to England. With...with Miss Whitehall."

TWENTY-SIX
THE DUKE OF PORTLAND

GRANDMAMA'S GRAND FOYER
FIFTH AVENUE, NEW YORK CITY
8 FEBRUARY 1889

Grandmama did not enjoy being interrupted, whether it was while reading a good book or choosing her next move in a game of chess. She most certainly despised being woken up at an indecent hour, forced to receive guests she wished to toss into the snow-covered streets.

She inspected Thomas in a way that made me reconsider whether or not I believed in the power of prayer. After what felt like an eternity, she nodded curtly. "You better be worth all the trouble you're causing."

Thomas flashed his most charming smile. The very same one he'd used on my father to get him to grant me permission to attend the academy in Romania, and then on the train ride there. A feat I was still impressed by, considering Thomas's reputation as an unfeeling automaton in London society. Because of his refusal to play by their rules, there were rumors early on that he'd been the ruthless killer we sought. Some still whispered his name in connection with the crimes. The idea that Thomas could be the notorious Jack the Ripper was too ludicrous to even consider.

"I assure you, Lady Everleigh, I'm handsome enough to hopefully make up for less appealing qualities."

I closed my eyes, preparing for Grandmama to crack him in the kneecaps with her walking stick. Instead she laughed. "Good. I like you. Now, let's see if we can shift that trouble to your father for a while."

"Nothing would give me greater pleasure." Thomas held a hand against his heart. "He's a very tactical man. Any upset in his carefully plotted plan will cause the greatest distress. And that happens to be something my sister and I are quite skilled at."

"Hmmph," was all Grandmama responded with.

Moments passed dreadfully slow, agitating my grandmother further. I held my breath as she stamped the floor with her walking stick periodically, muttering what I imagined were curses in Urdu.

While I couldn't hear it from the foyer, I imagined the lamppost outside hissed at the sleek black hansom that suddenly halted before the walkway. I held my breath. A curtain twitched back, though the occupants were cloaked in shadow, hidden from view. It was strange, coming to someone's home after midnight without there being a party or other occasion to do so. Perhaps the late hour was a method purposely used to be threatening. Thomas's father was establishing himself as the dominant figure—one who picked rules that suited him best, regardless of how troublesome it might be for others.

We waited, my grandmother, Thomas, the butler, and I, standing like soldiers preparing for war. Daciana and Ileana had taken over reading the journals, assisting us and also keeping themselves out of what was sure to be an unpleasant greeting.

No one moved from the carriage. Another moment ticked by. Then another. The seconds on the clock ticked, ticked, ticked, in time with my heart.

"What are they waiting for?" I asked, growing almost as annoyed as my grandmother.

Thomas tapped his hands against his sides. "Father knows stretching a moment out causes anticipation. It unsettles. Any bravado fades when what we expect to happen goes slightly awry."

"Well"—Grandmama's eyes narrowed—"he does not know with whom he's playing these games. Trying to unsettle a poor old woman." She shook her head. "What has the world come to?"

At this I grinned. Grandmama might be older, and her arthritis brutal, but she wore those years like burnished armor. Only a fool would think her an old helpless lady. She was the woman who taught my mother to sharpen her mind as if it were a blade.

Mercifully, the coachman hopped down from his seat, consulted with someone inside, then made his way to the front door. The butler waited until he knocked before opening it.

"Yes?"

The young man removed his cap, twisting it in his hands. "I've come to fetch Mr. Cresswell for his father."

Grandmama elbowed in front of the butler, scowling. "Do you believe he's a hound, boy?"

"Ma'am, I—O-of course not. It's just—"

"I will not have any guest who's staying under my roof be treated thusly. You may come back at a more decent hour." She nodded to her butler and he gladly slammed the door in the poor coachman's face. "Now let's see how your father enjoys such hospitality. The rudeness of some men is eclipsed only by their arrogance. Come"—she hit the ground with her walking stick—"let's go back to bed. We'll receive the duke in the morning. First thing, I'm sure."

Liza crawled under my covers, eyes wide as I told her each detail of Thomas's father's arrival. "The nerve!" she whispered. "He ought to fear your grandmother and her stick. The way she swings that thing about." She shook her head. "How do you think it'll go?"

I yawned, rolling onto my side. The sun was nearly up, which meant I needed to join it. The Duke of Portland would arrive soon, no doubt.

"He's a Cresswell," I said. "There's no telling how it'll play out."

Much too soon, Liza helped me into a rather complex gown for the early hour.

Considering the laboratory work that needed to be done with Uncle, it was hopelessly impractical. It was meant to be worn after my wedding—Daciana had insisted I change for the evening dinner celebration, so it was a dreamy, whimsical thing. Much too pretty for breakfast. Though I agreed it was best to appear as regal as possible while meeting Thomas's father for the first time. No matter the pain he caused, I wished to make a good impression.

If only to make him regret his meddling.

"Two interlocking braids pinned at your crown will show off your mother's locket." Liza lifted my hair to demonstrate the effect. "See?"

"Beautiful," I agreed, clutching the necklace. It comforted me, knowing Mother would be there in some fashion, offering me strength.

Liza had just finished pinning the last piece of hair up when Thomas entered my room. He stopped short, attention immediately going to my hips. The gold lace fit snugly against my body, allowing the tulle skirts to fluff out around it. The effect was like a sunrise peeking through a wispy cloud. Judging from his expression, Thomas approved.

I spun the engagement ring around my finger, frowning. "Oh. I-I keep forgetting to give this back."

I awkwardly tugged it off, but Thomas shook his head. "That belongs to you. Plus, my father ought to see it on your finger. Where it will remain, regardless of his demands." He glanced at my cousin, who busied herself by fluffing her own skirts.

She met his look, brows raised. "Would you care for a moment alone?"

I went to say it was unnecessary, but Thomas responded quickly. "Please. Thank you."

As she closed the door behind her, I found it hard not to run into his arms. He, too, had dressed meticulously well this morning—his suit smart and fashionable.

"Before you meet my father, there's something I'd like you to know." He didn't hesitate as he crossed my room this time; confidence was back in each step. He paused before me. "If you'll still have me, there is nothing in this world, no threat mighty enough, to keep me from you. I want my father to see us, a united front, and know we will not be broken."

"Thomas—"

"I'm rejecting Miss Whitehall directly after this meeting with my father. Yesterday, I visited a barrister originally from London and discussed the possibility of forgery. I did not write that letter. I heard from him earlier and I cannot be held accountable, nor does the engagement stand in court." Thomas took my hand in his. "When we go downstairs, I will be introducing you as my wife-to-be."

The Duke of Portland, Lord Richard Abbott Cresswell, reminded me of a slightly older, more cunning version of Thomas. He was intimidating not only in stature but in the intelligent gleam in his eyes as well. A flutter of unease settled under my skin. His dark hair was a shade or two lighter, but the structure of their faces was unmistakable. He eyed me as if I were a vase full of freshly cut flowers. Pleasing, but not worthy of much attention aside from a cursory glance.

I tried not to fidget on the settee Thomas had guided us to. My father and grandmother were fanned out to either side of us, sitting regally in two high-back chairs. The duke was on the settee directly across from us. Sir Isaac, unimpressed by Lord Cresswell, curled up near Thomas's feet. All we needed was a painter to capture this most uncomfortable joining of our families. I must have been close to hysterics, because the thought almost made me laugh.

"Was all of this"—the duke motioned around the room—"truly necessary? I'd have thought you'd outgrown your theatrics by now. Miss Whitehall's family certainly won't approve of such behavior. Private matters do not require an audience. You ought to have some couth. It's a wonder Miss Wadsworth's family have tolerated you thus far."

"On the contrary." My father set his tea down. "We find your son to be most agreeable, Your Grace. He's been a pleasant addition to our household and has brought out the best in my daughter."

"As she has in me, Lord Wadsworth," Thomas said, the picture of impeccable manners. I imagined by his use of "lord" he was reminding his father that my family was also part of the peerage. "Which is why I'm so thrilled you traveled all this way, Father. Now you've had the pleasure of meeting your soon-to-be daughter-in-law, Miss Audrey Rose. Shame you'll miss the wedding. You're leaving for England when?"

The duke adopted the regretful look of someone who hated that they had bad news to share, though a certain glint in his eyes belied the fact that he might enjoy delivering it. He turned that calculating gaze on me. "You're exceptionally lovely, Miss Wadsworth, and I wish I could welcome you into our family. I truly do, but I'm afraid Thomas is already promised to another. Most unfortunate—and embarrassing—to drag your family into this, though I'm sure you understand I cannot deny the marquess's wishes. It would be most... impractical."

I drew in a breath, hoping to leash myself before I sprang across the parlor and strangled the duke in front of too many witnesses. How impractical indeed to marry for love. Were my title that of a duchess or marchioness, I was sure he'd welcome me quickly enough.

It was my grandmother—who believed leashes were meant for mutts, not people—who spoke first. "I trust you're knowledgeable about the peerage system in India," she said, lifting her chin in challenge. "The very one Her Imperial Majesty was so *kind* to implement after that messy war business between our countries."

Thomas clutched my hand in his. Grandmama's tone was cordial enough, though the way she sat taller in her chair and clicked her walking stick when she said "war" hinted otherwise. Lord Cresswell blinked slowly, realizing he was approaching a trap of some sort, but unable to locate an escape. "Indeed. Her Majesty was right in knighting a few deserving families."

"Mm. Were you aware she also granted a baronetcy to a select few?" she asked, a catlike purr in her voice. The duke shook his head. "Ah, well. I suppose foreign affairs are quite boring to a man such as yourself. You must be extremely busy, ordering people about."

"When I'm not traveling the Continent, I spend most of my time in London." He smiled wanly. "I find the city air suits me more so than the country. Sadly, there are too many pig farms for it to be pleasant in the summer."

"I imagine keeping company with pigs would be loathsome," Grandmama said.

Thomas held my hand so tightly I nearly lost feeling in my fingertips. I stole a glance at him, noticing the unencumbered glee on his face. He might have just fallen in love with my grandmother. My father called for another tea service, looking like he wished for brandy instead.

"Well"—Lord Cresswell clapped his hands together—"this has been lovely. I'm afraid I must take my leave with my son and—"

Thomas pulled out the letter he'd received from the barrister, passing it over to his father with smug satisfaction. "Apologies, Father, but I'm afraid you'll be traveling back to England alone. Unless you'd prefer to stay here. I could always send this information to the House of Lords. I'm sure forgery and blackmail aren't qualities they openly enjoy in the peerage."

I watched Thomas's father closely, expecting to see an outward sign of defeat. Or fear. Thomas had practically declared him a criminal in front of my family. The scandal alone could cause quite a nasty issue for him. He calmly folded the letter back up and slid it across the table, his expression neutral.

"Oh, Thomas. You really ought to pay better attention to detail." He stood, straightening his suit jacket. "That letter was no forgery. You left a curious amount of signed sheets in your room prior to leaving for Romania. I simply filled out the rest according to your verbal wishes."

"That's a lie! I never—"

"You never carelessly discarded sheets of your signature in one of our homes?" he asked. "Never? Not even on that atrociously messy writing desk of yours?" He shook his head. "Honestly, Thomas. Do you know what the staff might have done with that? They could own you. You must take greater care with your things."

Thomas clenched his hands at his sides. "Why worry about anyone else when I have a father such as yourself? Is this all a lesson, then? If I admit you've proven your point will you cease the engagement with Miss Whitehall?"

"It's abysmal, you know. Carrying on with this charade. Don't pretend as if you didn't beg me to send that correspondence for you."

"I'm carrying on a charade?" Thomas asked, anger lacing his voice. "Yet you're the one lying to everyone in this room."

"You're a degenerate. No matter how often I try to shape you into respectability, it's in your blood. Do try and show the Wadsworths some respect and pretend you're a gentleman."

"How disappointing." It must have taken a monumental force of will, but Thomas managed to shift his anger into something else faster than I could inhale my next breath. He held his hand up, inspecting his nails with a look of boredom etched into his features. "I've been called more scathing names, mostly by you. Surely you can do better than 'degenerate'?"

The duke inclined his head at my father. "It was nice meeting you, Lord Wadsworth. Lady Everleigh. I'm sorry it was under such dishonorable circumstances." He shifted his attention back to me and Thomas, a flash of triumph in his gaze. "I'll give you a few hours to say your good-byes. Miss Whitehall and I will meet you at the docks promptly at six. Good day."

TWENTY-SEVEN

A SWIFT DEPARTURE

GRANDMAMA'S PARLOR
FIFTH AVENUE, NEW YORK CITY
8 FEBRUARY 1889

"Well." Grandmama stood, waving off Father's offer of assistance. "That was as delightful as I'd imagined. Your father is as arrogant as you are, my boy, with none of your charm. Edmund, help me fetch my nib and ink. I've got correspondence that needs attention."

My father and grandmother went off in search of the writing supplies, leaving me and Thomas alone in the aftermath of the duke's exit. I looked at the grandfather clock's looming form. It was nearly ten. We had less than eight hours to find a way out of this abysmal situation, or Thomas would be forced onto that boat, heading back to London. Without me. I could no sooner imagine him leaving than I could picture solving this Ripper case alone.

"No wonder you hated Mephistopheles," I said, rearranging my gold and cream skirts for the fourth time. "Your father is like an older, crueler version of him. Without the fun bargains and circus costumes. He twists *everything* in his favor."

"Not exactly twists." Thomas leaned his head against the settee. "He searches for weakness the way I inspect people's shoes for scuff marks and deduce where the wearer has been. His powers of observation are—honestly, they're better than mine. He's always teaching lessons, always pointing out places I've failed. Moves I've left open. I should've burned those papers. I thought since he'd sent me to the Piccadilly flat, they'd be secure. He never visits that place."

I folded my hands in my lap to keep from fussing with my skirts anymore. "Why did you have blank papers with your signature?"

He was quiet a moment. "I was practicing."

"Practicing." I didn't pose it as a question, though he answered it.

"Before we left for Romania, I requested an audience with your father. I knew how much he worried over you, so I included all the reasons why studying abroad would suit you. I wanted—I was unsure of how to sign it once I'd written it out. I didn't want to sound pompous, but I worried he might not take me seriously as a suitor in the future, should I simplify too much." He blew his breath out. "I'd never worried about such foolish things before. I must have signed ten different pages, all near the bottom so I could lay my letter on top, getting a good feel for how it would read. In the end, I signed 'Thomas' on the letter I sent your father. Who knew my name could cause such trouble?"

"It's been causing trouble for me since we met," I teased.

Thomas didn't return my smile. Instead he faced me, his expression deadly serious. He took my hands in his. "Let's run away, Wadsworth. We can elope and change our names. We'll write to your family once we're settled. If we leave now, there's nothing my father can do to stop us. In a few years we can return to England. By then Miss Whitehall will surely have found a better match. And if not? She will not be able to do anything since we'll be married."

My immediate response was *Yes! Let's run away at once.* Temptation coursed through me. It would make our lives so much simpler to run. We could stay in America, settle into a new town or city, begin a new life. Perhaps in a few years we could build our own agency, one where we assisted with forensic cases and seemingly unsolvable mysteries. I longed to say yes. I wanted it more than I'd ever wanted anything else. And yet...

"I-I cannot, Thomas." I hated the words, but they were still as true today as they had been yesterday. "Running away...it would not prevent my family from being ruined. We'd solve your issue only to guarantee mine. Can you deny that?"

He clenched his jaw but shook his head.

"And what about Jack the Ripper?" I asked, gently pulling my hands free. "Would we run away from solving that, too?"

He shrugged. Thomas would set fire to the case—and the world—if it meant we could be together. Not out of malice or uncaring, but out of his love and devotion to me. It wouldn't be easy for him, but he'd do it. No matter how much I wished otherwise, I couldn't turn my back on it or my family—I'd be turning my back on understanding my brother and on speaking for all of the women who lost their lives. And all the others who were sure to die in the future if we didn't stop him. Thomas might believe he could walk away from it now, but I knew he'd come to regret it. Just as I would.

"Do you remember what we talked about, once we'd reached New York? About our work?" I asked.

"Of course."

I swore I was about to stick a scalpel into my own chest and twist it. "Then you must know our work has to come first. We cannot run from this case. Not when we've got so much left to do. We started it together; we must find a way to end it." I glanced toward the window, watching snow fall in heavier flakes. "If your father won't be reasoned with, perhaps Miss Whitehall will change her mind once she sees how important your work is to you. Maybe she doesn't care if you hate her, but she might mind a husband who would rather dissect cadavers than touch her. Surely she will hate the whispers around London about your disinterest."

He was quiet for a moment, absorbing my words. I hoped he didn't see it as a refusal of him. I'd give anything to have a simple life together. He exhaled.

"I loathe when you're reasonable." He crossed his arms, though his lips quirked. "One day it'd be nice if you agreed with one of my grand romantic gestures."

"One day when I've got nothing better to do, I might."

He narrowed his eyes and sat forward, his new look intent. "Relationships are about compromise, are they not?"

I was immediately wary of where he was heading with this. "Yes, but... our short-lived courtship is technically over."

He swatted away the technicality as if it were a fly. "Our *marriage* is compromised because of my father and his disinheritance threats. Let's think this through. If I cannot find proof of his deception, I have only one option, according to my father. I am legally bound to Miss Whitehall and will be on the next boat. Which leaves"—he glanced at the clock—"in a few hours."

Still suspicious, I nodded. "True."

"Your theory that the Ripper has moved on to another city...if we had a good reason for leaving New York—one your uncle would agree to—we might slip away before my father realizes I won't be at the docks and comes to collect me. Correct?"

"Thomas..." Involving Uncle in this mess was the last thing I wished to do.

"Audrey Rose," he said urgently, "if we can deduce where he's gone and continue our investigation there, it'll give us a legitimate reason to delay my departure. We'd have more time to solve the Miss Whitehall issue without ruining your family's name. Otherwise I have two options. I'll either be disowned and hunted if I don't get on that ship tonight, or I will be legally bound to another. Is that something you can honestly live with?"

I closed my eyes, envisioning Thomas stepping onto a boat, greeting his father and soon-to-be wife. The image was so crisp, so lifelike, I gasped. "Your father will not simply give up and travel back to London. He'll come looking for you. And who knows what he'll do then?"

Thomas took my hands in his again, his face earnest. "I will deal with his wrath. I need to know this is something you want."

"Of course I want you." How he could think I wanted anything else was beyond common sense or logic. A fresh wave of panic flooded my system. "What happens if we can't find a good lead for the Ripper? What if we don't have any other city to investigate by the time you have to leave?"

Thomas hugged me close. "We'll figure something out."

I shook my head. "Uncle will not leave here on a whim. I know him. He'll need convincing evidence to prove there's a good reason to go."

"We have a few hours." Thomas sounded a bit uncertain about this desperate plan for the first time. "We'll find something. We have to."

"And if we don't?"

He was quiet a moment. "Then I'll run. I'll disappear so thoroughly my father will never have a chance to find me."

We gazed at each other, absorbing that fate. If Thomas ran away from his father and responsibility, he'd also be leaving me behind. My head swam with worry, but I also needed to do something. Time was slipping away from our grasps.

"Let's hurry. We'll tear the journals apart if we need to. Or we'll scour the notes from Miss Tabram's case. There's got to be a clue somewhere." I accepted Thomas's hand as he helped me up. We made our way into the corridor arm in arm, and I wondered if his heart was beating as furiously as mine was. "What if—"

"None of those, Wadsworth." Thomas patted my hand. "When. *When* we find the information, we'll tell your uncle. When we're far away from here, we'll worry about consequences. For now, let's focus on our immediate concern. I'll go speak with your uncle and tell him our theory about the Ripper leaving New York. You start in on our notes or journals."

Daciana stood near the newel-post, clutching it tightly. Dark circles marred the skin under her eyes. She hadn't been sleeping much since the wedding went to hell. "Ileana and I would like to help. We're quite good at finding hidden clues. It's..." I had the impression she was choosing her next words carefully, but I was buzzing with too much worry to reflect on it. "We've had practice with the Order. If you'd like, we'll handle the journals and you can take the last murder case. It'll help if we all split the work."

Thomas considered this for the space of a breath. He nodded sharply, a slight gleam in his eyes. "Thank you, Daci. The journals are in Audrey Rose's chambers. You'll both need to hurry; there are... a lot."

The Cresswell siblings held each other's gazes for a minute, silently communicating. A moment later, Daciana grabbed her skirts and dashed up the stairs, calling to her love as she rounded into the corridor.

Thomas kissed my head and went in search of my uncle while I collected notes from both Martha Tabram's murder and Miss Carrie Brown's. Even though the police had arrested Frenchy Number One, I knew he was not the man responsible. This was our Ripper and he was only just starting his newest murder trail. I settled into a sitting room on the first floor with pages of notes scattered around me.

I tried not to look at the clock, but all I could hear was the wretched *tick tick tick* of the second hand counting off our remaining hours. Time was not our ally. It seemed to rush more quickly than my pulse. At some point Thomas joined me in the sitting room, his own pile of notes in larger disarray than mine. Uncle had agreed to changing locations, as long as we provided a good argument for where. The Ripper case haunted him, too, and he wished to end it.

Somehow, despite focusing all of my energy on our task and willing the clock to slow, there was only one hour remaining before Thomas needed to leave. Every muscle in my body was taut, ready to snap. He sat back and heaved a sigh.

"I need to pack my trunks, Wadsworth. I can't risk staying any longer, or else my father will undoubtedly be here and I'm sure he'll have hired *assistance* with getting me to that boat. He won't trust that I'll get there on my own."

He pushed himself into a standing position, defeat obvious in the lines around his mouth. Everything about this felt wrong. I stood, heart racing.

"Let's run," I said, a sob ripping through my words. Thomas froze for the space of one moment before he lifted me into his arms, holding me tightly to him. If Thomas and I eloped, it would help calm the scandal. As would the fact that we were in America and the rumors would be delayed. It wasn't ideal, but it could work. It had to. Then we could still pursue Jack the Ripper leads together. "Are you certain we have enough time to pack?"

Thomas let me go and looked at the clock, his face grim. "Barely. Pack lightly. We'll meet in twenty minutes. I'll have the coachman ready a carriage now."

He kissed my cheek and ran for the door. I didn't linger. I made my way upstairs as fast as my leg would allow, pulse pounding in time with the seconds. I shoved dresses and brushes and unmentionables into a trunk, relieved I'd left a decent portion tucked away already. I finished with a few minutes to spare and called down for a footman to retrieve my trunk. While I waited, I scribbled a note to Liza and then one to my father. I didn't have time to say good-bye, nor did I want to involve them in our scheme.

I was already waiting for Thomas in the corridor downstairs when he grabbed our trunks, helping the footman move more quickly.

"Are you ready?" he asked. I nodded, too afraid to say anything more. I couldn't believe we were running away. Wrong and right mingled together until I was no longer certain which emotion was the dominant one. He seemed to feel the same. He jerked his chin in an impression of a nod, then indicated the back exit. "Let's hurry. We don't want—"

"Wait!"

Daciana and Ileana raced down the stairs, nearly tripping in their haste to reach us.

"We've found it!" Daciana said, panting. "We know where he's heading."

TWENTY-EIGHT
SATAN'S COMPANIONS

GRANDMAMA'S MAIN PARLOR
FIFTH AVENUE, NEW YORK CITY
8 FEBRUARY 1889

"Who?" Thomas asked, setting our trunks down. "Father? I believe even the Vatican knows where Father's heading. He's made it abundantly clear."

"Jack the Ripper." Ileana seemed slightly more reserved in her judgment. "We're almost certain," she amended. "The clues seem to point to a certain city. Here."

She handed me one of Nathaniel's journals, open to a page with yet another quote. I read it, immediately recognizing it as another passage from *Frankenstein*. My shoulders slumped as I read aloud.

"'I beheld <u>a stream of fire</u> issue from an old and beautiful oak which stood about twenty yards from our house; and so soon as the dazzling light vanished, the oak had disappeared, and nothing remained but a blasted stump. When we visited it the next morning, we found the tree shattered in a singular manner. It was not splintered by the shock, but entirely reduced to thin ribbons of wood. I never beheld anything <u>so utterly destroyed.</u>'"

I gave the journal to Thomas. He raised a brow. "You've divined a location based on this?" His tone was skeptical. "Perhaps you ought to pursue fortune-telling. I know just the carnival in need of those services. Maybe you'll convince the world that vampires, witches, and demons do roam the earth."

Ileana and Daciana shared a long look, one that spoke of shared secrets. I narrowed my eyes. What did they know of vampires and other legends that made them uncomfortable? They hadn't seemed scared of folklore back in Romania. Finally, Daciana turned our way, handing another journal over. "Don't be too impressed with us yet. Here's this."

" 'Satan had his companions, fellow devils, to admire and encourage him, but I am solitary and abhorred.' " Another quote from our favorite gothic novel. The underlined bits didn't seem worth noting before, and, frankly, I wasn't as excited as Daciana and Ileana appeared to be. If anything, the heavy weight of defeat settled like a royal mantle around my shoulders.

I chose my next words carefully. "This is...interesting, but I'm afraid my brother was rather enthralled with this novel. He often quoted it."

"At first, we also feared it was nothing, but look closer," Daciana urged, handing over another journal. "Read this next."

I was enchanted by the appearance of the hut; here the snow and rain could not penetrate; the ground was dry; and it presented to me then as exquisite and divine a retreat as Pandemonium appeared to the demons of hell after their sufferings in the lake of fire...it was noon when I awoke, and allured by the warmth of the sun, which shone brightly on the white ground, I determined to recommence my travels.

I glanced up at Daciana's hopeful expression, wishing I could muster the same level of enthusiasm. I didn't want to be rude, but we were wasting the last of our moments on nonsense. Thomas and

I needed to sneak away before it was too late. "Fire and traveling through snow...I'm afraid I don't see the connection."

Daciana turned to her brother. "And you?"

"Demons holidaying in a city of fire?" he asked, sounding annoyed. "Isn't that what Hell is? Or perhaps it's a quaint description of their summer home."

She grabbed the journal back, then motioned to Ileana to set them down in the order in which we'd read them. Like a professor teaching unruly students, she marched over to them, one by one, pointing out the significance. "Look at the dates of each. Now, when read in order, the underlined passages refer to people traveling to a place. Where was there a great fire in this country? What also has 'white' as a nickname now?"

"A great fire? How should I—" Understanding dawned. I'd read an article in the paper this week about Olmsted's contribution to the fairgrounds in Illinois. How magnificent and enchanting they were. The White City. The Great Fire. Thomas and I exchanged our first hopeful look in days. I shifted my attention back to Daciana, finally sharing her and Ileana's excitement. "Chicago. The Ripper is heading to the World's Columbian Exposition."

Of course. It had been the talk of the world for months—a place where scientific invention and industry could shine and draw hundreds of thousands of visitors. There would be so many people wandering around, it would be—

A horrible realization sank in, the thrill extinguishing as quickly as it had come. Whoever brutalized and stalked the gaslit streets of London was about to unleash more terror in a new city. He was done with New York for now. His sights were set on an even bigger stage. One where victims could be snatched away easily. The World's Fair would prove a most intriguing place for murder and mayhem.

With a heavy heart, I headed for the door. "I'll tell Uncle to purchase tickets for Chicago."

Thomas nodded. "Hurry. We don't want to run into my father and Miss Whitehall. Though it would be rather satisfying to watch them from the window of our departing train."

"No. Don't even think such foolish nonsense." Daciana's tone brooked no arguments. "I will go to the ship and tell Father you're right behind me. It'll give you some time to flee without him coming straightaway. You two need to be on the next train to Chicago or you won't be leaving New York of your own free will. And you cannot run into Father or he *will* hunt you down and drag you back."

"Bring this with you." Grandmama emerged from her parlor and nodded to the butler. He darted forward and handed Daciana a telegram. "It's for your father."

Thomas knitted his brows together, shock registering in his features when he noted the sender. He had much to learn about my grandmother. I was glad he'd already set our trunks down or he might have dropped them on his feet. "Is that from... the *queen?*"

"Of course it is." Grandmama stamped her walking stick. "Her Imperial Majesty was quite fond of my husband. Especially after he'd made the introduction to my family." She turned her rich brown eyes on me, as cunning as always. "You haven't told him, have you?"

I felt Thomas's attention on me, carefully watching each emotion I was trying to control, and contemplated hiding under my skirts. He was far too observant to miss anything. "I didn't see any reason I ought to share *your* personal affairs, Grandmama."

She harrumphed. "My father was granted a title of raja. He lent money to Englishmen of the East India Company. We had much influence over commerce." She shook her head. "My granddaughter will inherit all my property once I'm gone, boy. She may not hold the title of marchioness, but her dowry could purchase your father's precious title a thousand times over. I simply requested Her Majesty's blessing on your engagement. To my *granddaughter.*"

"And?" I prompted, knowing there was more. There always was with Grandmama.

"I might have suggested a new wing dedicated to the queen would be nice at Oxford. Victoria can't resist such things. Now, off with you"—she motioned for us to leave, eyes sparkling with triumph—"I need some peace in this house."

Ignoring her wishes, I kissed each of her cheeks. "Thank you, Grandmama."

Thomas and I were not free to marry yet, but she'd done all that she could to assist our endeavor. Now it was up to Thomas's father and the queen. I didn't have much faith in either of them, but it was certainly the best we could hope for, given the circumstances. Now we'd simply need to wait and see. But we'd wait and see from an undisclosed location, hopefully too far for the duke to find us.

"Be brave." Grandmama cupped my cheek lovingly. "Now, go, save the world and that devilish prince of yours."

PART TWO

CHICAGO
1889

These violent delights have violent ends
And in their triumph die, like fire and powder,
Which as they kiss consume.
—*ROMEO AND JULIET,* ACT 2, SCENE 6
WILLIAM SHAKESPEARE

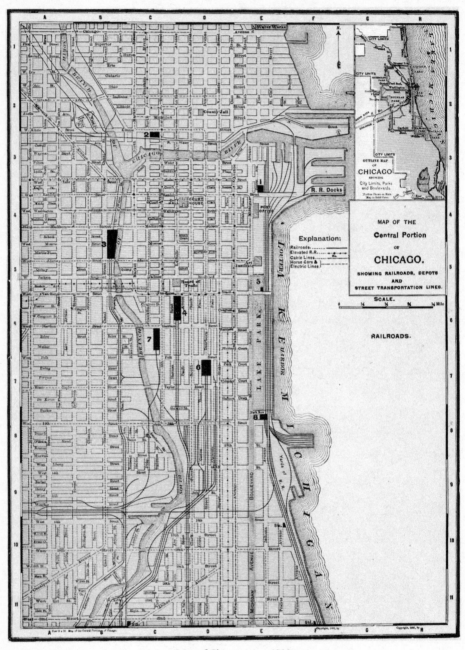

Map of Chicago, circa 1900

TWENTY-NINE
THE SECOND CITY

THE CENTRAL DEPOT
CHICAGO, ILLINOIS
10 FEBRUARY 1889

I'd read all sorts of unpleasant things in the newspapers about Chicago—how it smelled of slaughtered hog, smoke, and excrement. Some said the streets ran red with blood and black with ash. And it wasn't at all uncommon to come across a severed head or limb on the tracks—a daily danger to those who stood too near the rail cars. It was a city to be feared and avoided.

While some of those things were true, I found Chicago rather enchanting despite the tang of smoke in the air. There was an essence of grit mixed with hope that slipped into a person and made them believe they, too, might become whoever they wished to be. Anything was possible. Here was a city that had experienced destruction—it had burned to ash and had risen much like the mythological phoenix. It seemed to toss its arms wide, both challenging and welcoming. *Come forth and enter if you dare. Come and live freely.*

Welcome to Chicago.

I stood outside the train station, eyes wide, taking in buildings that reached toward the sky. They gleamed like blades in the setting sun. *Chicago*. I swore the city inhaled and exhaled in time to the trains chugging into and out of it. It was like a mechanical nervous system, the lines of tracks a constant movement of life. Wind whipped playfully at my hair despite it being an icy breeze that set my teeth chattering. Young women hurried along the streets, holding small leather cases, dressed smartly in long dark skirts. It hit me at once. They were alone. I blinked, completely and utterly taken with the notion of women traveling, without a chaperone, to *work*. I leaned on my cane, gaping. Surely this had to be a dream.

Thomas stepped beside me, taking in my expression and then the view. His mouth inched up on one side. "It's hard to be certain, but you appear almost as excited about the city as I was with that chocolate cake with espresso frosting."

"Don't be ridiculous; that cake was not of this world." I playfully nudged him with my elbow. "Look"—I spun slowly—"can you imagine? Living in a place where you needn't require an escort to go anywhere?"

Thomas looked at me a bit sadly, and I realized he *did* know what that felt like. He wasn't required to have someone watch his every move when he left his home.

A man ringing a bell scowled at people exiting the train station. "Sinners! This city is home to the devil. Wicked, wicked creatures running amok. Begone from whence you came! Flee back to the safety of your homes or you'll be taken by the demons stalking these streets!" He turned in my direction, his eyes as wild as untamed fire. "You! Go home to your mother, girl. Save yourself!"

My excitement and smile evaporated. I stared at him, all warmth gone from my features and my tone. "My mother is dead, sir."

"Come." Thomas gently guided me to the far end of the sidewalk. We waited, in silence, taking in the street noise while Uncle arranged for our trunks and medical equipment to be brought to our temporary home. The man continued his tirade. I ground my teeth together.

"Why is that man shouting about sinners and demons?" I asked, watching him ring his bell at a young woman who hurried past him, her face purposely turned away. "He's not referring to women, is he?"

"I imagine he is." Thomas inspected him. "Not everyone believes Chicago's such a magical, progressive place. I read an article that described it as a city where decency came to perish. It's a city under siege—wickedness is replacing morals. At least according to some." He nodded toward another young woman walking alone. "Men are keen on blaming women for the rise in sin. It's been something plaguing humanity since the Bible first accused Eve of tempting Adam. As if he had no mind to taste that forbidden fruit before she offered it to him. Everyone seems to forget God told Adam the fruit was forbidden. He created Eve later."

"Honestly?" I snorted. "I didn't realize you were so well versed in religion."

Thomas placed my hand in the crook of his arm, steering us toward my uncle, who'd just exited the station. "I enjoy causing discord when forced to attend parties. You ought to hear the arguments that break out from uttering something so supposedly blasphemous. The one question no one can answer is always, if Adam had been warned, why didn't he pass the message along to his wife? Seems he was more to blame than she was. Yet Eve is always the villain, the wicked temptress who cursed us all."

"Who *are* you?" I asked, only half jesting.

He stopped walking. "I am the man who will love you unto forever." Before I could collapse from either swooning or chiding him for his flirtation, he quickly added, "I'm also a student of observation. And a brother. The truth, Miss Wadsworth, is I've watched my sister navigate the world of men. Doing so with more grace than I ever could, were I in her position. I've watched you do the same. Biting your tongue when I'd want nothing more than to bite the offender. I delight in pointing out areas where man has failed, even if it changes only one mind. Or if it changes none. At least I feel as though I'm fighting on the side of women, not against them. Everyone needs to take responsibility for their own failures."

I clutched his arm a bit tighter. "You're remarkable when you choose to be, Cresswell."

He looked at me, a thoughtful expression crossing his features. "I long to live in a world where equal treatment is not something in need of commending."

Uncle stuffed his hands into his cloak, turning his face away from the increasing wind.

"Streetcars are available, but I've hired a carriage due to our trunks." He lifted his attention to the man still hollering about Satan. His jaw tightened as the man pointed to our group, cursing my family for bringing me to this den of sin. Uncle sighed. "You're not to go out unaccompanied under any circumstances, Audrey Rose. We're no longer on familiar ground, and I'll not worry about your whereabouts while we're investigating this case. Am I clear?"

"Yes, sir."

"Satan is coming for you! He's coming for you all. Every last sinner among you will be burned alive!" The man charged a young woman, waving a cross in her face. When she didn't flinch, he sank to his knees. "Angel of vengeance! Have you come to save us?"

I took an involuntary step closer to Thomas as the woman grabbed her skirts and ran out of the man's way. He was clearly suffering from some affliction of the mind if he truly believed angels and demons walked amongst us.

"Here's our transportation." Uncle motioned to a carriage. "Let's be on our—"

"Professor," Thomas began, "would it be all right if we met you there in an hour? I'd love to see the Sanitary and Ship Canal."

"I suspect you're asking permission to take my niece. To the sanitary." Uncle pinched the bridge of his nose when Thomas nodded eagerly. "One hour."

Thomas helped Uncle into the carriage, probably promising his firstborn to get us both home safely within the hour. Once the horses rode off, Thomas held his arm out for me, his smile near contagious. I hesitated only a moment before accepting it.

"We really need to work on your wooing skills, Cresswell," I said. "I'm afraid visiting a sanitary canal isn't the most romantic way to court someone."

He chuckled as we made our way down the street, steering us far away from the religious man's bell ringing. I noticed how tense his muscles were beneath my hand. "It's one of the most remarkable feats of engineering—they've reversed the flow of the river away from Lake Michigan."

"Since when have you become so enamored with engineering?" I looked up at him, brow arched. "It doesn't quite fit in with your science and deductions."

"Miss Wadsworth!" An almost familiar voice cried out. "Mr. Cresswell!"

Startled, I searched the crowd, which was turning out to be an impossible task. Five o'clock in Chicago was dreadfully busy. People rushed from sleek metal trains, green-and-cream-colored streetcars, and all manner of carriages both swift and more leisurely. Sidewalks bustled with workers emptying from the buildings, depositing dozens more into the already crowded walkways. We stood there, parting the crowd as if we were rocks jutting out from a raging river. No one came for us. Thomas shrugged, then gently guided me to the nearest building.

"In Bucharest," he said by way of explanation, "my mother used to say, 'If you get lost, stay put. It won't do any good if you're running about like a plucked goose.'"

I crinkled my brow. "Aren't geese plucked *after* they've been killed?"

"There, there, Wadsworth." Thomas patted my arm. "I didn't have the heart even at eight to tell my mother the error of her statement. Although," he said, as if coming to some new realization, "perhaps the absurdity of the image was meant to stick in my mind."

Finally I spotted a familiar young man with dark skin and a bright smile working his way toward us, moving against the flow of the crowd. Mr. Noah Hale. Our friend from the forensic academy in Romania. I couldn't believe our luck!

As he got closer, Thomas practically dropped my arm to rush to him. Catching himself at the last moment, he made sure I was all right before greeting our friend. "Noah!"

"Thomas!" The two young men embraced, a clap of hands on backs and gripped elbows. I rolled my eyes skyward. Men always seemed to have a secret ritual instead of simply hugging each other. Once they'd completed their greeting, Noah beamed in my direction. "What a surprise! It's good to see you both. Moldoveanu didn't admit it, but I think he missed you. The academy wasn't the same after you left."

"I'm fairly certain our old headmaster only misses taking out his hostility on me," I said, grinning back at him. Moldoveanu had despised almost everyone in our forensic course, though he'd taken greater exception to me and Thomas for the unforgivable sin of solving the murders taking place in his school. "Speaking of him, why aren't you at the academy?"

Not that I wasn't pleased to see him. Mr. Noah Hale was one of my favorite peers. I marveled at our good fortune of crossing paths with him here.

Noah's expression fell. I watched the gleam leave his dark eyes, replaced by something much sadder. "Momma got sick. I had to come back and help with the family. My dad works from sunup 'til sundown and the little ones needed me."

I gripped his hand in mine. "I'm sorry. How is your mother feeling now?"

One of the qualities I admired about Noah was how nothing ever seemed to keep him down for long. A smile lit up his face again. "Better, thank you. Don't feel too bad that I'm not suffering under Moldoveanu." He opened a flap of his overcoat, pointing to an insignia sewn onto his vest. It was an eye with WE NEVER SLEEP stitched around it. It was unfamiliar to me, but Thomas seemed impressed as he offered a low whistle. "I've been invited to apprentice with the Pinkertons. They gave me a filler case for now, but it's interesting."

"The Pinkertons, as in the famed detective agency?" Thomas asked, perking up further. "The ones who stopped the assassination plot against Lincoln?"

"How do you know that?" I stared incredulously. "That was before you were born!"

"As were the Romans, but we learn that history, too," Thomas said matter-of-factly. He turned his attention back on Noah, running all sorts of Cresswell deductions. "They haven't given you any problems, have they?"

"Mr. Pinkerton had a cabin about fifty miles north of here that used to be a stop on the Underground Railroad. Only thing he cares about is taking on the best people for the job." Noah buttoned his coat back up, breathing into his gloves. Snow started falling, twirling every which way as it tumbled to the ground. New York had been cold, but Chicago seemed born of ice. "You two here for the fair?"

Thomas glanced at me, perhaps searching for permission he didn't require. We had no rules or restrictions between us. "My uncle was called to New York for a case," I said. "Through a few strange twists, it brought us here."

"Oh? It wouldn't be the murder of that woman in New York, would it? The one they're claiming was done by Jack the Ripper?" he asked. Noah was always particularly astute, especially when it came to collecting details of things left unsaid. "I thought a man was found guilty of that."

"Yes, well, it's unfortunate but I don't believe it's the first time a man's been wrongfully convicted of a crime," I said. "You mentioned a case you're working on? Does it involve forensics?"

"Unfortunately, it doesn't. No body, no crime scene or evidence of any acts of malice in her home. I'm not even sure a crime was committed." Noah stepped out of the way of a harried-looking businessman. "It's as if she simply vanished."

"Her family is nearby?" Thomas's gaze traveled over our friend, no doubt deducing details of the case before Noah offered them. "Which is why you're here. How long has she been missing?" Noah didn't have time to open his mouth before Thomas nodded. It was impressive, even for him. "Ah. Not long. A week?"

"It's a bit unnerving when you do that, you know." Noah scratched the side of his neck, shaking his head slightly. "Miss Emeline Cigrande went to work five days ago. Left to have luncheon, then never returned. Her father expected her home for supper—she was his caregiver. When she didn't return…" I followed Noah's gaze as it settled on the man ringing the bell and spouting about demons. "Poor Mr. Cigrande. He's been out of his mind, hasn't slept since she left. He keeps ringing that bell like it'll bring her back home safely."

I softened at the hell that must be waging war inside of Mr. Cigrande's mind. His daughter was gone; he was unwell. No wonder he believed the devil was to blame.

"Anyway, enough about that. Have you been to the fair yet?"

Noah asked, changing the subject rather abruptly. I shook my head, pulling my attention back to the present. "You've gotta see it at sunset. The water in the Grand Basin looks like lava!"

"We won't have much time to see the sights once our investigation is underway." Thomas seemed intrigued. "We'll need to ask the professor's permission first, but why not go this evening?"

"I'm game if you are," Noah said. "I've got to speak with Mr. Cigrande and go over his story once more. Which should give you both time to send a telegram. Meet me near the *Statue of the Republic* around six thirty. You won't regret it."

Court of Honor, World's Fair, Chicago

THIRTY
ILLUMINATION

COURT OF HONOR
WORLD'S COLUMBIAN EXPOSITION
10 FEBRUARY 1889

We stood on the bridge overlooking the Grand Basin, admiring the domed Administration Building, waiting as the sun gracefully sank into a curtsy, its rays a rich tapestry of salmon, tangerine, and deep gold. Covered boats crossed from one side of the Court of Honor to the next, gliding across the otherwise still waters of the reflecting pool. American flags snapped in the light breeze, their sound swallowed by the large crowd. Every so often a flurry fell from the heavens, as if Mother Nature was adding a bit of her own magic to this shimmering city.

My gaze fell from one wonder to the next, drinking in each detail. From proud stone bulls facing east on the banks of the shore, to the *Statue of the Republic* before us, I could spend a lifetime traveling from building to building.

Noah and Thomas chatted about the architecture, commenting on the pleasing aesthetics of each cornice being built at the same height. What struck me was the neoclassical design—the creamy whites of each building, and the way they shifted to even softer hues as twilight cast its opal-colored net across the fair. I swore it appeared as if some celestial artist painted the buildings before our very eyes, taking care to gild their edges.

"It's incredible," I said. "How did they create such a palace so quickly?"

"Wait until the real magic starts," Noah said, gazing at a boat cutting through the water. "I've come at sunset at least once every week since I got back, and it never ceases to amaze me."

I inhaled the fragrant air. Potted flowers were surprisingly in full bloom in every direction, but other scents carried on the cool breeze. A couple standing nearby happily crunched on a new treat—caramel-coated popped corn called Cracker Jack. The Court of Honor was unlike anything I'd ever witnessed before—more ethereal and beautiful than even St. Paul's Cathedral. The buildings gleamed even at this hour. I couldn't wait to see them at the height of the morning sun. I found myself unable to fully describe the vast expanse of buildings fanned out around us, or how large they were. Giants could run from one end of them to the other, tiring even their long legs out well before they reached the end of the fairgrounds.

If heaven existed, surely this city must be fashioned after it.

I thought of Mr. Cigrande, the man whose daughter was missing, of his insistence that we were all walking blindly into Hell. He need only step into this White City to feel the presence of a higher power. Even someone like me, who wasn't sure what to believe, felt moved.

"...he didn't have much to add. Says the same story each time. Honestly, I'm not sure what to believe. I asked around and he did have a daughter, though neighbors recall hearing them argue at all hours. Dishes breaking..."

I tuned Thomas and Noah's conversation out, not wanting any hint of darkness to invade this most sacred of spaces. It was selfish, but after our ruined wedding and the horror of our job, I longed for one hour to be swept away in the fantasy of our surroundings. While the sun continued its slow procession past the horizon, I studied the *Statue of the Republic*—my pamphlet stated it was sixty-five feet in height. One hand held a globe with an eagle aloft, while the other gripped a staff. She was as fierce as a goddess and equally intimidating.

"It's almost time." Noah bounced on the balls of his feet. The sun was fighting for its last breath before the moon ascended to its heavenly throne. Pure golden light pulsed before twilight crept in. "Get your handkerchiefs ready."

Thomas puffed his chest up, no doubt ready to unleash an entire litany on why that would be unnecessary, when electrical lights flashed on across the grounds. My mouth hung open. Words failed me. My scientific-centered mind understood the engineering behind such a feat, but my heart raced at the brilliance. Never, in my whole life, had I witnessed such an event.

Thousands of lamps evenly posted from one end of the grounds to the next, from each building as far as I could see, all of it illuminated in unison. Brilliant white light reflected off the pond, shimmering. I reached for Thomas's hand the same moment he grabbed for mine.

"I-It's..." My eyes stung as I struggled to put my feelings into words.

"Magic." Thomas's expression held pure wonder. "The magnitude..."

Noah offered a knowing grin, but I noticed his eyes also misted. "There are over two hundred *thousand* incandescent bulbs, according to the program. Nikola Tesla's alternating current is going to be huge. You should see what else he's done in the Electricity Building."

"Tesla?" I asked, dabbing at my eyes with Thomas's handkerchief.

"He's here?" I'd read of his mechanical experiments—how he'd perform feats unlike any other for patrons in his laboratory. I gripped Thomas, ready to drag him all the way into the exhibition hall to meet a man who truly made magic from science. Nathaniel would have loved seeing him. I couldn't wait to—I sucked in a sharp breath. Sometimes, even now, I forgot my brother was dead. A bit of my mood darkened, but one glance at the shimmering lights and the sound of the cries of the people standing all around us kept my sadness at bay.

"Oh, Tesla's here, all right." Noah grinned. "He's showcasing his polyphase system. He's got fifteen feet of coil and oscillators in the electrical building. Steam hisses and sparks fly. It's incredible. Last time I was there, a woman stood frozen for nearly an hour. She thought she'd seen God."

"I imagine it would seem like that."

I glanced from one building to another. There was so much to do and see and I wanted desperately to do it all. It would be daunting, trying to hobble over so much ground, especially in heavy crowds. I'd hate to hold my companions back. Thomas watched me in that uncanny way of his. "Taking a boat ride across the pond would be fun. I'm up for it if you are, Wadsworth."

I bit my lip. We'd sent word to my uncle, asking if we might stay out a little while longer to visit the fair, and he'd instructed us to spend no more than two hours at the exhibition. We'd already been waiting an hour for the nightly illumination; judging from the size of the crowd, by the time we crossed the bridge and made our way to a boat, that'd take at least another hour alone. I wanted to go very badly, but I wanted to respect Uncle's wishes.

"Perhaps next time, Cresswell. Much as I wish to spend eternity in this heavenly city, we have a devil to catch."

Our carriage rolled to a stop outside a prim house that seemed to sneer at our arrival. I raised my brows. It was an interesting design; each arch was ornamented, reminding me a bit of—

"Is it me, or does it look like a witch owns this property and is gouging out children's eyes and setting them in jars for her spell work as we speak?"

"Thomas," I chided, swatting his arm. "It's very... gothic."

He snorted. "How magnanimous of you, Wadsworth. The spires look like fangs."

"Don't be snippy about the house," I warned, "or it might bite you back."

Ignoring Thomas's further commentary, I pushed his assessment aside. It was a grand estate—a favor from Grandmama. She'd made the arrangements for us, claiming to know the perfect location for our endeavors. I had no idea she owned property here, but she was full of surprises. It was much too large for the three of us, though after leaving the chaos and clamor of our families behind, the extra space would feel welcome. A much-needed respite from meddling dukes and vengeful fiancées. I smiled to myself. Grandmama always knew what I needed.

I accepted Thomas's arm as we got out of the carriage, tottering only a little until I secured my balance with my cane. I exhaled, my breath steaming in front of me, startled to see we weren't alone. Uncle paced outside our temporary home, either unaware or uncaring of the snow that had started falling in earnest.

Thomas and I exchanged glances. Uncle hadn't seemed to notice our arrival, either. His focus was directed inward, his hands clasped behind his back, his lips moving with words we couldn't hear. Thomas cleared his throat, and Uncle swiveled to us, his expression stern. Whatever magic and merriment I'd felt upon leaving the White City vanished. Thomas helped me up the stairs, his attention split between ensuring I didn't slip over the slick cobblestones, and my increasingly irate Uncle.

"Professor? What is it?"

"I spent the afternoon walking from one police station to the next, all across Chicago."

I drew my overcoat closer, trying to ignore the bits of frosted ice that pelted my skin. I'd no idea how long my uncle had been out here, but he'd catch his death if he didn't get inside.

"Uncle, we should—"

"It's the lack of bodies that troubles me." He stopped moving long enough to stare at the soft glow of a lamppost. "Do you know what I find most disturbing?"

"That you're not frozen solid after standing out here without a coat?" Thomas asked. "Or is that only me?"

Uncle flashed him a warning look before turning to me. "Well?"

"I-it isn't t-that unusual for a-a city, i-is it? P-perhaps t-the b-bodies are i-in t-the canal," I said, fully chattering. I leaned on my cane, the cold biting into my leg unmercifully. "May we please discuss this in the house? M-my leg—"

"There are no bodies. No body parts," Uncle said, motioning us all inside. Thomas kept his hand on the small of my back as we stepped through the ornate front door. "Even in a city of this size, corpses have a way of turning up. Miss Brown's body, for example, was discovered within hours of her murder. Why, then, are there no corpses?"

A footman helped me out of my coat. "Tea service is waiting in the drawing room, Miss Wadsworth. Your grandmother also arranged for assorted pastries."

I moved as quickly as I could into the room, standing before the fire, soaking in its warmth, mind churning over possibilities. "Our murderer…he might have some laboratory secreted away where he keeps the bodies." I accepted a cup of tea Thomas offered, shifting to meet his and Uncle's worried expressions. "He could dismember them, then toss them into the river. Or any of the canals or lagoons of the Columbian Exposition." I glanced at Thomas. The earlier beauty of the fair now took on a sinister aura. "There were many waterways. Perhaps they've gotten tangled up in the underwater mechanics."

"Theories are good, Audrey Rose, but facts are better at this juncture. There's no bloody clothing, no scarf or coat or bit of torn fabric or skirt or shoe—not one clue or trace of evidence that any crime close to the Ripper murders has been committed here." Uncle collapsed into an overstuffed leather chair, twisting his mustache. "Does that sound like the work of the Jack the Ripper we know? The very one who mailed letters written in blood to detective inspectors? The one who made a game of hacking off body parts and organs?"

Thomas and I were silent. As much as I wished otherwise, Uncle had a very decent point. It did not sound like the attention-seeking man we'd been terrorized by back in London. Nor did it sound as if it were similar to the New York murder. Each of those killings were spectacles in their own right—ways for the murderer to flamboyantly show off his ability to thwart police efforts.

"I fear we left New York on a whim," Uncle said. "Bits of poetry and newspaper clippings affixed to journals do not indicate Jack the Ripper lives. Or that he's chosen *this* city to taunt next, out of the whole of America, if he has survived. I want you both to tear those journals apart, find me a bit of irrefutable proof that this isn't some fanciful folly conjured up by your need to escape your father, Thomas." He turned his attention on me and I withered beneath his scornful gaze. "I sincerely hope you didn't insist on coming here so you might dodge your own responsibilities and live in sin."

Thomas didn't so much as breathe.

I drew myself up. "*I* wished to come here because I thought this was where the Ripper was. I am not ruled by my heart, sir. Nor am I running from my heartbreak. Coming to Chicago had nothing to do with what happened in New York." Even as I said it, I knew that wasn't entirely true. I was all too happy to rush from New York without a second thought. What he'd said about Thomas, though... I stepped forward, fists clenched at my sides. "And are you suggesting Thomas invented a lead for his benefit alone? You know him better than that, Uncle. He would never abuse your trust or our privilege—"

"It would not be the first time a young man has twisted the truth in order to get what he most wants." Uncle held up a hand, not permitting me any further liberty to speak. I was so angry I feared steam was spewing from my ears. "Find me proof that this is where Jack the Ripper is hunting now, or we'll return to New York by week's end." He met Thomas's gaze. "No matter how brilliant you are, Thomas, I'll deliver you back to London personally, should this have been an elaborate stunt to corrupt my niece."

THIRTY-ONE
DEVIL'S DOMINION

GRANDMAMA'S ESTATE
CHICAGO, ILLINOIS
10 FEBRUARY 1889

Sleet pelted the tin roof of our borrowed home, the drops steady and rhythmic. It took some getting used to at first, but soon it became comfortable background noise, almost lulling me to sleep despite our newest task. I took a sip of mint tea, relishing the fresh, clean taste. Thunder crashed in the distance, lighting the room in a flash of silvery white. I pulled my shawl closer. While I hadn't recently conjured up images of wolves or other dark creatures stalking the night, on evenings such as this, my mind played devilish tricks.

A second crash of thunder had me sucking in my breath. I looked at the window as the night sky was set ablaze. Thin lines of ice crept along the windowpane, as delicate as lace. Mother Nature was a fine seamstress, her stitches almost as carefully worked as mine when I closed up a corpse.

Thomas lifted his head from his own work, a slight smile starting. "Are you afraid of thunder, Wadsworth?" I gave him my most unpleasant look, not deigning to respond. He already teased me endlessly about clowns and spiders. "I wouldn't mind holding you under the covers until the storm passes. I would feel quite gentlemanly."

I inhaled sharply and the room felt as if it did, too. Images of our pre-wedding night flashed through my mind. Thomas watched me very carefully, his expression a mixture of desperate hope and unrelenting fear. Hope that I'd tease him back in our familiar way. And fear that I wouldn't, that his father had truly succeeded in driving us apart for good. My pause lasted only a moment, but it felt like forever.

"You would offer to do that, wouldn't you?" I said, finally collecting myself. "I'm surprised you didn't suggest we do so without our clothing. You're losing your Cresswell touch."

Relief instantly replaced the building tension in the room.

"Actually, I was about to suggest that next. And not for entirely selfish reasons, either." His expression was too innocent, which indicated trouble. "Did you know snuggling skin to skin releases endorphins which assist with increased brain activity? If we decide to forgo clothing and hold each other until the storm passes, we might solve this case faster."

"What medical journal did you read that in?" I narrowed my eyes. "I thought laying skin to skin was proven effective during hypothermia."

"Don't be cross with me." Thomas held his hands up. "I cannot help quoting scientific fact. If you'd prefer proof, we could we test this experiment out. Let's see who's right."

"Would that it were actual scientific fact and not an attempt for wanton follies, I might agree to it."

"What better kind of follies are there?"

My attention strayed to his lips, but I quickly banished any longing for them. If we didn't work on proving Chicago was the most likely place Jack the Ripper would strike next, I'd have to watch him leave for England to marry Miss Whitehall.

Ignoring that misery, I shoved the journal away. "Maybe Uncle is correct. Maybe the Ripper is truly dead and we're chasing his ghost."

"Or maybe he's here as Daciana and Ileana believe, and he's biding his time before he makes himself known." Thomas twisted in his chair, his fingers strumming along the tabletop. "I'm not sure if you've noticed, but my sister and I are fairly impressive when it comes to seeing the obvious and compiling an entire scenario from the slightest of hints."

"Your humility is also an attractive quality," I muttered. Thomas drew his brows together and I sighed. "You were about to impress me. Or you were boasting to yourself; it's hard to decipher sometimes."

"That's because it's often a bit of each, my love." He flashed a grin, then winced. Remembering to not call me his love was proving difficult. I wondered if his reaction was due to any shift in my expression. Each time I felt that invisible force punch my heart out. He stared down at his hands before glancing back up. "I've been thinking about Noah."

"Very productive to think of a different case while trying to prove you didn't fabricate an excuse to leave New York and your betrothed behind."

At the word "betrothed," his eyes darkened. He might not like the term or his intended, but until we found a way for him to be free of it, he belonged to another.

"Noah's case sparked an idea about ours. An angle we haven't considered. Your brother has several clippings of missing women scattered throughout his notes." He flipped his journal around, showing me an article. His flirtations were now gone, replaced by steadfast determination. "Why? Why would he bother making note of them if he wasn't responsible or if they weren't connected?"

I thought back to the man, Mr. Cigrande, who'd been convinced the devil had risen from Hell and stolen his daughter. It was highly probable that she'd simply had enough of his religious outbursts and had abandoned her old life. That was what Noah was trying to determine now.

261

"I admit the articles about missing women in London is a bit odd, even for my brother," I said. "But I'm afraid it's not enough proof for Uncle. We need something bigger—something he cannot possibly find fault with." I fiddled with my mother's ring. "He will not hesitate to make good on his promise. If Uncle feels we've lied to him, he'll drag you in chains back to England if he must. He despises deception."

"I haven't deceived anyone. In fact, I'm the one who's been deceived." Thomas blew out a frustrated breath, running his hand through his hair. "I loathe complications."

We fell back into silence, the sound of the storm and flipping pages our only talkative companions. I found a few more missing London women and added their names to my notes, not hopeful about their significance to this American case, but desperate for any links. As time dragged on, Thomas became more restless than usual.

He stood, paced about the room, and muttered to himself in Romanian. I worried he was becoming too agitated to find his calm center and see those clues only he could. If we didn't find a thread to tug on soon, this whole case would unravel before our very eyes.

I gently touched his arm, startling him. "Want to go adventuring tomorrow, Cresswell?"

"Do you feel that?" His agitation dissipated in the next breath. He pulled my hand to his chest. His heart gave an excited thump. "You make my dark heart sing, Wadsworth." He carefully turned my hand over, pressing a kiss to my palm. Electricity tingled over each nerve ending. I longed to touch him again, exploring as we'd done a few short nights ago. I curled my hand into a fist. I had no business wanting him as much as I did. "The real question is, would you care to go on an adventure with me *tonight*?"

I had a feeling he wasn't suggesting we go for a sleigh ride. My attention strayed to his lips; it would be so easy to pretend the last few days hadn't happened. But they had. I shook my head. "You know I can't do that, Thomas."

"Why?" he asked, brow crinkled.

"You know why," I hissed. "You are promised to another. We cannot succumb to wanton pleasures. Think of what it would do to our families."

"Can't we, though?" He brushed his thumb over my lower lip, his voice smooth and alluring in the dim light. "If the world thinks we're heading straight to Hell, we might as well enjoy the journey there. I'd rather dance with the devil than sing with angels. Wouldn't you?"

Hail tapped against the windowpanes, waiting for my response. I wasn't sure about angels or devils, but spending an evening with Thomas, alone, forgetting about our growing worries, was more appealing than it ought to be.

Sensing my wavering, Thomas dropped another kiss on my wrist, moving ever so slowly upward, his eyes fixed on mine. It was hard to tell who was in need of a distraction more. I thought of the notes I'd jotted down, of the girls who'd vanished in London. Most were my age or a little bit older. None had been given an opportunity to truly live. To explore themselves or the world around them. Life was short, precious. And could be snatched away by a villain when we least expected it. If tomorrow was never promised, then I'd seize today.

I tentatively reached over, running my fingers through his hair. If we didn't find information, he'd soon be gone from my life. I did not want to spend any more nights without him lying beside me. Our time could be extinguished in an instant. If I'd learned anything at all during our last few cases, it was to live each day in the present. I knotted my fingers in his hair, tugging him closer, worries of betrothals and complications melting into the past. He was right. We were already damned to Hell; it was silly to not at least enjoy our descent.

I brushed my lips against his, relishing the way his gaze darkened with the same longing I felt. I tipped his face up, wanting to fall into the depths of his rich brown eyes.

"Yes." I kissed him again, more fully. "I'd enjoy going on an adventure with you very much."

He gripped me by the waist, pressing me against the table, deepening our embrace until I worried we might not make it from this room before tearing each other's clothes from our backs. Most unexpectedly, he stepped away, his breathing uneven.

"Grab your coat. I'll go ready the hansom." His eyes sparkled with mischief as he rubbed his hands together. "You, my love, are in for quite a treat."

I stood there, mouth agape, trying to collect myself. It seemed our ideas of nighttime adventures were vastly different, though this turn was no less intriguing. After taking a few steady breaths, I called for my cloak.

⟨⚯⟩

Snow replaced ice and rain on our ride through the city, turning the buildings a riot of color. It was magnificent, seeing the multihued lights of theaters and saloons set against a backdrop of purity. Vices versus morals; the ultimate struggle of this city.

I glanced around, one hand gripping my cane, the other my cloak. While I'd envisioned cuddling in bed, Thomas had brought me to a rather questionable establishment. Snow covered much of the disrepair of the building like a thick layer of stage makeup hiding imperfections. Rats rustled in rubbish bins in the nearest alleyway.

"Well?" he asked. "Aren't you excited?"

I was cold, snowflakes were finding every chink in my wintry armor, and I'd no idea how this would aid our current investigation. Perhaps he'd brought us here to get stabbed for giggles. "You brought me to a bawdy saloon, Thomas. I'm not quite sure how I feel."

He grinned like there were more secrets he was keeping and held an arm out. "Once you sip some brandy and dance on the tables, I'm sure you'll feel fine."

"Honestly, what is your obsession with drinking spirits and dancing on tables?" I shook my head but followed him into the saloon, my curiosity piqued.

If the White City had been angelic, this saloon—appropriately named the Devil's Den—was most certainly its opposite in every way. The interior was like stepping into an empty body cavity or deep cavern—deep plum curtains, ebony walls, and a long bar made of a wood so dark it might have been inspired by the blackest of nights. I stared at it, noticing that carvings of devils with raven wings decorated each end.

Electrical chandeliers sat like spiderwebs above us, every other bulb burned out. Absinthe bottles glowed an unearthly green while looking glasses sat behind them, magnifying their etherealness. I expected there to be music, some hedonistic drumming, but the only symphony was the sound of voices.

Men and women chatted happily, if a bit drunkenly. Some women wore burlesque costumes; others were covered to their necks in finery. People from every class mingled, though some seemed more uneasy than others. There was almost something familiar about the—A young dark-haired man bumped into me, apologizing a bit too zealously.

"It's all right." I didn't spare him more than a quick glance. I was too worried I'd be swept into dancing the cancan like I'd done with the Moonlight Carnival. Which was exactly what this reminded me of—the performers-only party I'd attended on the *Etruria*. Thomas watched me carefully, his mouth twitching.

"What? Why are you smirking like that?"

He lifted a shoulder, his grin spreading.

"Let me buy you something to make up for my rudeness," the young man insisted. I'd already forgotten him. "Have you tasted the green fairy? She's quite delightful."

Pushing Thomas's amused expression away, I turned back on the drunken man, doing my best to hold both my tongue and cane in check. "That really won't be—*Mephistopheles?*"

THIRTY-TWO

THORNE IN MY SIDE

I blinked as if he were an illusion. He was not. There stood the young ringmaster of the Moonlight Carnival, as proud as a peacock, practically preening. "What on earth are you doing here?" I asked. He looked at Thomas, brows raised, and I braced myself. In any universe where they were conspiring, it meant trouble. "Did you arrange this meeting?" Thomas gave me a sheepish look. Letting that anomaly slide, I studied the ringmaster. "Where's your mask?"

"Safely tucked away for when we begin traveling again." He chuckled. "It's absolutely a joy to see you again, too, Miss Wadsworth." His dark eyes traveled to the ring on my finger as he took the liberty of kissing my hand. "Or is it Lady Cresswell now?"

I might have imagined it, but it seemed as if his question held a note of sadness. Misplaced if so, considering we'd only known each other for a little over a week.

"Easy now, Mephisto," Thomas interrupted. "She's not interested in your games or paltry two-bit bargains."

"*My* games?" he asked, rolling his eyes. "If I recall, Mr. Cresswell, you were the one who requested this meeting. And she seemed fond enough of our last bargain. I thought we'd become good friends." He sniffed as if injured. "It's rather rude, coming into my theater, spilling my drink, and flaunting your beautiful bride."

Before they could devolve into one of their ridiculous battles of wits, I cut in. "Your theater? What's going on?" I shifted my attention. "Thomas?"

Instead of responding straightaway, he studied the ringmaster. Another silent look passed between them. I found I didn't care for this newfound camaraderie at all. The two of them were too much for me on their own; together I didn't want to know what they could unleash.

"Do you remember what you said about Tesla earlier?" Thomas asked, catching me by surprise. "About his inventions?"

"Of course. But I still don't understand."

Mephistopheles signaled to someone across the room.

Faux lightning streaked around the darkened hall, hushing the crowd at once. Man-made thunder boomed, and the sound of waves crashing followed quickly after. People shifted, making their way toward a stage I hadn't initially noticed. A tapestry of a churning ocean hung from each wall of the room, as if we were all standing in the midst of a violent storm.

I glanced at Thomas. "What—"

"Boatswain!" cried an actor rushing onstage, silencing my questions.

"Here, master: what cheer?"

"You're putting on plays now?" I turned my attention on Mephistopheles, brows knitted. *The Tempest?*

"*Romeo and Juliet* seemed too macabre, though I needed some outlet these last couple of months." He motioned to someone before bending close, his breath tickling me. I leaned away.

Jian, the Knight of Swords, slapped me on the back in greeting, then handed the ringmaster a suit jacket studded with clear gemstones. Stars set in constellations. Andreas's old costume, I realized. As he quickly put it on, I spied thin wire crisscrossing on the interior portion of the coat. That was a new addition to it. He was up to more stage tricks.

Mephistopheles grinned. "Nikola's a good man. He's an even better showman."

"You've met Nikola Tesla?" My mouth practically hung open. "The *real* Nikola Tesla?"

"Well, he's certainly not the imposter Nikola. I've heard that guy is rather dull in comparison. We've spent some time together, exchanging notes." He nodded toward a contraption hanging above the stage. "You've heard of the Tesla coil, I presume?"

"Of course," I said, trying to work out the fact that Mephistopheles spoke of Tesla as if they were the best of friends. "It's supposed to be incredible."

Fake winds howled and the lights dimmed. "Ah"— Mephistopheles bowed—"that's my cue. Enjoy the show."

The curtains closed on the first scene and the ringmaster of the Moonlight Carnival disappeared behind them. I looked at Jian. "What was that about?"

"It's nice to see you, too." He gave me a sardonic smirk. "He moped around for weeks, you know. Human emotions are hard for him." Jian crossed his massive arms. "Now you'll see what he's been up to. He likes putting his energy into inventions, helps occupy his mind."

The curtains flew back as if on a huge breeze. Mephistopheles stood, his hands spread wide, as man-made thunder and lightning crashed and banged all around him and us. It was as if we were all part of the stage...lightning struck the ground in fizzling pops.

He thrust his head back, holding his arms toward the heavens. Veins of electricity buzzed from the contraption in the theater, snaking from his hands and shooting back out. He twirled about the stage, electricity flowing and bending from his fingertips as if he alone controlled the raging storm. As if he were the tempest.

"Prospero," Thomas whispered. "Of course he'd take on the role of a wicked sorcerer."

He turned his attention on me, though I could scarcely take my eyes from the stage. It was magnificent, witnessing such a machine up close. That explained the wires in the ringmaster's jacket—it attracted the bits of electricity to him. I longed to reach out and touch a whip of white-blue electricity myself, just to see if it tingled like I imagined it did. I'd read that Tesla's coils didn't harm anyone; the ropes of wild electricity were just for show.

Thomas kissed my cheek right as sparks flew like glitter from Mephistopheles's hands. I felt him smile against my skin. "Look at that, Wadsworth; when we kiss sparks literally fly."

I twisted around, cupping his face and laughing as we kissed again. "You certainly have a way of making the impossible possible. Thank you for this. I know you don't care for Ayden."

"I'm glad this didn't...disturb you," he said, biting his lip. "I-I wasn't sure if it would be another horrendous miscalculation."

I tore my gaze from the magic, noting the worry etched into his features. "Why did you think I'd be displeased? Because of Mephistopheles?"

"Your brother..."

He allowed the statement to sit long enough for me to piece together his meaning. I inhaled sharply. My brother's secret laboratory. The electricity that had shot through his body, leaving him convulsing on the floor. His death had been brutal. I hadn't been thinking of that at all. I glanced away, ashamed. Perhaps I truly was wicked. It should have been my first thought, not my last. Thomas wrapped an arm around me.

"Don't. It means you're healing, Audrey Rose. Cherish it. Don't condemn yourself for moving on, or for living."

I kissed Thomas sweetly, then stood in front of him, his hands anchoring me in place, while Miranda stepped onstage, demanding her father cease the tempest he'd started. I leaned my head against Thomas's chest, watching the storm rage. If only there were such things as sorcerers, I'd beg for a spell to find the devil before he struck again.

~⚬~

"Miss Wadsworth, Mr. Cresswell, I'd like to introduce you both to Miss Minnie Williams." Mephistopheles brought us backstage, where performers sat in silk robes, sipping tea or spirits and celebrating their nightly success. "She's an exceptional Miranda, but, alas, she's moving on to calmer shores."

Minnie wiped her makeup off, cheeks reddening from the damp washcloth. "Henry doesn't care for theatrics. He thinks they're beneath us. We're to be married this week, and I can't very well go around displeasing him."

She plucked a leaf from her hair, disposing of it on her dressing table. It must have been a leftover from the man-made tempest. True to his attention to detail, Mephistopheles had created an entire island of magic within the saloon's walls. No wonder the Devil's Den was the most popular destination in this part of the city.

"Plus," Minnie continued, "it's not as if I won't have anything to do. He's promised me I can be a stenographer. It's not the stage, but it's important work."

"Mm-hm. Very." Mephistopheles kicked his boots up onto the table, the leather gleaming as usual. "So? What did you make of the coil? It's got that 'razzle-dazzle' Houdini's always going on about. A real show-stopper. In recent shows, I've had half a dozen women—and men—require smelling salts after witnessing the electricity whip about like serpents."

"It is quite…shocking." That earned a groan from both Thomas and the ringmaster. Clearly they didn't appreciate good humor. "Is Harry here?" I asked, thinking of my cousin. She'd had little choice but to stay in New York with my aunt. I wasn't sure how she'd feel if she knew Houdini was here and she wasn't. "I didn't see the others."

"Not to worry, dear; they're all still employed by yours truly. This is a temporary stop for the Moonlight Carnival. We're heading to Paris next. I've got them spread out, going to other shows, learning new tricks we might improve upon. It's always best to study your competition, then obliterate it."

"So you're paying them to spy for you."

"Spying, learning"—he shrugged—"really, what's the difference? Anishaa's been studying that Wild West nonsense Buffalo Bill Cody's got set up." He blew out a breath. "She's become friends with one of his gun-wielding performers. An Annie something or other. Now Anishaa wishes to target practice with Jian. I supposed she could breathe fire while shooting, might be some sort of way we can spin it. What do you think of a fire-breathing sharp-shooting dragon?"

"I—"

"Not to interrupt," Minnie said, stuffing her arms into a heavy overcoat, "but I must be on my way. It was lovely meeting you both." She smiled at Thomas, then kissed each of my cheeks. "If you're ever near 63rd Street, do pop in for a chat. I'll be working at the pharmacy counter there while I take my course. I'd love to see you again. I just moved here from Boston and it would be wonderful to have a friend."

"I should like that," I said, hoping I'd be able to keep my promise.

Mephistopheles waved her off as she left. "One more woman running off with another man. I'm losing my touch."

"Have you considered you might be a Thorne in their sides?" Thomas asked. "You certainly can be a pric—"

"Thomas," I whispered harshly, pinching the inside of his elbow.

"How clever," Mephistopheles said blandly. "You've made my name into a pun. What other comedic brilliance will you think of next? I wish I could say I missed this"—he motioned between himself and Thomas—"but that sort of lying doesn't pay my bills."

"Nor do the gemstones on your suits," Thomas muttered.

"Are you still jealous about my jackets?" Mephistopheles grinned.

"For the love of the queen," I said, interrupting before they really got into it. "If we're moving on to more stimulating subjects, have you heard about the murder in New York?"

The cool, cavalier persona Mephistopheles had adopted was gone the instant his boots smacked the ground. He stood so abruptly, his chair knocked over. "Oh, no. No, no, no, my dear. It was lovely seeing you, lovelier still if you'd left that one at home"—he jerked his chin toward Thomas—"but I can't involve myself in any more of your brand of debauchery."

"*My* brand of debauchery?"

"Death-*defying* is wonderful. Death on its own is wretched for my line of work."

"Please," I said. "Just hear us out."

Mephistopheles crossed his arms. "Tell me why I ought to."

"I need you," I said, hating that I was desperate enough to utter those words.

He didn't so much as blink for a beat too long. When he finally did, his lip curled devilishly as he slid Thomas a taunting look. "Ah. I see I haven't lost my charm yet. Most women I meet say the same thing, usually whilst scantily clad. Should we remove a few of those pesky layers? It'll help clear my mind. Get me in the mood for charity."

"Only if you'd like me to strangle you with them."

"Still so violent I see." He lifted a shoulder. "I'm sure you make Thomas a very happy man. I always imagined his tastes were a bit depraved—what with all those dead bodies." Thomas plastered on a grin of his own but remained silent. Mephistopheles narrowed his eyes. "Did you two *actually* fall in love surrounded by corpses?"

"Don't be ridiculous. We—" I shut my mouth. Distilled down to its most basic element, Thomas and I had continued a flirtation in the laboratory. It could be argued we *did* fall in love while carving the dead. The thought was disturbing.

"You're both twisted and gnarled in ways too gruesome for even my mind." Mephistopheles grinned as if reading my thoughts. "You truly are perfectly matched."

"You're avoiding my inquiry," I said.

His smile vanished as if it had never been there to begin with. I couldn't stop myself from shivering in place. He was talented with casting illusions, almost too talented.

"Am I? I thought I'd been perfectly clear."

He ushered us out through the back doors of the theater, sticking two fingers in his mouth, whistling for our carriage. A shadow peeled off the wall, lurching toward us. I closed my eyes briefly, worried I'd imagined it. I opened them and it was gone.

My heartbeat continued to race despite the fact that there wasn't anyone lurking in the darkness, waiting to attack.

"While I hate ending our little rendezvous, you'll have to solve whatever mess you've gotten into this time on your own. I'm truly sorry, Miss Wadsworth, but I must look after the Moonlight Carnival. We were lucky to recover from that cursed voyage, having lost only one of our troupe. Getting mixed up with more murder will send us straight to the grave. No pun intended."

THIRTY-THREE
THIS DEVILISH PURSUIT

GRANDMAMA'S ESTATE
CHICAGO, ILLINOIS
11 FEBRUARY 1889

Once the maid finished helping me change into my sleeping attire, I lay back on the bed, going over the events of the evening. Mephistopheles's reaction had been odd, especially for the normally boisterous ringmaster. He'd never seemed to mind causing trouble or involving himself in it before, though maybe his reluctance was simply out of fear. The last investigation nearly ended his carnival for good. I supposed I ought to be happy for him—he'd rebuilt his illusions and was doing quite well. Still, I couldn't rid myself of unease.

Thomas slipped in like a shadow slinking around corners. I shook my head and turned the small lamp on, watching as he balanced an entire cake with two glasses of milk on one small tray. I moved over, making room on the bed for our midnight treat. He handed me a fork, his smile wide and bright. "I'm not sure how you're faring, but I'm exhausted."

"You're not too tired for cake," I said. Or for sneaking into my bedchamber.

"I'm never too tired for cake. Especially when it's chocolate."

I watched him dig into the fluffy confectionary, his concentration solely on the task of carving it up without a knife. I huffed a laugh and handed him a scalpel from my satchel. "Thank you for tonight, Thomas. I really enjoyed the play."

He flicked his attention to me, shrugging off the compliment. "Being selfless is terribly taxing. I don't suggest trying it."

I took a fork from him and tasted the treat. Chocolate and cherry tonight. I stuck another forkful in, enjoying its richness. "I'm surprised you didn't bring champagne. Aren't you always going on about getting drunk and dancing most inappropriately?"

"Why indulge in spirits when there's nothing more heavenly than chocolate?"

"Mmm." He did have a point. We sat in companionable silence, each happily finishing off our slices. It was nice, having him here at night, sitting together and doing something as mundane as indulging in a late-night treat. He finished his piece and stared longingly as I savored my last two bites. If the devil thought he was getting any of my cake, he was sadly mistaken. I was most unladylike as I licked my fork clean of icing. His dark gaze was suddenly entranced by the motion and I realized my misstep. My cheeks pinked.

"Why did you really take me to see that show tonight?" I asked, handing him my empty plate. "It wasn't simply for the Tesla coil, was it?"

"In truth?" Thomas stacked our dishes and set them on my nightstand. "I wanted you to see Mephisto again. Especially after everything that happened with my father and Miss Whitehall. I—" He glanced at his empty ring finger almost ruefully. "I'd heard he was here and didn't wish to keep it from you."

I narrowed my eyes. "And?"

"You're really getting quite good at reading me, Wadsworth. Too good." He leaned against the wooden headboard, smiling. "He still has feelings for you. That much is plainly obvious. I hoped he might be swayed to at least listen for any news about murders. He's got eyes and ears all over the lowly parts of the city. If anyone might know anything, much as I loathe to admit it, it's him."

"I see. So you decided to use me as bait in your little scheme? Your romantic gestures truly are something to behold, Cresswell. Be careful. You might kill me from swooning so hard."

His gaze swept from my crossed arms to my turned-down mouth. It didn't take his skill in deductions to figure out how annoyed I was. He held his hands up. "The main reason was to show you the Tesla coil. I know how much you wished to see Tesla perform it himself. I won't deny the added bonus of speaking with Mephisto about the case and seeing if he could assist." Thomas inched closer. "Trust me, I don't want to be selfless. Not with you. But I'll always stand aside so you have the space to make your own choices."

The sincerity in his voice and his expression softened my ire. He had much to learn about partnership and going about things in a more respectable manner, but he loved me enough to try.

"No more schemes unless I'm part of them, agreed?" He nodded. "Do you believe Mephistopheles will really involve himself in this? He didn't seem likely to, given how quickly he kicked us out once we'd asked."

Thomas held the covers up, an invitation to my own bed. I stared at the spot, pulse trickling into a flood of emotions. He didn't move, nor did he pressure me in any way to join him. He kept his focus on me, waiting to see if I decided to snuggle beside him.

"Thomas..."

"If you want me to leave, I will. No questions or guilt."

He made to get up, but I placed my hand on his arm, stalling his movement. I bit my lip, glancing around the empty room. I told myself we were mature enough to handle snuggling next to each other, and without further hesitation, I crawled into bed beside him. He carefully tucked us both in, his attention so palpable I swore it undressed me by itself.

This was a dangerous game we were playing. He'd need to be up and in his own room before the maid came in to light the fire. Or before Uncle called on us.

"Didn't you notice him whistle?" he asked, changing the subject.

I blinked, trying to focus on something more important than my raging heartbeat. Or the curve of Thomas's treacherous mouth when he noticed my attention on it.

"Of course I noticed. He nearly made my eardrums burst with all the racket." I rubbed my ear as if I could still hear the phantom ringing. "He was calling for a carriage."

"Oh?" Thomas drew closer. His warmth was much more enticing than any fire. I nestled against him, relishing the total calm. "Was that what he was doing? Strange, since I'd instructed our coachman to wait in that alley for us. Stranger still that when he went back inside, someone else slipped in behind him."

My pulse picked up speed that had a little to do with our conversation. I was recalling the way it had felt when Thomas lightly pressed his lips to the sensitive skin at my throat. And how much I longed for him to do it again. It was becoming harder to concentrate with him so near. "You believe he'll inquire around for us, despite his protests?"

Thomas played with the ribbons on my nightgown, his gaze fixed on mine. "Not for us. For you. I expect we'll hear from him once he's done his own snooping."

He took hold of one ribbon, slowly pulling it free. I wasn't sure what he was distracting me from. Maybe he simply couldn't hold himself back any longer, either. Perhaps we were both tired of fighting against our wicked hearts. He waited, ever a gentleman in this one area, for me to change my mind. No matter that we had shared a bed before; he would ask permission each time. Perhaps it was his consideration, or perhaps it was my own desire, but I moved my shoulder, allowing my nightgown to slip down and expose a swath of skin, successfully reigniting the fire in his gaze. I should tell him to go. To sleep in his own chambers. To stop this devilish pursuit until we were both free to do as we wanted, whenever we wanted.

We were being reckless with our hearts and it would only lead to breaking them further. He needed to leave at once. Instead, I unbuttoned his shirt.

I was no devil, but I never claimed to be an angel, either.

"Now, I recall a discussion regarding another adventure." He brought his mouth to mine, soft, teasing, and wholly intoxicating. "Before we left for the play, you seemed to want—"

"—you, Thomas."

I pulled him to me, silencing him with a kiss. He needed no further instruction or permission. Tonight was about forgetting the rules. There was no right or wrong. Nothing but the two of us, giving into our base desires. He had us both out of our clothes faster and more efficiently than any sorcerer casting a spell.

"Audrey Rose."

He whispered across my skin, murmuring my name until I lost all sense of time and place. I gripped him, never wishing for us to part. I'd choose Hell each time if it meant experiencing this feeling with him. This euphoria. I refused to think of darkness and evil deeds.

Tonight I'd focus on the way our bodies created the closest thing to Heaven I could imagine here on earth. I'd tried doing the correct thing: I'd pushed him away and my heart had torn in two. I was tired of denying what felt right. He and I were two pieces of our own private puzzle—we fit together perfectly.

If that made us wicked, wanton things, so be it. I gladly accepted my fate.

THIRTY-FOUR

WICKED SOULS

THE CENTRAL DEPOT
CHICAGO, ILLINOIS
12 FEBRUARY 1889

Noah eyed the journals piled on our table, brow raised. Mine were stacked neatly before me, while Thomas's were in haphazard heaps, ready to topple over if he so much as sneezed. Noah shook his head. "I was hoping you two might be able to talk out some of these facts with me."

I shifted my attention to a satchel he'd tucked under an arm. Crinkled papers poked out from the top end, trying to escape the volume he'd stuffed into the small leather case. I glanced at Thomas. If we didn't convince Uncle we were in the right city hunting the real Jack the Ripper, we'd be on a train for New York before we could blink.

"Noah, I'm sorry. We'd assist if we could; it's just"—I motioned to the disarray around us—"we're buried at the moment."

Thomas set his text down. The challenge of solving another mystery was too alluring for him, it seemed. He held his hand out. "What have you got?"

"Not a lot of facts, but a lot of chaos." Noah grinned as he rushed around the table, pulling notes out and scattering them like entrails. I went back to my own task, ignoring the twinge of worry that we were doomed to let the Ripper slip away once again. "Mr. Cigrande says the devil took his daughter, right? That demons sneak around, capturing women as prey. It sounds like the rantings of a madman, until you notice this." Curious, I glanced up as he pushed a newspaper toward Thomas. "Here's another woman. Missing. Same age and appearance as Miss Cigrande." He pulled another paper. "And this woman. And another. Every week, multiple women are reported missing to the police, but nothing's being done."

Thomas read the papers, frowning. "You said Mr. Cigrande claimed to witness the devil or a demon abduct a woman?"

"Yes." Noah nodded, swallowing hard. "He said he saw a devil coax a young woman into a streetcar, took a package she was carrying, acted like a gentleman."

"I imagine that's true." Thomas pushed his chair back, the limbs screeching over the hardwood. He walked to the fire, staring blankly into it. It was fitting, watching him get lost within an inferno while speaking of capturing the devil.

Fully intrigued with this new mystery, I leaned across the table. If there were a large number of missing women, we might have finally located a connection to our crimes. Maybe the Ripper *was* involved. Perhaps either his tactics had changed—as we'd feared earlier—or he was getting better at hiding the bodies. "Would you mind if I took a look at that?"

"Not at all," Noah said, sounding relieved. "Any help or ideas you can offer will be greatly useful. I can't, for the life of me, figure out where to search next."

I rummaged through the leather satchel, which contained page after page of reports of missing women. My blood chilled. There were nearly a dozen families begging Chicago to help find their daughters and wives.

"The police haven't investigated any of these?" I asked, flipping through more documents.

"Not a one of them." Noah shook his head. "Mr. Cigrande, mad as he may seem, marched himself into our agency, demanding we find his daughter. Then he started in with the demon-snatching nonsense, but with a little poking around, it doesn't seem so far-fetched."

A demon might not be truly stalking the Chicago streets for prey, but a different sort of monster was.

"Radu." Thomas abruptly faced us, his jaw set.

Noah and I exchanged worried glances. Perhaps Thomas needed to get some rest—he'd been under severe stress and it was obviously affecting his senses.

"He was an interesting man," I said. It was a kindness, really. Professor Radu had been our folklore instructor back at the forensics academy in Romania. He'd filled our heads with stories of vampires and werewolves—legends and myths he claimed weren't strictly fantasy. Why in the name of the queen Thomas was thinking of him at a time such as this was beyond me. Though, knowing him, he had his reasons. "I thought you were considering the missing women. How does Radu fit in?"

"Fantastical stories about horrific events take a person out of their terror—they're removed from it—therefore, we must pay close attention to the monsters he describes. They aren't fantasy at all." Thomas picked his cloak up from the back of his chair and addressed Noah. "I need to speak with Mr. Cigrande myself. Will you take us to him?"

Mr. Cigrande was hunched against the wind, his ungloved hands raw and cracked as he shook his bell at young women exiting the train depot. "Go back to your homes, heathens! The devil is coming for you! Run! Run while you're still able!"

The constant clanging of the bell was bringing on a massive head-ache and the icy wind whipping down the avenue wasn't helping to alleviate my growing discomfort. I held on to Thomas with one hand and my cane with the other while Noah walked along beside us.

"Let's inquire about a demon, shall we?" I asked.

Thomas's mouth quirked, but he didn't entertain me or Noah with any of his usual wit. His mind was now fully engaged in solving this new mystery. I could only hope it would unlock another clue for us as well. There *had* to be a connection to these cases.

Noah made his way to Mr. Cigrande first, waving as we all gath-ered around him. "Mr. Cigrande, I'd like to introduce you to—"

"Heathens!" The poor man shivered in place. "I won't talk to wicked souls."

"These wicked souls are good with locating impossible clues. If you'd like a better shot at finding your daughter, you'll reconsider," Noah said, his tone sharpening. "It might behoove you to speak with them."

Mr. Cigrande cast a suspicious look our way. I mentally counted to five; poking him with my cane wouldn't solve my problem of being deemed a heathen. I looked about for a way to get us all off the street, away from distractions. A sign fashioned to look like a teapot hung from the awning of one business. I pulled my shoulders back, adopt-ing my best posture for my best attempt at soothing him.

"Would you like to speak someplace warm? There's a little tea-room just over there." I nodded two doors down, saying prayers of thanks for the establishment being so close. "They advertise melted chocolate and milk. Might be fortifying if you've planned a long afternoon of..."

I bit my lip, at a loss for how to describe his screaming at young women. Blessedly, Mother Nature aided our endeavor by opening up the skies, shaking snow and bits of ice out of the clouds. Cold, miserable, and now wet, Mr. Cigrande grudgingly followed us into the warm tearoom. Freshly baked scones and buttery scents welcomed us in from the cold. I had no sooner inhaled the aroma when Thomas marched over to a glass display filled with tarts and tea cakes.

"Once you've finished your unholy flirtation with the dessert, you can join us at our table, Cresswell."

"Don't be jealous, my love. I assure you, nothing tastes as sweet as you."

His eyes flashed with amusement while I did my best imitation of Mr. Cigrande and cursed him under my breath. I quickly ushered Noah and Mr. Cigrande to a table in the corner, hoping we'd be far enough away from any poor, unsuspecting patrons who'd be harassed by either a religious zealot or my fiendish Thomas.

A few servers came to our table and offered choices of hot and cold breakfast items along with cake and biscuits and all manner of curds and puddings. I snagged a few pieces of bacon, an orange, and a soda scone. It truly was a treat to enjoy an orange during this season. I didn't know how they'd managed to get such fruit but was immensely grateful for their magic. Another server presented a chocolate pot for the table and I quickly nodded, my mouth watering for the richness of melted chocolate and frothy milk. Thomas wasn't the only one who enjoyed sweets.

"I'd like to know about the demons," Thomas said bluntly once he'd sat down. He popped a berry into his mouth, then poured some hot chocolate into his cup. "What do you recall of them?"

"*Them?*" Mr. Cigrande stared at Thomas as if he'd escaped from an asylum. "What them? I only saw one demon. And seeing one demon is enough for anyone."

"Apologies," Thomas said. "Describe the demon to me. Try and recall every detail, even the smallest."

Mr. Cigrande held fast to his mug of hot chocolate, his expression wary. "He looked like a regular man. A young man. Handsome, like you, but not in the way Lucifer is usually described in scripture. His eyes, though. They was something. That's how I knew he was a demon."

Noah drew in a breath but remained silent as Thomas subtly shook his head. "What about his eyes let you know his true self?"

Mr. Cigrande stared into his drink, mouth drawn into a frown. Without his bell and anger, he appeared to be a man who had as many wrinkles as gray hairs. He was worn and frail, his face covered in white whiskers. Much less imposing than he seemed while hollering at passersby.

"When he looked at me?" he said, meeting each of our gazes. "It was like staring into the eyes of a dead man. It's cold out, but those eyes..." He huddled into his coat. "They sent shivers down my back. They were like blades. Like he could see every thought in my head and knew exactly how to cut them outta me."

"Hmm. I bet his eyes were as pale as the ocean," Thomas said, doing that unnerving thing where he was now half in the mind of the so-called demon and half reading the impossible clues no one else bothered seeing.

Mr. Cigrande startled back from the table. "How did you know?"

"Are light blue eyes the best way to spot a demon?" Thomas asked, not delving into the complicated science of his deductions.

"Not just a demon," Mr. Cigrande said. "The devil himself. Only a creature of Hell could tempt those poor girls away." He shook his head, the color in his face flushing brighter. "I watched him for a bit, you know. Once I knew what he was. I watched him real close." He leaned across the table, glancing about the bustling tearoom. "He doesn't act like no demon; that's for sure. When he stole that last girl's soul? He seemed as angelic as anything. Asking if she needed help, if she was new to the city. He preys on the wayward ones. The wanton ones who've left God and their families. They're easy pickin'. That's why I try and scare them away."

"Do you believe good women who stay in their homes and memorize their scripture are safe from the devil?" Thomas asked. His eyes flicked to mine, silently asking for me to hold my tongue. I was more than happy to allow him the pleasure of having this conversation on his own. "The wicked are the only ones in danger?"

"Don't be crazy," the old man said. "Why would the wicked ones be in danger? They's already wicked." He folded and unfolded his napkin. "Women are safe at home. They can be watched after, cared for. They don't know what sort of sins await them in the world. The devil don't want the bad ones, mister. The devil wants to collect 'em before they turn wicked on their own. He needs 'em good. Otherwise, what's there to corrupt?"

"And the demons? What do they want?"

"To take more souls to the devil. They want to please him so he doesn't do his nasty tricks on them."

"What sort of nasty tricks do you believe he's doing?" I asked. "Aside from stealing them."

"What else?" Mr. Cigrande shifted in his seat, facing me. "He brings them to his castle in Hell and they never return."

Noah sent Mr. Cigrande home with promises to call on him the moment he discovered any news of his missing daughter. Thomas and I climbed into our carriage, and while we waited for our friend to join us, Thomas arranged the heating brick so I could rest my leg upon it.

"Well? What do you make of the demon?" I asked, stifling a moan. The heat felt lovely.

He settled the blanket around us, then stared out at the sidewalk.

I followed his gaze, noticing swirls in the light dusting of snow that reminded me of serpents slithering through it.

"He saw a man with blue eyes talk to a woman on the street," Thomas said. "That much I believe is fact. The issue I'm struggling with is his claim of seeing the same man with another woman, doing the same act."

"Do you think it's a fabrication?"

"No. His behavior was quite easy to read. Weren't you observing…" Thomas shook his head at my scowl. "Apologies, Wadsworth. What I mean is, when I asked about the demon's acts, Mr. Cigrande was able to give them without moving about. When asked about the devil or his desires, he had to think. To make up his own idea of what Satan might be after. It wasn't information he'd seen firsthand. I couldn't deduce if he'd truly witnessed the same man luring another woman away, or if he'd replayed it in his mind so often he confused the facts."

"Let's argue the facts, then," I suggested. "If what he claims is correct, how will that assist in us finding the man he claims is the demon?"

Noah rushed back to the carriage, clapping his hands for warmth. "Sorry. What do you think?"

"We were just trying to figure that out now," I said. "It's something."

The carriage driver snapped his reins, urging the horses into a trot.

"If he can recall where he saw the man abduct that first woman"— Thomas braced himself against the jostling of our ride—"you ought to sit nearby and wait. See if the kidnapper's brazen enough to return. He may or may not be telling the truth about the demon revisiting the site. It's worth investigating at the very least."

Noah flashed a skeptical look, his mouth pinched tight. "I don't see how anyone would be foolish enough to commit the same act twice in the same location."

"It's part of his fun," Thomas said. "The hunt is thrilling, but so is the idea of potentially getting caught. This man is besotted with the unknown. It's dangerous. Tantalizing. It makes his heart pound and his loins ache with desire."

I scrunched my nose, not wanting to think of anyone's loins, aching or otherwise. Silence filled our carriage, broken up by the clomping of hooves on cobblestones. I turned the events of this new mystery over in my mind, working out all the oddities. As much as I loathed to think such a thing, if we had a body to study I'd feel more confident in my own theories.

"Do you believe he's holding them captive?" I asked, already dreading the answer I knew was coming.

Thomas dropped his gaze to mine. "Perhaps for a time."

"So?" Noah asked. "What does he do next? Let them go?"

"He murders them." Thomas didn't notice the color leach from our friend's face. Or if he did, he paid it no mind. There was no such thing as delicacy when it came to murder. "I'm sorry to say, my friend, but this is a career murderer. It's likely no simple missing persons case."

I looked at Thomas, searching his expression for anything he wasn't saying. When he met my gaze, my stomach dropped. This career murderer was undoubtedly the same one we sought.

Poor Noah was unaware he was now tracking the most notorious killer of our time.

THIRTY-FIVE
DARK CREATURES

GRANDMAMA'S ESTATE
CHICAGO, ILLINOIS
12 FEBRUARY 1889

It seemed a terrible contrast to be so cozy and snug while reading about missing women who were probably dead. I stared down at my notes, nearly going cross-eyed trying to find a substantial clue that might link our case to Noah's. The missing women were of ages ranging from nineteen to thirty. Hair color and build varied as much as their backgrounds. The only connection they seemed to share was that they all up and vanished one day, never to be heard from again.

I hadn't realized I'd pressed my nib so hard until ink splattered across the page. I glanced up sheepishly, but Thomas seemed more worried than amused. Honestly, I was growing more worried with each passing hour, too.

Purplish black shadows under my eyes gave away how little I'd been sleeping. Though I was exhausted each night, my mind never ceased. It was a constant wheel of tension. Nathaniel. Jack the Ripper. Miss Whitehall. His Grace, Lord Cresswell. Missing women. Thomas. Uncle. Each person brought on their own set of worries until I was sitting up in bed, gasping for breath.

"I believe we ought to set this aside for tomorrow," Thomas said, his attention still fixed on my face. Knowing him, he probably read each of my thoughts before I even had them. "It's getting late, and while you may not require beauty's rest, I like to keep myself as pretty as possible."

I nearly snorted. Sleep. As if I could tumble blissfully into the arms of rest when my world was utter chaos. I flipped to the next page of my brother's journal and hesitated. It was the only page that had been folded over on itself—almost as if it were hiding.

Or marking the spot for someone to easily find.

"Audrey Rose?"

"Hmm?" I glanced up briefly, turning my attention straight back to the journal. A note scrawled in my brother's hand stared back at me. It almost read like a poem, though it was only the same sentence written on different lines in different intervals.

A burning sensation gnawed at the pit of my stomach.

i am guilty
of many sins, though
murder is
not one of them.
i am guilty of many sins,
though murder is not one of them.
i am guilty of many sins, though murder is not one
of them.

If this were true...I closed my eyes against the sudden feeling of the ceiling dropping down. I breathed in slowly and let it out. If I didn't calm myself now, I'd experience those waking terrors again. But if Nathaniel was being honest...

"I said I'm turning in for the evening, Wadsworth. Would you care to join me?"

"Mmmh." I tapped the end of my pen against the table; it was strange for my brother to have so many articles about missing women if he *didn't* harm them. I still didn't understand his role in this mess, but by his own hand, he hadn't murdered anyone. Whether or not he could be believed was another story altogether. It might simply be another well-constructed mask he'd created to disguise who he truly was.

"I've decided to farm spiders. I think training them to dance to show tunes will bring in a hefty sum. It may also cure me of my phobia. Unless you think dancing roosters are better."

I tucked a stray strand of hair behind my ear, half listening to Thomas and half staring at the confession. The more I uncovered, the less I knew anything for certain.

"Once, I hung naked upside down from the rafters, pretending to be a bat. Isn't that interesting?"

"Mm-hm?"

"Wadsworth. I have a confession to make. It's something I ought to have mentioned sooner. I am shamelessly addicted to reading romance novels. I may even shed a tear or two at their conclusion. What can I say? I'm a fool for a happy ending."

"I know." I pulled my attention from the journal and fought a smile. "Liza told me."

"That scourge!" He feigned being upset, clearly pleased he'd wrested me from work. "She promised to not say a word."

"Oh, not to worry, my friend. She more or less just showed me your secret stash under the bed. *Ravished and Ravenous* sounded like an interesting read. Would you care to discuss it?"

A troublesome smile played over his lips. If I expected him to feel shy about his reading tastes, I was hopelessly mistaken. "I'd much prefer to show you how it ends."

"Thomas," I warned. He mimed locking his mouth and instead of tossing away his imaginary key, he placed it in his inside pocket, patting the front of his jacket. "What do you make of this? *'I am guilty of many sins, though murder is not one of them.'*"

"Your brother wrote that?" Thomas scratched the side of his head. "Honestly, I don't know what to make of it. Nathaniel seemed to be Jack the Ripper, especially when we confronted him that night in his laboratory. Since we've got more murders done by the same hand, and he is most certainly deceased, we now know that his involvement in the actual slayings was a lie. At least in part. Who knows what else he's lied about?"

Frustrated, I returned to my work. I wasn't sure how long had passed, perhaps only minutes, but a similarity finally caught my attention. I set my journal aside and searched the newspaper. *There.* Quite a few of the women in both London and Chicago were either off to work or inquiring after a job. It was a tiny connection, but it was the only one that might be worth following. I read over the article about the latest missing woman in Chicago.

Her last known whereabouts was exiting the train near the World's Fair. I scribbled her information down, hating that there wasn't more to do. I wanted to scour the streets, knocking on doors and demanding people take notice. These were daughters. Sisters. Friends. They were people who were loved and missed. A few moments later, I found another missing notification. A Julia Smythe. She and her young daughter, Pearl, hadn't been seen since Christmas Eve.

I scribbled another note. Thomas fell asleep at the table, arms sprawled out in front of him, snoring ever so slightly. Despite my work, I grinned.

An hour later, the fire popped, waking him. He glanced around, coming alert as if someone had snuck into this room and attacked us. Once he relaxed and fully woke up, he settled his attention on me. "What is it?"

I pushed over several articles I'd clipped out from the papers.

"Why don't the police care?" I asked. "Why aren't more people out combing the streets?" I held up my parchment. On it alone there were nearly thirty women, gone in the span of a few weeks. "This is absurd. At this rate, a few hundred will have vanished in a year's time. When will it be enough for them to investigate?"

"Do you recall what happened when the lights all came on at once at the fair?" Thomas asked, all traces of tiredness now gone.

It was an odd segue, but I nodded and played along. "People wept. Some said it was magic—the most beautiful thing they'd ever seen."

"You know why they cried? That fair is quite literally a shining achievement of both art and science. The most talented people in America have poured their blood into making it one of the most surreal places ever to be seen. The Ferris Wheel alone is one of the most incredible feats of engineering. Over twenty-one hundred passengers can ride it at once, soaring nearly three hundred feet into the sky. If something that large can be done, anything is possible. What is the Gilded Age, if not dreams dipped in gold and outlandish fantasy sprung to life?" He shook his head. "If the police admitted there were a staggering number of young women missing, it would be a stain on this place, the ultimate American Dream. Their White City would morph into a den of sin. A reputation Chicago is desperate to mend."

"It's awful," I said. "Who cares if the White City gets stained? A man—most probably Jack the Ripper—is hunting women. Why doesn't that take precedence over some silly dream?"

"I imagine it's similar to war—there are always casualties and sacrifices that are made. We happen to live during a time when young, independent women are seen as expendable when pitted against greed. What are a few 'morally compromised' women in the face of dreams?"

"Wonderful. So the greed of men can condemn innocent women and we all ought to sit quietly and not utter a word."

"Unfortunately, I don't believe it's just men who want to keep this illusion up. This is a puritan nation, built upon strict religious notions of good and evil. To admit the devil walked these streets would acknowledge their greatest fears. Something that *looked* like the Kingdom of Heaven was actually the devil's dominion. Imagine what that realization would do? No place would feel safe anymore. Hope would be replaced by fear. Night would descend forever. If there's one thing man cherishes above greed, it's hope. Without it, people would cease to dream. Without dreamers, civilizations crash. Think about the police inspector in New York. One hint that the Ripper was in his city sent him spiraling into chaos."

I stared at the fireplace, watching flames lurch up and devour the shadows. Light and dark, forever in conflict. Our task suddenly felt more daunting than usual. I knew confidence when holding a scalpel and demanding clues from flesh. But there were no bodies to inquire after. No physical mystery to dissect.

"What about those missing women? What of their dreams?" I asked quietly. "This city was supposed to be their escape, too."

Thomas was quiet a moment. "Which is all the more reason for us to fight for them now."

I grabbed my paper, renewed in our mission. If a fight was what this murderer was after, a fight was precisely what he'd get. I'd not give up until breath left my body.

It was near midnight when I spotted a detail I'd overlooked. Miss

Julia Smythe, the missing woman with a child, had last been seen leaving her job at a pharmacy jewelry counter in the Englewood section of Chicago. I rubbed at my eyes. It wasn't much, but at least we had a goal for tomorrow—a hint of a plan. We could inquire around that neighborhood and see if anyone saw anything out of the ordinary.

Thomas watched, his gaze questioning, as I picked up the pieces of newspaper clippings and tucked them into Nathaniel's journals that also contained missing women.

"I'm bringing this to Uncle," I said. "He's the one who's taught us about there being no coincidences in murder. If he was unsure of the *Frankenstein* code, then this will be a bit harder for him to ignore. Something *is* happening here. It's only a matter of time before bodies turn up."

T. XLII.

99

100

102

101

Gem v. A. Gerasch Lith v. F. Gerasch   Verlag CARL GEROLD'S SOHN. Wien.   K. k. Hof Chromolith. v. Ant. Hartinger & Sohn Wien
Jede Art Vervielfältigung vorbehalten.

Birds of the crow family: four figures, including a crow, a raven and a rook

THIRTY-SIX
MURDER OF CROWS

SOUTH SIDE
CHICAGO, ILLINOIS
13 FEBRUARY 1889

Uncle, Thomas, and I walked into police headquarters, appearing like a murder of crows, swooping in with our black cloaks and sharp eyes. The sound of my cane reminded me of the *tapping* of Edgar Allan Poe's famous raven. I hoped the Chicago police would fear us haunting them forevermore should they ignore our evidence. Someone had to hold them accountable for their lack of effort. I was thrilled Uncle was back on our side.

It hadn't taken him long to start twisting the ends of his mustache when I'd showed him each piece of new evidence. He'd agreed: there was undoubtedly a career murderer stalking these streets. Young women didn't simply vanish on their own. At least not in the staggering numbers of the last few weeks. Someone was preying on them.

A lack of bodies troubled Uncle. He wondered where the murderer kept them. Surely he hadn't dug over thirty graves within the city of Chicago. So where were they? He didn't want to connect the crimes to Jack the Ripper without further proof, but even he couldn't deny the underlying suspicion that we were getting close. And now we were about to demand answers.

Uncle paused at a desk where a young woman sat, typing up correspondence.

"Good morning. I'm Dr. Jonathan Wadsworth, forensic coroner in London. I rang earlier." He cleared his throat when she still hadn't looked up. "Is the general inspector in?"

The young woman slid her gaze from Uncle to Thomas before landing on me. She shook her head. Back in England, Uncle's name meant something. We were no longer in England and her blank stare indicated she'd never heard of the famed forensic man. Odd, since he was mentioned in conjunction with the Ripper murders worldwide.

"I'm sorry," she said, not sounding apologetic at all, but still polite. "Mr. Hubbard is currently indisposed. May I take down a message?"

I studied the young woman. Young. Independent. Someone who craved to earn her own way without relying on anyone else. I imagined she wasn't originally from this city and had left comfort and familiarity behind with her loved ones. She was precisely the sort of person who appealed to our murderer. She very well *could* be next. Anyone could.

"It's quite urgent," I said. "We believe we've got information that might be beneficial to him regarding several missing women."

She seemed to hesitate at that, her own attention traveling over me with the same curiosity I'd shown her. I must seem equally intriguing—a young woman working with a forensic coroner. For a moment, I thought she'd break protocol for us.

"He really is indisposed," she finally said. "Do you have a card or an address he can use to contact you?"

Uncle stayed behind to make sure she'd taken his message and address down, while Thomas and I waited outside the building. Sunshine tried shoving its way through a thick wall of clouds. Its attempt at getting through was going as well as ours was at present.

"What are we supposed to do?" I asked, poking holes in the snow with my cane. "Sit around, sipping tea and eating cake, until a body turns up?"

"We could try speaking with friends of the missing women." Thomas watched me stamp at the snow. "Though perhaps we can wait a bit."

I glared at him. "You're not suggesting I'm incapable, are you?"

Without care or concern for the people walking past us on the street, Thomas tugged me by my overcoat until we were close enough to share breath. "You, my dear, are more capable than any person I've ever had either the pleasure—or displeasure in most cases—of meeting." He kissed my forehead. "I'm suggesting we see what Noah's come to say."

"Noah?"

He smiled down at me. "He sent a telegram this morning. He has new information he wants to share in person."

"Hey, you two!" Noah loped through the snow, his infectious smile in place. He held fast to his hat as he crossed the busy sidewalk and paused in front of us. "Have any luck?" He nodded toward the police station. After scanning the holes I'd punched in the snow, he answered his own question. "Don't take it personally. No one in this city wants to acknowledge bad stuff is happening. They think it'll scare people away from the illustrious White City. As if anything would keep people away from the Ferris Wheel." He rolled his eyes. "I'm heading there now and thought you'd like to come."

Thomas quickly assessed Noah, and I imagined he already knew the answer before he asked the question but was attempting to be polite. "Another missing woman?"

"Yeah." Noah scratched the side of his head, nodding. "She worked at the fair. Thought I'd poke around and see what I could find. The Columbian Guard is being tight-lipped about it."

"Columbian Guard?" I asked. "What's that?"

"An elite part of the police force." Noah seemed less than impressed. "The White City is so massive, it needs its own police. They wear stupid uniforms, too. Complete with capes. The council thought it would look good to, you know, be in theme with how regal the place is."

Costume choices aside, I shifted my attention to Thomas. He offered a slight nod. Here was a promising trail for us to follow.

I inhaled some of the icy air, already feeling more energized. "Let's go back to the White City, shall we?"

After Thomas ran inside and informed Uncle of our plans, we set off for the World's Fair.

Despite clouds covering the sky, the enormous Ferris Wheel cut like a blade through the gloom with its sheer might. In fact, it was hard to believe in anything other than magic in the White City. Even knowing what I did about missing women, I couldn't stop from gasping as I watched the mammoth wheel rotate high in the sky. It carried two thousand people into the heavens. And while I watched it happen before me, I still found it impossible to believe. I'd been impressed by images I'd seen of the Eiffel Tower during Paris's Exposition Universelle, but this was the most magnificent thing I'd ever witnessed.

Thomas stood beside me, watching the enormous wheel rotate. When he caught my eye, I saw a hint of sadness before he covered it up. I reached over and held his hand. He needn't utter a word; I knew how he felt. What he longed for. I longed for it, too.

It would be lovely to be the sort of young couple who could purchase boxes of Cracker Jack and stand in the massive line for the giant ride. We could talk excitedly about Buffalo Bill's stagecoach attacks, marvel at how authentic it appeared, our cheeks flushed with the thrill. Once we finally boarded the Ferris Wheel and soared into the heavens, perhaps Thomas could steal a kiss. But we weren't that couple. We had a murder investigation to conduct.

We followed Noah through a throng of people, Thomas holding tight to me so we didn't get separated by the masses. Despite the buildings and the new technology on display, the crowds might truly be the most remarkable spectacle yet. Tens of thousands of people meandered around. It was the most people I'd ever seen in one location.

It took nearly two hours of moving at a slug's pace, but we finally made it to a small building tucked behind the Court of Honor. Giant plants hid it from the view of passersby, and if Noah hadn't known where to turn, I'm positive we would have walked straight past it.

He knocked on the door, a tap that sounded like Morse code, then stood back as heavy footsteps marched our way. A stout man with red cheeks greeted us. "Mr. Hale, I presume?"

Noah stepped forward and tipped his hat. "Thanks for meeting with me, Mr. Taylor. These are my associates, Mr. Cresswell and Miss Wadsworth." He swung his arm to include us. The older gentleman narrowed his eyes. "They're here to observe," Noah clarified, lying smoothly. "Would you mind if we came in, or should we do this out here?"

Mr. Taylor blinked as if to clear his thoughts, then motioned us in. "It's best to not draw attention to ourselves. Come in."

Inside I was surprised to find a tiny but well-organized office. The limited space had been utilized well—four desks were split evenly on each side, creating an aisle; three of them were occupied by young typists. Mr. Taylor brought us to a fifth desk partially hidden with an ornate screen. He pulled a chair around and set it next to two others already there. "Sit. Please."

Once we'd arranged ourselves, Noah jumped straight into his inquiry. "What can you tell me about Miss Van Tassel? Anything about the last time you saw her, her mood, if anything was odd. Even the most insignificant detail might help. Her family is sick with worry."

Mr. Taylor sat forward at his desk, his hands steepled in front of him. "She never missed a day of work. Always came in with a smile. I believe she'd only been in the city for a few months, but she kept mostly to herself, so none of us heard much about her life outside of here."

"She didn't tell any of your other typists about her personal affairs?" Noah pressed. "No one she might be courting..."

Mr. Taylor shook his head. "When you rang earlier, I called a meeting with everyone. I asked them to tell me anything they knew. Prior to working here, she had a job at a pharmacy on 63rd Street. She never told anyone why she left it; we assumed for the pay. We've only been operational in this location for a little over a week."

Thomas tapped his fingers on his thigh but didn't interrupt Noah's interrogation. Noah glanced at us and I could see the defeat I felt mirrored in his eyes. "Did anyone ever meet her here or drop her off?"

"No, I'm afraid—" Mr. Taylor sat back, brows drawn together. "Actually, there was someone. A young man stopped by two days ago. He wore a bowler hat and matching overcoat. Seemed like a reputable fellow. I'm not sure—Dolores?" he called abruptly, flashing an apologetic grimace our way. A young woman poked her head around the partition. "Do you remember what that gentleman came here for? The one who talked to Edna?"

The young woman frowned a bit, then brightened. "I couldn't hear much, but he mentioned having her money." She shrugged. "I think he was her old employer, but she didn't say much once he left."

Noah thanked Mr. Taylor for his time and we all made our way back outside. Thomas offered his arm and I accepted it. We parted ways with Noah near the front of the Court of Honor. He had to stop by the Pinkertons' office and it was on the opposite side of the city.

We strolled along, each lost in our private thoughts, when one tiny, almost insignificant detail sprang to mind.

"Wait." I pulled Thomas to a stop, recalling what I'd seen on a map of Chicago. "Sixty-Third Street; I believe that's in Englewood. We need to go to that pharmacy straightaway. So far two missing women were last seen in that neighborhood, or had a connection to a pharmacy there—Julia Smythe with her daughter, Pearl, on Christmas Eve, and now Miss Van Tassel."

And Miss Minnie Williams, Mephistopheles's actress, had just started working there. I didn't know her well, but I didn't want her to cross paths with our murderer, especially since he seemed to stalk that neighborhood.

Thomas nodded toward the sky. It was a dusky rose tinged with purple and black. I stared at the sun dipping into the horizon, wondering how I'd not noticed how late it had gotten. Thomas called for a carriage. "I'm afraid our adventure will have to wait until morning. Most shops close at dark."

I wanted to argue, to point out that our murderer didn't care what time of day it was, that he'd still keep up his sinister pursuits, but before I could utter a word, the skies opened up. Hail clattered around us, ensuring that no one would be lurking around outdoors now.

Thomas held his coat over my head, trying to shield me from the worst of it before ushering me quickly into our hansom. We were both quiet as we watched the White City fade behind us. From here, the buildings jutted up from the horizon, like broken fingers reaching toward the sky. It was a morbid thought.

As our wheels clattered over stone and frozen rain tapped at our roof, I hoped it wasn't an omen of worse things to come.

Typical Victorian Pharmacy, Plough Court Pharmacy, 1897

THIRTY-SEVEN

A GRID SYSTEM

SOUTH SIDE
CHICAGO, ILLINOIS
14 FEBRUARY 1889

I blew out a breath, glancing from one avenue to the other. Chicago's streets seemed to devour those who weren't familiar with them, leaving no morsel behind. "Foolish," I cursed under my breath. Why I imagined it an easy task, taking a streetcar instead of hiring a carriage, I didn't know. Thomas left me standing on the corner as he dashed into the nearest store to inquire after our destination. At least I wasn't alone in my lack of direction.

"Miss, are you lost?" A man in his mid-twenties wearing a sleek coat and matching bowler hat stepped close, but not improperly so.

"This city is impossible." I tossed a hand up, indicating the whole area. "At least New York is laid out in a grid. There are practically a dozen 'Washington' streets alone!"

"Chicago's actually a grid, too, and it's fairly easy to navigate once you've had some practice." His eyes twinkled with amusement. "Townships keep getting swallowed up, which is why there are so many streets with the same names. You're from England, I presume?"

I nodded. "I'm from London."

"You're a bit far from home." He eyed me in a friendly manner. "Are you here for the fair?"

"My fiancé and I are here for a variety of reasons." Admitting I was here to hunt the White City Devil seemed a bit much to tell a perfect stranger. "Do you know where I might find this pharmacy?" I showed him the address Minnie Williams had scribbled down after our introduction at Mephistopheles's theatrical show. "I thought this was Wallace, but I seem to have gotten turned about."

He took the letter from me, then shifted. "It's right over there. See that jewelry store?" I followed where he pointed, barely making out a small sign. The building was still a good distance away. It had to be the same store where Miss Smythe was last seen. "Is your fiancé joining you? Or did you slip away on your own?"

An uncomfortable feeling slithered through me. I discreetly studied the young man—he was perfectly ordinary. Except for the almost cobalt-like hue of his eyes; they were quite mesmerizing. I tried imagining him stealing women off the streets, or ripping them apart, if he were the elusive Ripper. Mr. Cigrande claimed the demons who'd taken his daughter had light eyes, but this man's were a deep blue.

"Should we not tell your fiancé about this?" he pressed.

"My—"

Thomas rounded the corner that very moment, his attention immediately running over the young man in his usual manner. I knew he was identifying each detail and cataloging it for future use. His expression remained unreadable.

"You must be the fiancé," the young man said, turning up the wattage on his smile. "I was watching over your lady here."

"Yes, well, my lady hardly needs watching." Thomas didn't return the man's smile. "I enjoy obedience in my dogs, not my wife. She's free to do as she pleases."

I tried not to heave a sigh. I loved that Thomas never shied away from sharing his innermost opinions, but we'd have to work on his delivery a bit more in the future.

"No insult intended." The young man raised his hands. "If ever there was a city where young women were free to do as they please, it's Chicago." He was sincere sounding enough. "I hope you both enjoy your stay. Make sure to visit the fair at night—it's spectacular."

With a quick nod to us both, he crossed the street and disappeared around the next block. Thomas watched him go before looping his arm through mine. "Apparently you and I are stellar at details of murder but abysmal at locating storefronts. The address we're looking for is—"

"Right over there," I finished, grinning up at him. "Let's not tell anyone about our terrible sense of direction."

A bell jangled pleasantly above us as we stepped into the pharmacy. Thomas immediately abandoned me in favor of a table stacked with sugar cubes. He held a small box up, breathing in the scent as if it were a fresh bouquet. I all but rolled my eyes. We were here on a hunch regarding the Ripper frequenting this establishment, and here he was, mesmerized by candy.

"Lemon drop." He picked up another. "Mint." He clutched them to his chest, glancing toward me. "Imagine what these would taste like in coffee or tea?"

"Those infused sugar cubes are one of our bestsellers." A familiar young woman stepped around the table, her smile infectious. "Miss Wadsworth. Mr. Cresswell."

"Miss Williams," I said, hugging Minnie warmly. "It's lovely to see you again. How are you enjoying your stenography course?"

"It's good. There's always much to do, so I'm quite busy. I split my time between that and watching the counter here until Henry hires another girl. We rent a few rooms out upstairs and I tell you, I can't keep up. It's hard to find reliable employees lately. Everyone wants to be at the fair, not stuck behind a counter." Minnie plastered on a smile, though it didn't light up her face the way acting had. "Enough with talk of work; I'm so pleased you both came to see me! Just look at this!" She held up her hand, showing off a beautiful wedding band. "We married a few days ago. It was a private little affair, but I couldn't be happier. Henry's found us a place in Lincoln Park. We're almost settled in, and I'd love if you'd come visit. He'll be traveling for a bit and it'll just be me in that big old house. Not that I'm complaining—it's simply darling." Her attention strayed to where Thomas was still lifting boxes of sugar and breathing in their aromas. "You're welcome to take a few home, Mr. Cresswell. I'm sure Henry won't mind."

Thomas lifted his gaze to mine, his expression hopeful.

"I'm your fiancée, not your keeper, Cresswell."

Actually, I wasn't technically either. I must have frowned because his eyes darkened into two pools of trouble. I braced myself for whatever untoward thing was about to come out of his mouth to distract me. Sugar cubes forgotten, he tossed them aside and took a quick nip at my ear. "Who needs sugar when you're sweet enough to satisfy me, Wadsworth?"

Poor Minnie appeared as uncomfortable as anything. I gave Thomas my most exaggerated eye roll and shook my head. "Will you look around for anything else you might be interested in?" I raised my brows, hinting at our ulterior motives. "Perhaps you'll find something of note."

Thomas looked ready to dazzle me with another of his flirtations, and before he could utter something silly, I turned to Minnie. "The pharmacy is lovely. I've never seen so many tonics in one place. There must be over one hundred different jars."

"Oh, goodness." Minnie eyed up the shelves as she stepped out from behind the counter. Bottles filled with powder and different colored liquids were stacked two and three rows deep. "There's closer to three hundred! Henry is gifted with his elixirs. He's got tonics for headaches and backaches and even creams for smooth skin. People from all over the city come in to purchase his tinctures."

"Well, with a collection so grand, I can see why." We walked through the store, my cane clicking pleasantly. "Minnie," I began slowly, not wanting to frighten her, "have you heard about a Miss Julia Smythe? Or her daughter, Pearl?"

Her brow crinkled. "No, I can't say either name sounds familiar. Are they friends of yours? I might ask around if you need me to."

I caught Thomas's eye across the store; he gave me a slight shake of his head. A warning to not reveal too much. "No, one of our friends came across her picture in a paper. Julia worked at the jewelry counter on 63rd Street and was last seen on Christmas Eve. Her family is quite worried. A Miss Van Tassel did work here and recently disappeared, too. Have you heard of her?"

"That's awful!" Minnie's expression didn't shift, though her tone did. "Henry hasn't mentioned anyone by that name before, though the pharmacy across the street is run by that strange man. I wonder if that's where they both worked. He sells jewelry there, too." She seemed genuinely concerned. "I swear there's something not quite right about him... the way he watches each move a person makes like they're ready to steal from him. Henry's warned me to not draw his attention."

I was momentarily taken aback. I hadn't counted on there being two pharmacies in close proximity to each other. Now I was unsure if Miss Van Tassel and Miss Smythe and her daughter were linked to this one or the other. "Have you had many dealings with him?"

"Goodness, no." She shook her head. "I told Henry about the last time I stopped in there and he said to stay away from that wretched man and his shop." She shuddered. "My Henry never speaks poorly of anyone, so I took his warning seriously."

Thomas had inspected almost every inch of the store and was now standing close enough to overhear our conversation.

"I do hope you find that missing woman and her daughter," Minnie added. "If she worked for him, I wouldn't be surprised if he'd buried them in his basement. He seems the sort to have a collection of blasphemous things."

That certainly sounded as if it could fit with our suspect. "Thank you, Minnie, you've been very helpful. We must be on our way, though. We've got to speak with the proprietor of that pharmacy, too."

"Oh, he's not in," she said, nodding toward the giant window. "He drew the curtains and the CLOSED sign has been displayed for a week now. No one seems to know where he's gotten to. I can't say that I mind, though. The less I see of him, the better."

Thomas and I exchanged looks. We were getting closer; I could sense it in the way gooseflesh rose along my arms. Either we'd missed him by a week, or he was still inside, lurking in the darkened building. I hid my shudder as I faced Minnie again.

"I'm sorry to trouble you with one more question," I said, "but did anything unusual occur right before he disappeared?"

Minnie assumed her spot behind the counter and ran her fingers over the ornate cash register. "Nothing extraordinary. Except..." She bit her lip. "Except Henry did have a few words with him about frightening me. He told him to cease any foul ideas he might have, and that we were to be married soon. He told me all about it; it was terribly romantic."

I thanked Minnie for her time and promised to stop by for tea the next afternoon. Once she'd written her address down, I followed Thomas outside. Snow decided to join us, falling in excited clumps. We stood under the striped awning of the pharmacy, inspecting the pharmacy across the street. No lights flickered behind the curtains, no gilded outlines to hint at someone being shut in tight. All was eerily still, like it was watching us back.

Thomas tapped his fingers at his side, frowning. "If he's taking the missing women and holding them prisoner, then it's not unreasonable to think he could have some sort of...dungeon...in the basement."

"It would explain why he closed the pharmacy. He wouldn't want anyone overhearing any cries for help," I said. "Would he actually remain here, after being confronted by someone? If Henry noticed odd behavior and threatened him, he might have feared police involvement. Maybe he did slip into the night. He could be anywhere by now."

Thomas appraised the building, then shifted his attention to the alleyway beside it. "Someone's still there; look at the rubbish bins. They're overflowing."

"That doesn't prove he's the one who's filled them, though."

"True enough. But the number painted on them matches the number above the door." Thomas lifted his chin. "The rubbish bin beside it is also full, and matches the building to the left. While it is *possible* someone else took advantage and put their rubbish in his bin, it's not probable. A simple glimpse inside it might give us a better answer."

Snowflakes quickly stuck to the cold cobblestones of the street. The sun was ready to set and it would only get colder and more dangerous to be out. Digging in someone's rubbish hardly seemed like the sort of evening jaunt I'd care for with my beloved. I sighed. Wants and desires didn't take precedence when there were missing women and a brutal murderer running amok.

"Fine." I swept my arm out. At least I hadn't worn my favorite gloves today. "Let's see what clues we can find in the trash."

Two hours later police swarmed like angry bees around a hive. Thomas leaned against the pharmacy, arms crossed as he watched them collect the bloodied bedsheet. He had the decency of not uttering anything close to "I told you so," which was good for his health. I was cold and miserable, and my mood plummeted along with the temperature. I shivered under the horsehair blanket an officer offered me, teeth chattering as snow continued to fall in drifts. Winds whipped down the streets, lifting stray hairs and raising gooseflesh.

General Inspector Hubbard exited the building, his expression more grim than when he'd first disappeared through the doors. I tried not to glare in his direction, though he was the reason I was standing outside in the freezing elements, instead of investigating the scene. Heaven forbid I witness a body in any sort of indecent state, such as dead.

He motioned for the officers to gather around. "Put everything back where you found it. There's no sign of any wrongdoing here." He met my gaze briefly, though I wasn't surprised it didn't linger on me long. He addressed Thomas. "It appears to be a…" His attention wavered, and I rolled my eyes. "There's a space in the basement that appears to have been used as an abortion chamber."

He puckered his lips, his entire expression turning sour. His tone implied it wasn't the medical procedure but the women who'd seek such a service that bothered him. I immediately wished I could jab him with the tip of my cane.

"There were medical tools and bloodstained sheets. No signs of murder. No bodies." He stuck his fingers in his mouth and whistled. A carriage clattered to a stop in front of us and he opened the door, ushering us in. "Perhaps it's best if you stick to studying the bodies *we* discover from now on. It's better to not waste either of our time. We won't come on a fool's errand again. Especially not for a pair who seem to only be after fame."

"Pardon me?" Thomas asked, sounding too confused to be angry.

"Oh, I've heard of you two." The general inspector sneered. "And that doctor you're with. Thought you could come here and start that Jack the Ripper nonsense in my city, did you?" He jabbed his hand at the open carriage, his look free from any politeness. "I don't want to see you making any further problems. Have I made myself clear? One more slipup, and I'll have you both in custody."

Thomas and I glanced at each other. There was no point in arguing with this man—he'd already made up his mind about who we were, no matter that it couldn't be further from the truth. With nothing left to say, Thomas helped me into the carriage.

It seemed we now had one more complication to add to our never-ending tally.

THIRTY-EIGHT
BE MINE

GRANDMAMA'S ESTATE
CHICAGO, ILLINOIS
14 FEBRUARY 1889

I was in such a miserable state after our encounter with the general inspector that I hardly noticed the food on my plate. I stabbed at my vegetables, lost in my darkening mood. Thomas and I sat alone in the large dining room while Uncle sequestered himself away in his new makeshift basement laboratory, setting up his tools in a manner that pleased him.

We'd offered our assistance, but the feral look in his eyes had us back up the stairs in an instant. It was best to leave him to his work, lest he start tossing scalpels and bone saws about, disturbed by the intrusion.

I brought the fork to my mouth, still no closer to paying attention to my meal. I grabbed for my wineglass instead, taking a small sip and hoping my expression didn't turn as sour as the drink. Thomas sighed from across the table. I flicked my attention to him, not quite understanding the look on his face.

"Are you well?" I asked, unable to discern if he was sad or ill. Perhaps he was both. I looked at him, *really* looked, and saw smudges of darkness under his eyes. A haggardness that edged his beautiful features. I wasn't the only one who hadn't been sleeping well. "What is it?"

He set his cutlery down, then folded his hands together as if in prayer. Perhaps he was requesting assistance from our Heavenly Father. "I hate when you're upset, Wadsworth. It makes me..." He wrinkled his nose. "It makes me feel quite foul, too. It's abominable."

I raised my brows—I could tell there was more. His eyes didn't hold that usual glimmer of excitement when he teased me.

"I hate feeling out of control," I said, hoping by admitting my fears it might encourage him to do the same. I sipped from my wine, no longer bothered by its tartness. "The general inspector believes we're overreacting or fame-mongers chasing headlines. We haven't been able to assist Noah in his endeavors. Then"—I stumbled over our personal drama, unable to think or speak of the failed marriage more than I already did—"there's Nathaniel's confession and his journals. Which only add to my confusion and feeling of spinning helplessly, wildly out of control."

I inhaled a sharp breath. There was more to my growing anxiety. Things I hadn't wanted to share with him or admit to myself. I stared at the delicate lace on the table runner. It was so beautiful it made me want to slash it with my knife.

"Then there are my nightmares," I whispered, not meeting his gaze. "At night, I see a man with curved horns. Always in silhouette. He doesn't speak. Doesn't move. He stands there in the shadows, as if he's...waiting for me." A chill ran along each of my vertebrae. I finally worked up the nerve to look at Thomas. His face was a study of worry—worse than it had been moments ago. He nodded for me to continue. "He comes for me every night, stealing into my most private moments. I-I know it's not real, but it's hard to not think—"

I snapped my mouth shut, suddenly unsure I wanted to be quite so vulnerable. I knew Thomas wouldn't accuse me of madness, but I did not want to add to *his* growing worries by admitting the full truth. I wondered if the devil in my dreams wasn't haunting me, but waiting for me to willingly come to him. To accept my role as his mistress of darkness. The silent command emanating from him was simple: *Surrender,* he seemed to say without speaking. Part of me feared I'd set this inevitable path into motion the moment I decided to follow my own desires.

Thomas might be Dracula's heir, but I was the one who craved blood. I was the one who enjoyed sinking my blades into dead flesh more than I had any right to. Sometimes, if I gave in to my secret fears, I worried there was something gnarled and twisted in me. Perhaps our wedding had fallen apart because my true companion was Satan and I was destined for treacherous things.

Thomas moved swiftly around the table and sat beside me, taking me into his arms. He cradled me there, against his pounding heart, as if he could keep my demons at bay through the sheer force of his will. "How long have the nightmares been happening?"

I hesitated. Not because I couldn't recall, but because I wasn't sure I should admit they'd begun the same night we'd spent our first evening together. Right before our failed wedding. I didn't want him internalizing anything, thinking my subconscious was damning me for our desires of the flesh. I feared he'd stay far from my bedchamber forever, blaming himself no matter how wrong that was. And while I shouldn't miss his presence in my bed since he was promised to another, I wasn't ready to say good-bye to him yet.

"A few weeks."

He sucked in a breath. I could practically hear the gears of his mind cranking over the information. "How can I make them go away?" he asked, his mouth against my hair. "Tell me how to help you, Audrey Rose."

My first reaction was to pretend I could handle it on my own, but my mind was churning with negativity. I could not take the constant bombardment without a bit of respite. I wrapped my arms around him, uncaring that it wasn't the most comfortable position, sitting crookedly in our stiff dining room chairs.

"Tell me something I don't know about you." Recalling something he'd said during one of our former adventures when things had gotten a little too serious for his taste, I added, "Make it scandalous, too."

He grinned against my neck before planting a chaste kiss there. No doubt he was recalling when he'd said that to me—we were tucked behind the fern fronds in his family's estate in Bucharest. He ran his hand along my spine, soothing and gentle.

"Before I met you, I was convinced love was both a weakness and a hazard. Only a fool would allow himself to be swept up in someone's eyes, pen sonnets dedicated to them, and dream of the floral fragrance of their hair." He paused, but only briefly. "The night we met I'd gotten into a fight with my father. He was livid with me for ruining another potential match."

His tone was bitter now, and I remembered him telling me earlier their argument had been over Miss Whitehall. He instinctually held me tighter.

"My father called me a monster," he admitted. "The worst part was I believed him, that I was less than human, unable to *feel* things as others do. I accepted his appraisal of me, which made me harbor all the more animosity toward love. Why long for something that would never be mine? If I didn't believe in it, I could avoid the crushing disappointment that would inevitably follow if I ever did fall. Surely no one would truly want *me*, the monster. More obsessed with death than living."

I wanted to twist in my seat, to see his face, but realized because

I *couldn't* study him it was easier for him to confess. I sat very still, hoping to not break the spell of the moment.

"You're not a monster, Thomas. You're one of the most incredible people I know. If anything, you care too much for those around you. Even strangers."

He drew in a shaky breath and waited a minute before responding. "Thank you, my love. It's one thing for someone else to tell you you're good, but when you don't believe it yourself..." He shrugged. "For a long while I thought I *was* a monster. I'd heard the whispers around London. The way people mocked my behavior and accused me of being Jack the Ripper. Sometimes I wondered if they were right, if one day I might wake up and find blood on my hands with no recollection of how it got there."

My fingers curled into his lapels, gripping them tightly. I remembered those rumors, too. I'd encountered a bit of that animosity during an afternoon tea I'd hosted what felt like ages ago instead of mere months. I'd only just met Thomas—and couldn't stand him most of the time—and yet I'd defended him instead of sitting back and quietly agreeing, much to my aunt's dismay.

I loathed the way the people of so-called noble birth spread rumors of him like a plague. When they'd discovered Miss Eddowes, one of the Ripper victims, had a small tattoo that read *TC*, they went wild with theories. They were cruel and inaccurate. Thomas could never harm anyone. If they'd only given him a chance, they'd have seen what I did...

"Anyway, that night I made a vow to the heavens. I swore I would only marry science. I refused to surrender my heart or my mind to anyone. No one can think you're a monster if they don't know you. And those who already thought it? Why should I care? They didn't mean anything. I refused to let them."

He dropped a kiss on my neck, drawing a lovely tingling sensation on my skin there.

"When I walked into your uncle's laboratory, I'd been so consumed with the surgical procedure we were about to perform. It was the perfect distraction from my black mood. I hadn't initially noticed you. Then I did." He breathed in deeply as if preparing to reveal the secret I craved. "You were standing there, scalpel in hand, apron splattered in blood. Of course I noticed your beauty, but that wasn't what caught me off guard. It was the look in your eyes. The way you held that blade aloft, like you might stick me with it." He chuckled, the sound rumbling in his chest. "I was so startled at the odd surge of my pulse, I almost fell face-first into the open cadaver. It was a horrifying mental image. I was even more disturbed when I realized it mattered—what you'd think of that. Of me."

He gently stroked my hair for a few beats.

"I hadn't had a physical response to anyone before," he said, voice shy. "I'd never found myself intrigued by anyone, either. And there you were, within an hour of my declaration against love, as if mocking my resolve. I wanted to shout, 'I will not become a monster for you!' Because a foreign piece of me wanted to snatch you away and keep you all to myself forever. It was downright animalistic. I wanted to loathe you but found it impossible."

I snorted at that. "Yes, you certainly seemed bewitched by me. What with that icy reception. You didn't even speak to me."

"Do you know why?" he asked, not expecting an answer. "Because I knew, straightaway, there was only one reason behind my treacherous heartbeat. I thought if I could fight it, pretend the feeling away, freeze it, if necessary, I might win the battle against love." He shifted behind me, gently turning my face to his. This time, he wished to confess to me. "I knew from the moment I set eyes upon you there could be something special here. I wanted to forget the surgery and don an apron, too. I wanted to cast you under the same spell that you'd cast over me. Of course that wasn't logical. I needed to remember who I was—the monster, incapable of being loved. My coolness was directed entirely at myself. The more time we spent together, the harder it became to deny the change in my emotions. I couldn't pretend away my feelings, nor could I blame them on some strange illness."

I rolled my eyes at that. "How exceptionally sentimental. Believing your affection for me was nothing more than an *in*fection."

His laugh erased my remaining worry with its warmth. I all but forgot about the maelstrom in my head. "I had an inclination that you might feel that way. Which is why I penned this for you instead."

I stared at him for a moment, pulse pounding. "You wrote something for me?"

He pulled a small cream envelope from his pocket, his expression bordering on bashful as he handed it to me. My name was written with care—the script more beautiful than his usual hurried writing. A lovely flush crept up his collar.

Curious as to what would bring about such an unusual emotion in him, I quickly opened it and read.

My dearest Audrey Rose,

Poems and sonnets are meant to rhyme, but I find myself unable to pen anything other than the deepest longing of my soul. My world had been dark. I was so used to it that I'd grown accustomed to traversing through the lonely stretches of desolate land.

When you entered my life, you shone brighter than the sun and stars combined. You warmed the frozen parts of me I'd feared were incapable of thawing. I'd been convinced I had a heart carved from ice until you smiled... and then it began to beat wildly. I cannot imagine my world without you in it now, because you are my entire universe.

Happy Valentine's Day, Wadsworth. You are and will forever remain my truest and only love. I hope, though I have no right to, that you will be mine. As I will always be

Yours forever,
Thomas

My eyes brimmed with unshed tears and I clamped my jaws together to keep from crying. I didn't think the proper way of thanking him for his thoughtfulness was to snot all over his suit. Horror washed into Thomas's features. I tensed, unsure what had brought on his sudden shift.

"I-I didn't mean...you don't have to—" He ran a hand through his hair, tousling his dark locks. "It's all right if you don't want to be mine. I-I understand our circumstances aren't ideal. It's—"

Relief sluiced through me. He'd misunderstood the source of my tears. It was incredible that his powers of deduction were so lost when it came to reading my emotions. I touched his face gently, my hand fitting around the curve of his cheek, and brought his lips to mine. Showing him, without words, how much he meant to me.

Thomas needed no further explanation. He deepened our kiss, his hands gripping me tighter—but not uncomfortably so—as he closed the space between us. Whenever he held me like that, with his body molded so perfectly against mine, I swore I lost my senses. The world and all its problems settled into a corner far away. There were only the two of us.

I nipped at his bottom lip and his eyes shifted to a molten chocolate that started a fire deep within me. He scooped me into his arms, knocking my cane over in his haste to exit the room and any possible interruptions from the footmen should they come to check on our dinner.

We were fortunate to have made it upstairs to my chambers before we expressed our love more thoroughly. I yanked his shirt open, buttons popping in all directions, and gave him an impish grin as he set me on the bed. He seemed anything but disturbed by my exuberance as he returned the favor and relieved me of my corset. Tonight he didn't bother with slowly pulling its strings; he practically ripped it apart.

I traced the outline of his tattoo first with my fingertips and then with my lips, never tiring of the way he gasped beneath my careful touch.

If I lived to be one thousand years old, it would never feel like enough time with him.

"I love you, Audrey Rose. More than all the stars in the universe."

Thomas erased all space between us and gazed down at me as if I were the most perfect person in existence. When he kissed me again, it was so sweet I nearly forgot my own name. It was a good thing he kept whispering it across my skin.

I lightly trailed my nails down his spine and back up, marveling at the goose bumps that rose, the sensation seeming to drive him as wild as it drove me. He repeated my name like an incantation, his tone as reverent as those praising gods. He worshipped my mind and body until I, too, became a believer. Then he brought us both to another realm—one where we were nothing more than love in its purest physical form.

Hours later, after we'd professed our adoration—and while I lay cradled in the safety of Thomas's arms—the devil stood waiting for me. Silent and watchful as always, as he welcomed me back to his dominion of darkness.

THIRTY-NINE

STRANGE DISAPPEARANCE

1220 WRIGHTWOOD AVENUE
CHICAGO, ILLINOIS
15 FEBRUARY 1889

"Miss Wadsworth!" Minnie greeted me warmly at the door. "It's so lovely of you to call on me. Tell me, have you heard from Mephistopheles? I haven't been able to locate that scoundrel anywhere."

It was quite an odd opening, but I handed my cloak to the maid and shook my head. "I'm afraid I haven't spoken with him since I last saw him with you." I studied her expression, the nibbling of her lower lip, the crease in her brow. "Is everything all right?"

"I'm sure it is. I just heard a rumor that my understudy hasn't been seen for ages. It's a bit strange, given how much she loved playing that role." She brightened up again. "Come. Harry's allowed me to decorate the parlor to my liking. Shall we take some tea and coffee there?"

I wished to return to the subject of yet another missing young woman, but something else caught my attention. "Harry?"

Minnie blinked slowly as if awakening from a dream. "Did I say Harry? Goodness me, *Henry*. My Henry is such a lovely man. Wait until you see this wallpaper. It's from *Paris*!"

We situated ourselves in a lovely blue-and-white sitting room, the fabric as rich as any fine dessert. Gold thread shot through navy-and-cream stripes on our chairs. Little gold tassels tied back deep blue curtains that appeared to be made of velvet. A matching blue-and-white tea service was promptly brought out with a stack of freshly baked biscuits.

A proper household always boasted of polished silver, but Minnie took it even further. Crystals dripped off of shining candelabras and hothouse flowers bloomed fragrantly in vases nearly the size of a dog. It was quite a flashy show of excess.

"The flowers are lovely," I said, motioning around the room. "Are they for a special occasion?"

"Henry is a man of fine refinement and taste." Minnie poured me tea and herself coffee. "He enjoys beautiful things."

Her smile seemed to freeze in place, like there was more she wasn't saying aloud. I accepted my cup of tea, treading carefully. "Does that make you sad?"

"N-no, it's not that." She set her cup and saucer in her lap, staring down into the swirling cream. "It's just...my sister said something rather unflattering the other day when I told her we'd married. I haven't been able to get it out of my mind. I'm sure I'm simply being silly." She glanced at the tea service again. "Sugar?"

"No, thank you." I sipped my tea, enjoying the taste of vanilla and something richer. She added a few cubes to her coffee with silver tongs, seemingly lost in thought. "If you'd like to talk about what your sister said, I'm happy to listen."

She gave me a grateful smile. "Sisters are wonderful, truly. No one in the world will hug you when you're breaking and slap sense into you at the same moment."

While I didn't have a sister by blood, I thought of Liza and all of the ways that was true. There was no one who'd stand by your side and stare down demons with you as much as a sister would. She'd then kick you for being stupid and getting involved with demons after the fact, but a sister was always there when it counted. Images of Daciana and Ileana sprang to mind, too. I was elated to count them as my sisters as well, regardless of the ruined wedding.

"What did she say that upset you?"

Minnie drew in a deep breath. "I know I'm not...as I said before, Henry enjoys beautiful things. I know I'm plain. My hair is a dull brown; my eyes are utterly ordinary. I often wonder how I drew his attention, but when Anna said I was being foolish...that if he was as handsome and charming as I'd described—" She sniffled. "Well, she doesn't think his intentions are very pure. You see, we have a small inheritance. And I started thinking about—"

Just then, a man in a bowler hat and matching brown suit stepped into the room. He started forward, then halted when he noticed me. I nearly dropped my tea when I recognized his striking blue eyes. He was the young man who'd given me directions to the pharmacy.

Those same eyes fixed on my face, widening ever so slightly before he blinked. Warmth flooded his features. "Minnie, my dear, I didn't know you were entertaining. I'm sorry to barge in so rudely." In a few strides he crossed the room, bending to kiss his new wife. He turned to me, a small grin starting. "Miss Wadsworth, wasn't it?"

I nodded, impressed he'd recalled my name. "I apologize, but I don't remember..."

"Please, call me Henry." At Minnie's confused expression, he explained. "I ran into Miss Wadsworth and her fiancé on their way to the pharmacy the other day." He turned back to me, expression polite. "Did you find what you were looking for?"

The bloodstained bedsheet crossed my mind. It was alarming,

almost, how I could envision such garish things with startling clarity and pretend them away. "No. I'm afraid we didn't." I narrowed my eyes a bit. "You didn't mention owning the pharmacy."

"Quite right. I don't like boasting about my properties and businesses. I own several around Chicago alone. Well," he said, his attention flicking to the clock on the mantel. "I must be off. I just wanted to give my wife a proper good-bye."

He kissed the top of Minnie's head, warmth returning to his features. I studied him, trying to find truth in what Minnie's sister had worried about. To all outward appearances, he seemed to genuinely care for Minnie. The sparkle in his eyes didn't appear fake. Though he wasn't quite as perfect as she'd made him out to be. He was of average build and height, if not a bit on the short side. His face was wholly unremarkable except for his cunning blue gaze. That was shockingly magnetic. I imagined he'd get lost in a room full of men with similar builds.

"Don't wait up, my dear," he said. "I have a meeting all the way in the South Side tonight, and you know how that may go. If it gets too late, I may spend the evening in our rooms there."

With another polite good-bye, he left us to our visit. Minnie's demeanor had changed, her worry dissipated like morning dew in the sun. Her cheeks flushed pleasantly, and I wondered why she thought herself plain. When she looked at me, her whole face lit up. "Well?"

"He's very nice," I said. "I'm sure you'll both be exquisitely happy." She sighed dreamily. I wanted to ask further regarding her sister's worries about him being interested in her money but didn't wish to upset her again. At any rate, he had several businesses, so it appeared he was doing quite well on his own. "You mentioned your understudy has not been heard from. Is that something she normally did? Disappear for a few days?"

"Oh, no. Trudy wanted that role too much. She'd been a patient understudy, but you can always see the longing, you know?" She rearranged her skirts. "She'd stare at the stage as though it was the very source of her life. The electricity machine Mephistopheles crafted— when she watched it, it was like she'd seen an angel. I can't imagine her giving it up, not now. And I cannot understand why she'd leave without telling anyone."

"Did she travel anywhere out of the ordinary?"

"Not that I'm aware of. Trudy never liked to go anywhere alone—she'd even have one of the other performers walk her to the streetcar after a show. She was always so cautious."

"Was she afraid of being followed?"

Minnie lifted a shoulder. "I'm not sure why she insisted on being escorted to and from her boardinghouse. I imagined it was because her family's beliefs of a woman being unaccompanied was a sin. I guessed there were some rules she didn't want to break."

"When was the last time you saw her?"

"A few days ago, when I was married," Minnie said. "She came to the courthouse to be my witness."

I mulled the information over. It was hard to ignore that if she was actually missing, she was yet another young woman connected to Mephistopheles's show. We'd cleared the Moonlight Carnival of wrongdoing on the *Etruria*, but this coincidence was a bit much. As well as him being present on the ship, in New York, and now in Chicago, where the succession of crimes was occurring—that was a coincidence as well. And I knew precisely what Uncle said about there being no coincidences when it came to murder.

I started thinking of the enigmatic ringmaster and his stage name, of how it was based on Faust. In that legend, Mephistopheles was a demon in the devil's employ, sent to steal souls. That character used trickery and deceit to get what he wanted, manipulating everything in his favor. Much like the ringmaster did with his midnight bargains. Could Thomas have been correct about his fears? Was Ayden truly a devil hiding in plain view?

And if Mephistopheles wasn't the White City Devil, was there a chance he knew who was and aided him? There had been a circus in London during the Ripper murders; my brother and I had attended it. Chills ran icy fingers down my spine. It wasn't such a stretch of the imagination to think the ringmaster had been present there, too.

"Audrey Rose?" Minnie waved her hand near my face, brow crinkled. "You appear as if you've seen a ghost. Should I ready the carriage for you?"

FORTY

INFERNO

GRANDMAMA'S ESTATE
CHICAGO, ILLINOIS
15 FEBRUARY 1889

"Mr. Cresswell left this for you, miss."

"Is my uncle in?" I asked the maid as she assisted me out of my cloak.

"No, miss. He and Mr. Cresswell both stepped out. Would you like some coffee?"

"Tea, please. I'll take it in the library."

Americans drank coffee the way the English indulged in our tea. Thomas was thrilled, guzzling nearly three cups per day. Sometimes more when I wasn't around. The extra caffeine was the last thing he needed, though his buzzing about was a nuisance I adored. I smiled, recalling the way he'd used to smoke to get that jolt. Thank goodness he'd given that habit up.

I peeled my gloves off, then headed for the library, reading the note written in his hurried scrawl. He and Uncle were meeting with a coroner to consult on a case. It wasn't anything out of the ordinary, perhaps a death caused by being exposed to the elements. They'd return soon.

Lost in my own thoughts, I swore I felt a frostbitten kiss along my spine as I traveled the length of the corridor. It was dreadfully chilly at this end of the house.

When I got to the library door, I reached for the handle and hesitated. The iron knob felt like a block of carved ice. Trepidation entered my senses. Even if a fire hadn't been lit, the handle was much too cold for being indoors. Before I lost my nerve, I pushed the door open. I held fast to my cane, ready to wield it at whatever lurked inside the room.

Sheer curtains fluttered toward me, two pale arms reminding me of phantoms searching for their next victim to haunt. Panic seized me in its grip. Someone had broken into Grandmama's home! I bet they'd—I shut my eyes. My imagination was at it again, no doubt.

Gathering my wits, I glanced around, noticing the freshly polished wood, and a stick that was likely used to beat dust from the rugs sitting against the wall. Bits of the mystery unwound. No malicious entity or murderer had entered our home. This room was simply cleaned. The window had been cracked to let the scent of cleanser and mustiness out. Nothing more.

I exhaled, my puff of breath like a storm cloud as I closed the window and drew the curtains. One day I'd harness my wild imagination. I flicked the curtain back, staring down into the street. Night had fully fallen, cloaking the city in shadows. Lamps offered orbs of warmth, though I couldn't help thinking of them as glowing eyes, ever watchful, waiting for me. A pale face shimmered before me, two horns twisting above its head. A demon.

I drew back, screeching as I felt hot flesh behind me. I whirled, coming face-to-face with the specter from the window.

"Miss!" The maid dropped the tray with a clatter, her eyes as wide as the saucers she'd broken. "Are you all right?"

I stared at my trembling hands. It was no demon. There were

no horns. I'd simply seen her reflection in the glass—the cap she wore casting the odd shape. Memories of being haunted by delusions sprang forth, taunting me. It was happening all over again.

Realizing she was still waiting there, her expression tight with worry, I pulled myself together. "I'm a bit jumpy this evening," I said. "I'm dreadfully sorry I frightened you. And caused such a mess." I felt the beginnings of hysteria creeping in around the edges. "I...I'm going to my room for a nap. Please," I interrupted before she could offer to assist me, "I'll be quite all right on my own."

I rushed from the room, hobbling down the corridor, chills my constant companions as they raced along my body. The house seemed to delight in my terror. Sconces flickered as I hurried past, as if clapping flame-coated hands. I drew in breath after breath, my stomach twisting. Why now? Why were these hauntings assaulting me when I'd done nothing to evoke their rage? I climbed the stairs, mind churning. Had I ingested something hallucinogenic? There had to be a reason...I couldn't—

I halted in my doorway. "God have mercy."

Chairs were broken, their limbs tossed around. Clothing and jewelry were strewn on the floor. Shards of the shattered looking glass covered most of the Turkish rug; a thousand small versions of me stared back, horrified at what I saw on my bed through a haze of swirling snowflakes.

I bit my knuckle to stop from screaming at the golden-horned half-ram, half-man mask propped against my headboard. It was garish—evoking images of Shakespearean plays with nasty creatures playing vicious tricks. Distantly, I heard the roar of a fire but couldn't drag my gaze away from the trickle of red dripping down my nightstand.

"This isn't real," I whispered, closing my eyes. It couldn't be real. I pinched the inside of my arm, wincing as pain lashed up my limb.

I knew I wasn't conjuring the scene up. I slumped against the door-frame, knees buckling while old fears sprang forth, torturing me.

Thomas was out with Uncle. He was safe. My uncle was safe. We'd left Sir Isaac at my grandmother's in New York, so he was safe. It was not the blood of my loved ones. I silently repeated that assurance until my pulse steadied. I forced myself to glance at the pool of red once more. It looked like blood. But—I'd left my cup of hibiscus tea mostly untouched this morning, and now the rug was stained red where it had spilled.

Slightly reassured, I closed my eyes, granting myself a moment to become the scientist I was. When I inspected the room again, I did so as if it were a mutilated corpse I'd come upon. The description was chillingly fitting. My chaise had been ripped open like a wound.

Slices of the fabric were clean and precise, much like the blade work of the man I knew as Jack the Ripper. Cotton innards were yanked out, left dangling from the frame. Someone had torn my room apart searching for God knew what.

At first I'd been too shocked to notice the scent of burnt leather, or understand that the soft grayish-white particles dancing in the breeze weren't snow, but ash. As these details slowly registered, a sense of dread weighted my limbs.

"No." I limped to the fireplace, hardly feeling the jolt of pain that lanced through my leg as I dropped to my good knee. "No. No. No!"

I stuck my hands into the flames, screaming as I drew them back, empty. Footsteps clamored up the stairs and down the hall.

"Wadsworth?" Thomas shouted.

"Here!" I called, bolstering my nerve to snatch the evidence once more. I thrust my hands in again, hissing as the embers singed my flesh.

Thomas threw his arms around me, jerking me away from the fireplace. "Are you mad?"

"It's over." I buried my face in his chest, unable to stop the tears from soaking his shirt. "They're gone. All of them."

He rocked me, his hands stroking my back in even intervals. Once I'd stopped sobbing, he asked, "What's gone?"

"Nathaniel's journals," I said, feeling my emotions overtaking me once more. "They've all been burned."

I couldn't recall how I'd come to be perched on the edge of Thomas's bed, huddling into a blanket, a mug of hot chocolate pressed into my bandaged hands. Nor could I focus on the hushed conversation happening across the room. My mind tortured me with images of flames and paper. Ash and destruction. Not one journal remained. Someone had ransacked my room. They'd burned the only evidence we had of Jack the Ripper. They'd torched what remained of my brother; no matter how conflicted I'd felt over his actions, it was like losing him all over again.

"...we'll need to inform the police," I heard Thomas saying as if he was part of a terrible dream. "They have to make a record of this."

I didn't bother dragging my focus away from the cup before me as I waited for Uncle's reply. I didn't need to see his face to know he was twisting his mustache.

"I'm afraid it won't do us any good. What will we tell them? That we had newly discovered evidence regarding Jack the Ripper? That instead of turning it over straightaway, we'd kept it in a young woman's bedchamber?" At this I shifted my attention to Uncle. "No one will believe us."

"Someone has to," Thomas argued.

"Did the general inspector you two spoke with seem keen on entertaining that notion?" Uncle asked. "Or what of Inspector Byrnes in New York? Did he strike you as the sort who'd take our word that Jack the Ripper was here?"

"So we're to simply let it go, then?" Thomas looked appalled. "The world deserves to know everything about the Ripper."

"I don't disagree, Thomas. You're free to do as you see fit, but I ask you to leave my name out of this mess." Uncle shook his head. "Don't say I didn't warn you when they wish to lock you in the asylum."

"That's ridiculous," Thomas said, though he sounded uncertain. They *had* locked Uncle in an asylum during the original Ripper investigation. I shuddered at the memory of walking along the desolate corridors of Bedlam. They'd drugged and caged my uncle like an animal.

I set my mug down, wincing at my tender fingers. I thought about Frenchy Number One in New York, about how the police had fabricated evidence to lock him away. They were more concerned with preventing mass hysteria than they were with apprehending the real murderer. Finding the person who'd slain Miss Brown so brutally wasn't their main goal. I recalled what the White City meant for not only Chicago but America as well. This was where dreams jumped out of imaginations and into reality. I had no doubt Uncle was right—General Inspector Hubbard would not hesitate to toss Thomas into an asylum, blaming his ravings on lunacy.

"He's won," I said, startling them both. "We don't even know who he is and he's stolen our only chance at solving the mystery." I unwrapped the end of my bandage, then wound it back again. "Uncle's right, Thomas. We can't tell the police we had journals detailing the Ripper murders. They'd either think we were making it up or they'd think us mad. Without proof to back up our claims, we've got nothing. No one is interested in hearsay. They'll want facts."

"Then I'll write the passages in a new journal myself." Thomas met my gaze obstinately. "I recall enough of what they said. When we catch him, it will be his word against ours. Who will know the difference?"

"You will. I will." I beckoned him to come closer and sit beside me. "We cannot sacrifice who we are in the pursuit of justice. If we fabricate these journals, we'll be no better than the police who did that very thing to Frenchy Number One. We must search for another means of revealing him."

Thomas dropped beside me, shoulders slumping. "That's just the issue. Without those bits of evidence, there's nothing that ties this murderer to the crimes in London."

"We might convince him to confess," I said, not believing it myself. Neither Thomas nor Uncle bothered calling out the unlikelihood of that occurring. A bit of hope fluttered in my chest. "He didn't destroy one thing, probably the most important."

"Oh? I was fairly certain he'd obliterated what was left of our dignity, Wadsworth."

A smile ghosted over my lips. "He didn't succeed in breaking our spirits. Look how we're speaking: 'when we catch him.' We must not give up hope yet."

Uncle walked to the door, his own countenance anything but hopeful. "Regardless of whether or not we catch him, or whether or not we can link these American crimes to England's, one fact remains; he has found us."

He let the weight of that statement settle around us. Thomas whipped around to face my uncle, his gaze wide. I'd been so caught up in the horrible discovery, I hadn't yet been frightened by the fact he'd been *in* my room, gutting my things like they were his newest victims. Fear blew an icy breath down my neck, goose bumps rising at once. Jack the Ripper had been stalking us.

"He has crept into our home and destroyed evidence," Uncle continued. "The staff heard nothing, despite the chaos and devastation in that room. Which means he waited until almost everyone was out of the house, doing errands, before he struck." Uncle swallowed hard. "Do you know how he accomplished that?"

"By watching the house." I shivered in place. "He had to have been watching us for quite some time."

Thomas went very still beside me. "Stalking, not watching. He's been toying with us all. But now he's tiring of the game; he craves something more tangible than our fear." He slowly rotated until we were face-to-face, his expression shuttering. "I guarantee it's not me or the professor he's after. Not when his targets have all been women."

"Thomas," I said slowly, "we don't know that for certain."

"No." He swallowed hard. "But we soon will. It's only a matter of when—I suspect he's going to make his intentions clear in a dramatic showing."

I searched my heart for the fear that ought to be present. For the terror that had coursed as readily as blood through my veins earlier. A violent murderer who'd slain more women than we probably knew thirsted for my blood. A tingle started in my center, slowly unfurling until tendrils reached my toes. Most worrisome was its cause. Determination—not fear—settled in my chest like a raging lion. I had been stalked and hunted and had escaped harm thus far.

I'd now be the one setting a trap for this monster. "He's not the only one who tires of this game." I pushed to my feet, jaw set, as Thomas handed me my cane. "Let him come for me."

FORTY-ONE
AGAINST ONE'S NATURE

GRANDMAMA'S ESTATE
CHICAGO, ILLINOIS
15 FEBRUARY 1889

Back in London, what felt like ages ago, I'd sat in Hyde Park with my brother, watching birds fly across the pond, readying themselves for winter. They didn't go against their nature, never ignored the voice inside them urging them to seek warmer lands. Their innate sense of preservation urged them to flee to warmth and safety.

At the time, I'd wondered why the women who'd found themselves at the end of Jack the Ripper's blade hadn't listened to their own innate warning systems—the ones that whispered of danger. Now, as I stared at the golden ram's-head mask left to taunt me, I understood why.

I hated the way the horns twisted like serpents above goat-shaped ears. It looked like a devil's mask from Eastern European folklore. One where goat and man had morphed into one terrible creature. In fact, I was almost certain I'd seen something similar during our stay at Bran Castle. I abruptly stopped thinking about the mask and went back to packing. Little bells of warning jingled in my mind, calling me a fool. But I'd had enough. I couldn't stay in this house, waiting—no, *hiding* from my fate. I would not let fear make me its prisoner.

I shoved the last of my dresses into a trunk, sitting on it to shut it tight. Thomas knocked on my door, his attention immediately falling on my unruly luggage. His brows raised. "Are we leaving and I'm the last to know?"

"Not we. *I*." I huffed as I reached down to fasten the locks with no luck. The bloody thing was a beast thanks to the bold designs Liza had initially packed as part of a post-wedding surprise holiday. They were lovely, but highly impractical for travel. Thomas crossed his arms. His look promised a debate and I was tired of them already. "If I am on my own, he's more likely to strike. You know that's true, even if you don't care for the idea of it. I'll go rent a room somewhere near the fair, or see if Minnie has any rooms above the pharmacy left. I'll wander the streets during the daytime. Eventually I'm bound to catch his notice."

"Of course I don't like the idea of it, Wadsworth. I can't fathom anyone who would."

"It's a little reckless, but it's also a good way to provoke him into action."

"Please. *Don't.* You do realize what you're asking of me, right? You're asking me to stand by and wait for a cunning murderer to come for you. As if it might not break me to lose you." He gripped the doorframe as if to keep himself from rushing to me. "I won't ask you to stay. But I will ask you to consider how you'd feel if I was the one marching into death. Would you stand back and not fight for me?"

An image of him sacrificing himself as bait sent chills skittering along my body. I would sooner chain him to a laboratory table than permit him to do such a thing. He deserved credit for allowing me a choice when I'd rob him of his without second thought. "Thomas..."

I watched him swallow his fear down, saw the resolve set in. He wouldn't stop me. He'd watch me walk out the door and disappear into the night. He would be terrified, but I knew him well enough now to know he'd keep his word. We'd been down this path together before. One where our ideas of how to proceed during a case diverged. That time, I'd chosen my own way over trusting in our partnership. It was a mistake. One I did not intend to make again. I slid off the trunk, deflated. A tear slipped down my cheek and I angrily swiped at it.

"I don't know what else to do," I confessed, holding my hands out. The scent of lavender wafted into the air, the oil healing and soothing my burns. "How do we catch someone who might as well be a demon born of another dimension?"

Thomas crossed the room in an instant, taking me in his arms. "By standing against him together, Wadsworth. We will solve this mystery and we will do it as a united front."

"As touching and nauseating as this little scene may be," Mephistopheles said from my doorway, his hands shoved into his pockets, "I have some information that might assist in your endeavor."

The ringmaster strode into my room and settled on the bed as if he were the high king of the Fairy claiming his throne. He set his top hat on the golden ram's-head mask and kicked his boots up, the leather shining in the most annoying manner. "Cute mask. Do you wear it to set the mood, or..."

"You are completely ridiculous."

"Is this the first time you've realized this?" Mephistopheles raised his brows. "And here I thought you were quite bright, my unrequited love."

"Where have you been?" I asked, hints of my earlier suspicion returning. I couldn't stop thinking about how talented career murderers were. They were friends, lovers, family members. All leading what seemed like regular lives, except for one monstrous secret. "Minnie has been looking for you."

"She—"

"Let me guess," I said, losing patience and cutting him off. His usual response always involved mention of his...charms. I was not in the mood for jokes. "She wouldn't be the first woman or man to do so. Can you be serious for once?"

"What I was about to say, Miss Wadsworth," he said, amusement in his dark eyes, "was she must not have been looking too hard. I haven't been anywhere but my theater. In fact, I went to call on her today and her staff couldn't find her. Maybe she couldn't handle seeing a face this handsome again."

He glanced over my shoulder to where Thomas now leaned against the wall looking bored. I shook a sense of foreboding from my heart. I'd seen Minnie a couple of hours ago and she seemed fine enough. If he'd visited her after, that meant he was the last person known to be at her home. Maybe she saw him arrive and asked her staff to send him away. Or maybe he'd taken her...

"I did, however, manage to gather some information you both may find interesting," Mephistopheles continued, unaware of my growing worry.

"Oh, good. It has a purpose for crawling out from its hidey-hole at last." Thomas smiled sweetly, his eyes flashing with delight as Mephistopheles's jaw tightened.

"Weren't you the groveling soul who inquired after *my* expertise?" he said. "What other tasks are you not measuring up to? Or"—a slick, antagonistic smile spread across his face—"might I ask Audrey Rose instead?"

"Enough!" I exclaimed. "You're both infantile. Stop provoking each other and focus. What did you learn, Ayden?"

Perhaps it was the use of his true name, but I finally held the ringmaster's full attention. "Very well, then." He picked imaginary lint off his suit, his expression hurt. "There are two women and one child who were last seen in the Englewood neighborhood of 63rd and Wallace Streets. Some were known to be associated with a pharmacy there."

Any excitement or hope I'd felt withered. This wasn't anything new. We'd already visited the pharmacy and the police couldn't find any signs of a crime. My shoulders slumped forward. I was suddenly exhausted. We didn't even know for certain if Noah's missing women were related to our case, though I still believed they were.

"Thank you for—"

"I have people—let's call them information specialists—who also mentioned something about the World's Fair."

"How original." Thomas crossed his arms. "Who *isn't* talking about it?"

"The better question to ask yourselves is not who, but what. *What* aren't they saying about the fair? What do they worry about when those pretty little lights dim? It couldn't possibly be the blood they found near the docks. Or the bloody handkerchief outside the great, impressive Court of Honor."

Mephistopheles lifted his hat from the ram's-head mask, tumbled it down his arm, and stuck it on his head with a carnival-inspired flourish. It was hard to tell where the showman ended and the real young man underneath the sequined suits began. He might not be wearing a visible mask, but that did not mean he was without one now.

"Rumor has it... there's a body. They've got it locked up tight in the morgue near Lake Michigan. The Columbian Guard stands outside the door, day and night." He grinned at our stunned expressions. "Seems strange, doesn't it? A police force created entirely for the fair to be guarding a body in a morgue. Especially if she's a nobody."

"Speaking of bodies." I eyed him suspiciously. "Minnie mentioned her understudy is missing. What have you heard about that?"

He hopped off my bed as gracefully as a panther and stalked close. "I've heard that body in the morgue might be hers. Now I need *you* to tell me for sure."

I frowned at him. "You wouldn't have come here if you wouldn't benefit from the information, would you?" His answering smirk told me everything I needed to know about his motivations. "Don't you ever do things out of decency?"

An ancient sadness filled his gaze for a moment, stretching far beyond what his nineteen years should know. Little hairs rose along my arms.

Then Mephistopheles blinked and his eyes were once again filled with mirth. I must be in need of more rest than I thought. My nightmares were bleeding into my waking hours.

"I tried decency once." He wrinkled his nose. "I wouldn't recommend it. Leaves a bitter taste in your mouth."

"I thought that was just defeat," Thomas added, trying and failing to not look smug. "I've heard that's not so pleasant, either. Not that I'd know."

With a seemingly great amount of restraint, Mephistopheles turned to me, taking my hand in his. He leaned forward, pressing his lips to my knuckles, his gaze locked on mine.

"I do hope you're happy, Miss Wadsworth. And while I'd love to stay and be entertained by your court fool"—he flashed his teeth in what was supposed to be a smile at Thomas—"it's time for me to go."

I had a strange premonition that once he waltzed out that door, it would be the last time I set eyes on him. "You're leaving for good, aren't you? I thought the Moonlight Carnival only just arrived."

"Have we, though…only just arrived?" A secret danced in his eyes, one he had no intention of sharing. His expression turned serious again. "Once blood starts flowing, even the most angelic of places loses its appeal, Miss Wadsworth." His focus darted behind me. "Beware of trusting beautiful creatures. They hide the most wicked surprises."

Thomas stepped forward and wrapped his arms around me as I shivered in place. I tried to ignore the effect Mephistopheles's words had on my growingly superstitious mind, but I couldn't help but feel as if he spoke of the future. One he'd seen as clear as a cloudless day when the rest of us were stumbling in the fog.

"What about Trudy?" I asked, desperately casting about for a reason to make him stay. "Don't you wish to discover if she's the body in the morgue?"

"I trust you'll sort it out the way you do best."

He tipped his bullion-trimmed top hat, then vanished one last time. I could only hope we hadn't just allowed a murderer to roam free once more.

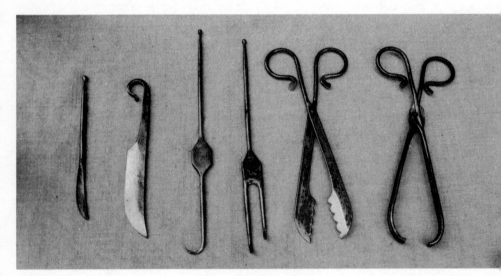
Vintage Post Mortem Tools

FORTY-TWO
WHITE CITY STAINED RED

WORLD'S COLUMBIAN EXPOSITION
CHICAGO, ILLINOIS
16 FEBRUARY 1889

One would never guess while walking through the heavenly city above that underneath it lay labyrinthine tunnels used by workers and laborers servicing the fair. It made sense, though. In order to keep the illusion alive and well, fairgoers couldn't be bothered with mundane things such as rubbish being carted and loos cleaned.

As we followed members of the Columbian Guard deeper underground, we passed rooms filled with props and excess items for the fair. A riot of flowers was in one, buckets of creamy white paint and an odd-looking spray contraption in another. Electrical devices and popped-corn machines and things to delight—all polished and ready to go. There were boxes of Cracker Jack, which everyone had been eating the last time we were here. A scent of caramel mixed with salt followed us as we wound down and through another corridor.

Even being in the bowels of the grand city above, I felt awed by the majesty of it all. Then there was the secret chamber we were headed to. The one not mentioned in any pamphlet or newspaper. Beneath the beating heart of the Court of Honor was a command station larger than an army's. Within its well-fortified walls, there was a morgue.

The lead guard paused outside a door with no name etched onto it. Unlike the others, it was closed, the lights out within. I knew where we were before he set his key in the lock and ushered us into the cool space. He flicked a light on, the slight buzz the only sound in the room. I scrunched my nose at the sharp scent. It smelled of bleach. My eyes watered and my throat burned. I wondered if they'd spilled a ten-liter jug or if they'd purposely used so much.

Whatever their reasoning, it was strange. Almost as if they were trying to scrub any stains from the glistening streets, even this far below.

Thomas blinked but, other than that, showed no discomfort. He was alert, his attention sweeping the room from ceiling to floor to the large drawers set into the far wall. The ones that held bodies, no doubt. I moved my own focus around, absorbing as much as I could of the sterile space. Everything here was white as well. The tiles that extended from the floor to the top of the walls. Everything was built of cool, smooth stone except for the ceiling.

A hose mounted on one wall featured an ornate crank, the only bit of beauty in an otherwise blank canvas. I caught a glimpse of familiar medical tools and aprons peeking out from an open closet door. Three silver tables were evenly spaced, the holes on top of them indicating they were meant for postmortems. A silver pail sat positioned under each and I fought my revulsion as I pieced together its purpose. I didn't see any sawdust, and the stench of bleach made sense. Bodily fluids would funnel into the holes and get collected in the pails.

The guard who'd unlocked the door cleared his throat. "Dr. Rosen will be here shortly to answer your questions."

With that, he stepped back toward the door, nodding to someone on the other side. Thomas and I both flinched as he shut the door behind him, locking it with a click that seemed to thrum in my chest.

I slowly inhaled and exhaled, ignoring the burning in my throat. I hated cages. "Why would they lock us in here?"

Thomas was quiet a moment, considering. Finally, he said, "I wonder if it's not us they're concerned with keeping in, but keeping others out."

"Do you believe our murderer is employed by the fair?"

Thomas shrugged. "Until we examine the body, we won't know if it's the same person who's killed in New York and London. Should we open the drawer and see what we find?"

A sense of calm radiated around me as I moved toward the drawers. My cane clicked loudly in the small room, though my pulse no longer raced in time with it. I paused at the only drawer with a label: Miss Trudy Jasper. The missing woman who'd worked for Mephistopheles.

I set my cane down and pulled the drawer handle. At first it wouldn't budge; then Thomas came over and we both managed to open it with our combined effort.

A marble-white body greeted us. Her hair was a lovely shade of auburn, reminding me a bit of flames. Her eyes were closed, though I imagined them being a wondrous hazel for some reason. No one had bothered covering her, and her wounds were immediately visible.

I was grateful I'd set my cane down or else I'd have knocked it over as I gripped the edge of the floating metal drawer holding her up. I squeezed my eyes shut, knowing it wouldn't do any good to stop the images I was seeing. Memories ran wild.

Suddenly, I was no longer standing in this strange crypt below the White City. I was back in London, in a foggy alleyway. The moon hung suspiciously low in the sky—yellow like a cat's eye, watching the chaotic world below as if it were a mouse to toy with.

"Audrey Rose?"

Thomas's voice was strained, like I imagined his expression to be.

I shook my head, not quite ready to answer him. I wasn't weak. I was overcome with the truth that sat before me. There was no doubt left in my mind that my brother's confession had been true. Nathaniel wasn't Jack the Ripper. I knew that because this woman's wounds were almost *exactly* like Miss Eddowes's. The second, unfortunate victim of the infamous double event. Even a cursory glance told me that much. I was certain a detailed inspection would prove my theory correct.

I wrenched my eyes open. I would not let him win. Jack the Ripper had left this body for us, knowing our tenuous connection to her—this was a proclamation and a dare. He felt untouchable and he mocked us. I slowly straightened up, giving Thomas a tight smile as I walked around the body, collecting each detail of her vicious demise.

A small bruise on her left hand—a detail that hadn't been known about Catherine Eddowes until her body had been washed. Part of Trudy's right ear had been cut away, again, just as Catherine Eddowes's had been. The familiar black stitching of the postmortem Y incision seemed to sag along with her skin over her abdomen. I'd wager my soul her kidney was missing, along with at least a foot or two of her intestines.

I swallowed hard. It was as if I was looking upon the body of Miss Eddowes all over again. I finally dragged my gaze up to her throat. An angry slash had ended her life. Her carotid had been cut, indicating she'd have bled out quickly. Other injuries were inflicted after death.

I glanced up, noticing that Thomas had already been watching me carefully. I wondered if he worried that this was becoming too much. If he felt the need to shelter me from the storm he thought was raging within. He had no way of knowing I was not afraid.

Blood pounded furiously in my veins. Months of devastation slithered into my bones, wrapping around my senses until all I saw was red. Anger. It was a beast that couldn't be tamed.

I'd believed beyond a doubt that my brother had been the devil. I'd ached at his death but felt justice had been served. I'd found peace, believing he could never harm another. No matter how much that thought had ripped my heart out and tortured me. I had spent *months* warring with my own sense of right and wrong, believing the world ought to know he was the monster who'd stalked Whitechapel streets and that they were safe from him forever.

I'd held my tongue, worried my father would not withstand the pain of such a public scandal. He'd been so fragile then. And selfishly, a part of me wanted to protect Nathaniel from hatred and scorn, even in death. I knew him only as my devoted brother, after all. I loved him.

I slid my gaze back to the body on the table. Trudy, like the women who'd come before her, did not deserve to die.

Thomas hadn't taken his attention from me, his concern obvious. I knew he recognized that Trudy's wounds were done by the Ripper as easily as I had. Before I could assure him of my composure, the lock slid free. A man with a crisp apron walked in. If he was surprised by our youth, he didn't let it show. This must be Dr. Rosen, then, an old pupil of Uncle's.

"Mr. Cresswell and Miss Wadsworth, I presume?" he asked. We nodded and he seemed to be going through the motions of formality. He glanced at the body, his expression unchanged. "I'm Dr. Rosen. Dr. Wadsworth sent a telegram this morning."

I nodded. "He sends his apologies, but he was unable to accompany us."

"Indeed. I see you've already helped yourself to the body." Dr. Rosen indicated the table.

There was no reproach in his tone, only cool fact sharing. If anything, he seemed pleased to not prolong our visit. He reminded me of Uncle in that sense. I had a feeling he got along better with the dead. He walked over to the closet with the supplies and emerged with a piece of torn paper. Everything seemed to move through quicksand after that. I watched as his arm slowly extended, the paper changing colors in the light as he lifted it up. Then I realized it wasn't shifting colors at all—what I was seeing were bloodstains.

Thomas was the only thing not suspended in quicksand; he moved seemingly with inhuman speed around the table, snatching the letter before the doctor handed it to me. I was grateful for his ability to read me. I needed a moment to collect myself. The body, the note—it brought about a strange ringing in my ears. Thankfully, it lasted only a few seconds, hardly noticeable to anyone but my very observant former fiancé.

He waited until I'd gathered up my emotions in my fist, then stood beside me so we could read the note together. The script was familiar—it had haunted my dreams on more than one occasion. It was not my brother's handwriting. It was Jack the Ripper's.

"These violent delights have violent ends
And in their triumph die, like
fire and powder, Which as they kiss
consume." A rose by any other name
does not deserve to live.
Why do you think that is?

I stared mutely at the note. I'd expected poor grammar and another reference to Milton. That seemed to be Jack's favorite back in London. I couldn't decide if I was more disturbed by the fact that he was quoting *Romeo and Juliet* or that he'd written it in blood. What on earth was he suggesting now? I glanced up at Thomas, but he'd gone deathly pale. In fact, I could have sworn Miss Jasper's corpse had more color, even drained of its fluids.

Unaware of or unconcerned with the reaction the letter had brought about, Dr. Rosen slid the mortuary drawer closed, removing the mutilated corpse from our sight. "The note was tucked into her bodice. We found it only after she'd been brought here." He seemed to deliberate on his next words. "It had actually been nailed to her body along with a rose."

Thomas had been otherwise distracted by the note, no doubt reliving the taunts sent to the police last autumn. At this, his attention snapped up.

"Where?" His clipped tone was neither polite nor merely inquisitive. I'd never heard him demand anything before. He could be arrogant and slightly obnoxious during an investigation, yes, but there was always a lightness to it. There was no such levity in his voice now. He sounded exactly like the dark prince he was. "Describe precisely where it was on her person."

Dr. Rosen faced us, crossing his arms against his chest. "It was nailed to her heart." He glanced from Thomas to me, coming to some other decision. "It's not going to be mentioned in the papers. You are here as a favor I owe Dr. Wadsworth. Do not make me regret my generosity." He nodded to one of the guards who was peering in through a window cut high in the door. "Speaking of, I've heard there's another body en route to your residence as we speak. A young woman who worked here, actually. Since she wasn't found on the fairgrounds, they didn't wish for me to examine her. You might want to hurry along. I'm sure Dr. Wadsworth will be waiting."

I thanked Dr. Rosen for allowing us in to see the body, though Thomas hadn't uttered a single word after demanding the information about the note. He kept to himself as we followed members of the guard back through the corridors, only reacting when I seemed to slip over the smooth floor in my haste to get out of the underground metropolis. He kept his hand at the small of my back, as if simultaneously assisting me and reassuring himself I was still there. I doubted he was aware he was even doing it. His mind seemed a hundred miles away.

I waited until we were tucked into the carriage before inquiring into his black mood. He sat across from me on a bench seat and turned dark eyes on me. I shivered.

"What's gotten into you?" I asked. I was disturbed that our doubts had been eradicated about Jack the Ripper, but there was something else happening with him.

He'd shifted back into that strange Thomas. The one who didn't move, who seemed to be frozen on the outside while a molten core seethed within. It took a moment, but he finally released the tension he'd been holding. He stretched his legs out in the carriage, but it still wasn't entirely large enough for him to be comfortable. He was careful to avoid hitting my leg, though I wasn't sure if it was out of worry over hurting me or his desire to not touch me. Either way, I recognized it for what it was: a show of nonchalance he didn't feel.

"Thomas?" I asked again. "Tell me."

He leaned forward and I instinctually met him halfway. Instead of whispering in my ear, he rapped the window of our carriage, grabbing the attention of our driver.

"Sir?" the driver called.

"North Side. Near the theater district. I'll show you where when we're close."

"Yes, sir. North Side it is."

Thomas settled back against his seat, watching me absorb our change of destination.

"Shouldn't we head straight to Uncle?" I tried not to let trepidation slip into my tone. "We really shouldn't dally. You know how he gets when there's a body to inspect."

Something I'd never seen directed at me flashed in Thomas's features before he reined himself back in. Anger. A leash I hadn't realized he'd been wearing slipped, if only for a fraction of a breath. Thomas was furious.

"I'm sure he'll understand. Especially when we inform him there's no longer any doubt Jack the Ripper has returned. Nor will he mind when he discovers our murderer has set his sights on someone else. Likely, he's been coveting her from the start."

His jaw clenched so hard I worried he might chip a tooth. I reached for him, trying to soothe his black mood. "Thomas..."

"A rose was nailed to her heart, Wadsworth." He seemed to be on the verge of combustion. I realized his anger was not directed at me. He was ready to attack the man responsible for all these deaths. I sat back and pulled my overcoat close. I wouldn't want to encounter this Thomas in a darkened alley. This Thomas seemed utterly lethal and unpredictable. "Do you find it a bit odd? That he'd leave such a dramatic gift?"

"A gift?"

"Yes. A gift. He's sent you his own morbid bouquet. Presented with a corpse you would never mistake for anyone's work but his own."

Thomas released a breath. The action brought some of his self-control back. I knew he would never hurt me, but it was still jarring to witness him transform into someone so deadly. It all crashed into clarity for me—Thomas would no longer simply slip inside the mindset of a murderer, should anything happen to me. He'd become one. He would destroy those who hurt me, and he'd feel nothing in the process of his methodical slaughter. I wanted to chide him for that, but knew I'd feel the same way should anyone hurt him. I'd disembowel the world and bathe in its blood if someone murdered him.

We were a twisted pair indeed.

"Audrey Rose. Who has a Shakespeare production happening? Who knew where that body was being kept?"

"Thomas," I started slowly, trying to shove my own suspicions away again, "we know he didn't commit the murders on the *Etruria.*"

"He didn't commit those particular crimes, but there were other crimes on that boat." Thomas shook his head. "I'm not saying he's responsible, but I want to see his reaction when we deliver this news."

On that much I could agree. It was best to unleash Thomas and his deductions on Mephistopheles; it would settle both of our minds and help our investigation.

We didn't speak for a while, both of us lost in thought. I knew Thomas's reaction was one of worry. He'd never forgive himself if something happened to me. But I couldn't bring myself to believe that the rose and note had been intended *just* for me. This seemed more directed toward Thomas. I believed it was sent to rattle him enough to make mistakes.

Jack the Ripper had had plenty of opportunities to attack me if he wished to do so. From London to the *Etruria,* New York, and now here in Chicago, I hadn't always ventured out with an escort. If he truly coveted me, as Thomas feared, he would have made himself known. He knew my brother; that much I was certain of. He had cause to be in my home. I couldn't imagine him staying his murderous hand for this long.

Unless I was never his intended target.

We rolled to a stop outside of the theater we'd visited just last week. Thomas cursed under his breath. The door and windows were boarded up; lights were out. A crudely painted sign said FOR RENT.

Even though I'd worried this might happen, I'd still hoped the ringmaster might change his mind and wait until we investigated his missing performer's death. But Mephistopheles hadn't wasted any time packing up his carnival and moving on to another city, leaving the bloody chips to fall where they may.

FORTY-THREE

COLD AS ICE

GRANDMAMA'S ESTATE
CHICAGO, ILLINOIS
16 FEBRUARY 1889

I stared at the body, the flesh the color of freshly fallen snow. I gently
pressed my fingers against her jaw, turning her head slightly to search
for marks. My skin burned from the coldness of death. Not one blem-
ish or laceration or outward wound to be seen. I set my cane against
the wheeled table holding our postmortem tools. We needed to call
upon Noah soon. This woman had been identified as Miss Edna Van
Tassel, one of the missing women he'd been investigating.

"Was she exposed to the elements?" I asked. It was unlikely,
given there weren't any signs of frostbite present. No blackened digits
or blistering of the skin. She appeared as if she'd simply fallen asleep
and never woke up.

Uncle shook his head. "No. The general inspector said the
woman who owns the boardinghouse where she rents a room didn't
see her for breakfast, so she went looking. The landlady was quite put
out that she'd let food go to waste and marched upstairs to give her a
scolding. When she entered her room, she found it empty. A few days

passed and she phoned Miss Van Tassel's family, wanting them to collect her things."

I inhaled. "Then her family explained she hadn't returned home."

"Correct." Uncle nodded. "Then they hired the Pinkertons through connections they had."

Which was how Noah became involved.

"After being missing for a week, our victim was found in her bed, tucked under the covers, her clothing folded neatly and left on a chair. The landlady is convinced she must have snuck back in to retrieve her things, then died in her sleep."

"That's absurd! Why wouldn't she think something more nefarious occurred?" I drew my brows together. "Did she hear anything odd?"

Uncle shook his head. "There were no sounds of struggle. Actually, there were no sounds coming from that room at all. The landlady happened upon her when she was about to show the room."

"Were there signs of a disturbance?" Thomas asked. "Any personal items missing?"

I sneaked a glance at him. He'd barely spoken the entire carriage ride home, his focus turned inward. What little he did utter wasn't happy news. He said there was no doubt remaining that Jack the Ripper sought me. Then he'd shut his emotions off and entered that land of frost and ice. He hadn't yet warmed from it.

"Not that the landlady noticed." Uncle took his spectacles off, buffing them with the corner of his tweed jacket. "The only oddity was Miss Van Tassel wasn't wearing her nightgown. The homeowner said she'd never sleep so indecently, but she couldn't fathom what kind of girl went off for a week without a word and snuck back in, either."

Thomas canted his head. Finally. He was coming around. He gazed at the body. "I suspect the loo was shared in a corridor or on another level of the home, which means it's unlikely she removed her own clothes before bed." He looked to my uncle for confirmation. Uncle nodded. "Regardless of her sleeping preferences, she'd likely have kept her nightgown on in case she needed to get up in the night. Not to mention, here where temperatures are frigid, it doesn't make sense for her to sleep without layers. At least not during this season."

He paced around the small basement laboratory, his hands near frantic as they tapped along his thighs. I knew he was pushing himself, trying to shove pieces of this impossible puzzle together in hopes of preventing the Ripper from stalking anyone else. Anyone such as me.

I waited for the worry to creep in, to hinder my own investigative skills. I almost felt relief, like I finally understood a part of his game I hadn't known existed before. If Jack the Ripper wanted me, then we could find a way to deceive him into thinking he'd won. I hadn't shared this idea with Thomas; judging from the wildness in his eyes and the promise of violence, I didn't deem it necessary just yet. I would let him calm himself before broaching that subject. And then we'd come up with a plan together.

"She was missing for a week but doesn't show signs of decay..." Thomas muttered observations aloud to himself, not expecting an answer. "A young person, dying in their sleep with no indications of disease or trauma. He killed her but how? And why return her to her chambers? What purpose does that serve?"

He paced faster, slowly becoming one with our killer, placing himself in the role of a demon. While he continued his descent into the mind of a murderer, a wide-eyed maid brought a tea service with stacks of lemon and raspberry tarts, pausing to consider which surface she might set it on. Her eyes lingered on the nearly naked corpse, and though her expression was perfectly blank, her throat bobbed with suppressed emotion. No one enjoyed the dead being on display, at least not in the way we set them like meat to carve.

"There, on the sideboard, please," I said, my tone as calm as possible. "Thank you."

After she'd retreated up the stairs, I made my way over to the teapot, pouring three cups. A hint of Earl Grey and rose cut through the slight odor of death. I put two rose-scented sugar cubes in Uncle's cup and four in Thomas's, knowing the extra sweetness seemed to aide him in his deductions. I was too rattled for sugar and left mine plain. I set the silver tongs and bowl aside, carefully bringing one cup and tart over at a time. It gave me something to do while turning over my own thoughts. If I could convince Thomas of my safety, perhaps we could set a trap. Would the Ripper be able to walk away from an opportunity to snatch me?

"Thank you." Uncle took his cup, sipping immediately. He'd practically finished the whole thing by the time I'd handed Thomas his. I glanced at the clock. We'd missed supper ages ago.

Thomas paused his pacing only long enough to shove in a few bites of his pastry before washing it down with tea. "Do we know who she was with or what she was doing prior to her death? There was mention of her possibly collecting wages from her old employer."

"The police were sorting that out when I was told to take the body. They also sent word to the Pinkertons, so your associate will be informed by them."

"We're missing something." Thomas seemed more agitated by the second. "What else? Was there anything in the room that shouldn't have been? Anything the landlady commented on, even in passing."

"Roses," Uncle said. "She mentioned a vase full of fresh roses on the nightstand." Thomas didn't so much as breathe as he swung around, his gaze landing on me. Either unaware of the sudden tension in the room, or maybe because of it, Uncle handed me and Thomas aprons. "Focus, the two of you. Let's see what answers we can find on our own."

I glanced at my untouched tart before setting it aside. It was just as well that I complete this portion of our work without a stomach full of sweet lemon curd. I placed my hands on the flesh like I'd been taught, pressing my blade hard enough for the skin to part like ruby waves as I dragged my scalpel from shoulder to sternum and exposed the red layers of flesh.

A sense of calm entered the room as I repeated the process on the other side, my Y incision nearly complete as I slid the blade down the torso. Without waiting for further instruction, I doused my rag in carbolic acid and wiped my weapon down before sinking it back into the flesh. In moments I'd removed the heart and viscera, handing them off to Uncle to be weighed and cataloged by Thomas.

He caught my eye briefly, looking up from his notes, his expression unreadable. I glanced at the liquid matter splattered up my pale sage velvet sleeves like tiny embroidered petals. Just as quickly as he'd studied me, he was back to his own work, his brow crinkled in deep concentration. Perhaps I'd imagined that his attention was directed toward me.

Once we'd taken note of every detail, I pulled the tray with the stomach close, preparing to do a full dissection of it. I'd be looking for any signs of poison. A drop of perspiration hit the metal surface, quickly followed by another. I jerked my attention up. Uncle removed a handkerchief from his pocket and blotted at his brow. It was quite cold in the basement of this house, especially in the dead of winter.

Petals of red bloomed over his cheeks. Not embarrassment. He appeared to be suddenly burning up with fever.

"Are you feeling all right?" I asked, trying to keep the concern from my voice. The last thing I wished to do was annoy Uncle. "Thomas and I can handle this if you'd like to rest—"

"It's nothing. I forgot my overcoat again and caught a chill." Uncle waved off my worry. "Mind your work, Audrey Rose. Stomach contents. Open it up now; unfortunately we haven't got all evening to study this body. General Inspector Hubbard will be here within the hour, and he'll expect answers. I suggest we try not to anger him again."

"Very well, sir." I picked up another scalpel, readying myself for the dissection of the stomach. I tried ignoring Uncle's hands as he gripped the edge of the examination table, his knuckles as white as the bones I'd just exposed. In quick, careful motions, I opened the outer layers of the organ.

"It appears—*Uncle!*" I cried as he collapsed against the table, the medical tools clattering onto the floor around him. "Uncle!"

I moved swiftly to his side, slipping my hands under his arms, trying to lift him back up. It was of no use; he'd lost consciousness. His head fell forward, his spectacles askew. I shot a look in Thomas's direction. "A little assistance, Cresswell?" I tilted Uncle's head back, my fingers searching out a pulse. It was faint, but it was there. He must be more ill than he'd let on. His lids fluttered, but he did not open his eyes again. "Thomas?"

I glanced up. Thomas stood against the wall, his fist gripping his stomach, his face screwed up in pain. The world became a narrow corridor, void of sound. Irrational horror spread through my limbs, weighing me down as much as my uncle's body.

Poison.

"Thomas!" I shouted, watching helplessly as he staggered forward, trying to get to me. I gently set my uncle on the floor, making sure he was on his side in case he began vomiting. I did not want him to asphyxiate on it. I sprang up, my heart now beating ten times too fast as I limped over and caught Thomas the moment before he slammed to the ground. I gripped him to me fiercely, as if I could protect him from this invisible demon. "You're fine," I said frantically, smoothing his damp hair back. "You're going to be all right."

A cough racked through him and he wheezed a laugh. "Are you commanding that?"

"Yes." I held his face between my hands, staring into his eyes, watching his pupils dilate. I forced the tremor from my voice, not wanting to scare him. "I command you, and if there's a God, then I command Him and His angels, too. You will not die on me, Thomas Cresswell. Do you understand? I will kill you if you die!"

Another coughing fit had him trembling in place. He could no longer speak.

"Help!" I screamed as loudly as I could. "Come immediately!"

I clutched Thomas tightly, forcing my mind to become the leader my heart desperately needed. It was clear they'd been poisoned. I focused on identifying which kind. Uncle twitched from his place on the floor, his breath coming in deep wheezes. His face was splotchy, as was Thomas's. I almost lost my battle with tears as I studied him.

Thomas gripped his stomach, indicating they'd ingested it. *Think.* It was both a command and a plea to myself. If I could identify the poison, I could find an antidote.

"Miss?" The maid from earlier stopped short, her attention bouncing from Thomas to Uncle to me, sitting there, cradling my dying love. A look of unadulterated fear entered her features. I wondered if she thought I was the monster who'd done this. "Are they..."

"Ring for a doctor immediately!" I said, thanking the marvels of technology for having a telephone in this old house. "Tell him there's been two poisonings. Possibly arsenic, given their symptoms, but it's working through their system at an advanced rate. It might be belladonna or something similar. Maybe even some strange combination of them all. Tell him he must come *at once.* Do you understand?"

She nodded too many times, her own body trembling. I made my voice harsher than it needed to be to wake her from her own daze.

"Hurry! They haven't got much time left."

FORTY-FOUR

AN AVENGING ANGEL

GRANDMAMA'S ESTATE
CHICAGO, ILLINOIS
16 FEBRUARY 1889

A heart was a curious thing. So contradictory. The way it ached in both good and bad ways. The way it leapt with joy and ceased with sorrow. It could beat madly and wildly during both pleasure and pain. Currently, my heart was steady. Too steady, as I watched blood drip into a waiting bowl, the rhythmic splatters hitting in time with my breaths. Perhaps I was in shock. It was the only rational explanation for how calm I was.

The doctor must have felt my gaze on him, probing. He flicked his attention to me, his fingers covered in wet blood—*Thomas's* blood—before returning to his patient. His name was Dr. Carson and he appeared to be one million years of age.

Each of his movements was slow and deliberate—an excellent trait in a doctor, but a horrible thing to witness when there were two people I loved in need of immediate attention. I wanted to shake him into action but forced myself to stand still, without any motion at all. Fearful of what I'd do should I begin moving.

He'd seen to Uncle first. I didn't wish to consider how torn I'd felt when he'd made that choice. He dabbed at the wounds he'd made on Thomas's forearm, his lined face tense. My grip on my cane tightened, as if I could crush my worry with my fist.

Worry wasn't the only emotion I felt. The more I considered how someone had tried to murder Uncle and Thomas—and likely me—the brighter the flame grew in my center. Anger was good. It meant there were still things left to fight for. I nursed it, coddled it, begged for it to surface, to kindle the fire I needed to raze the murderer to ashes. There were no guarantees that either Thomas or Uncle would live.

If Thomas died...

The doctor cleared his throat, the sound annoyed, as if it wasn't the first time he'd tried getting my attention. I shook myself from swirling thoughts. "Pardon?"

"Bloodletting is the best method to remove the poison," he said, voice gruff. Like the pale-faced staff, he probably imagined I was the murderess. I was, after all, the only one unscathed. "He's weak, though. I can't remove any more without a greater threat."

He tossed a dirtied rag into the second bowl of blood and I watched as he added a sharp-smelling astringent and set it aflame. Perhaps he worried I was a vampire or a bloodthirsty demon. As if I'd guzzle tainted blood even if that were true.

"Will he be all right?" I asked, shoving my treacherous thoughts away. "Is there anything else I can do?"

The doctor studied my face carefully. I did my best to hide each terrible thought, to soften my anger so as to not have it be confused with guilt. His eyes narrowed. "If you're a godly woman, I suggest praying, Miss Wadsworth. There's certainly nothing of this earth left for you to do."

He snapped his satchel closed and left the room without another word. I didn't bother watching him go. I remained at the end of the bed, guarding Thomas. His skin was so sallow—more pale and sickly yellow than I'd ever seen it before. Even when we'd nearly drowned in those water-filled traps under Bran Castle, when we'd been soaked through and freezing, he'd always gaze at me with that wicked half smile, his flesh flushed and vibrant with life.

Thomas Cresswell couldn't die. If he did…a darkness so complete as to truly be terrifying welled up inside me. I did not know who I'd become, should I lose him. But Satan would tremble at my approach.

I watched his chest rise unsteadily, his lids fluttering as Uncle's had earlier. I was grateful for the movement—it was the only indication he wasn't yet a corpse. I waited to feel as if I'd crumble this very moment, in this very spot. I'd already lost so many people I loved; I feared I'd cave under the pressure of my grief. All I felt was rage, coal-burning, crimson-tinted rage. Heat seared down my limbs in fast-moving torrents, my hands clenched automatically. If I knew who'd done this, I would stalk him to the ends of the earth, consequences be damned.

Thomas rolled to his side, moaning. I stood there helpless, feeling like I was twelve years old again, watching my mother's life fade until all that was left was the ghost of her memories. I'd prayed then. Begged God to spare her, to grant one blessing for me and I'd forever dedicate myself to Him. I'd promised anything, anything He could want in exchange for her life. I would have even given mine. God hadn't spared me a second thought when He'd taken my mother. I had little faith He'd listen to my pleas now.

Thomas began shivering so hard it seemed as if he were convulsing. I rushed to his side and tugged a quilt up to his chin, though it was quickly thrown off as he thrashed around. He was mumbling, his words too low and garbled to understand.

"Shhh." I sat beside him, doing my best to soothe his fit. "I'm right here, Thomas. I'm right beside you."

This fact only seemed to unsettle him more. He tossed his limbs about, their motions stilted and jerking. Arsenic attacked the nervous system, and I feared the poison had reached its intended target. He whispered something, over and over, his body becoming more agitated with each exhalation he made.

"Thomas...please, don't worry. Whatever you need to tell me can wait."

He coughed, his entire body trembling once again. "R-rose... r-r-rose."

I clutched his hand to my heart, hoping he couldn't feel it breaking. His skin was as clammy and cool as ice shards. "I'm here."

"H-hotel."

"We're in the home on Grand Street," I said gently. "The one you and Uncle and I are borrowing from Grandmama. It's that large one that reminds you of storybooks. Remember? The sort where witches brew tonics for bad children?"

Thomas sputtered, his voice no longer audible as his lips moved. I prayed then. A few quick words to a God I was unsure of. "Please, Lord. I beg of You. Do not take him from me. Heal him. Or if You cannot, grant me the ability to tend to him myself. Please, please, do not let this be how our story ends."

A knock on the door killed what remained of my prayers. "Come in."

The maid held up a covered tray. "It's plain broth, miss. The doctor said it might be good to try and get some in them both."

The hairs on the back of my neck lifted. This was the same young woman who'd served us our tea and tarts earlier. I refused to trust anyone until I discovered who'd poisoned my loved ones. "Did you make the broth?"

"No, miss." She shook her head vehemently. "The cook did. She's got a light course prepared for you…she thought you might not be too keen on eating something heavy."

"Have you tried the broth?" I asked.

"Of course not, miss. The cook doesn't allow it."

I took a deep breath. A dark, hateful piece of me wished to witness the cook take a spoonful, to be certain she wasn't the one who'd slipped the arsenic into our tea. I forced myself to clear those thoughts, adopting a smile instead. I motioned for her to hand me the tray. "I'd like to try them both first."

Looking a bit confused, she nodded, then went to fetch the second tray, meant for Uncle. Thomas groaned beside me. I balanced the tray on my lap, removed the lid, then dipped the spoon into the clear, rich-smelling broth. Green flakes of parsley floated around innocently.

I brought the spoon to my face, sniffing, though it was a pointless endeavor. Arsenic didn't have a smell or taste. Without hesitation, I sipped the soup. I made sure I'd had enough before setting the tray aside. I glanced at the clock. Now it was time to wait.

An hour later I felt as fine as I had before the broth, so I gently cradled Thomas's head, angling his face up, and managed to get a few spoonfuls down his throat. I kissed his forehead, leaving him to tend to Uncle. His skin looked slightly better than Thomas's—a flush crept into his face, indicating a fever. I hoped it'd burn the toxins out.

I sat with Uncle for a little while longer, silently watching as he fidgeted less and fell into a deep, restorative sleep. Once I was certain he was all right, I slipped out of his room and returned to Thomas's side.

I cracked his door open, hoping against impossible odds that he'd be awake. It was a fool's dream. If anything, his skin appeared more ashen, as if the poison was drinking every bit of life from his body in greedy drabs.

"Abigail?" I called down the corridor, forgetting I could have rung the service bell in Thomas's room.

Footsteps hurried up the stairs, followed by the maid. "Yes, miss?"

"I'd like more blankets for Thomas and my uncle," I said. "And if the fires could be a bit warmer, that would help keep the chill from their chambers."

With a quick nod, she ran off to accomplish the newly assigned tasks. That settled, I drifted back into Thomas's room, mind churning. What I needed to do was construct a list of suspects, all with cause to harm us. I sat down carefully, minding both my leg and Thomas's body, and settled against the headboard. In Chicago, General Inspector Hubbard wasn't our biggest supporter. He made it clear he didn't appreciate our inquiries and wished we'd be silent and enjoy the magic of the White City like the millions of other visitors.

Though I doubted he'd poison us, he could not be taken from the list.

Mr. Cigrande, the man who'd lost his daughter and believed demons roamed the earth, might be mad, but I couldn't imagine him sneaking in and tainting our food. Unless his madness was feigned... but I couldn't picture him accomplishing something quite so diabolical. Not without drawing attention to himself in the process.

Noah. Mephistopheles. They were aiding us. But it could be a ruse, especially where the ringmaster was concerned. I also couldn't forget members of our temporary household. I knew nothing of them or their lives or who they were acquainted with. It was entirely possible they wished us harm for reasons I couldn't explain. Perhaps they knew the man we hunted.

I sighed. Almost everything circled back to our case. People around the periphery were always suspect, based on the nature of their involvement, but I wanted the person at the center. If I could only piece together who Jack the Ripper was, I'd be able to stop him for good and reveal his wretched deeds to the world.

"R-rose." Thomas thrashed about, having another fit. "C-cubes."

My chest ached. "Thomas...I don't—Rose cubes...?"

The gears in my mind clicked as the puzzle slowly started coming together. Cubes. Sugar cubes. The ones doused in rosewater. Thomas had also muttered "hotel" earlier. There was only one place we'd come across the scented sugar cubes during our investigation.

I wasn't sure if it was an actual hotel, but Minnie's husband rented out rooms above their pharmacy. The very place that sold rose-infused sugar cubes. The pharmacy across the street had been a ruse on Minnie's husband's part. My few interactions with him collided in my mind. He'd walked in on me and Minnie during tea, knowing I'd be far enough away when he broke in and burned Nathaniel's journals. He also had a connection to Trudy, since he knew her through his wife. The tremble running down my spine confirmed their pharmacy was the place where the devil lived.

Soon, once I'd introduced him to *my* blades, it would be the place where he died.

Thomas retched and I grabbed a pail. Once he'd finished, I smoothed hair away from his brow in loving strokes and silently plotted murder.

HOLMES' "CASTLE"   (63d St., Chicago, Ill.)

Holmes' "Castle"

FORTY-FIVE
MORE WICKED THAN HE

GRANDMAMA'S ESTATE
CHICAGO, ILLINOIS
16 FEBRUARY 1889

It was comforting in a sense, to finally understand the reason darkness existed in my soul.

It was all so simple. To stop the devil, I had to be more wicked than he. I closed my eyes, picturing each deed that needed to be done in preparation. If there was one lesson I'd learned from Thomas Cresswell, it was to give myself over to that terrible place completely. To disconnect from my mind and judgment and become the thing I feared the most.

I had to consider each of the killer's moves before he did. I had to take on his wants, his desires. Each of his depraved fantasies would become my own, until I craved his blood the way he longed to spill mine. I visualized my blade tracing the lines of his body, glinting in a shaft of moonlight. A lone beam that illuminated my dark act.

Desire would course through my veins. Different from the craving I felt when lying entwined with Thomas, yet no less seductive or satisfying. I'd lay him out on a table, drugged but alive, so he might know what true horror felt like. Let him gaze upon me as tears slipped from his eyes.

Bloodlust. If it was his drug of choice, it would become mine. Tenfold.

The Ripper might have been practicing his dark arts these last few months, but so had I. I hadn't sat idly by, waiting for him to sink his talons into someone else. While he honed his deadly seduction, I'd done the very same. He was a tool for murder, but I'd mastered ways to hunt monsters. I was no longer the naïve, lonely girl who'd snuck about the London streets those many months ago. I now knew monsters were never satisfied. Thomas had been right all along—one taste of warm blood was never enough.

Every case that had come before this was practice—lessons in confronting the ultimate villain and defeating him. I'd lost my innocence and refusal to see the truth of people during the first Ripper investigation. Studying in Dracula's castle taught me to trust in myself, no matter how hard it was to see through distractions. While sailing on that cursed ocean liner, I'd played a role that convinced everyone, even Thomas, that my affections had shifted. I'd mastered emotional manipulation; I'd become a living sleight of hand.

Once upon a time, I'd sworn I'd be something better. That I'd never kill. That my work was only meant to help keep people alive. Now I'd seen enough of the world to know sometimes in order to fight darkness, you had to become a blade forged of heavenly fire.

The devil was a monster, but I would become his nightmare.

"If it's a war you crave," I whispered to the demon I couldn't see, "I'll bring the battle to you."

Part of me worried I'd lose my nerve. One ounce of fear or show of mercy would cost me more than my own life. It would damn those I loved most. I'd lost my brother to this depraved creature; I'd set up a queendom in Hell if he dared to touch Thomas or Uncle again.

Now was the time to confront my own demons.

I searched my heart for weakness, finding none. I was going to end this. I'd be the one who'd stick a blade into the Ripper's flesh, twisting until my hands were covered in his sins.

Thomas tossed back and forth, disturbed and feverish even in sleep. No matter how much I wanted him with me while I confronted Satan himself, I loved Thomas too much to involve him in this most treacherous pursuit. I was hunting the devil, and when I found him, I'd cut out his blackened heart.

"W-Wads—W-Wadsworth..."

I pressed my lips to his forehead, frowning at the dampness I found. His fever had finally broken. I pushed a few strands of hair back from his face, wishing I didn't have to leave him in such a state. His eyes fluttered open. It took him a moment, but he slowly reached for me, a slight tremor going through his arm. He was still so terribly pale. I swallowed a wave of emotion down. It would only make him worry if he read the fear in my face.

"Wadsworth? Are you really here?" He dropped his hand, his head rolling to the side. "I dreamed..."

"Shhh." I smoothed his hair back. "I'm right here, Thomas."

His chest rose and fell, his breaths jagged and uneven. I moved my hand down to his wrist, subtly checking his pulse. It was still too weak for my liking, though it was slightly improved. But not by much. Thomas was not free from death's grasp yet.

"I dreamed you were trapped in a castle," he said, his shallow breaths coming faster, "belowground. There were bodies and bats. Monsters. I saw...I saw the devil, Audrey Rose."

I pressed my lips to his temple; his skin felt like flames. It ignited the blaze I needed to consume lingering fears. I would murder the man who'd harmed my family. I would not be merciful. "It's only a memory, Thomas. An awful memory. We're not in Bran Castle anymore. We're in Chicago. Do you remember taking the train here? Or the *Etruria*?"

"Don't leave me." He felt around for my hand, unable to open his eyes. "Please. Promise you won't leave me."

"Never." I stared at the cloth and bottle of chloroform I'd uncorked and set on the nightstand an hour earlier. He was too weak for me to use it on him now. I wanted him to sleep, not die by my own wretched hand. He thrashed around, his nightshirt soaked through. I added another blanket to the bed, tucking him in as tightly as I could manage.

"Wadsworth. Wadsworth. You must promise. Don't leave me."

"Only in death." I stroked his hair until his breathing calmed. "Even then I will not leave your side. I hope you don't mind being haunted."

His lips twitched, but a smile never fully formed on his troublesome mouth. I waited a few moments, not wanting to stop running my fingers through his soft hair.

"But there is something I must do," I whispered as the slow, steady, rhythmic sounds of sleep drifted through the room, "and I have to leave you here. There's one journey I must take on my own. When I return, I promise we will never be apart again. Not if God wills it."

I waited a few more beats, watching and listening to his breathing. His sleep was deep now, and I doubted he'd wake until midday tomorrow. I memorized the shape of his face, the bone structure I'd been taken with from the moment I'd first set my attention on him.

In Uncle's class, I'd thought he reminded me of a painting or sculpture done by da Vinci. All angles and lines; strong and sharp enough to carve a person's heart out if they ventured too close. A smile started at the edges of my lips. I'd fought so hard against falling for him, never realizing I'd already been laid out on the ground, staring up into my future.

"I love you, Thomas Cresswell." I kissed him gently, before straightening. I permitted myself another stolen moment alone with him, then forced myself to stand and leave his side. I needed to complete my task and be home before he awoke.

Because I *would* come home to him again.

I tiptoed out of his chamber, taking careful pains to mind each creak in the floor as I passed Uncle's room. I paused at his door, hearing the same rhythmic breaths indicating deep sleep. Hopefully they'd both continue to mend. If I lost anyone else I cared for...

Vengeance settled around me like a demon on my shoulder. I slipped into my room and locked the door behind me, though I wasn't sure who I was locking out. Abandoning my growing worry, I flung clothing around my trunk, searching for a small leather pouch. It had to be here somewhere; I never traveled without it.

After upending nearly all of my dresses and underthings from my trunk, I held up the item I'd been hunting. I quickly undid the buckles, laying my scalpel belt across my bed. It had been quite some time since I'd last slipped it over my leg. I set it aside and stepped into trousers that were easy to move about in, then picked it back up.

My fingers shook as I fastened the scalpel belt together. As much as I longed to eradicate my fear, it seemed it wasn't quite ready to give me up. I took a few steadying breaths. I could not lose my nerve now. Not when so many lives depended on me.

I thought of Miss Nichols. And Miss Chapman. Miss Stride and Miss Eddowes. Miss Kelly, Miss Tabram, Miss Smith. Miss Jasper. Miss Van Tassel. And all the women we'd yet to connect to him.

I swept my hair up in a low knot, checked the weapon on my thigh, then grabbed my cane.

"I'm coming for you, Jack," I whispered to myself in the looking glass. It might have been a trick of the lighting, but I swore my reflection shivered.

"Hello, have you come for one of Dr. Holmes's famous tonics or are you interested in a room in the luxurious World's Fair Hotel?"

The young woman standing beside the ornate cash register was undoubtedly another victim in waiting. I eyed her pale blond locks, her expertly painted lips, her youth. She was handsome in the way that seemed to matter to Henry or Harry or whoever this man was claiming to be. From what Minnie had mentioned during tea, outward appearances held the most value to him, though lives didn't matter half as much; those he could toss away without a care.

"I am actually a friend of Dr. Holmes's wife," I said, noting the slight narrowing of her eyes at the word *wife*. Here was another secret he'd apparently kept. She needn't worry. I was quite sure his new wife was dead. "I was hoping to speak with him. I haven't been able to get in touch with Minnie and needed her sister's address. Is he in?"

She pursed her lips. After a moment of collecting herself, she offered me another polite smile. "I'm afraid you missed him by moments. He won't return until very late, or possibly tomorrow morning. It's only my first day working here, but Dr. Holmes seems to be very mysterious about his private affairs."

Her blush hinted that he'd already begun weaving a silvery web for her to get trapped in. Little did she know he was a venomous spider and not a handsome prince.

"I'll rent a room for the night, then." I slipped her an extra coin, her eyes going wide. "I'd like you to let me know straightaway when he arrives. I have other more...urgent...news."

She stared at the coin for a moment, hunger for it gleaming in her eyes. Holmes might be a decadent flirt, but apparently his generosity didn't extend to his purse strings. I hoped the anger writhing up inside me didn't show on my face. Her gaze slid behind me before she snatched the coin and stuck it in her bosom. She handed me a key with a brass tag that had the number 4 on it.

"I'll show you to your room now, Miss..."

"Wadsworth," I said, giving her a warm smile. "And you are?"

"Miss Agatha James."

Apparently her hospitality was being tested. Her response was clipped, as if each word cost her. She motioned for me to follow her to the end of the counter of tonics and other apothecary items lining the shelves and walls. In the far corner of the store, a door opened onto a narrow staircase. My heart beat furiously, but I wouldn't let fear stop me from what I'd set out to do. No matter if I was planning to murder a man who'd evaded police and had slain a countless number of women already.

"Will this be your first evening staying at the Castle?"

"Castle?" I asked, thoughts flashing back to the imposing fortress of Vlad the Impaler in Romania and the corridors that seemed to crave blood. A shiver started at the base of my neck, dancing down to my toes. In Thomas's fever dream he'd spoken of Bran Castle. "I thought you said it was named the World's Fair Hotel."

"It is."

She smiled demurely as she motioned for us to continue up the stairs. It was a dreadful little corridor. The walls were covered in a deep charcoal wallpaper, and I could have sworn they were closing in ever so slightly the farther up we went. I had the off-kilter sensation of being stuck in a carnival fun house. That impression grew when I noticed skulls carefully drawn into the design of the wallpaper. A peculiar choice for a hotel.

"Locals call it the Castle, though. It's so large, with over one hundred rooms—did you know it takes up an entire city block? Dr. Holmes is quite the businessman. Smart, too. He began construction on it right before they announced the World's Fair would be held here. He'd already predicted it would be a lovely, safe home for the young women who came here to work. Isn't that kind of him?"

I bit down on my immediate response to his *kindness*. This monster had grown tired of stalking women in the street. His new game was luring them into what they believed was a sanctuary, and then he unleashed his bloodiest desires.

After we crested the top of the staircase, I ran my hand against the wall of the long corridor, the other tightened on my cane, reassuring in its presence. Sconces were placed at uneven intervals, deepening that sense of unsteadiness that followed me up the stairs. It almost gave one the feeling of having had too much champagne.

Sweat beaded along my brow. I didn't feel right. Vaguely, I heard the quiet hissing of snakes. I squinted toward the sconces; they'd been fashioned after cobras. The bulbs bulged where their bodies coiled, their fangs exposed. It was creepy décor, fitting enough for a murderer.

Despite using my cane for support, I stumbled forward. The young woman caught me before I hit the ground, her brow crinkled. "You don't look well, Miss Wadsworth. Let's get you to bed to rest for a bit."

I dragged in a laborious breath, my chest burning.

"Why aren't you…" My lids drooped, my mind going sluggish. I staggered against her. My vision blurred and panic set in, chittering and clicking along my spine. Drowsy, I slid my focus back to the hissing serpents. If I squinted, I could just make out faint traces of mist. Oh, no. I'd not planned on being exposed to an airborne contagion. My father's worries came flooding back. "But I didn't eat or drink anything here."

I thought I'd been prepared for this confrontation, but he had created rules I'd never dreamed up before; Poison in the air. I stopped moving. I needed to get back to the stairs. My mind spun so quickly I had to put my head between my knees to keep from vomiting.

"Agatha, I…I don't feel well."

"Oh!" Agatha clutched my arm, keeping me from tumbling down into darkness and back down the stairs. "The fumes from the cleanser might not agree with you. Dr. Holmes is still perfecting the formula." She pointed to her nose. "Cotton. I almost forgot." She tied a scarf about her face. "Not everyone has a reaction to it, but I'm pretty sensitive to most strong scents. That's why Dr. Holmes makes me remember the cotton. I won't be helpful to him if I get ill."

I staggered a few steps farther, knees shaking. This was no cleanser. At least none that I'd ever encountered. "Why doesn't he give them to his patrons?"

"He doesn't run a charity, miss. If he handed out cotton to everyone who rented a room here, he'd be out of money. Plus, this doesn't happen with everyone. He said he only cleans the corridors like this once in a while. Today seems to be one of those rare occasions."

She left me and swiftly moved forward, pausing at the end of the corridor, opening doors that I swore were bricked up. I fell against the wall, fighting the darkness creeping into the corners of my vision. I needed to get out of this place. Immediately. My sense of self-preservation screeched wildly to hurry, but whatever he was poisoning me with worked fast.

With a final shove, I stumbled a few feet back toward the stairs, head spinning as a giant portrait loomed before me. It seemed as if the eyes followed me as I collapsed to the floor, trying desperately to crawl back the way we'd come. I heard the bones in my knees crack, the pain blinding in its fury. Two hands lifted me up.

"Now, now, Miss Wadsworth," a cool voice said. "Stop fighting me."

I feebly thought of my blade sheathed at my thigh. It was utterly useless to me now. All my preparations, my certainty. Gone.

"It's time you met your true match."

His voice was the last thing that tormented me before I plunged into blackness.

FORTY-SIX

CAPTIVITY: NIGHT ONE

MURDER CASTLE
CHICAGO, ILLINOIS
16 FEBRUARY 1889

My throat felt like hot coals had been shoved down it. My eyes leaked tears as if in mourning.

It was as though my body understood before I did.

The devil had come to claim me.

And I would soon die.

A hissing from somewhere above stole into the room, robbing me of consciousness.

Sleep, deep and endless. A blessing hidden inside the curse.

FORTY-SEVEN
CAPTIVITY: NIGHT TWO

MURDER CASTLE
CHICAGO, ILLINOIS
17 FEBRUARY 1889

Darkness greeted me as I cracked my lids. Oppressive like summer heat. I stirred, desperate to rouse from unnatural sleep. For a moment, I couldn't recall where I was. Then fragments of memory came back. Before I sat up, I heard the creaking of a door. A slice of yellow light spilled like entrails across the floor. I squeezed my eyes shut.

Counted my breaths.

This was a nightmare. Like the ones that had haunted me these past months. A trick of the mind. It wasn't real. It couldn't be real.

I opened my eyes, only to scream.

A figure with horns stood over me, and though I couldn't be sure, it sounded as if he hissed right before the darkness swept in to do his bidding once more.

FORTY-EIGHT

CAPTIVITY: NIGHT THREE

MURDER CASTLE
CHICAGO, ILLINOIS
18 FEBRUARY 1889

Drip. Drip.
   Drip.
   The scent of gasoline mixed with mustiness and other noxious odors twisted my stomach. It was different from when I'd last awakened. Another smell greeted me, an old familiar friend. Copper and pennies and metal. Vaguely, I wondered if the dripping I heard was blood. Something clattered nearby. It sounded like bones. Too many. I imagined an army of the undead, coming to claim me. I thrashed about, furious, as the hissing began in earnest. I knew what that meant. He was dosing me again. Toying with me until he grew bored.
   I screamed, the sound echoing around me, though there was an oddness to it. As if I was submerged in a chamber beneath the sea. I had a growing suspicion that no one could hear me. No one but him. Wherever I was, no sounds escaped.
   In the distance, I swore I heard the devil laugh in delight.
   A nightmare. I was having a nightmare and would soon be awake.
   It was the last thought I had before Satan dragged me back to Hell.

FORTY-NINE

CAPTIVITY: NIGHT FOUR

MURDER CASTLE
CHICAGO, ILLINOIS
19 FEBRUARY 1889

Drip. Drip. Drip.

An incessant dripping dragged me to the surface of a troubled sleep. Before I cracked my eyes open, I became aware of an icy chill seeping into my body. The surface below me was as hard as ice.

Drip. Drip. Drip.

I commanded my eyes to open, but they refused, the lids still too heavy to lift. Panic started at the edges, winding its way further into my consciousness. Fatigue could not account for my inability to rouse myself. Several moments passed, my thoughts fuzzy yet buzzing with an undercurrent of urgency. A puzzle piece I was missing. Tremors raked my body as my unbound hair tickled my neck. When had I taken it down? I swore snakes or worms were crawling over my skin. Perhaps even maggots. And I couldn't do anything about it. Imaginary walls seemed to heave and crumble with each breath. Was I buried in a grave?

Drip. Drip. Drip.

Open your eyes! I thought, furious my lips refused to form the words. Was I no longer in my body? I couldn't understand how nothing seemed to work. My mind was alert but the rest of me remained immobile. Then it locked into place. I'd been drugged. I tried sitting up, but it felt like a malevolent force had its knees in my back, keeping me shoved down.

A few terrifying moments passed and my fingers twitched. Bolstered by the improvement, I splayed my hands against the mattress, only to realize I'd been deposited onto the floor sometime in the night. My fingers slid over what felt like packed dirt. I rolled to my side and patted the ground for more clues and jerked my hand back. I'd touched something wet.

"T-Thomas?" I finally managed to whisper, reaching into the darkness for an anchor to keep me in this life, this present, this time. I did not want to be torn back into that place of nothingness. I did not want to contemplate the blood I was certain now coated my hands.

Drip. Drip. Drip.

Images of Thomas lying upside down, gutted and drained of blood, assaulted my senses. Were they fragmented memories? Fear propelled me up and out of the haze. Or perhaps it was love. There was no greater force on earth, nothing quite as powerful as love. Neither hatred nor fear could ever hope to possess the same amount of strength. I gathered those thoughts, clutched them close, and pushed myself into a sitting position, taking in the darkened room.

A lone candle flickered somewhere behind me. I blinked as my surroundings came into place. I seemed to be in some sort of storage chamber or cellar. From what I could make of it, the dripping noise, blessedly, was just an old leaky pipe.

I slumped down, focusing on the bigger worry of how I'd gotten here and why I'd been drugged. More images came back to me, though I was uncertain of them. A man with horns. Hissing. A room without sound. Now that I was awake, these seemed to be fantasy.

Except my current location was definitely a nightmare.

I glanced at my clothing—a thin nightgown—and froze. The trousers I'd had made in Romania were gone. As was my scalpel belt. Someone had undressed me. They'd touched me and I couldn't even allow my mind to process the violation of my person or I'd spin wildly out of control. Revulsion twisted my stomach until I choked bile down. I closed my eyes, forcing myself to breathe. To not lose myself to the horror. I would survive and I'd make him suffer.

I tentatively reached up, feeling for any lumps or injury. My hair was unbound and the bun had been removed, along with my hairpins. I frowned, running my fingers through the tangles, hoping to dislodge any of the missing pins. Nothing.

I forced myself to sit straighter, the motion prompting my body into a state of alertness. Followed quickly by nausea. I doubled over and concentrated on finding calmness again, breathing slowly until I was sure I wouldn't vomit.

More of the room came into focus, my clarity improving the longer the drug worked its way out of my system. What I'd first thought to be a cellar was similar in appearance to a laboratory of sorts. A shard of fear lodged itself under my skin.

"No."

I squeezed my eyes shut, feeling like a coward. Then I forced myself to remember what had brought me here to begin with. Whom I was fighting for. It became easier to recall I was fearless in the face of fear. I was capable of so much more than I'd ever imagined.

I'd been knocked down, struck time and again by those who did not believe I could accomplish anything other than smiling prettily. I'd been told I was wretched for my curiosity and scorned for following my heart. It was time to tell myself a different tale. One where I was the hero, battling against harmful words and doubts.

"I will not be afraid." I repeated it silently as I maneuvered to my knees, wincing as a new memory came to me along with the bright spots of pain. I'd forgotten I'd cracked my bones again. I prodded my leg, relieved it wasn't rebroken, just badly bruised from the feel of it. Determined to escape before the devil returned, I got to my feet and took in the full sights around me. "Don't be afraid."

It was a nice sentiment, though like most areas of my life, it proved false as the true horror of my situation came into view. I was not alone in this basement chamber.

Lying on a large slab, as if a tribute to the gods left on some unholy altar, was a female corpse. Half its face was missing its outer layers of skin, the angry red and white of meat and muscle glistening in the dull light. The other half seemed frozen in an eternal scream.

I clapped a hand over my mouth, praying that I could choke my own scream down before the devil found me. I was looking at what remained of sweet Minnie.

Her partially missing face was not the worst of what had been done to her, however. As my gaze slowly moved down what remained of her body, I noticed strips of flesh had been cut away, exposing the milky-white bone beneath. An image of the goat in the meatpacking district of New York City flashed through my mind.

One leg appeared to have been set in a vat of sulfuric acid—there was nothing left but charred fragments of skin and the pungent scent of foul eggs. Sulfur. I inhaled again, immediately regretting it as the sweetness of decay got stuck in my nose. It was a sickening aroma—worse than any I'd had the misfortune of experiencing before.

I'd woken up in Hell. And Hell smelled of rotten flesh and felt like eternal screams.

My pulse was near hysteria as it rushed through my body. I forced my attention on the rest of the room, all traces of the drug burned out as fresh adrenaline coursed through me. My body understood the laws of nature—it was ready for fight or flight.

Shadows and dust twirled and danced to their own macabre beat, spurring my heart into a greater frenzy. Nathaniel had created a hidden lair in our home to practice his dark deeds, but it was nothing compared to this castle built of blood and bone.

Barrels lined the walls, some larger than others. Human skulls were piled high in one, and I stared, unable to comprehend the magnitude of how many people had to die for the number of skulls needed to overflow from those barrels. I swallowed my revulsion, continuing to scan what must be hundreds of victims. Some barrels were small enough to fit a—

I squeezed my eyes shut as a tiny skull caught my attention. Was that Pearl? What sort of monster would harm a child? I knew who in an instant. It was the very same man who ripped women apart and left them in discarded heaps as if they were rubbish. The one we'd stalked and foolishly assumed was dead. This chamber reminded me so much of my brother's secret laboratory, and yet it was nothing like it. Nathaniel's had been dark and twisted, but it was focused on science. This...this was only a crypt filled with death. A tribute and prize of remembrance. A place of torture.

A shiny bit of metal glinted in the flickering light. I slowly moved toward it and wished I hadn't. It was my brother's prized silver comb. I stopped breathing. I wasn't sure how Holmes had gotten it, but there was no doubt in my mind it belonged to Nathaniel. Which meant the Ripper had snuck into my house in London sometime after my brother had died.

Even though it was the last thing I wished to do, I brought myself back to that fateful November night when I'd confronted my brother with the crimes I thought he'd committed, replaying each detail as if it were a moving picture.

I'd claimed Nathaniel was the Ripper.

I'd accused him of committing such violent acts. But, like

Mephistopheles had warned me time and again during that hellish carnival, I needed to beware of my mind conjuring its own tale. I knew now that it had been creating stories, but why hadn't my brother confessed the truth?

I closed my eyes, seeing that night clearer. At first Nathaniel seemed surprised, but then he'd recovered quickly. He'd fed me line after line, almost as if he'd made it up on the go. But why? Why lay claim to something so unspeakably horrid if he was innocent? Had he been coerced? What on earth would possess him to—The answer hit me so swiftly, I gasped. It was so simple, yet I couldn't process it. There was only one force on earth with that power.

Love.

Not necessarily romantic love. My brother likely felt so deprived of true companionship that he'd been led onto a dark, twisted path. I imagined the murderer had seen the hunger in him for the love and acceptance of a friend and exploited it. After my mother's death, Nathaniel was emotionally broken in so many ways I hadn't seen, but someone else did.

And used it against him.

My brother was mad about science and *Frankenstein* and reanimating the dead; perhaps carrying that dark secret had been a much bigger burden than I'd imagined. He could have shared those desires with someone who he thought understood. Who didn't judge him. Who encouraged his mad beliefs. All the while hiding the dagger behind his back.

If that were true…hatred coiled in my core. I would take pleasure in killing this devil not only for Thomas, but for my brother as well. Nathaniel had never been Dr. Frankenstein; he'd been twisted into the creature. One who'd taken the blame for his creator.

I was unsure how Nathaniel had managed to do so, but he'd tricked Thomas with his lies as well. In my mind's eye, I relived

Thomas stumbling down those laboratory stairs, his expression frantic, until his attention landed on me. Back then I didn't recognize the depth of his fear—how his own emotions had interfered.

I was both Thomas Cresswell's weakness and his strength.

When he feared for my safety, his deductions were rushed, less razor-edged than when he had no emotional ties. He'd claimed cuts on Nathaniel's fingertips had indicated he was the Ripper, but what if there was another reason for those? My brother had been handling sharp bits of metal, fusing them into his contraptions. Those actions could produce the same wounds. I opened my eyes, seeing the clues in an entirely new light.

"Dear God above." Terror, I soon realized, had its own taste. It was sharp and coppery, much like blood. Each hair raised itself from my body as if it hoped to sprout wings and take flight. If Nathaniel had help with creating his laboratory, then any deficiencies in the design had most certainly been worked out. This house was a weapon itself, ready to destroy those who dared cross its threshold.

My home was the prototype. This was the grand masterpiece.

I glanced at the skulls and poor Minnie's body, which had been partially skinned. If this chamber was located under the hotel—then I was only in one small portion of the underground maze. The hotel took up an entire city block. I almost sank to my knees. Getting out with my life would be nearly impossible. Maybe this was always how my story was supposed to end, in this earthly version of Hell. Perhaps if I let him have me, his murderous rampage would come to a close.

I stopped looking at the mangled corpse that used to be the bright and cheerful Minnie. Would her fate soon be my own? A cadaver ripped apart into something hardly recognizable as human? A flash of Thomas's body crumpled with poison battled against my fear. I promised I'd make it home to him. I would not let this murderous castle or its owner win.

This time when I scanned the chamber, I was searching for items to assist with my escape. Much to my surprise, my dragon cane lay against a barrel. I retrieved it, not looking any closer at the skeletal remains than was necessary.

For the sake of moving as stealthily as I could, I ripped my hemline into strips, then tied them about the bottom of my cane. Ignoring the ever-screaming corpse, I took a turn about the room, my breath catching at each muffled sound of my cane meeting the floor. It wasn't the best, but it would make it harder for anyone to hear me moving around.

I crept over to the door, pressing my ear against the cool metal, listening for any movement on the other side. I stayed that way, doing my best impression of a statue, until my good leg prickled with needles. Not one sound stirred. Slowly, I reached out, trying the handle.

I winced as metal slid over metal, creating a sound much too loud for my liking in the oppressive quiet. I froze, waiting for the door to swing wide as Holmes came charging from the opposite side, knocking me backward, but no such force came.

Bolstered by my small victory, I leaned against the door, adding more of my weight, ready to rejoice at freedom—it was locked. Of course. Part of me wished to kick it, to beat it with my cane until either it or I surrendered to this fate.

"Be still," I commanded myself as Liza had done after my ruined wedding. *"Think."*

I turned around and pressed my back against the door, staring at the room from this perspective. A smaller doorway was tucked near a corner, almost hidden by the overflowing barrels of bones. Unlike the door I rested against, that one wasn't closed.

With a quick reminder to be fearless, I crept toward my escape.

FIFTY

OF BLOOD AND BONE

MURDER CASTLE
CHICAGO, ILLINOIS
19 FEBRUARY 1889

As I stood in the small doorway leading out of my current night-mare, an even greater one greeted me. Suspended from hooks in the ceiling—reminding me much too closely of the butchers' row in New York—hung rows of corpses and skeletons.

The objects of horror were evenly spaced on either side of the small room, leaving a narrow path between them. It was wide enough for a person to pass through, but only just. I barely noticed that this corridor of death opened to another chamber. The skeleton nearest me moved, and the sound of its bones chattering like teeth sent shivers along my spine.

I couldn't tear my gaze from the skeletons. Some had been entirely stripped of flesh and bleached until their bones gleamed like the streets of the White City. Others hadn't yet been fully treated. Metal wire glinted from the joints where the bones had been fastened together. The less-stripped skeletons had wire piercing rotting skin. The decaying tissues from flesh stained those bones and dripped to the floor. A slimy, greasy puddle saturated the ground beneath them. Maggots crawled about, their little milky bodies teeming with energy, enjoying their feast.

The stench was strong enough that my eyes watered and I could no longer hold back my nausea. I turned and vomited the pitiful contents of my stomach, thankful I hadn't desecrated any other body. I wiped my mouth with the back of my hand, cringing at the sour taste of bile.

A lone bulb flickered above, sending shadows skittering. The room teemed with movement, though it was likely a trick of the light. I was not being watched by ghosts, even if a part of me wondered if spirits were haunting this murder castle, waiting for justice.

My stomach tightened again at the thought.

I closed my eyes against the image of a hundred pale faces emerging from darkness. No doubt the owners of these skeletons were seeking their revenge. Would they come for me, too? I thought of the many times my blade sank into flesh, the jolt of joy I'd tried unsuccessfully to tamp down. I delighted in my work, marveled at the secrets revealed to me. Perhaps the dead didn't wish to tell me their troubles. Perhaps they thought I was as wicked as the man who'd strung them up, their bones rattling in the gentle breeze.

My mind latched onto that realization with ferocity. *The breeze.* There shouldn't be any wind down here, unless...I spun in place, forcing myself to see beyond the forest of skeletons. My quick movement had them clattering together again, the sound setting my teeth on edge. I ignored the fear clawing up my spine and focused. There had to be—there! Wedged behind a trunk—its contents I refused to consider—was a large grate.

Hope rose from the ashes of my soul. It was small, but it wouldn't be impossible for me to wedge myself into it and crawl to the outdoors. Air flowed in, meaning it most certainly flowed out. If I could only work the grate free from the—My excitement dwindled as I got closer.

I stared numbly at the giant railroad ties that secured it to the wall. There was no chance I'd be able to work it free, even if I ripped my fingers to shreds in the process. I considered sticking my cane in the grate and using it as a lever, but it would snap.

Defeat reached out, begging me to collapse in its waiting arms. Giving up would be so easy. I could sit here quietly waiting for the Ripper. If I gave him what he wanted, it might be over quickly. Perhaps he'd be disappointed to not find me cowering in fear.

I wondered if that would enrage him into carving my body into his finest horror yet. The pain would be unbearable, but if he stayed true to his previous murders, he'd strangle me or slash my throat before his real work began. Either way I'd lose consciousness within minutes, followed by my life. Maybe this was the way the darkness always meant to claim me. Maybe I was supposed to die on the *Etruria*. If I'd been living on borrowed time, I did not regret the weeks and months I'd gotten to spend with those I loved. With Thomas.

I recalled the way it felt to share my whole self with him, the way his eyes shone with the same love I felt. Our wedding was terrible, but at least I'd seen him at the altar. If I died, I would focus on that. His radiant smile, his unsteady breath. How close we'd come to being husband and wife. My memory taunted me with images of my father next. Followed by Uncle and Aunt Amelia and Liza. I'd be leaving them all behind.

I sagged against the doorway, no longer listening to the bones play their chilling death march. I had no hope of winning a physical fight. And the realization that I would never see my family or Thomas again, never press my lips to his and hear his heart pound in time with mine...it was almost too much to bear. I suddenly wished to call out, to beg for death to come swiftly.

But I kept seeing Thomas's face. I heard my promise to him. And I remembered why I'd ventured here to begin with. I straightened, slapped hopelessness away, and marched over to the grate. I *would* find a way out of here.

I stuck my fingers through the openings and tugged, really pulling with all my weight, and almost fell on my behind. The grate didn't budge. Refusing to give up, I tested its strength again, wondering if I could find something to pry it off the wall with. A few threads of an idea began to weave together. The Ripper had made a mistake when he'd left me here. He imagined the corpses and skeletons would terrify me. I'd wager anything he was counting on it. He wanted horror to override my senses. I was certain nothing would please him more.

He must not realize how much I craved the knowledge hidden between layers of flesh. I might not make cadavers to carve as he did, but I enjoyed the process no less. Since I understood the process of death, I understood the grandest mistake he'd made yet.

This room was used to clean bones. He probably had some scheme where he sold full skeletons to academies. It was the only reason I could see why he'd take such good care of them, bleaching the stain of his sins from each bone. It was revolting—the way he'd not only murdered for his pleasure but then profited from it. Shoving my disgust for him aside, I refocused on this chamber. If there were metal wires used to tie the bones together, there must be shears to cut them. And if there were hooks nailed to the wall, there must be a hammer to set them there. And if there was a hammer, then the opposite end of it might be the perfect pry bar.

At the very least, this butcher of women must have a decent blade he used to dismember them. If he was careless enough to leave me down here with my cane, he might have made another fatal mistake. My pulse sped. If there was an axe, I'd break through the damned wall and chop off his head if he dared to attack me.

I put pressure on my good leg and searched for the object I was sure was here. Unfortunately, this seemed to be only a storage room of sorts. I didn't want to venture back into the chamber with Minnie's corpse, but...

I turned slowly, remembering this corridor of skeletons led to yet another room. It was dark in there; no light glimmered except for a strange orange-red glow.

My bravado vanished. Images of demons with hooves for feet and tails with tufts entered my thoughts. I forced myself to steadily breathe in and out. It would do no good to lose my nerve now. Pushing against my growing fears, I slowly moved down the corridor of bones. No matter how careful I was, they still rattled as I passed by.

Little hairs along my arms and neck rose. I was almost in the next chamber and there was a new, strange combination of odors to contend with. I paused on the threshold, trying to adjust my vision to the strange light. It took a few moments, but dark objects slowly took form. The hellish glow was not a fire from Hell, but a long, coffin-shaped metal box. It took only a second to piece together what it was—an incinerator.

I bit down on my lip to keep from making a sound. No wonder he hadn't left bodies in the streets of Chicago. He'd created the perfect playground for himself. One where he might torture and dispose of his victims without ever being caught.

I inhaled sharply, immediately regretting it. The tang of gasoline was faint but there. I squinted up at the ceiling, where pipes crisscrossed like spiderwebs. I followed them, trying to sort out why there were so many and why they extended in different directions. Up close, I spied what appeared to be spigots. I cursed under my breath.

These gas pipes were his new weapon of choice. He no longer needed to dirty his hands with knives and blood; he could simply target the hotel room of his choice by turning on a spigot and his prey would be rendered unconscious from the toxic carbon monoxide fumes. Just like I'd been. I hadn't been drugged at all. I'd been brought to the brink of death time and again.

A boot scuffed against the floor, the sound raising the hairs along the nape of my neck. It wasn't hard to picture monsters dragging their talons over the ground, their nails caked in gore. If I wished to make it out of this murder castle alive, I needed to become what terrified me. I took a deep breath and stepped fully into the incinerator room.

At first I didn't notice him, standing near the corner, his body nothing more than a dim silhouette. He'd been here the whole time. Silent and still. Waiting. That frightened me more than the thought of impending death. Something in his hands glittered in the darkness, conjuring images of metal claws. I forced my gaze up his form, swallowing panic as I took in the tall, twisted horns. It was the scene of my recurring dreams made flesh.

The devil was here.

He'd finally stepped out from my nightmares and had come to claim me.

Goat Skull with smoky background

FIFTY-ONE

SATAN EMERGES

MURDER CASTLE
CHICAGO, ILLINOIS
19 FEBRUARY 1889

He stepped from the shadows into the burning light cast by the incinerator. His skin was tinged red from the flames, which seemed to grow in his presence, his eyes dark from the shadows, which had yet to relinquish their hold in this underground dominion. It took a moment for my mind to cast my demons aside and realize he'd turned the fire up on the incinerator. He was planning on burning another body.

Mine.

In a sudden panic, I stumbled toward the corridor of bones, cursing wildly when I noticed what I'd tripped over—a dismembered torso. I'd interrupted him disposing of another victim. I fell to the ground, ignoring the pain that shot up my spine as I scrambled back, away from the White City Devil.

My fingers dug into the packed earth, my nails splintering as I searched for purchase. Something sliced my palm and I nearly cried out as warmth flowed down my hand. I bit my tongue instead, taking the blade with me as I moved backward. I didn't dare glance at it, but it felt like a long, thin dinner knife. It was the exact weapon Uncle had described during that first lesson I'd attended about Jack the Ripper's kills. I held on to it like it was my only salvation. I was almost certain he hadn't seen me grab it. Since it was covered with dirt, he'd probably dropped it a long while ago and forgotten it was there.

He left his dark work and stalked after me. I was grateful for the dim light—it would make it hard for him to notice the trail of blood I knew I was leaving.

He was silent in his pursuit, taking steady, unhurried steps. I needed to become fearless, but it was hard when faced with my personal nightmare. I finally managed to heave myself into a standing position and stopped in the center of the bone corridor. My sudden halt made him pause. I didn't think he was used to his prey growing their own claws and striking back.

He stood just inside the doorway between the incinerator and the skeleton corridor, giving me time to think. I needed to come up with a plan. And it needed to happen this instant. I knew the door in the room I'd woken up in was locked. There was no getting out of there. If he cornered me in that space...I refused to think in those terms. I was not prey, but predator.

"A devil mask is a bit theatrical," I said, surprised to hear how smooth and unafraid my voice sounded. He canted his head to one side, seeming as surprised by my statement as I was. "I didn't think you'd enjoy such things. But then I recalled your letters to Scotland Yard. You've always had a flair for the dramatic. The devil...I suppose I understand in theory why you chose it, but it seems a bit contrived."

My taunt worked as well as I'd hoped it would. I'd been playing this game with Jack for too long now. He might believe he knew me, but I'd gotten well acquainted with him, too. His vanity would be his undoing. I was counting on it. If I could get him to talk about himself and his crimes, it might give me an opening to spring my own trap.

A skeleton that hadn't yet been strung together lay in a heap near the door to the incinerator. If I could trick him back into that room, I could secure him inside by wedging the femur in the handle. It would purchase me time to work the grate off the wall. Then I could flee without him capturing me and making me into his latest prize.

"Is the concept of a devil truly far-fetched?" His voice was another part of his deception. It sounded pleasant. Charming. His conversational tone was meant to be disarming, and if I hadn't known who he was, I, too, might have fallen for his façade. I'd learned, though, that fallen angels were beautiful creatures. Mephistopheles had reminded me to be wary of them. "You of all people should know that darkness walks among us. Satan might be a fantastical legend meant to frighten, but aren't his acts real?"

"No," I said. "Men are monsters who use fantasy to ease their minds. They find it easy to blame their actions on good and evil. It's much harder to face the truth—that you enjoy the pain and fear you inflict, for no other purpose than your own wicked pleasure."

"We are all wicked. More than flesh and blood, our very souls harbor evil. Don't you see it in the bodies you carve? In the choices people make? The man who beats his wife is as terrible as the person spreading lies out of spite."

I must have a made a disgusted noise, because he paused.

"No?" he asked. "Who sets the scales for what's more evil? Why is physical violence deemed terrible, yet an assault on one's mind or emotions less so? What of the person wounding you with their words? What of their desire to watch you bleed tears? They, too, guzzle your pain. Their hearts beat with hate. They gain pleasure by spreading their noxious negativity." He shook his head. "Hatred. Jealousy.

Vengeance. Evil is all around, Miss Wadsworth. There's a devil in us all as much as an angel. Right now, which one is speaking to you?"

He glanced at the blade I slowly held up, no doubt recognizing the determination coursing through me. I hoped he might step backward. He knew I'd seize upon any opportunity to kill him. And how sweet that justice would be—having a woman use the very blade he'd slain so many other women with to end his cursed existence.

He didn't move. And now I'd revealed my hand.

"Is your evil dressed up in righteous indignation?" he asked, taking a small step forward. "Do you walk that morally gray line of what's 'good'? If you thrust your blade in my heart, what lie will you tell yourself at night, what story will you spin, casting yourself as the hero?"

For a moment, my resolve faltered. I bit the inside of my cheek, regaining my senses. "By taking one life, how many others might be saved? How many have you murdered in this castle of horror alone?" I didn't take my attention from him, but I motioned at the skeletons clattering around like a morbid audience. "One hundred? Two? How many more will you collect and kill and maim to satisfy your wretched hunger?"

He smiled. It was the sort of angelic look that convinced countless women to trust him, never remembering Lucifer had once been an angel, too. He prowled closer, yet was careful to stay out of reach. Here was one man who remembered my claws were also things to be feared.

My grip tightened on my found blade, which only seemed to delight him more. Thomas had been correct—he'd coveted me. He'd been savoring the idea of this encounter for months. He wanted to draw this out for as long as he could before his knives tasted my blood.

"You, my dear, may be more of a villain than I am. I accept my horns; I know the blackness in my soul. I was born with the devil in me. But so were you, Miss Wadsworth."

"I do not believe in such nonsense as Heaven and Hell."

"But you do fear your darkness." I cringed and he smiled knowingly. "I recognized it in you the moment I first saw you. I wanted to help you, you know. Unleash the potential I knew was writhing in your soul. It was difficult, holding myself back."

He was a cat batting a mouse around before it snapped its neck. I would not be toyed with. I lifted my blade, hand steady. "We've only just met in Chicago."

"Have we?"

He shifted, his devil mask catching the light. Here, outside of the incinerator room, I saw it had been dusted with gold. It looked like metallic flames danced across his flesh. No matter how hard I tried, I could not contain the shiver that vibrated through me.

"Or did I first make your acquaintance in a London alley?" he asked. "For a moment, I was certain you'd seen me, lurking in the shadows we both love. You remember, don't you? The finger of trepidation that slid down your spine, the shiver despite the summer heat."

"You're lying." I glanced around the room, noticing a thick door I hadn't spotted before, propped open on one side. It appeared to be a vault. It would take maneuvering, but if I could lead him to it, it might be even better to lock him in there than in the incinerating room. I'd have to weave through the hanging skeletons, though. I took a careful step back, my shoulder brushing into someone's limb, and hoped he'd mirror my action.

He prowled in the opposite direction, stepping between the row of skeletons farthest from me. I'd not succeed in tricking him into a corner. He was an unsparing predator—a murderer with untold skill. If I was to beat him, I'd need to be more cunning, more ruthless.

I'd need to become bait before I raked my claws over his throat.

"I wanted to follow you home that night. Your brother…" He shrugged. "Let's just say he wasn't keen on the idea of you and I meeting. That's why he sent you home with that annoying companion of his." A smile flickered across his lips. "I don't believe he ever fully trusted me. Wise of him. I hardly trust myself. I have these urges, you see. They're like feral creatures. Do you know what it's like, having something wild and untamed writhe about within you? To hunger for things that other men tremble from?"

His hands fisted at his sides as if he were fighting off the unholy transformation this very moment. I swallowed hard, my sense of flight taking over. If I did not strike out at him, I would not leave this murder castle alive.

"I yearn for blood the way most men yearn for wine and women. When I lie down at night, I imagine the ecstasy of witnessing life leave a person's eyes. Being the one who decides who lives and dies is the most intoxicating feeling."

His lids fluttered shut and he tilted his head back as if in the throes of passion. A moan escaped him, and the sound made me freeze. My heart urged me to run, but my mind commanded me to hold my position. I thought of predators in the animal kingdom, how whether hungry or not, if a creature ran from them, their hunting instincts took over.

For this hunter, my fear was his favorite perfume. He was doing all that he could to make me afraid. He needed my terror. And I would keep it from him out of spite.

"You see, I feel so very little. I often wonder if I am human at all."

His gaze followed my slow procession, calculating and adjusting himself so I was never completely out of his reach. Though I was careful to not bump into the skeletons, the movement of my body was enough to disturb the space around them. Bones knocked together like macabre chimes. I gritted my teeth, refusing to be disturbed.

"Should I plunge my knife through your chest this moment, Miss Wadsworth, I'd feel nothing aside from pleasure, watching you bleed out. It's an incredible sensation—so at odds with itself. The warmth of blood flowing as the body cools. The flame of life being snuffed out by death. It's all so short-lived, though. The satisfaction never remains for long before hunger strikes again."

"Is that why you killed so many so quickly in London?" I asked, hoping he'd admit his role as Jack the Ripper. I needed to hear him confirm it. "You strangled them and then carved them open, why?"

He cocked his head, his eyes narrowing behind his mask. I wondered if he was growing bored of entertaining me. He was still shadowing my movements, like we were two magnets rotating around a small circle. Soon he'd be near the vault. Though I was now closer to the incinerator again. I'd have to be quick to reach him before he got too far from there.

"Well?" I asked, letting impatience slip into my tone. "Why did you kill those women one way and begin murdering others here differently?"

"Oh, I've found the method of killing isn't what excites me. It's *death*. Whether I strangle someone or flay them open, exposing their innermost secrets, or watch as they slowly asphyxiate behind a closed door, it's their pain, their inability to conquer death, that thrills me." He pushed past a skeleton, not nearly as careful as I was while weaving through them. "I wanted to be enthralled by the thought of using body parts to conquer death and reanimate them, but I couldn't. It was your brother's dream, not mine."

"What?" I whispered. I hadn't been anticipating hearing about my brother just yet. My curiosity spun out of control. I *needed* to know how he was involved in all this.

And Dr. Holmes knew it.

A cruel smile touched his face. It was a calculated strike and it had hit its mark.

"Your brother and I didn't share the same vision or desire. I'd hoped he might join me, but then I watched *you* and there was no doubt of your nature. I wanted you to be mine. Tell me, Miss Wadsworth, how many have you killed and then lied about?"

FIFTY-TWO

HEAVEN OR HELL

MURDER CASTLE
CHICAGO, ILLINOIS
19 FEBRUARY 1889

I could barely hear past the blood pounding through my ears. "I have *never* taken a life." I snapped my mouth shut. He was testing for holes in my emotional armor, searching for another place to land a blow, to distract me. I had not murdered anyone, but I would kill him before this battle was through. I practically growled, "How did you know my brother?"

He inhaled. It was the sort of sound that alluded to a long story about to be told. Or perhaps he was frustrated his attempt to rattle me had been in vain. I imagined he'd envisioned this meeting a million times and it wasn't living up to his fantasy.

What a pity that I should disappoint him so.

"Nathaniel and I met at a pub. He was openly hostile, never afraid of shedding his mask. His convictions were strong enough to be appealing. I watched him watch the women plying their trade, his disgust practically vibrating off him. Here was a man barely leashing his rage. He loathed the way prostitutes spread diseases. You should've heard the way he'd rant about their destruction of good families and all the religious nonsense he associated with sin."

I *had* heard my brother speak of such wrong notions, and I knew how that hatred had started in him. After our mother died from scarlet fever, Nathaniel became obsessed with how disease spread. It was a fear my father had passed along to each of us, though I rallied against it by using science to refute his claims. Nathaniel's solution had morphed from good intentions to a gnarled, ugly beast. He'd used that same fear to experiment, hoping to rid the world of death. He preyed on those he deemed to be the cause, and I would never condone what he'd done.

"I did understand him, though," Holmes continued. "I recognized a part of myself in him. I knew what it was like, trying to fight against the darker urges. Watching him, the seed of an idea was planted. You see, I couldn't find a good reason to prevent that thought from flourishing. Not that I tried too hard to stop it."

He smiled, I assumed from recalling the imagery. If my hands weren't otherwise occupied, I'd have curled them into fists. I wanted nothing more than to shred that smirk from his face. I all but forgot my purpose as I let the rage over my brother's unfortunate encounter with this demon's spawn consume me.

As if sensing my fury, he continued his twisted tale. "It didn't take much grooming on my part to make him my creature. He was only too willing to follow me, playing spy while I let my blade sing. Well, now, not *my* blade, exactly. Your brother always lent me his when the time came. He wanted to belong. I gave him that comfort."

Bile seared up my throat. "Did he . . . did he watch the murders?"

He moved ever so slightly toward the vault, leaning against the wall. My breath caught. I had to move straightaway, but I couldn't seem to. The desire to understand my brother's role in this treachery warred with locking this villain in his own chambers. My hesitation cost me. Holmes stepped to the side, now closing in on where I stood near the incinerator room. My strategy was coming undone at the seams, all because of my cursed curiosity.

"Turns out, he didn't much have the stomach for murder. He had no such issue with accepting their organs for his science, though. Does that ease your mind, knowing his brand of devilry has limits?"

"Of course it doesn't." I shook my head. "Instead of turning you over to Scotland Yard, he accepted gifts in the form of kidneys and ovaries and hearts. Had you not burned his journals, I'd have given them to the detective inspectors when I returned to London. You need to pay for what you've stolen. And so does my brother, deceased or not. He hated the women you killed. I saw that hatred in his heart and in the way he spoke of them the night he died. He was not innocent."

At that, a slow, malicious smile spread across his face. He held up a blade, a silver gleam in the flickering darkness, matching the glint in his eyes. It was as if I was standing in my laboratory watching Nathaniel do the same maneuver. The blade had been hidden up his sleeve, just as Thomas had deduced all those months ago. I was so caught by surprise at the clashing of memories, I could scarcely breathe. Nightmares and reality came together until I wanted to drop my knife and cane and cover my ears.

"Do you know what the most dangerous weapon is, Miss Wadsworth?"

Somehow, he must not have noticed the panic swirling about inside me. Through some miracle I'd kept my expression blank. My association with Thomas had proved most beneficial. Something he'd joked about a long while ago. I swallowed hard, never removing my attention from Holmes. I did not focus on the knife, recalling my time with the carnival. Sleight of hand was a dirty trick. It always made you look at the wrong target.

417

"I suppose a pistol or a sword." I lifted a shoulder. "It depends on the circumstances."

"Is that what you truly believe? That some tangible object is what's to be feared most?" He exhaled, the sound laced with disappointment. "What of the human mind? That's the most dangerous weapon. How many wars would be waged, swords drawn, cannons readied and fired, without that one weapon being deployed first?"

He watched me with the eyes of a shark, emotionless yet predatory. I couldn't help but feel as if I was wading in waters much too rough to survive. I refused to be afraid as I stepped into the incinerator room.

Heat licked at my calves. Our time together was coming to an end. Only one of us would leave this murder castle alive. I pictured Thomas standing at the altar. Uncle instructing us in his laboratory. My father's glistening eyes as he set me free. My aunt and cousin and Daciana and Ileana—the two other sisters I'd come to love as if they were my own blood. Mrs. Harvey and her traveling tonics and warmth. I had much to fight for, aside from avenging the women he'd brutalized. I would not be an easy target.

"A mind is a powerful weapon, but it doesn't have to be used wickedly," I said. "That's a choice."

He roughly parted the sea of skeletons before him, no longer patient with our game. He strode toward me, leaving them chattering loudly in warning. They needn't have bothered. I knew the monster was about to emerge. Running was no longer an option. It was time to fight.

"We are all wicked. More than mortal flesh and blood, our very souls harbor evil. It knows no beginning or ending."

He paused on the threshold of the room and I silently prayed he'd take one final step inside. All I needed was to complete our dance. One last circle around until I could lock him in here with his latest victim. Anticipation coursed through me.

I spied a stool off to the side with a gas can. I'd try throwing it at him and run. Or I could swing the metal can at him—it seemed hefty enough to stun him for a moment. He stepped forward and I immediately moved back, edging farther into the blazing room.

Sweat beaded on my forehead. Soon it would soak through my nightgown. I shivered at the thought of this man undressing me. He smiled as if he knew my thoughts.

"Your soul longs for the very things mine does. Don't trick yourself into thinking you're better because you haven't crossed that line yet, Miss Wadsworth. I see your desire to end me. It's so strong I can practically taste it. Like a fine berry wine, your darkness is sweet."

Silence had many roles. It could be either a villain or a hero depending on when it was called to service. I decided to keep my mouth shut. Let him entertain himself with his lies. I might desire to kill him, but not for the reasons he believed.

"Have you nothing more to say? That's a shame. I was enjoying our chat together."

When I slowly swept around the outer edge of the room, he didn't shadow me like he'd done before. He remained where he was and I knew it was only a matter of moments before the rest of my plan joined him in Hell. I braced myself for whatever was coming next.

"I saw you in New York, you know. I'd gotten to hold you a moment. I wanted to slice your throat then and there." He smiled shyly. I searched my memory, unable to locate—I swallowed hard. I had bumped into him. He'd been the clumsy young man I'd chided Liza for being rude to. "Delayed gratification is the basis of euphoria."

I sensed the charge in the air—an invisible building of pressure before lightning struck. I hoped I was strong enough to finish this. I squeezed my cane in one hand and my knife in the other. I'd use them both in any fashion I needed to. As I eased up the pressure on my dragon's-head knob, I heard the softest *swoosh* of a stiletto blade sliding free. My heart stuttered.

Thomas. My brilliant, cunning, prepared man. I'd forgotten that he'd had a weapon built into the end of this cane. His gifts were beautiful and practical. Had he deduced my need for this before either of us understood just how important it would be? I didn't have time to ponder it.

The devil had been coiled like a rattlesnake, and while I was expecting his attack, when he sprang at me, I flinched. It was a costly mistake. He grabbed a skull from the pile just outside the door and in one fluid motion was across the room, smashing it against my head.

A loud, sickening crack echoed around me. My vision swam.

Dark glitter tinged in red flashed across my eyes. It was different from when I'd lost consciousness on the *Etruria*. Then I'd gotten swept into that in-between state of wake and sleep because of blood loss. It was an odd combination of white spots fighting the encroaching darkness. This was like pain exploded in my brain, all-consuming and terrible.

Warmth trickled down my forehead and into my eyes.

When I blinked, I saw blood. Our battle had begun and I was already losing.

FIFTY-THREE
CAPTURING THE DEVIL

MURDER CASTLE
CHICAGO, ILLINOIS
19 FEBRUARY 1889

I would not go quietly into the darkness.

Pain shifted from my tormentor into my ally. I used it to fuel my rage. Each drop of my blood was my sister-in-arms. I licked it from my lips, the throbbing of my pulse pumping it out in torrents. What a sight I must be, drinking the very blood he spilled to terrify me.

I thought again of Miss Eddowes. Miss Stride. Miss Smith. Miss Chapman. Miss Kelly. Miss Nichols. Miss Tabram. Minnie. Julie Smythe and her daughter, Pearl. The names of countless others he'd maimed becoming a silent refrain urging me on. I was not alone in this room with this monster. I was surrounded by his victims.

I'd been wrong before—they did not wish to attack me. They wished to join me as I delivered their justice. I didn't know what happened after death, if anything, but I believed they'd be waiting to greet him as he stepped from this world into theirs.

It was time to send him where he belonged.

I lifted my head, teeth bared, and an almost inhuman snarl ripped itself from my throat. I don't know where it came from, but the devil hadn't been expecting it. He took a startled step back and it was enough. More than enough. If he wished to taste my darkness, I hoped he recalled poison could also be sweet.

I dropped my knife and grabbed my cane with both hands, swinging it blade first in his direction as hard and fast as I could manage. I heard the satisfying sound of it hitting its mark. Fabric ripped and I felt the edge catch in his flesh as I followed through.

A warm mist hit my face. His blood, I realized.

He screamed and scrambled back, holding one hand against his side. Blood continued flowing warmly down my face; distantly I knew I ought to worry. Eventually I'd become weak. But at present, I'd never felt more alive.

"A mind *is* the best weapon." I smiled with bloodstained teeth. "And Thomas Cresswell wields it well. He made this for me, you know."

I slashed my cane in an arc toward his throat, missing by inches. I screamed in frustration, the sound shrill enough to tear my throat. He threw himself backward, toppling the stool. The smell of gasoline filled the air. I didn't need to glance down to see he'd spilled the can. Liquid spread long fingers, pointing to the demon I needed to destroy.

I scented his blood in the air, my focus falling on the crimson slash that smiled from my first strike. His body trembled at my approach. His fear *was* intoxicating.

Perhaps his assessment had been correct—perhaps he and I were alike. The thrill of his retreat vibrated in time with my pulse. I'd let the demon out of me and there was no locking it away again. Except maybe I'd never been born with the devil in me as he suggested. Maybe my monster was more vampiric in nature. I did not crave death; I craved blood. *His* blood.

"This is for Miss Nichols." I jabbed him in the leg with my blade, unable to control my bloodlust. I was a shark in the water, circling my prey as I scented its life-force leaking out. I struck again as he turned his own knife on me. I felt blood splatter onto my nightgown and wanted more. "And Miss Chapman."

I flung my arms back, intent on ending him at once. His hand struck out, as quick as a cobra, and wrested my cane from me. In a matter of seconds, he'd disarmed me and had his hands around my throat. It had happened too fast to avoid. I struggled against him, digging my fingers into his eye sockets. I managed to knock his mask off and stared into those electric-blue eyes that would haunt me, should I survive.

"Intoxicating, isn't it?" he whispered against my jaw. "The power. The control." I wheezed as the pressure on my throat grew impossibly tighter. It wouldn't be long before the blood vessels in my eyes burst. "Have you known pleasures of the flesh, Miss Wadsworth?"

He practically purred. Black spots crackled around the edges of my vision. I clawed at his hands, nails breaking. Suddenly, Nathaniel fluttered in and out of my thoughts. He screamed in warning. I lost all sense of my surroundings, focusing solely on my dead brother. His lips moved but I couldn't hear him. Strange I would think of him before death. Though maybe he was coming to fetch me.

"This is better than even that."

I blinked the hallucination away, focusing on the man before me. His eyes were wild now, knowing the end was near. Nathaniel flashed into my mind again. Insistent. This time it was a memory of our childhood. I watched the two of us playing on the grounds of Thornbriar.

I recalled the day vividly—he'd been teaching me methods of fighting off unwanted pursuers. The White City Devil let up on his stranglehold long enough to pull me back to the present. Apparently my death wouldn't be delivered swiftly after all. He wanted to play cat and mouse.

"Once I'm through with you, I'll see to your intended. I'd like nothing more than to wipe him from existence. If he's not already dead. He didn't look—"

With my last burst of energy, I brought my knee up into his groin as hard as I could manage. It was the move my brother had taught me all those years ago. He'd also told me to not hesitate to run away. I'd only have a few moments. I wrenched myself free as the devil howled in pain. I limped for the door, but my head spun so badly I couldn't manage a straight path. As I neared the threshold, Holmes ripped me back by my hair, yanking a chunk out.

My throat was too raw to scream anymore. Not fully recovered, but spitting mad, he pinned me to the ground with his body. His hands were vises around my neck again. This time his eyes were black. His pupils seemed to have swallowed the blue entirely. His rage was something I'd never encountered in the flesh before. In this moment, he was no longer human.

Staring into those burning eyes, I knew my death was imminent. I scrambled to find something. A weapon. A prayer of a chance at leaving this place with my life. My fingers clawed through wet dirt. I bucked around, knowing I was losing more oxygen, but I had only one chance left. As the darkness swept in again, my hand closed over the handle of the gas can. With the strength of my will and that of the women who'd been slain before me, I smashed it into his skull.

He tumbled off me, knocking into a switch. Hissing sounded from above. He'd put the gas on. He was still stumbling around, gripping his head, as blood blinded him. This was my chance. I limped toward the door, hoping he was sufficiently distracted so I could escape. I was almost to the corridor of skeletons when I heard a *whoosh*. A blast of heat swept over me. I half turned, unable to see what new horror was heading my way.

While he'd been stumbling around, he'd somehow knocked the

incinerator door aside. Flames and gasoline didn't mix well. Unless creating a fire or explosion was the goal. I spun around, dragging my battered body to the door. I'd lock him in and never look back.

I'd made it to the skeleton room, wrenched a femur from the victim he'd yet to string together, and slammed the door shut, sealing him in with the fire. I stared as smoke gathered and slipped out from the cracks around the threshold. It would be so easy to leave him here to burn. It was what he deserved. Police would think it was an accident. I would be free.

I swallowed the lump in my throat, wincing at the pain.

He began screaming. I stared at the bone I held. *Tell me, Miss Wadsworth, how many have you killed?* he'd jeered. The satisfaction of making him pay for his crimes would be great, but if I became his judge and executioner, I'd be robbing the families of his victims of their right to see him stand trial for his crimes. Though it might be worth it just to feel him bleed.

My choice should have been easy, but I'd be lying if I said it was. Through the darkness something Thomas had once said came back to me, a flickering beacon of light to cling to. *I will not become a monster for you.* I would not become Holmes's monster, either.

"I am my own monster." And it was time to slay that wretched part once and for all.

With a growl that tore at my throat again, I yanked the door open, coughing at the black, rancid smoke billowing out. Holmes was on the flooring, wheezing. I gritted my teeth and rushed to him, shoving my hands under his arms and pulling with strength I didn't know I had.

Our procession was long and the sweltering heat from the angry flames made it more difficult. I could scarcely breathe in the endless smoke. I managed to drag him into the room farthest from the incinerator and swiped the keys from the inside of his waistcoat. I fumbled until I found one that opened the lock. I glanced back at him, but he was no longer incapacitated by the smoke. He had rolled onto his side, his cold gaze locked onto me once more. I had seconds before he'd come for me again, and I would not survive another skirmish.

I stumbled into the corridor, fighting tears as pain shot up my leg. I couldn't stop moving, though. Tears slipped over my cheeks, each step more painful than the last. I had no idea if I was traveling in the right direction, but I hoped the stairwell led somewhere good.

Pain pounded in my head and my leg, overriding my thoughts. All I could concentrate on was to keep moving, keep going. I swore I heard Holmes shuffling behind me, but I refused to turn. I saw a hint of light at the end of a corridor and used it as a guide.

Life distilled into two all-consuming elements: pain and light. I had no idea how I made it outside. I wasn't even sure if I exited from the pharmacy or if a hole had been gouged in a wall. One moment I was traversing through darkness; the next I was blinking at the setting sun. It was so jarring, I froze in place. I didn't trust that this was real. Wind whipped smoke away.

Flames roared behind me and the ground shook. I turned in time to see a wall collapse. Rubble scattered not ten paces from where I stood. If I'd been another minute behind, I would have been crushed. Dust flew into the space around me and I couldn't stop from choking on it. Part of me wanted to curl up on the ground right there.

In the distance, I heard sirens wail. My teeth began to chatter.

"Wadsworth!"

I shielded my eyes against the brightness of the sun and squinted through the thick covering of dust. It seemed winter had been banished while I traipsed through Hell. Or perhaps this was Heaven. And Thomas was coming to greet me at the pearly gates. My heart stopped for a moment—If I hadn't died...Thomas was out of bed. He was well.

I staggered forward, then stopped. Ash and soot rained around me, making it almost impossible to breathe. There was so much debris, I couldn't see more than distant shapes and silhouettes. But I needed to get to that voice—that tether attached to my soul.

"Audrey Rose!" Thomas shouted, running so hard and fast I almost jumped from his path. He broke through the smoke like an avenging angel and scooped me into his arms, tears streaming as he kissed me everywhere. "Are you all right? I thought—if he'd..." I nodded and he clutched me tightly to his chest, his heart pounding against me. "Do you have any idea how terrified I was? I went mad with fear, imagining all the ways you might have been harmed." He ran his hands over me, as if convincing himself I was real. "The thought of never seeing you again, never hearing your voice or watching you elbows-deep in viscera—it nearly killed me. If he'd hurt you I would have—"

He would have turned into the monsters we fought.

"You're alive!" I kissed him, long and deep. I poured each emotion into it, each flutter of longing and passion and apology. Each moment I thought I might never see him again. Never hold him near. Never thread my hands through his hair or feel his body mold itself perfectly against mine. I pulled him closer, and his grip on me tightened as if he might never let me go, so long as I wished to stay.

I heard others join us, but society and propriety and everything else be damned. I didn't care who saw me kissing the man I loved. Uncle barked orders to the police and Noah, drawing my attention briefly. "Grab Holmes. He's crawling away."

Several men—including our friend—rushed to the murderer, who'd fallen to his knees, choking on the smoke. His murder castle was no more. He would never harm another young woman again. I didn't end his life, but I had ended his life of murder. It was a victory I'd cherish.

Noah glanced over at us and nodded, his expression mirroring the emotions I felt as he helped drag the murderer away.

"Wadsworth?" Thomas touched my face as if he still couldn't believe I was real. Before I could inquire about anything, his mouth claimed mine once more. We kissed as if our lives began and ended in that embrace. The devil hunted the White City no longer. I'd stopped him.

I held tightly to Thomas, trembling as my actions finally caught up and shock wore off. Or perhaps my shudders were the result of it being winter in Chicago and I was only in a nightgown. Thomas swiftly removed his jacket and placed it around me.

"I almost killed him," I confessed, my voice breaking. "I almost became the evil we fight against. I…"

Thomas placed his hands on either side of my face, his gaze straying to the gash in my head. I'd forgotten I was covered in my blood and Holmes's.

"But you didn't," Thomas said. "Were I in your position, I'm not sure I'd be able to lay the same claim. You are far stronger than I am, my love. Don't doubt your actions now."

I stared into his loving eyes. He was right. I couldn't dwell on what *could have been,* on a temporary weakness. In the end, I remembered who I was. I buried my face in his chest, never wanting to leave his side again. "It's finally over."

"And you went and had all the fun on your own again," he said, feigning injury. "It really is quite inconsiderate of you."

"Not true, dear friend. You had the joy of being poisoned. Not many people can live to tell the tale."

"We both know you're the hero." He grinned. "It actually makes my dark heart race, seeing you take on the world."

"Are you suggesting you're impressed?"

"Let's see, Wadsworth." Thomas ticked off points on his fingers.

"You've carved open dozens of bodies from London to Romania to America, been held at gunpoint beneath a castle once owned by Vlad the Impaler, got stabbed while defeating a deranged carnival, and have just captured the White City Devil. All before turning eighteen. I'm downright woozy with want. I beg you to ravish me now before I lose my mind."

"I love you, Thomas Cresswell." I kissed him gently. "With my whole heart."

"Beyond life. Beyond death"—he nuzzled my neck, whispering— "my love for thee is eternal."

"I adore when you say that." I smiled against his lips. "Tell me, though. How long have you been practicing it for this moment?"

He nipped at my neck, eyes brimming with mirth. "Not nearly half as long as I've been plotting our next adventure, you delightfully cruel thing."

"Oh?" I raised my brows. "Where shall we adventure to next?"

"Hmmm. There's the issue of Miss Whitehall we still need to contend with." He traced the line of my jaw, his expression suddenly serious. "However, I believe that trouble is behind us."

I tightened my grip on him, feeling the first buds of true hope sprout. "Don't toy with my emotions, Cresswell! Why do you think it's over?"

"My father sent an extremely agitated telegram yesterday. Apparently he'd been at the palace, convinced he'd be getting the queen's blessing for my nuptials with Miss Whitehall, when she wished you and me the best of happiness in our marriage. In front of a roomful of people, no less. So many witnesses. My father could hardly argue."

My heart near ceased. "The queen did that? How?"

Thomas grinned. "Her telegram requested an audience with my father immediately upon his return to England. It simply said it was regarding the betrothal. He assumed she'd been speaking of Miss

Whitehall since she's the daughter of a marquess. Imagine his surprise when she announced our names in front of court." He sighed dreamily. "I would've paid a large sum to witness the look on his face. He can't go against the queen. Your grandmother is my new favorite person."

Excitement turned to worry. "But your inheritance and title…"

Now his grin was that of a cat who'd swallowed a tasty bird whole. "In light of obtaining the queen's favor, my father has removed all threats from both me and Daciana. He's even offered me one of our country estates, Blackstone Manor, as a showing of goodwill."

I stared at him a moment, trying to absorb everything. "How did you manage to solve these issues? I've only been gone—"

"For four horrendous days. If the poison wasn't about to kill me, I swear the thought of losing you was." He shuddered, then swept me into his arms. "Perhaps we should think of taking a holiday. No murders. No angry families. Just the two of us. And Sir Isaac."

"Mmm." I smiled against his lips. "I rather fancy that idea."

"Where would you like to go next, Miss Wadsworth?"

He placed me back on the ground. The sun gilded the tops of the buildings as it crawled behind them. In the distance I saw the gleaming White City, its magic glittering without darkness at last. If I could go anywhere on earth, there was truly only one place I longed to be in this moment. Somewhere Thomas and I could be alone. Fighting another grin, I turned to him.

"I believe you mentioned something about a country estate. If I recall correctly, you made it sound as if we might send the staff away. Where—"

Thomas swung me into his arms once again before I could finish my sentence. "I was hoping you'd say that, because I cleverly purchased two passages before we left New York. I'd been watching the way you stared at your ring. That determined set to your jaw. You know, that stubborn bit of chin lifting that indicates you're about to wage war?" Completely unaware of my eye roll, he continued on. "If we hurry, we can make our ship by week's end."

"Where, exactly, *is* the country estate?" I asked, looping my arms around his neck. "England? Romania?"

"That, my dear Wadsworth, is a surprise."

He'd promised me a lifetime full of them, and it seemed Mr. Thomas Cresswell—the crown fiend and love of my life—delivered on his promises. We'd finally emerged from the darkness that had stalked us all these months. Night no longer held dominion over our souls.

I tipped my head back, closing my eyes against the last rays of the sun, excited for wherever we were headed to next. Like the stars shining madly above, the number of our future adventures was infinite. I had no idea what tomorrow had in store for us, but I knew one thing with utter certainty: no matter what new chapter awaited, Thomas and I would turn that page together.

H. H. Holmes, circa 1880s/Early 1890s

EPILOGUE
CRIME OF THE CENTURY

THOMAS'S FAMILY HOME
BUCHAREST, ROMANIA
ONE YEAR LATER

"H. H. Holmes didn't confess to the murders in London, though he's written an account of his crimes at his now-infamous murder castle from prison." I all but snarled as I read a snippet of his words aloud to Thomas. "'I was born with the very devil in me. I could not help the fact that I was a murderer, no more than the poet can help the inspiration to song, nor the ambition of an intellectual man to be great. The inclination to murder came to me as naturally as the inspiration to do right comes to the majority of persons.'"

I closed the paper, wishing I could burn it with my fiery gaze. Even after all this time, Holmes still enjoyed the sound of his own voice. No matter that what he was saying was horrid.

"Who allowed him to publish such rubbish?" I tossed the paper on the bed. "He's earning more now as an inmate than he did with all of his scheming. Don't they realize they're giving him everything he's ever wanted? Fame. Fortune. It's appalling."

"His *mustache* is appalling, or...oh. Am I the only one who loathes the thing?" Thomas dodged the pillow I threw at him. "We could try again to prove his guilt over the Ripper murders, you know. Perhaps he's not the only one who can write an account of the events that have transpired. Why not publish your own account? Some people might believe it's fiction, but some people also believe *strigoi* walk amongst us. Though most know vampires aren't real, I'm sure a large enough group would believe us. We can keep fighting until we win over the masses."

The thought was tempting. It was *always* tempting. However, we'd traveled down that path and no one wanted to hear the truth. I understood, in a way, that without any evidence to support our outrageous claims, there was no proof that the charming American con man was also the notorious Jack the Ripper. He vehemently denied any connection to the crimes, and without a confession, there wasn't much anyone could do. Ripper madness had died down in the hearts and minds of people, and it seemed no one wished to reopen those wounds. Apparently a few dead "whores" weren't a top priority any more. Not compared to the crime of the century.

When we returned to London, I'd even gone as far as telling Detective Inspector William Blackburn about my brother and his journals. I'd brought him to the laboratory in my family's home, and he claimed all it proved was Nathaniel's affinity for science. Something I ought to understand. I wondered if the detective inspector was being loyal to my father or if he truly couldn't pursue that lead.

Uncle tried pressing the issue of connecting the crimes—pointing out forensic similarities between the two murder sprees. He showed proof that Holmes was in London during the murders and was in America when they ended. He'd secured samples of Holmes's handwriting—which was startlingly identical to the notes Jack the Ripper had taunted police with. No one in a position to do anything cared. His colleagues laughed or sneered at him. They thought he was a fame-monger, wishing to see *his* name back in the papers. Feeling so helpless was abysmal.

Rumors began in upper-class circles that saw Thomas's name swapped out for more salacious perpetrators: royals. No one spoke of the American killer, nor did they care he was in London during the Autumn of Terror.

They didn't care that he'd also left a few bodies on the *Etruria* when we crossed the Atlantic. Nor did they care about a drunken brute whose neck had been nearly sliced clean off in an alleyway behind the Jolly Jack public house. Those cases remained unsolved, begging for attention they wouldn't get. They were unfortunate, terribly sad, indeed, but that's the way life was. At least that's what I'd been told.

H. H. Holmes and Jack the Ripper were now becoming as mythic and legendary as Dracula. They were scary stories told during tea, in bawdy halls and gentlemen's clubs. How quickly fear could be replaced with laughter. It was always easier to laugh at the devil when we believed he'd been captured.

I angrily swiped the paper off the mattress, flipping to the next ridiculous headline. Witches and vampires and werewolves were apparently having a war in Romania. Villagers blamed scorched plots of land, dead crops, and bloodless goats on the monsters. I sighed. It seemed the only true war was raging between fantasy and reality.

"You're upset." Thomas gently touched my face, his expression soft. "Understandably, and I'll stand by your side, fighting to locate any shred of evidence we can to convince the world who the real Ripper is. I will devote my life to the cause if it would please you."

I couldn't help the smile that twitched across my lips. He was certainly dramatic. A trait that was wholly Cresswell. And I wouldn't have him any other way. "I thought you wanted to start our own agency. Will that be our only case?" I shook my head. "We'll starve. Though I suppose we can also go about proving vampires don't exist."

Thomas took the paper from me, quickly scanning it as he set it aside, chuckling.

"You know, I am quite talented with a sword, Wadsworth. I'll hunt dinner for you. Or demons and werewolves." The teasing slowly left his eyes. He picked up my hand, playing with the massive red diamond. He slipped it on and off my finger, almost absently. "Is that your answer, then? You wish to open our own investigative agency? I know we spoke of it..."

My attention shifted to the headline again, and I hardened my resolve.

H.H. HOLMES
AN ARCH-FIEND'S RECORD

"I don't want to have another case like this one go 'unsolved,'" I said. "With your deductions and my forensic skills, we will be quite a force to be reckoned with. Consulting on investigations—I can't imagine a more fulfilling vocation. Our partnership and combined expertise will be beneficial to many. If they won't listen to us about who Jack the Ripper is, we'll keep searching for definitive proof, but we'll also do our best to never allow another career murderer to go unpunished."

Thomas held the ring in his hand, squinting at it as if it might speak to him. After a moment, he bit his lip. One of the signs he was stalling.

"Well?" I asked. "What sort of smart, witty remark are you debating?"

"I beg your pardon, dear Wadsworth." He drew back, holding a hand to his heart. "I was imagining our very own sign hanging above the door to our agency."

I narrowed my eyes. "And?"

"I was trying to picture what we'd call it."

The tone he used was innocent enough, which indicated trouble on the horizon. I pinched the bridge of my nose. I was slowly turning into my uncle. "Please. Please do not suggest that combination of our names again. No one will take us seriously if we call ourselves the Cressworth Agency."

His eyes flashed with mischief. It struck me that that was exactly what he'd hoped I'd say, granting him the perfect opening for his real intentions. I waited, breath held for the truth.

"What do you think of Cresswell and Cresswell, then?" His voice was casual; however, his expression was anything but. He held the crimson diamond up, never taking his attention from mine. Always and forever watching for the slightest hesitation. As if he would ever not belong to me wholly. "Will you marry me, Audrey Rose?"

I glanced around the room, searching for any upturned bottles or signs of elixirs.

"I thought I already agreed ages ago," I said. "You're the one who slipped the ring off my finger. I fancy it right where it's been."

He shook his head. "I realized I'd never asked you properly. And then the debacle at the church..." His voice trailed off as he looked at the ring. "If you've changed your mind about taking my name, it won't bother me. I only want you. Forever."

"You have me." I touched the curve of his lips, my pulse racing as he playfully nipped at my fingertips. "Is it not enough that we've made the happiest of memories this past year? Traveling and living as husband and wife in every sense of the term?"

"I do rather enjoy that part. Now if you'll just drink too much wine and dance inappropriately, I will die a very happy man."

His wicked mouth pulled into a grin. He slipped out of bed, ring in hand, and went down on one knee. A sweet vulnerability entered his features as he presented me with the crimson diamond once again. Sir Isaac Mewton, who'd been tolerating our movements in bed thus far, flicked his tail and hopped to the floor. He offered us one annoyed look before dashing out the door. Apparently he was through with declarations of affection for now.

"Audrey Rose Wadsworth, love of my heart and soul, I long to spend forever with you by my side. If you'll have me. Will you do me the tremendous honor of—"

I wrapped my arms around his neck, our lips brushing as I whispered, "Yes. A million times over, Thomas Cresswell. I want to spend forever adventuring with you."

My bounty is as boundless as the sea,
My love as deep; the more I give to
thee,
The more I have, for both are infinite.
—*ROMEO AND JULIET,* ACT 2, SCENE 2

WILLIAM SHAKESPEARE

OUR ADVENTURE BEGINS

Audrey Rose

&

Thomas

Request the pleasure of your company

to celebrate their wedding.

TOGETHER WITH THEIR FAMILIES

16 October at 7 in the evening

BLACKSTONE MANOR

ISLE OF WIGHT

BEYOND LIFE, BEYOND DEATH; MY LOVE FOR THEE IS ETERNAL

CRESSWELL'S COUNTRY ESTATE
ISLE OF WIGHT, ENGLAND
ONE YEAR LATER

Thomas and I waited, side by side, on the grounds of Blackstone Manor for the exact moment the sun turned the color of sleep. It was a drowsy pink—the kind of lazy shade that took its time fading into darkness. Thomas had charted the colors of the sky each night over the last two months, capturing each shade of tangerine or rose, calculating down to the minute how long we'd have before it collapsed into the purply black of night.

Waves lapped at the shore, the mist rising around the craggy bluffs. It reminded me of spirits, and I wondered if our mothers had managed to bridge the gap between life and death after all. They were certainly represented in both my ring and the heart-shaped locket I wore.

I heard a rather loud sniffle and fought a grin. I'd expected Mrs. Harvey to be sobbing into her handkerchief; I did not expect to see my aunt bawling with Liza's arm slung about her.

I met my father's eyes and saw joy shining in them. Uncle sat beside him, trying to ignore Sir Isaac as he settled onto his lap. If I didn't know any better, I'd believe a few tears had also slipped from his eyes. Daciana and Ileana sat together, their gowns sparkling like magic dust in the setting sun. Next came Mrs. Harvey and Noah, both dabbing at their eyes.

The most surprising addition was Thomas's father. The duke sat with my grandmother and gave us both a small nod, the action enough to inspire hope for cultivating a better relationship with him in the future. In the end, Thomas and I were surrounded by the people we cherished the most, the ceremony small and focused solely on love.

Thomas kept his gaze locked onto the slow procession of the sun, holding his pocket watch in one fist. A peacock strutted down the path, its head bobbing in time with my heart. I grinned. The bird was his idea, unsurprisingly. Thomas flicked his attention to me, his expression softening. "Ready, Wadsworth? It's time."

I inhaled the salty scent of the sea. "Finally."

I took his bare hand in mine, my heart fluttering like a bird in a cage of bone as he smiled back at me. Each shared memory flashed through my mind. From the moment I first saw him rushing down the stairs in my uncle's laboratory, to the first time we made love, and every second in between our first adventure and today. He stole my breath now just as he'd done then.

His suit was midnight black, edged with champagne whorls at his cuffs and collar to match my dress. My capped sleeves fluttered in the light ocean breeze and I flushed as Thomas slowly scanned me, his attention pausing ever so slightly on my sweetheart neckline.

This time, my gown was my own design—I chose a sheer white that bordered on a frosty blue, reminding me of sunshine illuminating a glacier. The bodice featured what resembled a golden butterfly with its wings spread wide.

Delicate gold and champagne appliqués cascaded down my waist in thin tendrils before fading into the dreamy ice-blue white layers of my skirts. The bottom of the gown was my favorite part—the same champagne appliqués gathered en masse at the ground and carefully faded into the fingers of the smaller design. It was ethereal in all the right ways.

We stood facing each other, wearing what I imagined were similar expressions of flushed excitement, as the sun slowly descended toward the horizon, turning my dress brighter shades of gold and champagne. The hour had finally arrived.

This time, the priest we'd requested was more than happy for us to say our own words. "You may begin exchanging your vows now."

Thomas took a deep breath and stepped closer, his smile genuine and sweet. It was amazing to me, after these past few years of exploring the world and each curve of our bodies, that he might still appear so shy. So blissfully, beamingly in love.

He looked upon me today the way he'd done from the moment we both knew there was no turning back, no fighting our fate. He and I were two stars in the same constellation, destined to shine brightly together each night of forever.

"My dearest Audrey Rose."

Thomas gazed unabashedly at me, as if his soul was speaking directly to mine. Tears threatened to choke his words before he could get them out. I gently ran my thumb over his hands, my own eyes glistening.

"You are my heart, my soul, my equal. You see the light in me when I'm lost within darkness. When I'm cold and distant, you're as warm as autumn sunshine, bathing me in your glow. If I am the night, then you are the stars lighting up my endless dark." His voice broke, wrenching my heart. "My best friend, the absolute love of my life, now until forevermore, I call you my wife."

This time—with just the gilded clouds and autumn-colored tree branches swaying in the soft twilight breeze, along with our joyous families on this private estate—there was no one to interrupt Thomas as he slipped the wedding band over my finger.

"Beyond life, beyond death," he whispered, his breath warm against my ear, "my love for thee is eternal, Audrey Rose Cresswell."

My breath hitched. The priest turned to me, his voice kind and encouraging. "Do you accept this man as your husband, to have and to hold, until death do you part?"

I gazed at Thomas, seeing a range of emotions that were entirely him; mirth, love, adoration, and a wicked gleam that promised a lifetime full of surprises and adventure.

I placed the ring on his finger, never taking my attention from his; I didn't want to miss one second of this moment. His lips quirked crookedly and I knew, without a doubt, that he'd read the same promises in my face. I could not wait to spend forever with my best friend, the dark prince of my heart.

"I do."

AUTHOR'S NOTE

Before I wrote *Stalking Jack the Ripper,* I read a jailhouse confession written by Herman Webster Mudgett, aka Dr. Henry Howard Holmes, or H. H. Holmes, the con man dubbed "America's first serial killer." His book started the all-important "what if?" scenario my muse craves. There are many theories and arguments about who Jack the Ripper really was, but there was something about Holmes that always made me wonder if he was indeed the infamous serial killer who terrorized London.

There were a lot of puzzle pieces that seemed to fit nicely with the "Holmes as the Ripper" theory—the personality, the medical background, the fact that he was in London at the time of the murders, his handwriting closely resembling Ripper letters sent to police, an eyewitness claiming an American was the last person seen with a Ripper victim, and more.

For those of you who enjoy details: Holmes actually traveled on the RMS *Etruria,* the setting I chose for *Escaping from Houdini,* before he began building that labyrinthine murder castle in Chicago. He was a con man and opportunist, much like Mephistopheles, which gave Audrey Rose the much-needed lesson in dealing with sleight of hand and its many applications before this final showdown.

One of the more interesting things that emerged about Holmes being the Ripper came from his great-great-grandson—Jeff Mudgett—after he'd read two of Holmes's private diaries (*Bloodstains,* 2011). One theory claimed Holmes had trained an assistant to kill the women in London, and that his true mission was to harvest their organs so he could make a serum to increase his life span. Whether this is true or not was never confirmed.

That possible motive was where the idea of Nathaniel harvesting organs to cheat death came from. Speaking of Nathaniel—one of the reasons I made *Frankenstein* his favorite novel was because Holmes's most trusted associate—Benjamin Pitezel—had been called his "creature" in real life. I used this detail and played with their roles in the Ripper killings in *Stalking Jack the Ripper,* and once again when the truth behind Nathaniel's involvement is revealed in *Capturing the Devil.* Benjamin Pitezel was not included in these works of fiction, but he was part of the inspiration behind Nathaniel's character.

Another rumor circulated about this infamous killer calling himself "Holmes" as an homage to Sir Arthur Conan Doyle's famous detective, which also planted the kernel of an idea to give Thomas Sherlockian deduction skills to track this predator.

Now, I'm not fully convinced Holmes *is* the Ripper, but it certainly gave me lots to work with while crafting this series. One of the best parts about any mystery is researching and coming up with your own theories. Who do *you* believe Jack the Ripper was? Maybe one day we'll finally have an answer to that question. For now, I'd like to imagine that Audrey Rose and Thomas solved the crime, only to be thwarted—once again—by the slick con man, who burned their only evidence the way he incinerated bodies in his murder castle.

Like Audrey Rose in this final installment, I have a chronic condition. It was important for me to write a character who also wasn't able-bodied, in hopes that others might see themselves, too. I believe it's invaluable to see characters with all different backgrounds and abilities starring in their own stories. I based most of Audrey Rose's symptoms on my own, and am so proud that a cane-carrying, scalpel-wielding goth girl in STEM defeated the ultimate villain.

In order to continue Audrey Rose and Thomas's story without a large time lapse, I took some liberties with historical timelines. Here are a few:

The World's Columbian Exposition, aka the Chicago World's

Fair, opened in 1893, not 1889, and more than twenty-seven million people visited it. The Paris Exposition Universelle also hadn't opened until May of 1889, though Audrey Rose references the Eiffel Tower.

H. H. Holmes began working on the World's Fair Hotel, his infamous murder castle, in early 1887. In 1888 he was sued by a company he'd fired (and hadn't paid) to build part of it, and fled to England briefly that autumn.

The murder of Carrie Brown took place on the night of April 23, 1891, not January 22, 1889 and her body was discovered on April 24, 1891. Many details of her autopsy scene were kept quiet, mostly because the police didn't want people to panic at the thought of Jack the Ripper stalking American streets. The interior of the East River Hotel described in my story is fiction.

Frenchy Number One and Frenchy Number Two were both real suspects, and police did arrest Ameer Ben Ali. All of the evidence that Audrey Rose points out is historically accurate—there were no bloodstains leading to his room or anything other than the slightest circumstantial evidence tying him to the case.

Thomas Byrnes was really an NYPD chief inspector who didn't think highly of Scotland Yard after Jack the Ripper slipped from their grasp.

As with all good mysteries, there are still many debates about the actual body count for both Jack the Ripper and H. H. Holmes. All of the victims mentioned in this story were real or suspected victims. I gave some of them their own backgrounds, mixing fact and fiction. For instance, Holmes was known to take ads out in newspapers, hoping to hire young women to work in the shops below his murder castle. Once they were there, they usually didn't survive. Mr. Cigrande was not really anyone who yelled about demons or who was an eyewitness to the Holmes crimes, but his daughter was one of the suspected victims. Minnie Williams and her sister were both thought to be murdered by Holmes. Minnie was said to once be an actress, which is why I made her part of Mephistopheles's Shakespeare play. (She also really was hired by Holmes to be a stenographer.)

Queen Elizabeth did grant peerages to a few Indian families, though only one family was granted a hereditary peerage plus the title of baron in 1919. It was the first and only baronetcy awarded.

The wedding and engagement practices mentioned are all historically accurate, though as Audrey Rose points out, their brief engagement period was unusual.

H. H. Holmes fled Chicago in July of 1894 and was going to build another murder castle in Texas when he was arrested and jailed briefly. While there, he told a fellow inmate of an insurance fraud scheme and inquired about a lawyer he could trust if he faked his death. The scheme failed, but Holmes was undeterred. He tried again with his partner in crime Benjamin Pitezel, but instead of pretending to kill him, he actually murdered his longtime associate and collected the ten-thousand-dollar insurance policy. Frank Geyer, a police officer from Philadelphia, hunted Holmes as he traveled from Detroit to Toronto to Indianapolis with Pitezel's children. (Holmes ultimately killed them—Geyer discovered their bodies in the various locations where they'd stayed.)

The Pinkertons finally tracked Holmes down and arrested him in Boston in 1894. He was executed in 1896. (Though rumors circulate that he pulled the ultimate sleight-of-hand con and convinced someone else to die in his place.)

Alas, his murder castle wasn't destroyed in the fiery battle with Audrey Rose, but in the summer of 1895 police did investigate the building, horrified when they discovered greased chutes that dropped to the basement, an incinerator that reached three thousand degrees, vats of acid, soundproofed rooms and vaults, and gas pipes that Holmes had control over (amongst other horrors). A fire did gut the building in 1895 under mysterious circumstances. It was ultimately torn down in 1938. For readers who may be interested in visiting the site: a post office now sits where the World's Fair Hotel once did.

For history buffs: I recommend reading *Devil in the White City* by Erik Larson—it's a wonderful book that weaves together the story of Holmes's dark fantasy and America's gleaming beacon of hope. One tale was a dream and the other a nightmare, but both were centered around the Chicago World's Fair.

Any other historical inaccuracy not mentioned was done to enhance the world in this fictitious tale of murder, mystery, and romance.

ACKNOWLEDGMENTS

When I first started drafting *Stalking Jack the Ripper,* I wanted to write a story about a girl who loved forensics as much as I do. While Audrey Rose had many Victorian-era obstacles to overcome, she also had a core support team in Uncle Jonathan, Thomas, Liza, Daciana, Ileana, and her father, who all helped her pursue her dreams. I'm blessed to have an equally phenomenal team supporting me, and each of them has played a role in making my dreams come true.

Mom and Dad, thank you for all of the weekend trips to the library and bookstores growing up, for teaching me to never give up, no matter how dark the road gets, and for your unwavering love and support. I couldn't have done this without you both.

Kelli, thank you for letting me use your store's name in this book for Audrey Rose's gowns—*Dogwood Lane Boutique*—and for being the best sister and early reader. I'm so excited about our collaboration for *Stalking Jack the Ripper* series merchandise and love it (and you!) to jewel-toned pieces.

To my family, Ben, Laura, George, Aunt Marian, Uncle Rich, Rod, Rich, Jen, Olivia, Bob, Vicki, George, Carol Ann, Brock, Vanna—thank you for being my cheerleaders.

None of this would've been possible without my agent, Barbara Poelle. There will never, ever be enough words to thank you for fighting for me and for believing in this series. Everyone should be lucky enough to have a fierce (Godzilla stain) coffee-spilling agent (and friend) on their side and in their life. Cheers to prosecco in hotel bars, endless laughter, suddenly getting weepy over completing this series, and everything in between. Love you, B!

To the entire team at the Irene Goodman agency for all that you do every day. To Heather Baror-Shapiro for getting my books into readers' hands in so many incredible countries. To Sean Berard and Steven Fisher at APA for the Hollywood treatment Thomas Cresswell adores.

To Jenny Bak—I cannot believe I was lucky enough to find a home with the best editor around, who's also turned into a wonderful friend. Thank you for being one of the first Thomas fans, for begging me to add that one kiss in *SJTR* that changed it all, and for working your magic on my second and third drafts...and all of that bonus content I surprise you with! I am so happy we get to continue our next adventure together! Best partner in crime publishing *ever*.

To JIMMY Patterson Books, I still pinch myself when I think about working with each of you, the ultimate publishing dream team. Thank you to Julie Guacci (aka Momma Julie!) for always making sure my tour and event schedules are manageable for me. Erinn McGrath, Shawn Sarles, Josh Johns, T. S. Ferguson, Caitlyn Averett, Dan Denning, and Ned Rust—you're all amazing. Huge shout-out to Tracy Shaw and Liam Donnelly for not just one, but two magnificent covers for *CTD,* plus each cover before it! To Blue Guess, the Hachette Sales team, and Special Sales team, infinite thanks for getting this series into so many places for readers to choose from. Linda Arends and the production team—you are formatting magicians, and I'm so happy I get to work alongside you. Many thanks to James Patterson, who continues to support my writing and books in amazing ways.

To Sabrina Benun and Sasha Henriques—thank you for every bit of magic you both offered to this series. It has been an absolute joy to work with you on all four books!

Stephanie Garber, I can't thank you enough for all of our brainstorming sessions, for chats about life outside of publishing, and for the gift of your friendship. Here's to new adventures and our book club!

To Traci Chee, Evelyn Skye, Hafsah Faisal, Alex Villasante,

Natasha Ngan, Samira Ahmed, Gloria Chao, Phantom Rin, Stacee (Book Junkie), Lauren (Fiction Tea), Anissa (Fairy Loot), Bethany Crandell, Lori Lee, Kristen (My Friends Are Fiction), Bridget (Dark Faerie Tales), Brittany (Brittany's Book Rambles), Melissa (The Reader and the Chef), Brittany (Novelly Yours), Gabriella Bujdoso, Michelle (Berry Book Pages), and the Goat Posse, you bring sunshine into my life. Thank you for all of the smiles both online and in person.

Booksellers, librarians, bloggers, bookstagrammers, artists, Fae Crate, Beacon Book Box, Shelf Love Crate, Fairy Loot, and lovers of fictional worlds, thank you for falling in love with these goth kids obsessed with STEM, and for being so excited about this series.

And to you, dear reader. Thank you for going on this final adventure with Audrey Rose and Thomas. Getting to share this series with you has been an absolute dream—a wild, unbelievable, wholly precious dream I still can't believe came true.

I encourage you to pursue your passions and live life authentically, just like Audrey Rose. You are incredible, and there are no limits to what you can achieve. That is a fact more tangible than any of Thomas Cresswell's deductions. Beyond life, beyond death, my love for thee is eternal. xoxo

ABOUT THE AUTHOR

Kerri Maniscalco grew up in a semi-haunted house outside New York City, where her fascination with gothic settings began. In her spare time she reads everything she can get her hands on, cooks all kinds of food with her family and friends, and drinks entirely too much tea while discussing life's finer points with her cats. Her first novel in this series, *Stalking Jack the Ripper,* debuted at #1 on the *New York Times* bestseller list, and *Hunting Prince Dracula* and *Escaping from Houdini* were both *New York Times* and *USA Today* bestsellers. She's always excited to talk about fictional crushes on Instagram and Twitter @KerriManiscalco. For updates on Cressworth, check out Kerrimaniscalco.com.